Praise for B. Catling's

The Vorrh

"One of the most original works of visionary fiction since Peake or Carpentier. . . . For all its page-turning story, it is a poet's novel, a serious piece of writing."
—Michael Moorcock, *The Guardian*

"I am glad to have the book as a companion on my own dark quest."
—Tom Waits

"A dizzying trek into the dark heart of fantasy. . . . *The Vorrh* is not only a work of alternative history, but of alternate literature. . . . It's a testament to Catling's skill as a sculptor of words that such otherworldly ideas and images not only connect, but resonate to the bone."
—NPR

"B. Catling has not constructed a book so much as a happening. *The Vorrh* is bold, shaggy, and surprising; often beautiful, arresting, or both."
—*Slate*

"A sprawling, expansive, even fierce piece of storytelling, transporting us to realms both familiar and alien. . . . In a class by itself."
—*SF Reviews*

B. CATLING

The Vorrh

B. Catling is a poet, sculptor, painter, and performance artist. He makes installations and paints portraits of imagined Cyclopes in egg tempera. Catling has had solo shows at the Serpentine Gallery, London; the Arnolfini in Bristol, England; the Ludwig Museum in Aachen, Germany; Hordaland Kunstnersentrum in Bergen, Norway; Project Gallery in Leipzig, Germany; and the Museum of Modern Art in Oxford, England.

The Vorrh

➤ A Novel

B. CATLING

VINTAGE BOOKS
A Division of Penguin Random House LLC
New York

A VINTAGE ORIGINAL, APRIL 2015

The Library of Congress Cataloging-in-Publication Data
Catling, B. (Brian)
The Vorrh / Brian Catling. — First edition.
pages ; cm
1. Africa—Fiction.   I. Title.
PR6053.A848V59 2015   823'.914—dc23   2014037260

Vintage Books Trade Paperback ISBN: 978-1-1018-7378-6
eBook ISBN: 978-1-1018-7379-3

Book design by Jaclyn Whalen

Printed in the United States of America
10   9

For David Russell and Iain Sinclair,
who gave me the compass, map, and machete
and insisted on this exploration.

I cannot think back to those days without recalling, over and over again, how difficult I found it in the beginning to get my breathing to work out right. Though I breathed in technically the right way, whenever I tried to keep my arm and shoulder muscles relaxed while drawing the bow, the muscles of my legs stiffened all the more violently, as though my life depended on a firm foothold and secure stance, and as though, like Antaeus, I had strength from the ground.

EUGEN HERRIGEL, *Zen in the Art of Archery*

The vitality of the demonic—what is guided by genius in the most literal sense—dies of course with the renunciation of a limitless lebensraum (formation of colonies).

LEO FROBENIUS,
Paideuma. Umrisse einer Kultur-und Seelenlehre

Near the same tree two more bundles of acute angles sat with their legs drawn up. One, with his chin propped on his knees, stared at nothing, in an intolerable and appalling manner: his brother phantom rested its forehead, as if overcome with a great weariness; and all about others were scattered in every pose of contorted collapse, as in some picture of a massacre or a pestilence. While I stood horror-struck, one of these creatures rose to his hands and knees, and went off on all-fours towards the river to drink. He lapped out of his hand, then sat up in the sunlight, crossing his shins in front of him, and after a time let his woolly head fall on his breastbone.

JOSEPH CONRAD, *Heart of Darkness*

The Vorrh

PROLOGUE

That which is marred at birth Time shall not mend,
Nor water out of bitter well make clean;
All evil thing returneth at the end,
Or elseway walketh in our blood unseen.
Whereby the more is sorrow in certaine—
Dayspring mishandled cometh not agen.

RUDYARD KIPLING, "GERTRUDE'S PRAYER"

*T*he hotel was ponderous, grand, and encrusted with gloom. Its tall, baroque rooms were grudgingly fortified by vicious light that desperately tried to penetrate the heavy curtains and starched formalities. The Frenchman's room was a suite, the hotel's finest, but drab and without the illusive flair that sometimes makes audacious architecture appear natural.

He stood naked and shrivelled in the marble bathroom, the last feeble surface scars on his neck and wrists throbbing red, the deep plucking of his other wrist stitched back together. The dose of barbiturates had done nothing and he was being mocked by flights of gilded putti and ignored by the wafting indifferent female figurines that shared the room. He stood with his cock in his hand, trying not to see his reflection in the gigantic mirror before him. He was small and prematurely old. He could summon no image to instigate the action, even though he had witnessed many and imagined more. He knew that Charlotte, his *maîtresse de convenance*, and his servant were waiting for him in the next room. He knew that the chauffeur might have brought him some fruit of the gutter or the docks to arouse him. He knew that they were as bored as he. He knew that he had invented everything in their lives. Maybe in the world. Sometimes he thought he had dreamt reality itself. Dreamt it outside of sleep, which now eluded him continually.

The drugs sometimes coddled him a bit. But even the right combinations of doses would become unstable, wringing out the softness, the blur that he so craved. He made Charlotte write it all down. The quantities, the mixtures, the times. It must be there, concealed in the broth of unbeing.

He sometimes doubted Charlotte's ability to keep accurate records. She could be making careless mistakes or lying about the doses. They were not working in the way he wanted. They had argued over the last few days. She claimed to be doing exactly as instructed, trying to calm him with her infuriating patience. But he knew she was tricking him with her cunning servant's slyness. Some nights and most mornings found him on the floor, crawling on hands and knees towards the thing that was strangling his heart. He had begun to sleep on the floor. The terror of falling off his shaking bed was too much.

He stood before the smirking mirror.

Last night, there had been a carnival and fireworks outside. Music and gaiety had clawed at his upper windows. This morning was wet. He could hear the grit and spent festivities being swept away in a quiet rain. A tinge of sulphur and nitrate in the air.

He raised his eyes. Max Kinder was standing in the gilded frame where the glass should be, naked and looking exactly like him. He lifted his tired arm and Max mirrored it perfectly. This had been the comedian's great invention: the live reflection. And here it was. An act that would be copied throughout the century and beyond. His comic gestures of abrupt shock and dazed examination carved out the first continual comic character to grace the new flickering screen. He tugged his moustache and Max did the same. Then Max pointed at the open wound in his arm, deeply vented and bloodless. He had died nine years before, at the height of his fame, in another grand hotel, his wife cutting first, his hand gripping hers on the razor. This was a very different mirror dance. The Frenchman nodded and averted his eyes as Max stiffened back into glass. He knew he had exhausted his imagination, his wealth, and his libido. He knew he had lost a precious gift. He knew he had once been Raymond Roussel. He knew the hollow longing and guilt were growing stronger and that there was no money or memory to hold on to. There were no facts to grip and the fictions were worn out. He then realised it was time to die, and he did.

➤ *Part One*

The eyes have fallen into disuse in their method of stringing them. Nor is the notch frontally in the middle ends of the bow.

LEO FROBENIUS, "THE BOW" IN "ATLANTIS,"
The Voice of Africa, VOL. 1

CHAPTER ONE

*T*he bow I carry with me, I made of Este.

She died just before dawn, ten days ago. Este had foreseen her death while working in our garden, an uncapping of momentum in the afternoon sun.

Este was born a seer and lived in the expectancy of her departure, a breeze before a wave, before a storm. Seers die in a threefold lapse, from the outside in.

Her long name was Irrinipeste, and she had been born to Abungu in the Vorrh, the great brooding forest that she said was older than humankind.

We said goodbye during the days leading to her night. Then all of my feelings were put away; there were more important rituals to perform. All this I knew from our first agreement to be together as it had been described, it had been unfolded.

I stood before our wooden table, where her body lay divided and stripped into materials and language. My back and hands ached from the labour of splitting her apart, and I could still hear her words. The calm instruction of my task, embedded with a singsong insistence to erase my forgetfulness. The entire room was covered in blood, yet no insect would trespass this space, no fly would drink her, no ant would forage her marrow. We were sealed against the world during those days, my task determined, basic, and kind.

She had explained all this to me while I tried to serve her breakfast in bed on a rare rainy morning. The black bread and yellow butter had seemed to stare from its plate with mocking intensity, the fruit pulsing and warping into obscene ducts and ventricles. I perched on the edge of the bed, listening to her simple words glide with the rain, while my fear turned them into petrol, burning into my oxygenless, hidden core.

I shaved long, flat strips from the bones of her legs. Plaiting sinew and tendon, I stretched muscle into interwoven pages and bound them with flax. I made the bow of these, setting the fibres and grains of her tissue in opposition, the raw arc congealing, twisting, and shrinking into its proportion of purpose. I removed her unused womb and placed her dismembered hands inside it. I shaved her head and removed her tongue and eyes and folded them inside her heart. My tasks finished, I placed the nameless objects on the wooden draining board of the sink. They sat in mute splendour, glowing in their strangeness.

For three days I lived with the inventions of her and the unused scraps, the air scented by her presence, the musk-deep smell of her oil and movement. The pile of her thick, unwashed hair seemed to breathe and swell against the bars of sunlight that turned the room towards evening. These known parts of her stroked away the anxious perfumes, the harsh iron of her blood, and the deeper saturated smoulders of her unlocked interior. On the third day I buried her heart, womb, and head in the garden in a small, circular pit she had dug with her very hands a week before. I covered it with a heavy stone.

I obeyed with perfection, tearless and quiet, picking up the arrows that she had made and walking back into the house for the last time.

The bow quickened, twisting and righting itself as the days and the nights pulled and manipulated its contours. There was a likeness to Este's changing during her dying, although that transition had nothing in common with all the deaths I had witnessed and participated in before. With Este, an outward longing marked all, like sugar absorbing moisture and salt releasing it. Every hour of her final days rearranged her with fearsome and compelling difference. Every physical memory of her body, from childhood onwards, floated to the surface of her beautiful frame. I could not leave her. I sat or lay next to her, fascinated and horrified, as the procession gently disgorged. Her eyes waxed and waned memory, pale transparency to flinted fire. She was dimly aware of me but able to instruct and explain the exactitude of the living object she would become. She did this to dispel my anxiety and pain; also to confront the ecstasy of her control. In the evening of the third day, the memory in my dreams began to show itself. It refined our time together, the constancy of her presence. Since leaving her village, we had never been apart, except for those strange weeks when she had asked me to stay inside while she dwelt in the garden day and night. When she returned, she was thin and strained.

The bow is turning black now, becoming the darkest shadow in the room. Everything is very still. I sit holding the two wrapped arrows in my hands. Out of their turnings come hunger and sleep, forgotten reflections of my own irredeemable humanity.

From the cupboards and the garden I juggle anticipant food, flooding my senses with taste and smell. Citrus and bacon rise in the room; sage and tomatoes, green onions and dried fish, unfold.

My hands tremble holding the bow, the arrows between my teeth. The moment has come. The two arrows that Este made are white, an infinite, unfocused white without any trace of hue or shadow. They absorb the day into their chalky depth and I grow sick looking at them. I lift the bow, which I must have strung in my sleep, and nock one arrow into its contrast. The other is wrapped away and saved to be the last. She said it was for another to shoot, a bowman who would come after me. I will make all the other arrows.

This was her last instruction. I draw the bow back with all my strength and feel this single gesture brace every muscle of my body, feel the tension lock in as the grace of the string touches my lips. I feel as if the world stops to hold its breath. I raise the bow skywards.

The arrow lets itself go, vanishing into the sky with a sound that sensually pulses through me and every other particle of substance and ghost, in or out of sight.

It is still travelling the spirals of air, sensing a defined blood on its ice-cold tip. For a moment I am with it, high above these porous lands, edging the sea, its waves crashing endlessly below. Above the shabby villages and brutal tribes, singing towards the Vorrh. This arrow is in advance of my foreseen journey into the depth of the forest, but it will never be my guide. She said that it was for me, but never to follow.

The pain calls me back as I stand dazed in the garden. The inside of my arm is raw from where the bowstring lashed it, removing a layer of skin with the ease of a razor, indifferent and intentional. Stepping forward, I pick up my sack and quiver, steady my looping stance against the bow, and begin to walk into the inevitable.

➤—→

Tsungali sat, a lone black man on the mud parapet wall of a colonial stockade.

Far to the south, twilight was tasting the air. Swallows darted and looped in the invisible fields of rising insects, restless arrowheads spinning in the amber sunlight. One moment, black silhouette, Iron Age. The next, tilting to catch the sun, flashing deep orange, Bronze Age. Dipping and rotating in giddying time: Iron Age, Bronze Age, Iron Age.

Watching them were his yellow eyes. Tsungali attempted to gauge their distance and speed, making abstract calculations across the infinite depth of sky, a solemn assessment of range and trajectory for a shot that could never be made. Across his knees lay his Lee-Enfield rifle, a bolt-action firearm of legendary durability, in perfect working condition and untouched by any other hand since he was given it in his early manhood. The excitement of possession, matched by his pride at becoming a member of the bush police.

He and the gun bore cuneiform scars and indentations. They had been written into. Prophecies and charms marked his face, talismans against attack from animals, demons, and men. The butt of the Enfield was inscribed with the tally of the twenty-three men and three demons it had officially dispatched. It had been years since Tsungali had worked for the police and by extension the British army. So he was confused and disturbed at being called for, summoned to the enclosure he had known so well and loved as home, the same compound he had seen turned into the bitter kraal of his enemies.

They had come looking for him, not with troops and threats like before, but quietly, sending soft, curved words ahead that he was needed again. They wanted to talk and forget the crimes of before. He had smelt this as a trick and set about carving new protections, constructing cruel and vicious physical and psychic traps about his house and land. He spoke to his bullets and fed them until they were fat, ripe, and impatient. He waited in docile cunning for their arrival, which had proved to be calm, dignified, and almost respectful. Now he sat and waited to be ushered into the fort's headquarters, not knowing why he was there and surprised at his own obedience. He gripped the Enfield to fence it off.

———

The Possession Wars began when the True People, Tsungali's people, rebelled against the British occupiers. Once a policeman, Tsungali then became a leader in that bloody uprising. Tsungali should have hanged for treachery and murder, for betraying the position of responsibility given to him. Over three days, a peaceful and obedient community had turned into an inflamed, rampant mob. The church and school burnt down. The resident officers butchered in their astonishment, radio equipment torn to pieces. The airstrip and the cricket pitch had been erased, scrubbed out. Not a single straight line was allowed to exist anywhere.

By the time the British officers had arrived, they found a squalid churn of destruction. Everything that had been achieved with, or given to, the natives had been intentionally eradicated, mangled back into their own stinking, senseless history. Tsungali stood at the centre of the carnage, triumphant and exhilarated, wearing only his tunic jacket and his peak cap, ridiculously turned inside out. Feathers, bones, and cartridges were entangled in his hair, and his teeth had been resharpened.

Before this, when the colonial forces had first appeared, they were mysterious and powerful. Their ignorance of the world was forgiven. The quantity of wonderful goods they brought and the manner of their arrival startled the True People. Cautiousness made their hands hesitate and quiver over the treasures they were offered. There were gifts for everybody. Tsungali and his brothers watched their kindness with distrust and bewilderment, watched the endless flow of impossible things: animal meat in hard, shiny shells without bones, killing irons of great power and accuracy, rainbows of cloth, talking cages, and a swarm of other things and powers with no name.

When the strangers were given permission to cut the trees and shave the ground, nobody could have expected the consequences. Tsungali had seen the first ones in the sky when he was small. They floated belly side up like a dead lizard in a pool, streaking the sky with straight white lines. Tsungali asked his grandfather what they were, those dagger birds with long voices. His grandfather saw nothing, heard nothing; the sky was empty; they did not exist. There was no template in his perceptions for such a thing. And, if some did see something, then it must be from another world, and therefore dangerous and best left alone. The magicians said they were the dreams of young fathers still to be born, and that their growing frequency told of a vast future fertility. No one had an explanation when one came down to nest on the shaved strip in the jungle; the strangers simply had great power to be able to catch one so easily. Tsungali walked to the clearing with his grandfather, hand in hand. They stood and stared at the gleaming hard bird. Its shell was the same as the shell around the meat without bones. The old man shivered slightly and saw only the clearing with the strangers hurrying back and forth. He saw them because they were men, or creatures in the shape of men.

The excited child stepped forward but was yanked into a standstill by the old man's rigidity. He was rooted to the spot and his tugging grandson would not unbind him. The boy knew better than to argue, and tears of frustration filled his eyes. The old man wept too. One solitary tear crept through the scars of his face, through the diagrams of constellations and the incised maps of influence and dominion. A liquid without name, it being made of so many emotions and conflicts, each cancelling the other out until only salt and gravity filled the moment and moved down through his expression.

The airplane was full of possessions, more than had ever been seen before; astonishing things that made the young feel rich and honoured, making them far greater than neighbouring tribes, who had nothing. The plane also carried a priest. Over the next few years, the strangers settled in and brought families and new belief to the village. They said they had changed, coming from different lands now with different ways of speaking, but this seemed untrue, like so many other things that were discovered later. They instructed the True People in the way of the one world, with its god that was ashamed of nakedness. They taught them how work might bring them those precious things that were previously given. They brought books and singing and exchanged the splendour of an invisible god for all their carved deities of wood and stone. And somewhere in that sickly trade, suspicion became woven into the fabric of trust. The insistence of guilt was converted into the notion that the True People must have already paid the price for something, something they had never received, something that just might be possessions.

The airstrip was carefully maintained and the goods continued to arrive. The empty planes were filled with the disgrace of their vanquished homes. Old weapons, clothing, gods, and kitchen tools were stacked inside to be sent away, shabby totems of a discarnate history, expelled. Clean pictures, metal furniture, and uniforms filled their spaces, or at least appeared to.

The flint to the great conflagration was a man named Peter Williams.

>——→

Peter Williams had joined the far-flung outpost just after the rainy season. His journey there had begun in conception. Khaki bedsheets, stained dark by khaki spunk, his father having carried the rifle and the flag for three generations. There had never been any doubt; he was to be a soldier. From the day of his birth to the day of his disappearance, there was only ever one road.

A great yellow sun had spun in the bluest of Wiltshire skies. His birth had been abrupt and easy, his brilliant red head bouncing in the warm light. The sun was always to be his principle, and he sought to embrace it.

He had been given a choice of posts, and the remote back-water was his most favoured. He desperately wanted to escape Europe, and England. The scars left by the gutting rope of the Great War were still fresh, if those words could ever be used in the same sentence. The rotting trenches had carved gangrene into the heart of the old countries, which clung together like so many old maids in a storm, friends and foes alike. He had been in a slithering ditch at Passchendaele for two years, where no sun ever warmed the forsaken earth. When there was daylight, it was contaminated and heavy, so that it hung densely on the black thorn hooks of splintered trees, the few verticals in a sea of mud, smoke, flesh, and metal. The only clear light he remem-bered was the light that had not existed. He had been one of those who witnessed spectral visions floating over the smeared remains of men and mules. Angels of the Somme, they had been called. An illumination of purity, squeezed out of corruption to flicker in the wastelands. He never really knew what he had seen, but it had helped him survive and erase the impossible reality of that carnage.

At the age of twenty-three, he had been ready for a far-off land of heat and life. From the moment he'd stepped from the plane and onto the rough-shaved clearing, he had felt satisfaction, as if the place had greeted him with a smile. There was something about the aroma of the jungle and the humidity, something about the teeming life that pulsed in every inch of the land, that had reassured him. Perhaps it was the ecstasy of opposites or the certainty that what he had witnessed could never happen there. Whatever it was he inhaled into his soul that day, it had grown stronger as he had walked through the singing rain forest to the barracks, with the step of a prodigal son.

The outpost was to the southeast of the Vorrh, two hundred miles from the city and two thousand years away. The tribe who owned the enclosure had been there since the Stone Age; their land was an isthmus at the mouth of the great river, which ran from the sea to be swallowed by the great forest. They said it was the other way around, that the forest bled from its heart to invent and maintain the sea. They called themselves the True People, and they had been that forever.

The sublimation of the True People had led to the survival of their race and the obliteration of their meaning. As the twentieth century had made its entrance, it was deemed necessary and desirable to focus on the tribe's development, especially if the trade route via the river was to thrive after a long period of poverty. Three European countries had forcibly assisted their evolution. The British were the last to join the noble crusade, and they did it with their characteristic munitions of charm, cynicism, and armed paternal control.

The outpost was an elaborate undertaking. When he had arrived they were just finishing the roof of the church, complete with a joyless bell to summon the newly converted. There were six professional soldiers, two with families. A priest and a dozen bush policemen, aged between forty-two and fifteen, had been wrangled from the more significant members of the tribe. They took their positions very seriously. What they actually policed was a matter of speculation, since no set of formal laws had been introduced, and the previous mechanisms of agreed existence were fast being rubbed out. At least that's what the invaders had believed.

Williams had been an armourer in the Great War, and he was there to equip and train the new police force with weapons beyond their expectations. He had arrived with a cargo of arms and ammunition, which he lovingly unpacked from their solid crates.

All the hopeless carnage he'd experienced only proved to him that greed, pride, and blindness, once rolled together, created a mechanism of appalling velocity, and that humans outside of imagination are best kept caged and regulated by severe controls. Never, in all the conflict and the infinity of wounds, had his love and enthusiasm for the firearms changed. Yes, these beautifully designed and crafted machines had only one purpose, but they did not breed it. He knew that their sole purpose, the taking of life, would have been operated anyway, even if the tools at hand had been sharpened sticks and heavy stones. Indeed, he had seen trench warfare move into hand-to-hand combat, where the bayonet was too distant a weapon, where handmade clubs and honed steel had hacked flesh apart in slippery, sightless fury. If men were to be butchered, then better it be done professionally, with a precise tool in skilled hands. With this dislocation as a balm, he could continue.

He had been unpacking a crate of Lee-Enfield rifles when he realised, to his surprise, that they were not reconditioned stock as expected, but a batch of gleaming new models in mint condition. In fact, none of the order had matched his paperwork at all. Among them was a special prize, a Gabbett-Fairfax Mars pistol. A self-loading semiautomatic with an astonishing ballistic power, it looked like an axe or a hammer and possessed a rudimentary L of a body, an ugly, unique elegance of top-heavy dense steel, smooth and uncluttered. The rear end of the pistol was infested with a knurled mechanical contrivance of the breech, hammer, and sights. The Mars was intended for military mass production, but it entered the world backwards, and at the wrong time. It came with the same consideration that sent the mounted cavalry into the gas and machine guns of the First World War, with the pedigree of a medieval killing field: It could stop a horse. It sounded like the end of the world. Its recoil could break the shooter's wrist and spit hot, spent cartridge cases back into his face. The imagined accuracy was never achieved because its marksman, having taken the first shot, shivered and flinched so greatly before squeezing the trigger that it was impossible to aim. It was the most powerful pistol ever conceived or constructed at the turn of that century, and nobody ever wanted to use it. Fewer than a hundred were manufactured.

He understood little of the local people. Their language was impenetrable, their ways oblique, and though their humanity was blatant from the beginning, all of their methods were questionable. But he had begun to be fascinated by the way they watched without looking, bemused by their laughter, which seemed disconnected to events, and intrigued by their shock at new objects and gestures. In fact, his curiosity was fusing him to them in direct proportion to the extent that he was becoming separated from all the other colonists of the outpost. He had not known this. His day-to-day work of demonstrating the weapons and organising target practice had consumed introspection and nullified his nagging doubts. It was only the incident with a girl named Este that forced his dislocation and pinned him up against isolation and the threat of court-martial.

Williams knew that the Dutch priest was a man of one gear: forward. A dauntless missionary, he had finished his church in a record two months. It was filled with the faithful every day, or at least what looked like the faithful. But on this day it sounded woefully empty as he stood outside, sheepishly peering into the moaning interior. A group of onlookers had started to form around the newly painted entrance steps, and the abnormality could be heard by nearly the whole village.

"Padre, what's wrong?" asked the first of the senior officers to arrive at the priest's side.

"It's one of the women," he replied. "She has gone mad."

The lieutenant pushed past the priest and opened the double doors to take control. The church still smelt of paint, its whiteness disorientating and off-key. In the aisle, halfway to the altar, a young woman knelt on the floor, surrounded by books, with one heavy foolscap tome open before her. She was naked and menstruating heavily. A low, inhuman groan rumbled constantly from deep inside her, the kind of sound that is heard at a distance, from the centre of a glacier, or lethally close, when it growls from the sleek, unseen darkness of a big cat.

The lieutenant looked back to the priest and understood his reticence. "It's only a girl," he said, the greatest lie he could manage, because he, too, had begun to shrink back in fear. His testicles were sucked up into his pelvis and his hair was standing on end. Whatever was in the church was a girl only in the curves of its black surface: Its essence and action were not from the known world. What was in the girl was altogether alien to a trained modern mind, and it was rewriting the rules of phenomena in a language that had an irremediable taste of pure terror.

A second officer and a group of onlookers had begun to bustle at the entrance of the church. The officer had a revolver in his hand already and had pushed it through the door like a crucifix, ready to dominate anything into submission. He saw a blur that shivered. Its sound unbound him, made him want to flee. He smelt the fear of all those around him, and his bladder started to weaken and leak. Pointing his shaking defence down the length of the aisle at the hideous black confusion, he shut his eyes and squeezed the trigger.

Nothing happened. The hammer had dropped, but only onto the flesh of the left-hand ring finger of Peter Williams. He had grabbed the pistol and restricted the action, twisting it around and down, forcing his colleague to his knees in yelps of pain. He took the gun away and tucked it into his belt. After looking down the aisle for a moment, he walked to the young woman, knelt beside her, and closed the book. The silence was instant, the fears and shuddering vanishing immediately.

"Coat," he called back to the door.

Moments later one had arrived and was brought almost to

him, it being thrown for the last few feet. He covered the girl and helped her to stand, then slowly escorted her from the church, a trail of blood left on the new floor. Once outside, he had expected her to walk off or to be collected by one of her own. But this did not happen. Instead, every time he stopped, so did she; when he moved, she began to walk. So they walked out of the camp together, and thirty minutes later they were deep in the bush.

It was then that he stopped to look at her, wiping the sweat from his face with the backs of his hands. She was now calm and without the faintest sign of perspiration. Lifting her head, she stared through him, her eyes the colour of opals, bright and unnervingly clear as they gazed into a distance that he preferred to ignore. Then she spoke a word that seemed out of sequence with her mouth: "Irrinipeste."

He did not understand until she said it again. He heard it deep in the back of his head, in a place where the old brain skulked. Only part of it clung, and he repeated it: "Este."

She nodded a kind of agreement and waited. To hear his name, perhaps? He said it slowly. Halfway through its second pronouncement, she started to twitch, then shake. He thought that perhaps she was going to spasm again; the blood was flowing down her legs at an alarming rate. But she gathered herself and walked forward, pulling him behind her.

They walked on, into a clearing with six or seven large and ornately decorated dwellings. A few chickens scurried about in their passing, and a peacock watched them and shrilled. He looked about them and was ready to call out, when the old man was suddenly there. His tattooed and bangled arms held out for the girl. She folded into them and let Williams leave the clearing. As he looked back, he saw her beauty standing between them. It was detached, older, and breathtaking.

➤—➤

Tsungali unwound his sitting body and dropped soundlessly to stand, waiting a few seconds before he was called inside. Slow-motion dust clouded around his long, shoeless feet. He walked behind the soldier who escorted him to the barracks door. As he entered, the soldier grabbed at the Enfield, gripping it midway. Tsungali barked a word or a sound that was a crossbreeding of multiple ferocities, one taken from cats and snakes, birds and winds. The hand sprang back to hang limp and tingling, as if electrocuted, at the terrified soldier's shivering side. Tsungali's eyes drummed the officer's attention. He swallowed his contempt and waved him away. The shivering soldier left the room.

Tsungali walked in and smelt himself there years before, the rush of memories filling the hollows of his previous nervous system. For so it is among those who shed lives every few years: They keep their deflated interior causeways, hold them running parallel with their current usable ones; ghost arteries, sleeping shrunken next to those that pump life. Hushed lymphatics, like quiet ivy alongside the speeding juice of now. Nerve trees like bone coral, hugging the whisper of bellowing communications.

That old part of him swelled with an essence of himself before, nudging the now in a physical déjà vu, becoming two in the stiff interior of his body, ignoring the even stiffer officer who glared in his direction. The overhead fan waded in the congealed air, stirring heartbeats of a larger beast and giving rhythm to the mosquitoes queuing to taste the sweating white skin of the officer, who choked out, "You have been asked to come here"—the claws of the word "asked" scratched the inside of his throat—"for a very special purpose."

Night and insects.

"We are looking for someone to hunt a man, someone we can trust. Someone with all the skills, a bushman warrior."

"Trust" nipped at Tsungali's balls and diaphragm.

Even the officer heard the condescension, and it halted him, giving him time to look more appraisingly at the man before him. He was tall but slightly bent. His formidable skeleton had been broken and repaired many times. The flesh and muscle were hard, dark meat, pliant and overused, solid. The skin was losing its once blue-black sheen, a faint grey opalescence dusting its vitality. The uniform was worn-out and rearranged, mended into another version of itself, turned into how he had wanted it to be: the opposite of its function of uniformity and rank. Its blueness was waning, building a visual alliance with the man's skin. He looked like a shadow in the room and perhaps he was: a static shadow being cast by what was now happening in his swirling being, a gap of light spun out of a space in time.

In this second, the officer was given a moment to look at Tsungali's face, which was now still—not in calmness, but more like a single frame taken from a fast-moving film, held in blur at an unnatural rest. It had been some years since the officer had been this close to him. He had been in chains then, manacled to the courtroom floor. The ferocity of that man's face had been in the wild passion of its movement and malice. Now it was formalised.

The officer stared at the polished bolt of the rifle; polished not by pomp or fetish, but by use.

"Where is he from?" said Tsungali. His voice stopped the mosquitoes and caused the room to listen.

For a moment, the officer was jarred back into the abhorrence of their business and didn't understand the question. Then he said, "He's a white man."

Both men grew tired of each other's presence. The work had been done, the arrangement made. Tsungali had agreed to the hunt. He would take the unknown man's life and empty it somewhere, out in the endless wilderness.

Walking into the night, he was in control of his world. He would shape it with the gods and demons into an understanding of forces, each with its own price, marked in blood. He walked to the back of the compound, where his purloined motorbike skulked in the shadows, a puma skeleton of upright metal. He knowingly placed the Enfield in a brass scabbard on the bike. The rifle was named Uculipsa—"lullaby" in his mother tongue. It sat snugly in the dull, scratched metal, itself scratched and dented by abrasion and impact, but with a dense slumber of nonferrous richness that kept all moisture at bay. Uculipsa was safe here, the flesh of the wooden stock and the muscle and bones of the mechanism protected in the tight, resounding darkness, which smelt faintly of metallic blood. He drove past the sentries and the thick wooden gate, out of a past home and into the darkness of his unflinching confidence. The tyres rumbled and bucked a regular pulse against the red earth as he drove towards his encampment and a task he would enjoy.

He had no hatred of the white men—that would have taken energy away from his purpose. He just knew them all to be thieves and liars. When they made him a police officer in his early twenties, he was already an important visionary for his tribe, a neophyte priest waiting for greater manhood to achieve full status. The prized Irrinipeste herself had seen his value and praised his courage. To be noted by a shaman of such power was a great blessing. When she had asked for the headphones of his cousin, he had willingly given them to her.

His cousin had died the week before Tsungali's promotion, after the incident with the invaders. Many of the True People had worked hard to understand and adopt the new ways, converting the foreign senselessness into some usable part of the real world. His cousin had been one of those. He had watched their ways and seen the fetish that they held dear. He had made copies of the things they guarded and held in reverence, assuming that likeness would clarify everything, even make their words become clear, so that all could share the great wisdom. He made compressions of leaves and earth, bound together with spit and sap. He moulded them into the black steps that the white holy men called Bibles. He even carried his own, pressed against his heart like the padre of the invaders held his.

Yet they had responded badly to his dedication and confiscated all the imitations that he had given out. When he'd retreated into the forest and had started building the hut, they seemed relieved and glad of his departure.

The hut was just big enough for him to enter. Above it, he had erected a very long stick, tying together a collection of the straightest reeds and branches he could find. From this rickety mast dangled a long vine that he had tied to its very top. The vine passed through the roof of the hut, where it was connected to two halves of coconut shell, joined together by a bent twig. This sat on the head of his cousin, one half held over each ear. He, like the whites, was listening to the voices of ghosts floating in the air. His mast caught them on its line and drained them, down to the cups and into his head. He sat there for days, his eyes tightly shut, concentration absolute. When the invaders found him, they laughed until tears ran pink out of their eyes. He had laughed, too, and had given them the headphones, as they called them, to hear the voices.

The officer had taken the shells, still wiping the laughter away from his eyes, and cupped them over his ears. His smile had dropped immediately and he'd thrown the things away, casting them from him as if they were a serpent. He shouted at the cousin and told his men to burn the hut down. But the cousin refused to leave, saying that the spirits wanted it this way and that the fire would pass through the wand, over his hut, and into the air, where it would wait to enter the wand on the white man's hut at another time. He had burnt there. Tsungali had picked up the discarded headphones and watched with the others as the hut, and the spirit mast above it, collapsed about the squatting figure in the smoke.

Nobody had understood the incident then, even the invaders who said prayers for the fire and for his cousin's soul. That understanding would take several years to fully ripen.

It was after that debacle that they had made Tsungali a policeman. To balance things, he thought, and because he'd never accepted one of the solid Bibles. He was an excellent policeman from the first day, obeying all orders and achieving all of his tasks. It was simpler than it looked—he explained to his people what they must be seen to do, they agreed, and so it was done, and the new masters believed their wishes had been carried out. So good was he, in the eyes of his masters, that three years later they rewarded him by flying him from his land into theirs, a long and meaningless journey to show him the magnificence of their origins. By the time he had arrived in the grand European metropolis, he was without compass, gravity, or direction; his shadow had remained behind, bewildered and gazing at the empty sky.

They dressed him in smooth cloth and polished his hair. They put gloves on his feet and pointed boots; they called him John. They took him into great halls to meet many people; he had conducted his duties perfectly, they said. He was trustworthy, they said, a new generation of his clan, a prize in their empire.

He just watched and closed his ears to the drone of their voices. He touched everything, felt texture and colour to remember the difference, the size, and the fact that all things there were worn down, smoothed out, and shiny, as if a sea of a million people had rubbed against the wood and the stone, curving its splinters and hushing its skin. The food they gave him made his mouth jump and sting, burnt him inside and skewered him so that he had to shit continually; even this they kept contained. He was not allowed outside into the clipped gardens, but locked in a tiny room, where all his waste had to be deposited, washed away in a cold stone cup. He could endure all of it because he knew he would return soon.

It was the museum that changed everything and explained the volume of their lies. Like the churches he had been to, it was lofty and dark; everyone whispered and moved quietly, respectful of the gods who lived there. One of the army men had guided him through, showing him box after box of impossible things, all caged in glass. They told lies—the scenes, the guide—about men, living in ice and sleeping with dogs; pointing to tiny totems that glowed in the dark; murmuring their magic; nodding together. Steadily growing more sickened, he had walked ahead and turned a corner, coming to a standstill before the next great case. In it shone all the gods of his fathers. The prison of glass and wood held them, cleaned and standing proud, so that all around could see their power and worship them. But on the floor of the prison were the prized tools and cherished possessions of his clan, all mixed and confused: men's and women's tokens, implements and secrets, entangled and fornicating, lewdly exposed and crushed under writing. Manila tags were tied to each, scrawled white-men lies gripping each cherished thing, animals in traps; the poached, the stolen, and the maimed. All those things that had been taken away, discarded as shoddy and replaced with steel. And there, at the centre, was his grandfather's sacrificial spear. The one that had been handed down towards him for centuries, its wood impregnated with the sweat and prayers of his family. The one that he had never touched. He had walked into a trove house of all that was significant, all that was cherished—all that was stolen.

The visitors were humbled before these objects and deities, quietened into reverence by their influence. One of the uniformed elders got down onto his knees, nose almost touching the glass, to come closer to a carved manifestation of Linqqu, goddess of fertility and the fields.

On the far wall were pictures. Almost in a trance, he walked closer to these, into a memory of his village, pinned to the wall and drained of colour. This was the final sacrilege; the exposure of the sacred, the dead, and the souls of the living.

His sponsors were enjoying his visit, pleased with his attentive behaviour. They watched as he stared at a photograph of an elder of his tribe sitting before an elaborately carved dwelling. It was a significant image of anthropological value, a first-contact document that showed an uninterrupted culture in domestic vigour. Tsungali stared at his grandfather. The old man had never been photographed before, and he'd had no idea why the stranger was covering his face and shaking the box at him. Sitting on the steps of their longhouse, legs holding an animal-tailed flyswatter, the other hand quietly trying to cover his balls; his expression was confused, his head cocked slightly to see around the box, trying to look at the photographer's face. His grandfather's eyes and mouth had just been wounded by strangeness; he was too dazed and absent to ward off the event. The outside of the longhouse was encrusted with climbing, crawling, and gesturing spirits. All of their carved and painted faces were alive, talking to the stranger, laughing at his manner.

The old man looked through the box, through the stranger, through to his reflection, and appeared to shudder. The doorway to the house was dark, but another figure could just be seen inside. A boy, happy and grinning, all teeth and eyes in the darkness, open, smiling amazement. It was Tsungali, caught young, and in opposition to his beloved grandfather's nakedness, bewilderment, and pain.

Tears filled his eyes as he secretly begged the print to move, to turn away or turn back, to do anything but confront his memory with such resistant loss. He could look no more. To find his grandfather trapped behind glass and nailed to a wall, so far from home and his earthly remains, was beyond sacrilege and blasphemy. It gnawed into him, along his genetic ladder, an emotional, hidden thing, chewing back into extinction. He slid backwards into the crowds and quickly became dissolved among their throng. He ran from that place and became lost in the streets of liars outside.

He was, of course, found and returned to his homeland, where it was trusted that he would explain the splendours and dominion of the masters. Instead, he explained that the True People's gods had been stolen and replaced by cross sticks, that all they once were, all they had once worshipped, had been given to others. He explained that their masters had cheated them, had stolen their ancestors and locked them in prisons of glass. He explained that there was only one way to treat such wicked profanation: On the third of June, on a bright spring afternoon, he began the Possession Wars.

By the next day, two-thirds of the invaders were dead or dying, their houses burnt and the church torn apart; the airstrip was ripped up, desecrated beyond recognition.

Peter Williams vanished into myth. So had the blessed Irrinipeste, Este, the child who never grew old, daughter of the Vorrh, kin to the Erstwhile and the living heart of the True People.

>——→

I set my path by the night and walk out of the village, the velocity of the moonlight polishing the miles ahead.

I walk between banked walls of white stone as if in an empty riverbed, a road hollowed out by time, weather, and the continual passage of humans, as migratory as birds. Tribes crossing and recrossing the same gulley, desperately trying to draw a line against extinction. It is with this herd of ghosts that I travel, alone.

After some hours, I pause. I have been aware for some time of tiny movements in the edges of my vision, fish-like punctuations breaking the solid wave of stone on either side, catching the light in dim flashes for less than a blink. Every time I stop, the phenomenon ceases. When I continue, the glinting peripheral shoal follows me. There is wonder at first, but it has now turned to unease, and I fear sentience or hallucination. Neither is wanted at this time: I seek only loneliness and distance, not wanting association or introspection, it being necessary to seek one dimension to understand with clarity. Complexity has crippled me before, and the healing from it took too many years. I will not go there again and share my being with all those others who would claim and squabble over my loyalty. I need only to breathe and walk, but at this time of night, in this albino artery, I hear fear tracking me.

The bow comes to my hand, wand-like and unstrung. She gives off musk. I become calm and weightless, ready for the attack. Nothing happens. I stand, as still as a post. After a time, I tilt my head slightly to see if anything moves. At first nothing, then a flicker, a single, tiny glimmer. I focus on this sprite and move towards it in the manner of a cat stalking a sound. It is not in the air, but in the walls of white stone. I can see it embedded in its cretaceous library. Starlight has ignited it, and a resonance of dim brilliance quivers about its edge. It is a fossilised shark's tooth, a small, smooth dagger encrusted into the stone, its edges bitterly serrated and gnawing against the distant celestial light.

These teeth were once greatly prized and, as I recall, had offered a small industry to the local inhabitants, who dug them out and exported them to political cities, where they were mounted in silver and hung in a cluster on a miniature baroque tree. It was called a credenza, a name that became synonymous with the side table that once held it. The Borgazis and the Medici owned rich and sumptuous versions. When a guest was given wine, he or she was shown to the tree and allowed to freely pick a tooth and place it in the chalice, its delicate chain hooked over the rim. If the tooth turned black, the wine was poisoned; if it stayed unstained, the credence of the wine and the host was proven and business and friendship could commence.

I stand in the black night, musing on distant tables and forgotten aggressions, in a stone river of teeth, some of which I can use; their compact hardness and perfect jagged edges would make excellent arrowheads. In the approaching morning, I will dig them out and clean them, find straight wood for the shafts and hunt swallows; their wings will be my fletching. The wings are only perfect when cut from the bird alive, so I will have to make nets to trap their speed.

Twine, splinters of wood, and weightless teeth shards lie with the wingless bodies of twenty swallows at my feet, their strange, streamlined eyes looking in all directions. The shape of their eyes is echoed in their wings, the same wings that now grace my arrows. A sea fog rises at my back, and the horizon is gated, hinged on shadow. I am ready to leave these bleak, soft lands.

On a brilliant sunlit morning, I shoot another arrow. The curve of its fletching sings in the vibrant air as it flies out over my path of hard stone, which rises into the distant hills.

With each step I seem to climb out of the past, lift away from the flat gravity of waiting. From now on, memories will flow only forwards and await my arrival, the way it happens in dreams, where they give continuity and momentum. In the same way, the arrows went before to sense the void, taste its colour, and name its happenstance. She had written my understanding of this high in the continual pathway. What waited in my dreams to resume the path will be explained to me between the flights of the arrows. My walking between them will unravel the knowledge, while my feet erase the path of all arrivals.

CHAPTER TWO

*I*shmael was not a normal human, but he didn't know this because he had never seen one. He was raised by the Kin—Abel, Aklia, Seth, and Luluwa—gentle, dark-brown machines that nurtured him from infant to child, child to adolescent. They looked like him in shape but were made from a different material. He had grown in their quiet, attentive care, knowing he was not the same but never dreaming that he was a monster. There were no monsters in his world, deep under the stables in the old city of Essenwald.

Essenwald was a European city, imported piece by piece to the Dark Continent and reassembled in a vast clearing made in the perimeter of the forest. It was built over a century and a half, the core of its imitation now so old that it had become genuine, while the extremes of weather had set about another form of fakery, forcing the actions of seasons through the high velocity of tropical tantrum. Many of the old stone houses had been shipped in, each brick numbered for resurrection. Some of the newer mansions and warehouses had taken local materials and copied the ornate, crumbling splendour of their predecessors, adding original artistic brilliance in their skeuomorphic vision of decay. It was prosperous, busy, and full of movement, with solid roads and train lines scrolling out from its frantic, lustrous heart. Only one track crawled into the dark interior of the forest. Into the eternal mass of the Vorrh.

For years, it was said that nobody had ever reached the centre of the Vorrh. Or, if they had, then they had never returned. Business expanded and flourished on its southernmost outskirts, but nothing was known of its interior, except myth and fear. It was the mother of forests; ancient beyond language, older than every known species, and, some said, propagator of them all, locked in its own system of evolution and climate.

The banded foliage and vast trees that breathed its rich air offered much to humans but could also devour a thousand of their little lives in a microsecond of their uninterrupted, unfathomable time. So vast was its acreage, it also made its demands of time, splitting the toiling sun into zones outside of normal calibration; a theoretical traveller, passing through its entire breadth on foot, would have to stop at its centre and wait at least a week for his soul to catch up. So dense was its breathing, it dented the surrounding climate. Swirling clouds interacted with its shadow. Its massive transpiration sucked at the nearby city that fed from it, sipping from the lungs of its inhabitants and filling the skies with oxygen. It brought in storms and unparalleled shifts of weather. Sometimes it mimicked Europe, smuggling a fake winter for a week or two, dropping temperatures and making the city look and feel like its progenitor. Then it spun winds and heat to make the masonry crack after the tightness of the impossible frost.

No planes dared fly over it. Its unpredictable climate, dizzying abnormalities of compass, and impossibilities of landing made it a pilot's and navigator's nightmare. All its pathways turned into overgrowth, jungle, and ambush. The tribes that were rumoured to live there were barely human—some said the anthropophagi still roamed. Creatures beyond hope. Heads growing below their shoulders. Horrors.

The logging roads skirted its perimeter, allowing commerce to gingerly nibble at its unprotected edges. There were no commercial means of ingress or egress from its solid shadow, except for the train. The mindlessly straight track that ran towards its heart was laid, line by line, with the hunger for wood. As it grew forwards, it forgot its immediate past. The iron rail carried sleep in its miles of repetition.

Most of the train that ran on it was composed of open platform and iron chain, built to receive the freshly cut trunks. But there were two passenger carriages, made for short and necessary visits or for those whose curiosity outstripped their wisdom. There were also the slave carriers, basic boxes on wheels designed to carry the workforce into the forest's interior. The slaves had changed before the eyes of their owners. They had transformed into other beings, beings devoid of purpose, identity, or meaning. In the beginning, it was thought their malaise was the product of their imprisonment, but it soon became clear there was no personality left to feel or suffer such subtleties of emotion. The forest itself had devoured their memory and resurrected them as addicts.

The city of Essenwald fed on the trees, consuming the myriad of different species that ferociously grew there. Sawmills and lumberyards buzzed and sang in the daylight hours, rubber works cooked sap into objects, and paper mills boiled and bleached the bodies naked, ready for words. All this appetite was allowed by the forest. It encouraged the nibbling at one of its edges and used it as another form of protection—a minor one in comparison to the arsenal of defence that kept the Vorrh eternal.

Essenwald's declaration of power and continuance was written throughout the twisting streets, like a labyrinthine manuscript. One such crooked causeway was called Kühler Brunnen, its handwritten name nailed high on its sunless side. A house of significant age stood at its middle; its core was among the first to arrive and be sunken into the heated ground, on the site of a more sacred enclosure that some said was older than humanity itself. Parts of its later exterior had been copied in anthracite-rich stone, mined from a long-extinct quarry. Its proportion and whereabouts were stolen from one of the bitter-clad cities of northern Saxony. Its windows were shuttered. It quietly brooded, while deflecting any attention. Its small, neat stables contained three horses, a polished carriage, and a working cart. Cobbles and straw gave movement and scent to its courtyard's stillness, while far below, beneath the blue and yellow, the brown ones hummed and fussed over the white thing they grew. The air was filled with their scent of ozone and phenol and the slight singeing of their overly warm bodies, an odour of life that led to cracking and brittleness, emitting its own distinctive hum, in the same way we age with wrinkles and softening.

Four Kühler Brunnen wanted to be empty. The house thought it had completed its business with full-time occupancy many years before.

Yet while the house contained no people in the poised hollowness of its rooms above ground, in its basement was a well of astonishing depth—if it were ever given sky, it would reflect the most distant galaxies in its sightless water. The old, dark house was always alert and guarding what occurred beneath it.

There, under 4 Kühler Brunnen, among the crated machines and stagnant presses, boxed carboys and empty, stained vessels, Ishmael was becoming a man. His docile white body was beginning to toughen and shape itself for a different purpose, though it would never be as hard as the Kin. He was made of flesh, like the animals, and they were made of Bakelite, like the furniture. Their bodies were perfect in their gleam and the depth of their polished surfaces. Each was a unique, beautiful variation of form and appointment—he forever marvelled at their splendour, while examining the flabby imprecision of his own shell.

Over time, he had become more and more intrigued by Luluwa; she was unlike the others. Not because she was female. That had been explained to him before. There were four kinds of things like him in this world: men, women, animals, and ghosts. He was a man, like Abel and Seth. Luluwa was a woman, like Aklia. He was just a different kind. Men had tubes and strength, women had pouches and gentleness. He had a little of all.

He had first felt heat for Luluwa when she killed an animal for him. Snapping it in her long, shiny fingers, she had opened it for him to taste and smell and had explained that its insides were a copy of his, made in the same materials, unlike her own, which were modelled from a different substance. She had described how the thick, soft covering kept the animal warm, and that in time, he, too, would have such, and that if he looked carefully near the lamp he might see tiny traces of growth already there on his pliant skin. She had extended her smooth, graceful arm and shown him the absence of "hair." He had flushed, felt ashamed and badly made. He'd wanted to hold his breath and suck all the traces of animal back into his shell, wanted every hair to shrivel and glaze over, towards her perfection.

She had explained before that he was too soft to grow, to expand from the inside out, to puff up. She was fully formed and inflexible. This made no sense to him—why would he have to grow into something while she was already there, immaculate? She tapped her brown shell and said that her skin was stiff and brittle while his was pliant and cuttable, that they were both vulnerable in different ways.

She touched the back of his neck, stroking him with two perfect fingers, reassuring him of his place, his distinction, and her affectionate acceptance. The solidity and coolness of her touch excited him and tightened his lukewarm softness into tumescent mimicry. She pretended not to notice and drifted away from his shock on a wave of ductile clicks and internal hisses, sounds he would remember throughout his tangled life.

He lifted his gaze from his awkward lap to watch her move across the long room. Her walk was purposeful, smooth, and exact, as if each of the hundreds of minor adjustments needed for propulsion and balance was consciously thought about, carefully considered in fractions of time that were impossible to contemplate. He knew if he thought about walking like that, he would fall after a few steps. Such perfect control was unattainable to his jarring and ridiculous motion. Luluwa was graceful and constant, while he was becoming more and more clumsy and random. Surges of emotion and eruptions of ideas tossed his motley, leaking being in unpredictable tides, causing him to invent doubt as a companion, to construct anxiety as a mirror in opposition to flawlessness, knowing that only he would be seen in it and that the others would quietly continue without reflection.

Sometimes, when he watched them sleeping, becoming charged, he became fascinated by their stillness. He would sit very close to Luluwa and one of the others and watch for movement. Once, Seth, who was standing behind him, asked why he was looking so closely.

"Because I think they are dead," he said, without a moment's thought. Seth put his hand on the boy's shoulder and made a rotational sound in his throat. "It's like the animals when they are broken," the boy said over his shoulder, without taking his eye off the sleeping woman. "Before they break they are entirely made of movement, and then it stops. Where does the movement go?"

Seth moved to the boy's side and knelt, looking with him. "It is true that all living things move and the movement is unceasing. It is also true that the dead do not move. But sometimes the movement is concealed in smallness and hides from sight. I will show you."

Ishmael broke his stare to watch Seth speaking, looking at the words unfold from his toothless mouth, focusing on the shudder flap dancing in his jaws.

He slid away to a cabinet across the room and opened a drawer. He returned with quick purpose, carrying a glass tube as long as his arm and a small glass funnel. Kneeling again, this time between Luluwa and the boy, he rested one end of the tube on the sleeper's brow and attached the funnel to the other end. He put his finger to his lips, hissed, and winked. The boy understood the agreement and they moved stealthily, so as not to awaken her. Seth put the cupped end of the funnel to the boy's ear, delicately placing the other end in the corner of the sleeper's closed eye. He froze there, half-turning to watch the listener's face.

At first Ishmael could hear nothing but his own agitation. Then, in the tube, he heard a diminutive sound. Yes, and again, a fluid hiss, like the sound of spit in one's mouth, so faint that it could have been from the other side of the universe. Yes! There again—irregular but fast and flickering, a whisper of pulse. He stopped and took his ear away from the tube.

"What is it, that noise?" he asked.

Seth became intent and modestly smiled. "It's her eye moving," he said. "Beneath the hard lid." He stared deep into the boy. "She is dreaming."

➤→

Sigmund Mutter, a trained, tight-lipped servant, would visit 4 Kühler Brunnen every Sunday to mechanically attend to its upkeep. After finishing his duties that day, he turned the key in the heavy lock, which jarred against its closure, causing him to totter in the street. A tarry, wet cigar, chewed into the corner of his badly shaved mouth, accentuated his shallow breath in the cold air. He was returning home to the rich, swollen musk of his wife's lunch, and his attention was slurred between last night's schnapps and the saturated sleep that wallowed on the other side of the thick food of the afternoon; perhaps that is why the lock wasn't quite properly engaged and he fumbled the keys, dropping them into the icy mire.

"Good morning, Sigmund," fluttered a voice above his mittened stooping. He groaned himself into an upright attention to respond to the shining woman smiling over his moleskin hump. There stood Ghertrude Eloise Tulp. Her height was accentuated by the full-length beige winter coat that glowed around her, her radiance framed by a brightly patterned scarf, which held a wide-brimmed hat over stacked curls of auburn hair. Her green eyes shone with a strength that was uncomfortable.

"Good morning, Mistress Tulp; a fine, cold day."

For a moment they were suspended between gestures. The street became narrow as it rose, funnelling from a broad hip for carriages into a stilted neck of roofs, the chimneys crooked and attempting to mimic the calligraphy of trees, burnt black against the madder sky. High in the nape of the street was a clock, unworking and roughly painted out, an act of erasure that had no story. Like its blind face, the meeting below seemed equally gagged.

"How is Deacon Tulp?" Mutter blurted out, with a barked volume that disclosed his need for departure.

"My father is well," she said kindly, knowing that she could play with this stupid man's inferiority. A fierce gust of wind wrestled in from the cathedral square and paused her calculated sport, agitating the heavy door just enough for her to see that it was unlocked.

"Do give my regards and affection to your wife and the little ones," she piped. He blinked clumsily at her, not quite believing the ease of his escape. "And do tell her not to worry about the lateness of the rent; my father understands that things are hard at this time of year."

This sent him scurrying away, stuttering his beaten hat against his flaky head with felicitation for all of her kin. She was left in the empty, windblown street with her excitement distinctly rattling in the mouth of the half-open lock.

Mutter's main task was looking after the house and the horses, beasts that he and his family had the use of when not ferrying crates from locations across the city to the cellars below and vice versa.

Each week he collected a numbered crate from a warehouse an hour's drive away, brought it to the house, and exchanged it for the previous week's used one. He had no idea what was inside the beautifully made, simple wooden boxes, and he did not care. Such was his temperament; it was fiercely consistent, as it had been with his father and hopefully would be with his sons. It wasn't his or their concern to pry into the business that had kept them secure and employed for the last eighty years. Anyway, such enquiries were not the property of his class. Imagination was always inevitably a disastrous activity when operated or purloined by those in service.

The boxes were of varying weights, and he occasionally took one of his sons along to help with the heavier loads. It was good training for the boys, to see and understand the house, to repeat their duties and guard the quiet. They had known the building from the moment they could walk. It had been the same with him when he was a lad, standing behind his father's legs as the gate was opened, terrified by the size of the horses and the richness of their smell, mesmerised by the stillness inside the lofty, empty rooms, and always waiting to see the masters appear. But they never did. He never saw anybody there, because the house was empty. Only his father had keys.

One day, when he was twelve and waiting in the kitchen, swinging his feet from his perched seat, he thought he saw something in the far wall, a brown, polished shadow of something that moved out of his sight. He sensed, even then, that he must not see it, so he unbound it from his memory and never spoke about it, especially not to his father.

He was in the same basement kitchen now, gingerly dragging the box across the room to the middle wall, where the dumbwaiter was concealed behind a panel of polished wood. The kitchen was dominated by a rectangular marble table that occupied its volume with a dignity of purpose. This would have been the focus of the entire kitchen staff when preparing food for the household or when resting at the end of the day and feeding themselves.

Mutter panted as he straightened up and steadied himself, gripping the cold stone and wiping his red, wet face with a towel that he always kept folded near the sliding wall. Over the years, he had perfected a technique of lifting and sliding the boxes in and out of the interior of the dumbwaiter, but now it was getting difficult. Not because of weakness, but from a slowness that seemed to be dissolving his energy, like a flame passing over the wax of a candle. The image of a cold, sallow puddle, flooded on its white saucer, its bristling wick tilted and sinking, made a chill run through the bulk of his body. He gathered himself and heaved the crate into the lift with an echoing thunder that was swallowed into the depth of the shaft below the floor. The dumbwaiter worked in reverse. Instead of servicing the rooms above, as would usually have been the case, it travelled downwards into a self-contained and undisclosed part of the house. He had always assumed the queerly shaped elevator had something to do with the well that must be down there, giving the house and the street their name.

He closed the lift door and slid the panelling back into its position of concealment. Dragging the lighter, used crate out of the room, he slowly closed the door behind him, pausing momentarily until he heard the lift begin to be winched down on its long, thick ropes.

He listened, not out of curiosity, which would have been impermissible, but out of a sense of impending satisfaction. His duty and his task were again complete.

>→

Ishmael knew the crates were a teaching library. Each box contained poignantly selected examples of the world outside: Its structures, materials, animals, tools, plants, minerals, and ideas were represented for explanation. Some were preserved samples, sealed in jars; some fresh; some alive. There were also photographs, prints, and reproductions.

The Kin would open the crates away from their pupil. They would become silent and stiff, their heads in the boxes. Ishmael thought they were listening for instruction or having their memories prompted. But he never heard a voice, just a long, piping whistle.

They would take turns to explain the wonders to Ishmael. Sometimes they specialised in certain subjects. Abel would delineate materials and processes; Aklia would explain plants, minerals, and the earth in which they grew, also their attendant insects; Seth would demonstrate tools, act out history, and show inventions; Luluwa would illustrate the animals, how they worked and how they might be used.

There was always a small box inside the large one. This was taken out and examined in the kitchen and would then be turned into food for him. He loved the word "kitchen"; it was one of the first he'd learned. It was nourishment, perfume, and warmth, and he smelt its sound long before he tasted it. It also made the others' mouths go very strange. He watched when one of them said it, all of his attention turning to the speaker. It was the first thing he remembered making him laugh—not knowing why, just in response to their reactions. It somehow got better when they did nothing but stare blankly back.

They only ever laughed once, some days after he had shown them how he did it. They had watched his demonstration with such solemn attention that it had turned his perfunctory titters into full-blown guffaws. But when they came back and laughed for him, it was horrible. He could not explain why. It was simply wrong, the grating opposite of what he'd felt and heard during his spontaneous outburst. They had been practising it for him, for his sake, to join in, but they had no depth of reference. It was not in any of the crates. They promised never to do it again. In return, he promised never to scream again, never to sob uncontrollably.

Their care and tenderness were much better expressed through action and movement and touch, through the gentle unfolding of knowledge, companionship, and food.

The day that Luluwa showed him how his body could extend into her and produce nectar was overwhelming. She had cleared away the lesson of flies and he had posed a question about the thing she had called "pleasure." He knew it was like the dry white "sugar" or the thick yellow "honey," not outside or on the tongue, but all over. She said that his kind had many ways to find it and that they were all connected to knowledge. She said pleasure was made of cream, like her motor.

Some weeks before, Abel had shown him a small part from one of their bodies—the curved hollow of a Bakelite shell. Its interior was notched and ingrained with tiny lines, small dents, and channels. Bumps covered its surface, very different from the smooth perfection of its gleaming other side.

"We are hollow, only fluid inside," Abel had said, "not like you and the other animals, packed full of matter and organs. We work in another way. All of our forces are held in a thick cream contained within us; all that we are is alive in that cream, and it feeds and talks to the inside of our shell through these complex ducts and circuits." He pointed to the inside of the fragment in his hands. "We know nothing of its workings; it is forbidden that we question and examine its process. We have a greater knowledge of you than we do of ourselves."

Ishmael wanted to know more about pleasure and pressed Luluwa for a description. She said there were no words to explain it. "Your kindred have a connection between their breeding and their sweetness, a swelling of both that works like the magnets in Lesson Twenty-Eight. Their conception also follows the same construct."

He wanted more.

"Yes," she said. "It is time to show you. You are like the animals that we have seen—you must place your tube inside the pouch of the female to breed. The seeds then pass to fertilise the egg. This you know. But what you will learn is that its action is layered with pleasure."

Ishmael understood her words but not their consequence.

"When you release your seed," she said, "there is a great song of warmth."

He stared and spun inwardly. She coiled down closer to him. Her hard, gleaming hand stroked his thigh. The firmness of her shell drew an erection. "I will show you that I have been fashioned like your kind to explain these marvels to you. These lessons of humans have been clearly taught to me alone, for you."

She showed him a latch in the crease between her legs, normally hidden by its underside position. She asked him to move it and, with chattering fingers, he felt the mechanism of this secret thing. After a while she joined in, her nimble fingers sliding its notch down the entire length of her division, leaving the long cleft open.

"Touch inside," she said.

It was warm and soft. He looked closer, some of his hand now within her, fingers moving the folded layers.

"Kelp," he said. "It's made of kelp." Kelp had been in Lesson 17. Jars from the sea.

If she could have smiled, she would have. Instead, she stroked his head and said, "No, but very like it. It's a material you have not yet seen." She pushed the notched bulb in a little further and moisture flooded his touch.

"You leak like me," he said. "Like me and the animals. You never did before."

"This is not the same. This is not the passing of waste fluid, but a special oil to let you move inside me without friction or hurt."

She guided him towards her, positioning her prone body, and with the same attentive concentration that she showed when peeling the animals apart, she drew him into her. An inner clasping made Ishmael flinch, but she rectified it with the pressure of her left hand in the small of his back and a series of whistling clicks that he knew were declarations of satisfaction, the same sounds she made when he understood her other lessons. A growing wave of succulent achievement overcame him, and he began to push deeper inside her. His hands gripped the hard perfection of her curved hips, making the contrast of her hot interior a wonderful benefaction.

This was different from all the other things she had shown him. The understanding was in his whole body, churning with sugars that gave him a direct power he had never dreamt of before. He tasted might and dominance and the impossible joy of retreat as she fed his anxious childhood into the past. They rocked together while he cried, sobbing pleasure, locked in her arms, sensation boomeranging sensation with continual vigour. Suddenly she began to shake, every joint shuddering, her voice impaling itself on an imprecision of sound. This had never happened before, and she had no understanding of its purpose or meaning. Only Ishmael knew that one of her inner ventricles had been flushed directly to the shunt mechanism of her sleep and recharging mode, had switched into total response as he reverberated against her, causing her to flick in and out of sleep in a fast stutter of consciousness and oblivion, producing something like pleasure constructed of surprise in her old, servile body of juice and stringency. As long as the rule regarding her Kin was in place, she would never be able to comprehend her reaction. The mystery would be for Ishmael alone to understand.

Ghertrude Eloise Tulp was an only child. She was "only" in a great manner of ways: in the way that a single child is given all; in the way that it is received and understood as a sign of natural superiority, growing into unquestionable rightness; in her luscious delight in solitude and satisfaction without a trace of loneliness.

She was the pride, construct, and admiration of her father, the third-generation owner of the city's second-largest timber merchant, who had long since left the basic details of his inherited empire to his servants and turned his razor-keen appetites to politics and the church. She was modest in her skin, charming in her manner, with a tall, willowy vagueness, which mostly concealed the centre of her hunger. Her twenty-two years had been filled with kindness and education, but none of it had thawed her hurt at being born unknowing. She wanted to find out and possess all. Quickly.

She had always hated being excluded. Not many dared to attempt it socially—her power was too far-reaching and influential to be toyed with. But most had tried to lock her out in more literal ways, with brass and iron puzzles that fooled their owners into trusting their blind servitude. From the age of seven, she had begun to understand their mechanics and principles and, with that realisation, what delicious power and satisfaction lay on the other side of their manipulation. She had gained access to all hours of the day and night. She had tiptoed in forbidden places. She had seen a royalty of secrets: her parents becoming the beast with two backs; treasures being hidden; the dead, rotting in conversation in the catacombs beneath her home. She had seen intrigue, incest, deceit, lies, and pleasures, all closed to the assumption of sight.

Now she stood in the shadow of 4 Kühler Brunnen while the buffoon Mutter disappeared home. She waited a tantalising time, watching the street set into stillness, enjoying the restraint before she touched the door to see if her curiosity really had a menu. She walked quickly across the empty space and pushed the cold gate. It moved, heavy under her calfskin glove.

Her joy spun and silently shrieked: This was forbidden and ecstatic. The house had been a great secret for all of her life, the only thing denied to a child who was given everything. No one in her family would talk about it.

"Ah, *ja*, the Kühler Brunnen house," they would say, and then change the subject. She had stared at it, glared at it, and watched it in passing all the days of her life, from her pram to her womanhood. Something in it had tapped at her shell, stirring the wakening within. And now she had breached its outer wall, closing the gate behind her in protection from all vulgar intrusion.

She lingered over the stables and the basic construction of the courtyard, drawing out her anticipation before approaching the entrance to the building. To her delight and surprise, the lock was simple, an old and well-known type, the kind she had been surreptitiously picking for years in her family's homes. The door of this house would be no match for her skills, and she thrilled at the thought of devouring the secrets it had concealed for so long.

She returned through the courtyard. Once back at the gate, she looked again at the lock and laughed, almost too loudly. This was the ridiculous contraption that had held her at bay for so long? She could have opened it years before. It had only taken Mutter's pantomime of stupidity to give her permission and scrawl the ticket to her fulfilment.

She shut and padlocked the gate and walked along the darkening street, humming her way home and savouring her strength and the sweet weakness of everything around her. There was no rush now; she already had the conclusion to the enigma firmly in her grasp. She would relish all the possibilities rather than leaping into the outcome; it would pay back all those years of frustrating exclusion. She now owned every imagined room.

Six days later, when Mutter had again left, she entered the house.

CHAPTER THREE

The Frenchman was the only modern being to have explored the Vorrh, to enter its interior and scribble down some of its detail. The only one—and all his perilous journey had been fiction. What better way was there to trespass on the sacred and the forbidden?

He had, of course, read or held the weight of every volume related to its existence. He had absorbed all the obscure and fantastic accounts of travellers who had returned by the skin of their teeth, having been hunted by the anthropophagi, the Artabatitai, the dog-headed Hemikunes, and all manner of fabulous denizens, representative of every forest in the world, which had been sucked into the mythical whirlpool of the Vorrh. He knew of the saviour of the forest, the fabled Black Man of Many Faces, and saw in it another reworking of the Green Man of Europe; he owned copies and private translations of Euthymenes the Massilian and late medieval renditions of Scylax of Caryanda; he had marvelled at the tall tales of Sir John Mandeville, stories of the horrors and wonders to be found in the uncharted depth of unknown lands. He had ploughed through the works of Abu Abdullah Muhammad Ibn Battuta, even tried to find the famous mummies that had been bought by René Caillié and shipped, on a tortuous route through Timbuktu, back to France, where over the latter years of forgetfulness they had become "misplaced."

He had read all the fact and all the fiction, and in later days of need and intrigue, he had created his own version, cut out of the jungles of all the other words, their slippery shadows of meaning translated into a rich weft of description. He had re-seen each moment and the backdrop of the eternal, savage forest. His writing had given it life, with all the detail of its population.

The Frenchman, Charlotte, and a reluctant chauffeur had driven into Essenwald, through the outskirts of mud and rushes to its fired foundations of imported German dogma. Their huge car heaved and jolted on the deeply rutted road. It was the first-ever motor caravan, a grandiose collision of baroque parlour and expensive, petrol-driven truck, which he had invented specifically for long-distance travel. During the day, the three travellers would be separated, each sweating in a different compartment of the vehicle, the varnished dark-brown interiors sweltering in the buckling heat. The chauffeur was forced to wear his uniform at all times, even in the blistering temperatures. Only at night would his nakedness be tolerated and his name allowed.

Charlotte was paid to stay close, to be the lifelong companion to her neighbour in the eighth arrondissement. She did this with understanding and gratitude, and because she was drawn to such stray dogs—even the noble ones.

The Frenchman's mother paid for Charlotte's attentions, paid for everything. She knew of her son's weakness and something of his genius. She doted on him, and her love would have devoured him completely if she had not had a greater suitor. That suitor was heroin, and it determinedly won all conflicts of emotion and care. So Charlotte was employed to be her stand-in, the visible female pillar to which the Frenchman would be publicly leashed. This way, he could strain against something external and always have a place to return to, scratch against, and abuse.

Charlotte had a face that should have been loved. Her over-powering eyes said everything that was sensitive and feeling, on a level that hurt. Indeed, hurt was what coloured her gaze, not for herself, but for those around her, who pained and leeched their existence into permanent sadness. She was strong because she was quiet. Not silent, but still. Hers was a beauty of listening and a strength of giving; there was knowing, more than under-standing, in the smoulder of her gaze. She saw and felt it all; she gave more love than she received, more than she was ever paid for.

They had been driving for an hour when the Frenchman ordered the car to stop. He smelt blood. They'd been passing through the outskirts of the city, swerving and bumping towards its stony European heart. A shrine tower, one of the many tall, red buildings with wound-like windows, had given off a pun-gent aroma, its dried-mud surface still showing the prints of the hands that had made it. Goats had been slaughtered there each day for centuries, and one side of the tower was saturated black with blood and milk. He stepped out of the car into the blinding sunlight, the dust still spinning in circles around the stationary wheels.

In this part of the fabled city, the streets were immaculate in their filth. Taking a pair of bone spectacles from their seal-skin case, he arranged them over his eyes; the slits narrowed his vision and gated the sun. They had come from Greenland, purchased from a recent explorer of that frozen, barren place.

He was the most ridiculous of travellers, brilliantly pre-pared for all events, so long as they never happened. His hand-made shoes were instantly discoloured by the red earth, as was his cream suit. He stood and glared at the tower, waiting to be noticed by the throng of local passersby. They had seen him, the little man stamping in the ground of arrival, but they were much more interested in his vast, grunting cart, enclosed on all sides.

They slowed their pace and drifted towards its metal body, some daring to touch it on its blind side. Soon, the Frenchman would meet the young man who was to become the most significant person in his overcast life, but for that moment the crowd was pressed against the car's windows, trying to glimpse the interior. The woman inside gripped her small clutch bag. Hiding in the perfumed darkness was her silver derringer, a palm-size pistol of American origin; it sat like a bright comma in the umbered pouch. It was made to fit snugly in the hand when discharged. It was blunt and inaccurate but delivered a lethal slap at short range. The Frenchman had never had any feelings of masculine protection for the fairer sex, even the few he had tolerated and liked. He and his paid companion had been locked in a crude democracy forged from selfishness, desire, and humiliation.

Turning his back on the angry chauffeur and the twitching woman, he walked towards the tower in the open street.

A young man had stepped out of the sun, the halo of his head blasted by brightness. "Which is your way, Father? Are you lost?" he asked. "Where is your way?" he asked again, in a French that reflected the rippling mirage of sand that surrounded them.

He stared at the young man, speechless as his face came into focus. There was a resonance in his tone that had stirred a place yet unravelled, but nonetheless known, in his scarred heart. In a voice that was eerily subdued, he told the young black man that he was here to see the Vorrh, to gaze on the fabled forest.

The man's eager smile broadened, and he looked out over the dust and the Frenchman's shoulder. He pointed a tattooed finger towards the horizon. The Frenchman turned quickly to follow his direction, to look through the crumbling gap between the rows of buildings, where a dark curtain closed off the northern-most aspect of the city with shadow and solid contrast. The redness of earth, animals, plants, and buildings ended at its massive edge.

Its suddenness instantly reminded him of a stage set and returned him to the opera he had seen as a child. It had been vivid and overwhelming, its story indistinct, its music brash and bellowing. But its set had transfixed him, a forest of painted darkness stretched across the stage, blindingly artificial, its leaves, roots, and hanging tendrils filling his hungry imagination with a longing that had gnawed at all other realities with an unrelenting insistence; the same scene would pass through the last millisecond of his life, as he lay, seeded in oxygen, choking for absorption in the tiled indifference of a hotel bathroom.

That was only the second time he had been to the theatre, though his mother had often told him of it. She would come to say good night while he was in the bath, his nanny stopping, mid-sponge, to stand back in admiration while the apparition wafted in. She was always dazzling, in her society gowns and gleaming jewellery. She would tell him of the theatres and balls she was going to; of ballet and the opera; their stories of princesses and kings, demons, maidens, magic, and spells. Sometimes she would touch his back or arm with her silken gloves, sending a shiver through his damp, excited body. But she never stayed, and the nanny was always left to dry his cooling hope and dress it for sleep. His mother's perfume stayed in his heart for hours afterwards.

At last within sight of the Vorrh, he understood why he had travelled so far. Yet as he took an automatic step towards it and everything else that had unbalanced his life, his chauffeur had begun to pound on the horn of the car—his forgotten companions had become completely engulfed by a solid wall of in-lookers. The discordant screech, his memories, and his stumbling curiosity knotted against movement in time, cutting his next step away from beneath him, causing him to fall forward in stupid surprise towards the red earth. The young man swooped and caught his awkwardness in long black arms, before righting them both.

The Frenchman struggled against the embrace. He liked to be touched only when and where he commanded. He was about to shriek at the outrage, when something of its firm gentleness crept through his disgust. He looked into the face of the tall shadow who held him. His rescuer was now totally silhouetted against the blinding sun, his features and eyes hidden. Yet his expression could be perceived; his eyes radiated grace. Grace was holding him up, tottering on the sanguine earth. The young man said nothing, but extended a long, thin arm, shivering with bangles, towards the shade of a low building. The Frenchman leant into the grip of the other and allowed himself to be guided forward. Without speaking, they walked into the shade of a pungent bar, where they sat and drank mint tea and tried to talk. The young man started by introducing himself, explaining that, despite his rags, he was of noble blood.

"I will call you Seil Kor," the Frenchman announced.

"But that is not my name, master."

"That does not matter. Seil Kor was a great hero and I know his name well. For this adventure, you shall be he."

The young man had frowned at this strange way but accepted his play name to make the little man more comfortable. The conversation became more serious, and when the Frenchman declared he would traverse the entire forest, the space between their knowledge and understanding broadened and split.

Seil Kor turned his gaze away from his new companion and looked out towards the horizon. "Thou canst walk to the derelicts of the saints," he said with firmness and distance, "but no farther. More is forbidden. From there is barred; you must turn away. No son of Adam is allowed, for God walks there."

The Frenchman's sense of intrigue and challenge was ignited by such bold and ultimate statements. "The gods and monsters that live there must be more savage at the centre." He smirked.

At this, Seil Kor's countenance gained an expressive patience, and he turned to stare back into the conversation, while making a gesture over his heart. "Not gods of old people," he said gently. "The one God. Your God; my God; Yahweh. The great Father who made all things and gave Adam a corner of his clearing, so that he may dwell in it and grow. He walks there. It is his garden on earth. Paradise."

A sudden silence opened around them.

"Seil Kor, my friend, are you telling me that the Garden of Eden is located in the Vorrh?"

"Yes, it is so. But Eden is only a corner of God's garden; the rest of the clearing is where God walks, to think in worldly ways. It is impossible in heaven, where all things are the same, without form or colour, temperature or change. In his worldly garden, he wears a gown of senses, woven in our time. He lets rocks and stones, wind and water, clothe his invisible ideas. He pictures our life in the matter that makes us."

The Frenchman was shocked and moved by such faith and by the clarity that bound it. Delaying his cynicism, he tried desperately to shape his next question outside of his normal patronising indifference. "How do you know this?" he asked.

Seil Kor was confused by the question. Could his companion really be so obtuse? "Because he has told us," he replied.

Any further questioning the Frenchman may have been tempted towards had been silenced. They parted ways, agreeing to meet the next morning and begin their journey to the lip of the Vorrh.

He returned to his servants and found their hotel, solidly located at the centre of the city, on sturdy roads where all dust was banished. That night, the Frenchman had hardly spoken to Charlotte. Lying on his bed, listening to the moonlit sounds outside, he had prayed for sleep. He wanted to dream in biblical weight and in the brightness of a lush garden, untenanted by man for thousands of years. But the dreams that awaited him were without pity and had the predatory grace of a jackal.

He awoke the next day drenched in sweat, his pillow turned pink—dazed, he searched his head and body for a wound that might explain the stained fabric, but nothing could be found.

The dream had hollowed him; no trace of rest remained as he crawled into the morning, defeated and abused. Hot water did nothing; the stain of the night was indelible. He dressed grudgingly, tightly buttoning himself into a costume of scratchy, irritant lies. With one gulp of bitter black coffee, he walked out of his room and into the day, speaking to nobody. Outside the hotel, the heat had waited, ready to pounce.

Seil Kor stood in the shadow of a palm tree across the street. "*Bonjour*, effendi!" he called, one hand waving in the intense blue sky, as the blindingly white suit stepped into the sun. The Frenchman, barely able to get into his stride, had found himself exuberantly propelled along the street.

"We go directly to the Vorrh," said his acquaintance. "But on our way, I want to show you something."

He mumbled agreement but was inwardly horrified by the idea of walking. He had had no intention of making the journey on foot, yet discovered himself being dragged down the main road of the filthy town by a stranger. His irritation began to rise with the heat of the day; the claws of his previous night were prickling, envious, and alive.

Walking on the raised wooden pavement, under arcades of curved sandstone, he was reminded of the precise architectural splendours of Bern, where he had spent some time with his mother, shopping in the days before Christmas, the snow falling without intention, light and constant. Not a single flake had touched them as they moved from shop to precious shop, the vaulted Altstadt offering a snug tunnel of civilised proportions, the pleasure of warm cinnamon wine and pine trees scenting the frosted air.

As suddenly as he'd fallen into the fantasy, the perversity of the comparison had spat back, giving him no time to relish or ponder; his own mechanism of creative invention had turned on him once again. It had begun to happen more and more by then; the brilliance of his literary deceit had a vindictive twin, who could not see why his little word game, if it was so clever, should function only in his languid fiction. Each day it had started to apply the same rules of composition and invention to his life, twisting pleasure and experience into worthless jokes. It grabbed at his memories and perverted them with elaborate motivations, succulent in their weirdness, making stupidity and pride fuck on the hallowed ground of his genius. Here, everything was made of rotting wood and was held together by the stink of collapse. It was nothing like the elegance of Switzerland; even the grand stone houses paled into insignificance.

His irritation had mounted, turning inwards with a voracious glee. It chased him with accusations: The base of the comparisons had been exhaled from some dim childish sentiment— surely it should have been beaten out of him years earlier? And what was he doing there, anyway? He never left his rooms or his car. Why had he agreed to meet this stupid savage?

So it had continued. A swarm of flies buzzed around his head, a halo of carrion, just to emphasise the point. He spluttered one out of his mouth, waving his hands about wildly to fend the others off and dropping his cane, which clattered off the boardwalk and into the soiled road. Seil Kor only laughed at his new friend's pantomime. Indignant at the best of times, the Frenchman was entangled by an instant rage and spat abuse into the face of the ignorant black peasant. Nothing happened.

Seil Kor did not register shock or anger. He hadn't even flinched, but converted his open laugh into a serious, frowning smile and waited.

The hiss of the final expletives drained away; the Frenchman was ready to turn and stomp back to the hotel, when, with a smooth and simple action, Seil Kor took a fine, silken scarf from his head and loosely knotted it about the red and raging throat of the small man before him. The world dropped away. The blue of the silk and the sky melted together, a fresh breeze cooling his heart and soothing his mind.

With all the venom and distress gone, Seil Kor took his hand and led him on, bringing them to the doors of a nearby church. He directed his dazed companion inside, and they sat in the cool of the interior, on one of the dark, carved pews. The Frenchman tried to find words of apology, but it had been so long since he'd used them that he remained dumb.

"I have brought you here to understand the Vorrh," said his guide. "This house of God is for those travellers who pass near its sacred heart. The Desert Fathers founded this church before one stone was laid on another, before even a single tree was cut. They came out of Egypt like the prophets of old, came to guard and wait, to protect us and those travelling through us."

The Frenchman looked around the chapel. Images of trees dominated the iconography; trees and caves. Black, kohl-rimmed eyes stared out of a face that looked like it had been carved with an axe. Dark, shoulder-length hair and a tangled beard framed the whiteness of the Father's staring expression. In one hand he held a Bible, in the other a staff. He sat in a cave, surrounded by the deep green of an impenetrable forest. The scene had been set on a square piece of thick and gnarled wood. The Frenchman stared at the icon while the tall black man spoke over his head.

"The Vorrh was here before man," he said. "The hand of God

swept over this land without hesitation. Trees grew in its great shadow of knowing, of abundance. The old silence of stones was replaced by the silence of wood, which is not quiet. A place for man was made, to breathe and be thankful. A garden was opened at the centre of the shadow and the Vorrh was given an occupant. He is still there."

The Frenchman's eyes unlatched from the gaze of the saint. He turned to look up at Seil Kor. "The Bible says the children of Adam left the sacred lands and moved into the world."

Seil Kor made a gesture over his own head, a cross between wafting a scent and stroking a halo. "Yes, so it is written—but Adam returned."

They continued to talk while the heat of the day prowled around the chapel. The Frenchman had given up the last remnant of sexual desire for his companion. It had been present from the start, a rich, thick musk of fantasy that had excited their meetings. He had seen no reason, initially, why he should not possess the black prince and add him to the list of urchins, sailors, and criminals who had spiced the gutter of his sexual greed. He was handsome and presumably well-endowed; his obvious poverty would have made him easy to purchase for a short time.

But the words in Seil Kor's mouth—the certainty of his vision and the kindness in his eyes—had washed away those stewed perfumes, replacing them with an ethereal distance that shocked back the very pride and circulation of his vital cynicism. The tired ghost of his ennui had been offered colour and hope. He had begun to sense, with some fear, that Seil Kor tasted of redemption. He even found himself giving weight to the ludicrous myths of the Vorrh and the salvation that might shudder in them. They talked of the serpent sin, of deliverance, of the starry crown and the origin of purpose; Adam's house in paradise, his generations, Eve's punishment, and all the crimes of knowledge. During those moments, his eyes had wandered back to the saint and to his brothers lining the walls. He took in the black-and-white prints of angels; some he'd recognised as being pages from a book, torn and framed excerpts of Gustave Doré's visions of heaven and hell. The images were solid, almost marble in appearance, so different from the glowering Desert Father patriarchs of the icons, who all had the same eyes, an impossible combination of tempera infinity and point-blank, chiselled authority. It had occurred to him that Seil Kor had younger versions of the same eyes and that they would mature into that same gaze of stern wisdom.

As the conversation came to an end, the Frenchman noticed another painting. Smaller than the rest and set in a far corner of the chapel, away from any source of light, it was made on the same dense, gessoed wood, but something had obviously gone wrong with its process, for the pigmentation of varnish had turned black. He drew closer to examine it; it was as if the picture was empty, or contained only painted night. He put his fingertips on its crusted surface, discerning a raised outline, the contours of a head, the painting's swallowed occupant invisible in the tarry depth.

"What is this one?" he asked of his guide.

The young man looked bashful and evasive and refused to look directly at the block of darkness.

"What is this one? Please tell me."

"Some of the stories from the Vorrh are older than man and they become confused with the Bible," replied Seil Kor. "I think this is one of those. It is said that a being will come to protect the tree, after all the sons of Adam are dead. He is called the Black-Faced Man. This might be him."

The Frenchman looked closer at the picture. As he did, Seil Kor turned away, saying that he thought they would need a complete day to discuss the Vorrh's entrance, and that this day had been sidestepped to catch a different knowledge. It was the way of life, to scent the direction of the breeze or a man's falling. That day had been about the chapel and their place in the wheel of time. He noisily picked up the Frenchman's cane from one of the pews and gave it to him—it was warm and light. A whisk of dust swirled from its tip, looking like smoke in the shafting rays of the afternoon that waited outside. They never spoke about the tablet of darkness again.

CHAPTER FOUR

$\mathcal{E}$dward Muggeridge was a hollow man. Born that way. A camera without an aperture. Closed and hoping that nobody would ever see the volume of his dark interior. He worked hard on the panelled walls that framed him, changing his when he felt it could add gravitas and solemnity. He left England to start a new life and roamed the Americas starting modest businesses, scratching a respectable living selling other people's images of the world. Until a fateful day in 1860, when he missed the boat and instead left San Francisco by stagecoach. In mid-Texas velocity, concussion and blood changed the signature of Edward Muggeridge forever.

Before the accident he was a thirty-year-old man filled with vapor, aimless and devout, seeking a place in the world where he might gain weight and merit. When the speeding stagecoach had tripped on the unseen root, it had spun into the air and splintered, mangling and spilling all the lives it carried. He alone survived, tossed among the wrenched luggage and the broken, kicking mustangs. He had cut himself out of the canvas, a petticoat from a dead woman's luggage staunching his head blood, swooning clear of the hooves, which were now running against the sky, trying to gain purchase on the dying clouds. He now saw horses all the time, galloping in headaches, their iron hooves sparking the dendrite fuse wire to the fire in his brain.

He saw them cantering, all turning to white, eyes rolling, savage. He heard them walking, their echo mocking the vacant night streets below his hospital bed. They paced his beginning and his demise with an equal, measured step.

The aperture that had been gouged into his brain had no lens. It was permanently sick in double vision and raging in pain. After fifteen months he took the compensation from the Stage Company and set sail back to England, to find a cure or a focus.

First he changed his name to Edward Muygridge. Second he sought a doctor. Upon his return, the capital was swarming with horses; their stink and their volume made him shiver as he crossed London Bridge. His first consultation waited on the other side of the teeming river. He was early for the appointment; this was something that happened constantly. He deplored tardiness and overcompensated for it in every aspect of his life. He would rehearse the most trivial of deeds: framing the minor in advance of its time; having keys in his hands four streets away from home; talking under his breath to have a convincing answer to questions that would never be put to him. He forced himself to stop on the bridge and allow the slowness of actual time to catch up to his velocity. Placing his hands on the gritty stone, he looked down into the frantic activity of the Pool of London; cargo ships were moored three deep along its banks, their masts creaking against a spiny forest of cranes and the new verticality of the smoke from the steamers, all extending higher than the buildings that clung, crablike, to the land; dozens of barges obtusely nudged and grated one another in the restless tide and the wake of commerce; hundreds of small craft ferried to and fro, carrying pilots, passengers, and information. Every surface seethed and bristled with workingmen; stevedores and lightermen moved tons upon tons of goods and exchanged cargos in what looked like ceaseless confusion.

At times, the river could not be seen at all. The vast activity smothered it, and the detritus it bred was like a rough woven carpet, heaving over a secret turmoil. It was impossible to believe it was the same river that so gently flowed through his hometown. In Kingston, its broad ripple gave reflection and beauty; it was for fishing, idle boating, and rumination. There, you could smell its vitality. The tar, smoke, sewage, and proximity of Billingsgate gave the stretch in front of him a very different signature.

He pulled the great watch from his pocket and flipped it open. It had been the only thing he had kept of his family while on his travels; they had given it to him to ease his departure and secure at least one dimension in the distant colonies. He squinted at the Roman numerals. Time had finally caught up with him, and he started to walk briskly towards the Surrey side.

Dr. William Withey Gull was on schedule. His consulting room sat high on the brow of the building, facing the river. The spire of Southwark Cathedral and the dome of St. Paul's could be aligned from his oriel window.

Like them, the two men were almost cartoon opposites: Gull, opulent, padded, slick; a man grounded and in possession of his life; he retained the bones of his labouring family, held them in check with fine but simple tailoring; he wore his growing eminence in saturated gravity. Muygridge, lean and dry, a longing husked in doubt; frowning himself into biblical status; nervous, darting, and ill.

They shook hands, each gauging the other. Muygridge sat and proceeded to relate his medical history: the condition of his skull since the accident, the shifts of perception. Gull stood behind him as he talked, examining the cranium of the agitated man, feeling the words reverberate beneath Muygridge's scalp. He held the cup of the occiput and moved his hand forward, until it felt the ridge in the bregma, the overriding bone. He fingered the coronal suture, sensing its tension under his controlled pressure. The motion of his square hands under the long, matted hair made it look like a bizarre tableau of ventriloquism; he moved them farther forwards to determine the displacement or division in the nasofrontal suture. He then sat back down behind his Jurassic desk and began to make notes of his observations.

"Was it your face that took the impact of the crash?"

The patient put his hand to his face and covered his eyes and forehead. "Here," he said.

"Tell me," the surgeon said, "when you came to after the crash, what sensations did you feel? What sensory images do you remember?"

"I smelt cinnamon, and everything was blurred, like a double exposure, for days." His hand fingered the scar where the bone had peeped through that terrible day. "Cinnamon and burnt leather; a numbness in my hands; and the horse. I was lying on the earth, near one of the dying horses, staring at it, as it lay on its back, a slithering superimposition of many bodies, multiple legs outstretched. I did not know which of us was upside down."

"What is a double exposure?" asked Gull.

"Oh, it's a term used by photographers; it's when two images are fused together, one picture on top of another."

Gull stared at him. "It's an optical fixture of two different times, then?"

"Um, yes, that could be said."

"How do you sleep?"

"Badly. Sometimes not at all."

Unsurprised at the answer, Gull nodded and made a mark in the open book on his desk.

"Is that a bad sign?" asked Muygridge.

"No, not for you. Sleep is a complex matter; the body only needs an hour or so. But the mind requires more, and so the soul sometimes becomes involved, and greedy."

"I'm not sure I understand, Dr. Gull." But before Muygridge

could press his confusion, Gull had sealed the matter and continued in a different direction.

The questions lasted for twenty minutes. Then the surgeon moved across the room to one of his glass-fronted cabinets and selected an instrument from within. He carefully wound its clockwork mechanisms and strapped it onto his patient's head. It was made of brass and glass, with a delicate set of folding blinkers and mirrors, some darkened by plating. The surgeon pulled up a chair to face his patient and adjusted the metal discs, close to the sides of Muygridge's worried eyes. Both his hands worked the device, bringing his face so close to Muygridge's that each could smell the other's breath. Tiny ratchet clicks announced the adjustments.

"It's a peripherscope," the surgeon explained. "It should interest you, being a scholar of the optic world."

"I am no such scholar; I have only read a little and recently bought my first camera."

Gull ignored his comments and moved his chair and physically turned the patient's head towards the oriel window, setting a clamp on his neck and chin.

"This will be just like a photographic portrait," he said mildly. "Now, look through the central panel of the window and focus on the dome."

The patient wanted to correct him about the old-fashioned portraits, in which the sitter was secured in a metal frame, held still while the slow camera collected his or her deathlike image. He had already thought of a way to dispense with such artificial contrivance.

"The dome, please!" the surgeon demanded. The middle pane of glass was different from the rest, clearer, with a greenish hue. The distant dome was framed in its bright confines. The patient stared. "Now, please, do not move; just stare at the dome."

These were the surgeon's last words, as he paced from one side to the other, behind the patient. He touched the headset, activating spinning discs and minute reflections of light, almost out of vision, like the suns and moons of distant planets, contained in an unstable darkness inside the corners of the patient's eyes. A night that shimmered with endless space, drawing light particles from inside his vision, from his surroundings, even from the glowing dome. Outside, time was changing and the tide of the seething river had turned back towards the sea. Something in the space between the double dome fluttered and shifted in unison.

When the motors were stopped and all movement ceased, the day had vanished. He sat in a twilit room, growing chilled as the stars rose outside in the frosting air. Dr. Gull lit a lamp and put a shawl about the patient's shoulders, gently removing the device from his head. He sat, unclamped and stiff in the wooden chair, his attention still fixed on the oriel window.

"Please, make yourself more comfortable, Mr. Muygridge."

The surgeon's voice seemed far off and above him. The continual, dull pain in his head had gone, and he felt exhausted. A growing sense of euphoria was making him feel curiously weightless.

"It's the angels," Gull said. "The angels of silence that hide between the whispering gallery and outer dome of the cathedral. They have crossed the Thames and are fluttering in your head; it's quite normal to feel a little dazed."

He smiled broadly at Muygridge, who was gripping the surgeon's words like a vertiginous handrail in the gallery of St. Paul's.

"Your eyes are, miraculously, undamaged. The zygomorphic bones of your face conducted the impact of the accident backwards and upwards, into your brain. I surmise that the force of the shock was considerable but caused no long-term structural damage." Gull leant back in his leather chair and looked dramatically into the photographer's gaze. "There may be side effects," he said, "but I think I might have alleviated or at least diluted those this afternoon. The peripheral vision and its territories of sight and sense are virtually unexplored. My device measures and takes litmus of their emotional potential, their mental humours; do you understand? I have also made some inward adjustments, without the need of the scalpel or the saw."

He got up and made the necessary movements to conclude the meeting. As he conducted Muygridge towards the door, he said, "Are you planning to return to America?"

Muygridge nodded. "Eventually."

"I would do it soon, if I were you. Better to be in a landscape away from people for the next few years. Use your camera to take pictures of that wilderness; force your sight and your imagination outward. It's better for you."

They stood on either side of the door, their handshake passing through. "Will you send your fee?" Muygridge remembered to say.

"No, I think not," said the surgeon. "We will meet again and I might have a favour that needs your skills." He smiled again and gave his patient a white envelope. "Read this in the future," he said, and closed the door.

On a ship back to America, Muygridge had opened Gull's letter and was trying to taste the time that had vanished in the high room at London Bridge. The time that had been leached had been used to cleanse the wound in his head; he had no doubt of that. Gull and his peripherscope had cured a chasm in him. He would return to America a different man. It would be another three decades before he could thank the physician and offer his services in return; in the meantime, some part of him relished the prospect of that day, and he became dedicated to catching invisible time with his own device, so that they might share their notes as equals. Little did he know that their weighty conversation might be stolen by the machine itself.

For now, the wilderness called to him, and he would become lost in its magnitude. He would head north into the Yukon, then west to roam the open plains; he would suck their essence into hand-ground lenses and encapsulate their magnificent bleakness into paper that had been eclipsed under his strengthening hands.

He knew this because he had already seen it all, in the space where the pain used to live, projected brighter than life itself. Held in a place between sleep and waking, and contained by the sides of his vision. The only disadvantage was that he sometimes shared this space with something else, something akin to an ominous, rising moon. That was why he now stood on the deck, gazing at the real moon, high above the black waves. Away from the public lighting of the ship, he opened Gull's crumpled envelope again, in the white incandescence. The surgeon had known of this afterimage and how its blur might haunt his future clarity.

What you will see is the afterburn of my investigation and suggestive treatment. It will manifest as an absence in your mind, a glowing hollow that will sometimes disturb you, but mostly can be ignored. It is the negative of the dome that you looked on for so long in my rooms, and my joke about angels was only partially a jest.

I will not prescribe drugs to clothe its manifestations, nor to banish it. I suggest hard work at your given science, fresh air, and large quantities of solar and lunar light. After a while, the form of this genie will change, and you and it will live in unity. I wish you good health and success with all your endeavours.

W. W. GULL

The motion of the sea settled Muygridge. The moon bathed its interior other, as the written words began their transformation from diagnosis to prophecy. The ship ploughed through the darkness, a pinpoint of light skimming the great curve of water. A million beasts rolled, fled, and laughed in the vast distance beneath it, while the stars multiplied and roared in the perpetual silence above.

Upon arrival in America, he followed the doctor's advice to the letter. He was so far removed from human society that he had almost died of starvation three times. A legend of this thin man's endurance had begun to spread across the Great Plains, reaching as far as the Indian nations. Many such foolhardy explorers were scavenging this land, tipping themselves from famine-haunted homelands, from frozen pogroms and relentless oppression, to step into the burning sun and huge, endless spaces. They sought gold and silver, pelts and land. They had arrived to be reborn and to take everything they could with their pale, bare hands.

But he was very different. It was said that he was hunting stillness and that instead of picks or shovels, guns or maps, he carried an empty box on his back, a box with a single eye, which ate time. Some said he carried plates of glass to serve the stillness on. He would eat with a black cloth over his head, licking his plate clean in the dark.

The Europeans and the Chinese gave him a wide berth. Such behaviour was unchristian and suspicious in these new lands, where anything might propagate and swell to dangerous consequences. The other whites said his box stole the souls of all he placed before it, but how could those who had no soul to begin with ever know? The natives were intrigued by the stories and wanted to see the hunter of quiet. He had found their sacred places and stayed close to them. He had not interfered with or desecrated their energy and power. He had sat with his box in their presence for many hours, sometimes days, and then silently moved on.

He had found a race of humans that he could tolerate, and they welcomed him into many clans, even though he was a Lost One, a most-feared being in all small, tight societies. He was a man who survived outside the tribe and the family, a man turned loose and wild. But this one had understanding and silence and was dedicated to motionlessness; all qualities the Plains tribes cherished. He was allowed to photograph the great chiefs and their medicine men. Eventually, they would let him see and photograph the Ghost Dance. He sent back to England prints of lonely desolation, stunning landscapes of untouched, gigantic purity and pictures of powerful, noble men, who looked into the camera without seeing themselves. Many he sent back to the wise surgeon, to demonstrate his improvement and to reiterate his gratitude; his instinct told him that the man high in the oriel window at London Bridge would understand.

Muygridge began to feel himself healed; his growing confidence stood upright in the hollow lava beds of the flat plains of the Tule Lake. He turned his box on the Modoc War, shovelling up images of the vanquished lands and their shivering occupants. The enemy paid him well, so he became the official photographer for the U.S. Army; the stillness could wait while his plates were filled with the pumice of defeat and exile. At the end of it all, he gathered his new fame and his obsessively accumulated wages and travelled back to the city lights and the crisp linen of San Francisco, to embark on the joys of marriage, parenthood, and murder.

CHAPTER FIVE

*F*or Ghertrude Eloise Tulp, the quietness of the house was a thrill, heightening her expectations and making tiptoeing from room to room all the more delicious. She opened doors slowly against her discovery, moving with a certitude that caressed the moment. Searching in the complete freedom of night served only to increase her pleasure.

Some years before, she had read "The Tell-Tale Heart" in its third impression, taking in Poe's description of cunning, and standing alongside as his protagonist crept in to watch the victim sleeping. She had marvelled at his ability to describe such a contained act of evil against the common, dull speed of life; how he had known the precision of stealth and could put into words the silent, skilful malice. The modern American author's little story had moved her and given her hope. Even though it had almost been spoilt by a suggestion of mania, she knew that he truly understood the control and vision of a superior intellect, one that was ultimately engaged in the divinity of its own development.

Now, in this old, empty house, she could practise her own talent. Armed with a bull's-eye lamp, she listened for the sound of humans, that whisper of movement and breath that always betrayed their presence. Her ears strained for any sign of them but heard none of the faintness of life. Convinced she was alone in the mansion, she let her feet settle out of stealth. As she moved quickly through the lower passage, she almost missed the locked door to the basement.

Raising her lamp to inspect her collection of steel pins, she found two that were twisted in the right deception and applied them to the brass eye. She made the usual turns of leverage, yet nothing shifted. She changed the picks for a sturdier set; this lock was different, its inner workings more resistant, possibly newer. She mumbled under her breath as she strained. It should not be this difficult; what was she doing wrong? She stopped and listened to the empty house again. Nothing had changed, so she inserted the picks and suddenly realised what was different: It was a sinister latching, a set of left-handed tumblers cunningly set in a right-handed lock. She turned the probes upside down and twisted them against all logic. It yielded.

She opened the door and found herself in a distinctly separate space at the top of a flight of stairs, peering into the murky depths of the basement. Its entrance was in keeping with everything she'd already seen, but the difference in its atmosphere was plain—something in it lived. The palms of her hands became damp and her mouth was suddenly parched. She felt thrilled and nauseated at the same time. She had not seen, heard, or smelt the change, but every fibre of her sentient being told her she was no longer alone. Another indicator tinged her already heightened senses, poised, as they were, on the brink of discovery: warmth. A minute rise in temperature had perfumed the static, neutral musk of absence. Someone was down there, hiding under the house.

➤

Ishmael's demands to practise mating had increasingly punctuated their daily lessons; his diet had been adapted accordingly, to compensate for his change in habits and his loss of fluids and minerals. The eternality of Luluwa's patience had been clarified by her limitation of function, a trait that had, evidently, endowed her with a continuous enthusiasm for all things.

Some days they mated for hours. The others walked around and about their action, carrying food and lessons, ignoring them or sitting and watching, mildly bewildered by the energy and repetition of the acts. On one occasion, Seth adjusted their angle, to prevent them from sliding off the table on which they shuffled so.

Ishmael still learned from the crates, but his preference was for the damp, wordless classes, his enthusiasm limitless, until fatigue slowed him to sleep. Luluwa would then put him to bed, darkening the room and lowering the heat. She swaddled him in a deep, aching sleep before leaving the sanctity of their chamber to go into the house itself, silently entering the basement kitchen, where humans had once lived. She removed the casements of her internal mechanisms and cleansed them in the ancient porcelain sink. She did this in the dark, because machines do not need light to function, even when they have been given only one good eye.

The sound of the water made Ghertrude start. Now she really knew there was someone else there, that she was the trespasser. She also knew that, whoever they were, they did not wish to be found out; their clandestine tenancy was evidence enough. Yet her excitement outweighed any trepidation over her crime, and anyway, nobody would ever lay a hand on a Tulp.

The water stopped. Her attuned hearing caught the sound of a door's latch and she followed it down the staircase, elevating her long body and trying to become weightless, her toes delicately testing each step for betrayal before trusting it with her load.

It took her more than an hour to make the descent, by which time dawn had begun to murmur through the night. The old basement kitchen was vast and empty. Dim spider light filtered in from the high windows on the east side. The garden above was overgrown at its edges; matted vines, dusty leaves, and a gauze of webs flavoured the light on its journey downwards into the still room. She stood in the doorway and listened. Nothing. For the first time, she felt a chill of unease—not fear, but a slight soaring of the thrill that she was so enjoying. She looked around the room to gauge its current purpose and count the doors. Between the marble table and the hatchway of the dumbwaiter were the remains of a crate. Splinters of wood and a short crowbar had been discarded, probably by that fool Mutter. Then she saw the light in the cupboard; the door was too small to be anything else. She crouched down to examine its closeness. There was no keyhole or handle; it sat flush against the wall. It would once have been undetectable, so snug that it would have been impossible to see. But age had loosened its boundaries, so that now a sliver of light proclaimed its other side.

Putting the lamp down, she picked up the crowbar and, without hesitation, levered the stoic door open. Not a cupboard, but a curving, downwardly spiralling corridor appeared before her. She bent her height into its tunnel and started to walk-crawl, making her way down its length.

Unaware of her imminence, Abel and Luluwa were in the dim sleeping room with the quietly snoring Ishmael, tending to various details for the next day's class—"Lesson 314: The Signatures of Trees." Aklia was in an adjacent room, her concentration engaged with an open crate, her head cocked and staring into it, as if reading something contained within. Seth was charging in the rack, receiving energy for the next day.

Neither Abel nor Luluwa noticed the door in the wall begin to open; they did not register its occupant, as she attempted to make out their form. As her eyes became accustomed to the room beyond the light of the corridor, her brain tried to make sense of her discovery. It allowed for tricks of perspective; it suggested illusions brought on by tiredness; it even prompted dream as an explanation for what she now saw. But reality slid its frozen tentacle along her spine and she winced with a reaction of revulsion, fear, and hunger.

Her involuntary spasm unhinged the door, sending it flapping into the startled room. The brother and sister jumped to attention, blocking her view of the waking boy, adopting a predatory stance of defence, half-crouching, braced like cats. Ghertrude eased herself into the room, propelled by the wonder of this unique moment and too fearful to turn her back on the small, lithe creatures. She slowly unfolded herself into the space, holding the crowbar poised at breast height like a hesitant truncheon. Her head touched the ceiling; the creatures came up as high as her shoulder. As the morning light continued to rise, she saw that they were not creatures but machines, and the twisted reflex of her superiority felt secure. Her rind of confidence was gaining a voice, and she was just about to speak when Abel opened his jaws and let loose a high, sibilant shrill. Aklia and Seth appeared at once in the far doorway, both in the same stance as their kin. Ishmael, awakened by the commotion, rubbed at his face and turned sleepily into the conflict. His somnolence evaporated the moment he saw Ghertrude blocking the exit. Her face provoked horror, and he drily retched at her deformity: She had two eyes.

For a moment, everything in the room was locked rigid in an icy tension. Only Ishmael's gagging divided its glacier of time.

Then he feebly warbled, "Oh, oh, help!"

Abel became unleashed by the pathetic command and took three fast paces towards Ghertrude, his eye glaring at her pale, looming face. The other Kin converged behind him. He was within a metre of her, and closing, when the crowbar splintered his neck and shoulder. His head clattered across the floor, still attached to a sliver of his upper torso, the mouth chattering wildly, the single eye spinning in his cracked face. His body fell to its knees and stiffened, causing a judder to slop his interior cream out of the jagged rim of his fractured body. Even in the midst of the action, Ghertrude was instantly reminded of her dissections of beetles, years before. The same brittle carapace splitting under her blade, the same white pus escaping from the hollow of the shell. It had slipped over the chocolate-brown edge and splashed on the tiled floor.

The others were now making the same sound as the splintered head, chattering their hard gums together, working uncontrollably. Ghertrude's teeth rattled in unison, infected by the noise coming from these devices and the horribly deformed child crouching in its metal cot. But the staccato of her teeth was imbued with the adrenaline of exhilaration, so that its insistence dominated the choir.

The boy moaned and covered his eye against the ugliness of the giantess's symmetry. Suddenly, the Kin retreated, walking backwards, without turning, towards the far door; stepping with delicate poise, never taking their eyes from the invader, still half-crouched as if for attack, but reversing, rewound. They reached the door and disappeared beyond it. Luluwa was the last to leave, and just before she disappeared forever, she glanced at the boy, who felt her eye but turned too late to see her. All that was left of his protectors was the door, closing behind them.

➤→

The woman's voice boomed in a sluggish yowl. It was hideous but human, and Ishmael recognised something of himself in it. She was the first of her kind he had ever seen or heard, and she was a monster—oversize, with a face that made him retch repeatedly. The shock of being alone with this creature chilled his bones.

Misinterpreting his disgust as fear, Ghertrude tried to say something kind to the imprisoned child, something that would tell him she meant him no harm. She was practising kindness and the novelty made her feel righteous, in the purest sense she had ever known.

She spent a long time almost motionless, speaking softly to demonstrate her distance and restraint. Ishmael began to look at her less warily, moving his hand away from his protected eye and gradually standing up in his bed. She saw that he was not a child, but a stunted adolescent, diminished and grossly deformed, but very human.

High above, the sun had risen in the tangled garden, shooing off the clinging mist and unveiling a bright-blue sky. Its radiance dazzled the kitchen, sending thick, curling rays that shafted through the basement windows. Without breeze or any other movement, dust was lifted into its magnitude to be exalted in the stillness. The room sang to itself and rejoiced in its unoccupied beauty, as all rooms do when left for such long periods of time: When they are untainted by even the slightest trace of rearrangement or the hectic purpose of humans, their invention and design become their own once more.

Ghertrude had cautiously begun to cross the room to make contact with the youth; hands and arms wide, the crowbar left behind, she felt possession flood her future and justify her present. She moved slowly past the leaning remains of Abel, but her caution was not enough to stop him toppling over, spilling the remnants of his fluid in a noisy pool. It triggered an unexpected rage in Ishmael that leaked into every part of his fear. They had left him. Luluwa had abandoned him without a word. The Kin had failed to defend him—all the care of their work and time together had, in the end, meant nothing to them. He looked at the broken Bakelite body, slumped stiff and clumsy in its milky puddle. Abel's lifeless head lay on the other side of the room, but the memories of their conversations had already begun to elude him. His confusion and anger were meeting at a crossroads, and the shadow of this giant woman was waiting there to greet him.

She had quickly become accustomed to the pained squint of the shrunken adolescent, feeling a surge of protection towards him, which was an innovation and added sanctity to her confusion. She had never experienced such emotions as when she touched Ishmael, but he shrank back from her contact—its softness was without meaning, and queasy. He pulled the light-blue bedsheet around his nakedness and bit into his hand.

From a vocabulary of fiction, Ghertrude said, "Shush now; you're safe." In her hot mouth, the words bunched like his improvised loincloth. "Those creatures are gone, and I will protect you."

He knew what the double eye meant but could not understand what had caused her to say it. In the voice of the Kin, a brittle flutter, he said, "They were my family, my friends."

Ghertrude was incensed. Not for another second would she let those abominable puppets stay in his deluded head. Sweeping aside the last traces of unfamiliarity, she helped him out of the cot with both hands, pulling his face close to hers as she knelt, saying, "They are monsters, keeping you here, away from your own kind. They are abominations." He blinked and dribbled. "They will be found and destroyed for what they have done to you and your poor face."

She sat him on the floor and wrapped the sheet tightly around him, tucking its ends beneath his shivering weight. "Don't move," she said. "I'll be back soon."

She quickly crossed to the point where the Kin had vanished and looked into the next room, where another door was left ajar. Cautiously, she squeezed past the charging bays and the open crates, reaching the tiny kitchen on the far side of the room. The open doors there led to a spiral staircase with darkness at its base. There was hollowness below, far greater than its architectural structure. A resonance sounded towards her, a solid emptiness that tolled in silence: This was the infamous well.

Nothing moved there except volume itself, stretching downwards in a shaft of waiting echo. She could not tolerate its dominance and shouted into its length.

"*What!*"

The word found itself in her mouth without passing through her brain. It spat itself out, not as a question, more like a challenge or a curse, a gob of noise to state her territory and show that she would not retreat. It should have been defiant, but it quivered. Too late, she understood that it was the last word, in any tongue, to choose to screech into such a rifled abyss. Such questions must be answered at some point, and she prayed that it would not be now, for fear was finally invading her sense of control. What came back to her was a shattering rumble that described how far out of her depth she really was. The reverberation of "*What!*" crashed up the stairs, hissing and booming between the magma and the stars. For a micro-eternity, everything inside her gave up its colour and mobility. White blood blocked her heart, filled her ears, and coagulated in her eyes, cracked stiff in the capillaries of her brain; white breath's film stopped in the gate of her lungs; white muscle glued to white bone; white urine waited to burn white legs; and her white nerves clicked with opacity and hid in the transparency of water.

As the echo still shuddered, she jerked back into life and bolted. Crashing the door behind her, she sprinted through the careful congestion of the next room, colliding with packing cases, straw, and specimen jars, upsetting tables and gashing her leg. She barged the next door, scooped Ishmael up in her arms, and ran towards the cramped, upward corridor, slithering on the congealing fluid that had once been Abel, sending his head clattering once more across the wet floor. She pushed up hard into the bright tunnel, her dress squealing in friction against the smooth walls. Panting against the boy's sobs, she slipped on wet hands and feet into the quiet kitchen, through the splintering panel of the secret door. The slanting sunlight glazed her, offering benevolence, but she barely registered it as she fled with her charge, through the room to the upper stair, bursting at last into the still dignity of the old house. She slammed the door and, taking a deep breath, used one hand to turn the skeleton key, while her other arm propped the limp boy between her hip and the wall. The bolt turned into place. Tears flooded her eyes. Her relief was poised for release when she heard something move behind her. She spun around, summoning fury in a spray of voice, sweat, tears, and the nameless gruel from the broken Kin. Teeth bared, hands like claws, she came face-to-face with Sigmund Mutter.

→

It was difficult to know who was the most shocked. They had shuddered into the dining room of the old house without a word, Mutter swallowing loudly, trying not to look too obviously at either of them, but continually dragging his eyes up off the floor to make sure of the vision before him. Ghertrude was ruthlessly busy, daubing and scrubbing the mess from her clothing with a rag she had snatched from Mutter's pocket.

And Ishmael? It was impossible to guess what the half-naked little cyclops was thinking behind his hands, which had locked over his face the moment Ghertrude had released him from her protective grip. It was she who broke the silence with a command.

"Mutter, you will tell no one of this."

He looked up into her dominance, which was rapidly drying

off her humiliation, the steam it produced smelling of anger. Mutter nodded automatically.

"You must help me hide this poor, hurt child." She put her arm around Ishmael to emphasise the point. She had ignored him while repairing herself, and the sudden embrace made him jump. "Does anybody ever come here?" she demanded.

Mutter assured her that he was the only one with keys and that he had never seen the owner or anyone else here; neither had his father.

"Good," she said to herself. She was thinking fast now, and the clarity pleased her. "Do you have the keys to the rooms upstairs?"

"Yes, mistress, but all the doors are unlocked," Mutter said, a tone of unease creaking in his voice. The room was beginning to feel cold, and she became aware of the boy's shivering.

"Go and fetch some clothing for him," she said. "Anything will do. And light a fire in there." She pointed to the reception room next door. "Go, man, and say nothing."

He nodded and made for the door.

"Oh, and . . . ," she called out, as he made to leave. He turned to question her and she met him halfway, pushing four heavy coins into his hand. "Bring food and drink, something hot."

With that, he was gone instantly. She returned to Ishmael and pulled the sheet more closely about his white body.

Two hours later, the boy was dressed in hand-me-downs from Mutter's children. They had eaten and the room was warm. The exhaustion had put the cyclops to sleep and left Ghertrude free to make her plans. She questioned the anxious servant about his unseen masters, the house, the crates, and how his family had been paid over all these years. When she realised that he knew nothing, she started to build her palace of lies.

The foundations of this baroque edifice were dug in need and fear: Mutter's fear of becoming unemployed, or being held responsible for the damage and strangeness that so deeply perplexed him, gave her a foothold with which to begin her journey of deceit. She had explained in some detail that kidnapping was a crime punishable with the gravest of verdicts; that he was the only person with keys; that many would have seen him take food to the house each week. Moreover, there was nobody else there and any statement from Ishmael would be inadmissible, if he was allowed to speak at all.

The need, however, was hers. She wanted to keep the little monster to herself, to find out more and not share him, yet, with the many and the mindless. But she lived in her father's house. She needed another place to hide him, and 4 Kühler Brunnen was perfect. She would seal off the lower floor and any abomination that lived there and keep him in the attic or the rooms on the third floor. She would visit him every other day; nobody would know. Mutter was the key to making her plan work. He would be the engine to drive the day-to-day mechanism of concealment, and she would stoke the fires of that engine with dread and money. The only unknown in all of this was the response of his invisible masters, when they learned of her trespass and the destruction of one of their puppets.

She waited for their appearance, but it never came. Meanwhile, Mutter carried on as usual, collecting the crates, taking them to the house, opening them, shuffling their contents, nailing them shut, and taking them back. He brought regular food; he cleaned the stables and looked after the horses. Now he had two wages for doing the same job and keeping his mouth and his eyes shut.

The upper floor had been full of furniture, so it would be easy to make a usable suite of rooms. She could set about making a home that was comfortable and discreet. But before that, there was work to do in the basement. She told Mutter to bring tools, locks, and a gun.

Drawing a chair up to the door of the basement, she instructed him on what had to be done below. With his keys in her hand and his shotgun across her knees, she told him only what was essential to make him do the work, calling instructions down the stairs that she had so recently escaped. He was to go down, beyond the old kitchen, and into that shrunken place. He was to take the remains of that repulsive thing and drop them down the well shaft. He was to change all the locks and board up the doors. She would guard the house and listen to his progress from the stairs.

Mutter was not an intelligent man, but he knew that he was her litmus, her canary in a cage, to go down there and test for horrors. His skin crawled as he descended. She stood listening, her body in the hall, her head in the dark stairwell, the barrel of the gun pointing into expectation. After three hours, and a lot of banging and sawing, he returned, relieved to be out and buoyant in his fulfilment. She was beaming, as happy as he to have this work done, until he told her that there had been nothing left to clean, just a stain on the floor. The remnants that she had so horribly described were gone. She questioned him again and again to be sure that he was in the right room, and then gave up. Someone or something had moved the evidence and rewritten all of their parts in this strange event.

During the first weeks, her plan seemed to work. She made many excuses to her family for her growing bouts of absence. She enjoyed the cunning complexity, the drifting sideways past the walls of the house and slipping in without being seen. Her family believed everything she said. They had no reason to doubt it, and it kept her out of their hair and from under their feet. She had stopped her daily forays to the kitchen to give advice to the cook and no longer demanded to go through the housekeeping expenditures with the butler. She had less energy to expend directing her mother's attention to the new fashions and modes of entertaining, and no time at all, it seemed, to offer the converse point of view in her father's affairs. The family home was at rest and off guard. It was even rumoured, belowstairs, that a man had entered her life, that she had finally found a suitor who could keep up with her copious expectations. Much smirking and giggling occurred at such a prospect, as the servants huddled around the kitchen's circular table.

Mutter did as he was told. Occasionally, she would send him downstairs to check on the lock and listen for movement behind the boarded-up room, but nothing was ever heard. Once, she crept down with him to double-check his reports. She smiled at the growing layers of dust and the firmness of the barriers. She detected nothing and was content. Her plan was working, and a regularity forming that created a pleasing rhythm of mundanity in the strange old house.

The greatest surprise was how easily the cyclops had adapted to his new environment. He was calm and self-reflective, using the time alone to read books she had bought for him. He seemed to have forgotten, or at least disregarded, his time spent in that squalid hutch of a space under the house. He never mentioned the abominations that had imprisoned him. He had stopped calling them the Kin, after she explained how distasteful it was. He seemed content in his new home and to be growing into his new role as an adult.

It was in the fifth week that she noticed Ishmael was beginning to grow in more literal ways, stretching the cast-off clothing into a parody. By the seventh week, he had outgrown a second set of new clothes, which she had carefully picked out only days earlier. He was taller; his frame had gained bulk; he was eating the same food, albeit larger helpings, but that alone would not produce such a startling effect. She wondered if it was the room.

She had seen something like it, years before, when they moved her pet goldfish from its small glass globe into a much larger aquarium. She had been six years old at the time. So remarkable was the change in the small creature, as it ballooned to a size more relative to its expanded surroundings, that she had accused everybody within earshot of exchanging it for another animal. Even at that age, she had been unflinching in her certainty; no amount of explanation had been able to persuade her that it was a natural phenomenon, and she had held a smear of malice against the unidentifiable perpetrators of the conspiracy ever since. Now, for the first time, she had doubts. It was easy enough to replace a fish with a bigger, older specimen of the same kind, but to find another human cyclops? That would surely be impossible. So it must have been true: He was growing to fit the proportions of his new space.

Unfortunately, it also coincided with a change of temperament. He started to become listless and morose, finding her visits less and less interesting. A flicker of seething was pulling the strings, manoeuvring his body in sullen, bored lurches. His eye was avoiding hers, purposefully. She knew these movements well—they had been a significant part of her vocabulary for many years, but nobody had ever dared to use them against her.

It came to a head on the evening of a storm. She arrived later than usual, running up the stairs, shedding her soaking raincoat. He was waiting, his mood thickened and dark. She made little of it at first, busying herself with arrival, removing her wet hat and gloves, manipulating speed to slice through the tension he was broadcasting throughout the room. But this night it did not work.

"Where have you been?" he said in a cracked and guttural voice, three octaves deeper than the one she knew. "Why have you been so long away?" The unmistakable emphasis was on "where" and "why," the words bitten into the air.

"I'm sorry, the rain was very heavy and my class ran on so—"

"*Your* class!" he boomed. "*Your* class? I used to have classes! Now I just sit here, with nothing and nobody."

She was taken aback by the vehemence of this statement, the anger and sorrow strangling the space between them.

"You say I must not think or talk about those who kept me before; you say they were unclean and dangerous. *I say they cared!*"

She noticed, through the coagulated light, that a red rash was forming around his neck, and his ears were burning scarlet.

"I brought you books," she ventured limply.

This was enough for him to close in on her. *"Books are nothing! Your books are nothing!"* he bellowed, snatching one up and hurling it across the room. It hit the shuttered windows and ripped its spine, falling twisted and broken, like the game birds she had seen on her father's estate. *"I was taught before."* A gulp of memory seemed to well up through the house to prompt him. "I was taught with care, taught with meaning," he said, choking on the ashes of his rage.

An appalling silence telescoped the room into a reverse perspective, separating each of them to either end of its numbing distance. Mutter had long since crept away, preferring to keep a distance by busying himself with the crates downstairs. He wanted nothing to do with this drama or with the emotions of the situation, keen only to get on with his work, uninterrupted. He left the house quietly, tiptoeing clumsily across the cobbled yard.

Water dripped noiselessly from the fingertips of her discarded gloves, slipping off the table and onto the muted carpet. One page of the crumpled book turned in rictus, dreading to be seen in its last moments.

Finally, she said, "I will teach you."

He grunted a sound that should have been a derisive snort of doubt, but with his new and unused voice sounded closer to a cough laden with phlegm.

The next day was still wet, but without the lashing horizontal wind, which had come from the warm sea and driven the rain so relentlessly. Mutter remembered during breakfast that he should have collected another crate. The slab of bread lost its taste mid-mouthful, and he groaned through the melting butter. He decided to go back to the house immediately, when he knew she would not be there.

Harnessing the horse to the two-wheeled carriage, he led it out of the stables and across to the double gates. While unlocking them, he took a cautious glance up to the third floor. He knew he would see nothing at the windows; he had fastened the shutters tight and padlocked them closed, as instructed. Even so, he could feel the straining thing expanding against the glass, wanting to wash its eye in the city.

Forty minutes later, he had arrived at the warehouse on the other side of town. After climbing, achingly, down from the creaking carriage, he unlocked the padlock—bigger than his heart and six times as heavy—and swung the gate inwards, pulling the horse and carriage inside. He entered the warehouse, dragging the empty crate behind him. He used to do this mechanically, enjoying the constancy of repletion. There were no questions, just an exchange of objects. Since the dramatic change at 4 Kühler Brunnen, he had dreaded meeting the master of the house. He would be seen as betraying his responsibility, that which his family had been given and conducted without doubt or deception for two generations. Had he damaged that beyond hope? Then he saw the blinding whiteness of an envelope, intersecting the path between the door and the crates, and he suspected that he had. He panicked. A letter, the rectangular diagram of his ignorance, little paper blades that had threatened him all his life. He could not read, but it had never been a problem. His world of work and muscle, endurance and abeyance, had never required letters to direct it or describe its essential importance.

He picked up the envelope gingerly, so that its venom could not rise to touch him. He saw the spider ink trails of writing on its surface and had no idea what to do.

Then the voice said, *"Sigmund Mutter, you are a good man and we trust you."* Mutter gave a start and looked around bewilderedly, amazed and relieved at what he was hearing. It came from the entire warehouse, and yet it felt intimate, close by, somehow. *"The Mutter family has pleased us for years. Your father, you, and your sons, will always be trusted by us. All of your work and confidence is greatly valued. Take this letter to Mistress Tulp and say nothing of our conversation. You are protected and your family will endure."*

On his way back, Mutter sat as if in a dream. The ebony carriage flexed and curved through the streets, the wheels and the hooves talking through the reins to his cold hands. He stabled the horse and crossed to the house, holding the letter before him like a dead fish or a live centipede, at arm's length. Entering the mansion, he came upon Ghertrude, fluttering aimlessly in the hall. She feigned disinterest at his arrival, until his changed manner intruded upon her senses. Looking up, she noticed his unpredictable focus and the letter in his hand. He pointed it towards her and said nothing.

G. E. TULP,

You have committed the crime of trespass, housebreaking, and false occupancy. You have corrupted my servant. Nobody knows of this. Nor do they know of the other acts that you have undertaken to perform.

I do. However, I want the same as you: silence.

You are in my house and you have my child. I was at your birth; your parents are in my knowledge and influence. Do not doubt this, or you are lost.

You will be trusted to follow your own plans. You will be protected. Do not leave or subtract your stolen responsibility. I will speak to you again in one year.

CHAPTER SIX

I walked for days. The land has become depopulated. Too much effort is needed to keep the parched fields active enough to grow clinging tomatoes and dusty, dwarfish melons; it is a country of the old, tending their patches of earth out of habitual purpose, the last days of the clock ticking through daily ritual, the weights almost unwound from their creaking spool. There are no young people to reset it, no one to wind the well each day and sprinkle the ravenous earth into function. The young have left for the cities and for slave labour abroad. They are underground, digging fossils for other people's heat. They are in venomous sheds, weaving chemical cancer. They are automata in chains of industry that do not need identity, language, or families. All their saved money is endlessly counted as escape. Some come back to the fields to help the old and infirm raise the dented bucket and spade; others attempt to return as princes, buying expensive and bland new homes in the crumbling villages of their origin. This will fail, and their children and the land will turn on them and intensify the shuddering fatigue. The scuffed tracks of their efforts are erased under my feet, walking through the few occupied remnants of community.

It will take me three days to clear these places, another three or four to cross the low mountains and be farther out at the rim of the wilderness. We had lived in this place for eleven years, healing the gashes and fractures of our past, using the sun and dust to staunch the jagged memories. This peninsula of abandonment had given much, and a part of me ached to plan a return, even though I know it will never be possible.

The heat of the day has become saturated with weight, the brightness sullen and pregnant with change. Clouds have thickened and coagulated with inner darkness; water is being born, heavy and unstable.

This is the breath of the sickly wind called Burascio by the natives of the land; a wind that sucked rather than blew, its hot, inverted breath giving movement but not relief. It toys with expectation by animating suffocation, tantalising the arid earth with its scent of rain, while beneath the reservoirs, caves and cisterns strained their emptiness towards its skies.

This was the reason we had lived here. Este said the isolation was part of the treatment, but the mending and evolution of the body and spirit could take place only above a honeycomb of hollows. The skies and the sea would be heard in those places. Their vastness and motions would be echoed down beneath the taut earth, swilling and booming the darkness into quiet against their unseen mineral walls. She spoke of their unity of voice, from the humblest well to the vastest cathedral cave, how they are like pipes of different sizes in a mighty organ. An organ constructed to shudder in fugues and fanfares of listening, not playing; where a cacophony of silence was counterpoised only by insistent drips of water.

She knew it was their action that influenced the minute physical and the immense mental and spiritual spaces inside human beings. I think of this as I walk across the lid of their meaning, of her unfolding these wonders to my baffled ears. I think of her voice, very close, very clear, and I stare in shock at the truth of holding her bones and flesh in my sweating hand.

During the night, lightning can be seen far out at sea. Above the horizon, soundless dendrites of storm flicker, marbling the curve of the earth on their way towards here and the waiting dawn. I take shelter in a dugout shepherds' cave at the edge of one of the poorest villages. The terraced fields here are worn down, losing their boundaries in limping disrepair, survival and oblivion quarrelling among the falling stones and parched plants. In this domain of lizards, flies, and cacti, the human signatures were being erased.

My shelter feels like it has not been used for years, the stitched-together sacking that made its rudimentary door falling apart in my hand as I try to unhook it. This crouching space had been scratched out from the soft yellow stone, just big enough for a small man or boy and a few goats. There are still remnants of occupation: a low bed or table blocking the far end; a few tools bearing the labour scars of generations; a car wheel, its tyre worn smooth; dry, sand-encrusted empty bottles; and a few exhausted shotgun cartridges. Hanging on a nail is a fragment of rusted armour, an articulated breastplate of diminutive size. Whether this is a genuine artefact dug up from some unknown battle, or part of a carnival costume from one of the gaudy pageants that once marked the saint's passage through the year, it is impossible to say. The hot land and the salt wind have etched and cooked it into another time, a time that never stained memory, because it was too ancient to have yet been conceived.

The cave's bare interior seemed at once empty and brimming with occupation. I curl into the sanctity of this most human shelf and taste the joy of its simplicity with the edge of my sudden tiredness.

The thunder enters my sleep. It slides between the laminations of dreams with the grace of a panther, its first sound being no more than a whisper or a vibration. Each mile it runs it gains volume and power; each mile it flies it trains my unconscious to not respond, each growing resonance being only fractionally louder than the last. The hours are eaten in its stealthy approach, my nightmares absorbing the shocks until it is directly overhead and its massive percussion shakes the ground with light; a huge whiteness, battering the pale morning with a fury that refuses all kinship.

The village is awake and active, people darting from one house to another as the sky opens and torrents of rain fall to meet the rising earth's unbridled appetite. Within minutes, the fields have drunk deep and are forming lakes. The streets and tracks of the village are alive with rivulets and yellow tributaries of fast water. The villagers fall upon these eddies with a great frenzy of action. Rolled-up sacks and hessian are used to divert the flood into wells and gulleys, which lead to other cisterns. Logs and stones, even items of clothing, are improvised to divert this precious storm. The feuds and squabbles that fossilised the village are forgotten, water and its capture going beyond blood and its boundaries. The rain is constant and spiteful; the villagers are determined and drenched with mud. People slither and run, shout instructions to the very young, scream for more sacks, laugh and fall with the very old, who curse. Those who are normally locked away join the rush, limping and screaming with exhilaration and confusion. The entire village turns into mud beings, a chaotic, purposeful mania rattling under the rains. Some animals watch from their stables and doorways, surprised and indignant at so much energy, water, and noise.

I cannot stay outside of this circus vortex, so I carefully stash the bow and other goods high in the cave, away from the flood and beasts, and run to work alongside a toothless elder who is trying to build a dam of rocks and rags.

His efforts are useless against the power of the flow. His slowness gives a pathetic humour to the event, and his wall tumbles away every few minutes while he methodically continues to pile, seemingly unaware of the gleeful water and his mechanical futility. Together, we manage to turn the stream, sending it into the corner of the courtyard. It pours into the mouth of an open well and falls into its resounding depth with echoing splashes. As I watch our minor triumph, in a flash it occurs to me that I have no memory of Este bleeding, no picture of the blood leaving her body, just a vague blur of its presence drying everywhere in the room. Have these sounds caught a reflection, cupped the act in a palm of memory?

The old man tugs at my sleeve and clears my vision. He has started work on another stream and needs my help. We continue directing the water for two hours, soaked to the bone but satisfied. The storm passes, the rain stops, and the steaming earth has begun to dry. Birds noisily make use of the orange puddles before they return to dust. A saturated heat begins to rise, forcing all labour to cease.

The family of the old man insist I join them in their dripping home. Our celebratory feast is simple but powerful: We drink a coarse red wine made from the family's parched, hard grapes and eat a dish of fat rice and dark meat cooked in pomegranate juice, punctuated by delicious bread with black onions baked into its crust. There is much merriment and we share that language of need and alcohol, where the native and the foreign are overrun by excitement, and delicacies of grammar are jolted loose by emotion.

The old man concentrates on his food as if it were his last. I make some slight comment of jest about this and am carefully told that the rains and the old have a special relationship in this land. I had heard rumour of this before, but our isolation had kept most things at a distance; our contact with the neighbouring communities had been remote. But the spring rain ritual is true, and my host explains its necessity and the intricacies of its operation between mouthfuls of food and wine.

The old are a burden on their poor economy, becoming

increasingly incapable of work. So, once past their useful stage, they are given to the mercy of the spring gods and placed outside their homes with food and drink for three days. At that time of year, the rains are soft and constant, very unlike the autumn deluge we had just suffered. They would sit in silence, knowing that conversation or pleading would not help their condition; better to save strength. After their allotted time, they are welcomed back inside and returned to their anxious beds. They understand that this was a more civilised and kinder test than those conducted by their forefathers. In those distant days of famine, the old had been taken to steep cliffs and forced to find their own way home, the gods growing fat on their torn and fractured remains.

A quarter of the old will die during the coming weeks; night chills, influenza, or phenomena being the divine intervention. The rest will be celebrated, fed, and honoured for another year. The old father cleaning his plate with his last scrap of bread has survived six spring rains and has the intention of surviving many more.

In the afternoon, I say my farewells and return to my cave, where I sleep a peaceful and dreamless journey.

■→

Tsungali knew his prey would have taken one of two routes. The first, the main commerce artery, led directly into the city without any diversions, straight through its main street and its industrial flank, and then to the Vorrh. The other was an older track, which meandered through the long valley before entering the city by its layered history. That road splintered at a hub of old buildings, where the river and six other roads met, and then crawled towards the city, the Vorrh, and other, lesser-known extremities. These routes were slow and hardly ever used by normal travellers; they were reserved for those who wanted to taste the past, those who had something to hide, those who did not wish to mix with normal men. Often it was a combination of all three. He knew that, while his prey did not want to be seen, he would still have to rest and buy food and information on his approach. The old road would be perfect for his needs.

Approximately a day and a half's walk from the city, there was a scarred bridge, attached to a working mill and a scatter of huts. It was notched into the bend of a steep, carboniferous limestone valley. Glaciers had edged their razoring weight through, cutting twisting canyons and gouging out riverbeds, so that overhanging walls of jutting cliff leered above. At one point, by the mill itself, the lofty, sheer sides almost touched, either side approaching the other with a heightened tone of suspense; remembrance, perhaps, of historical connectedness. It was rumoured that sunlight could sometimes penetrate at that point for an hour a day; at other times, it proved impossible and darkness loomed beneath.

The mill and its attendant buildings had an equally murky history; most travellers would go to great lengths to avoid its shadows and crimes. But a man could stay there without being asked questions and could enjoy its muffled expectations without catching the eye of its threat.

Tsungali sat among a group of rocks, looking down on the bridge. Its four spans of the river were mighty and compact in their solid structure. It could withstand the dry, burning heat of percussive summers or the vicious frost of a chiselling winter. It eerily echoed a feeble stream in its arching curves. It would stand fast against floods that hurtled full trees against its stanchion and would catch light from the water beneath, casting polyphonies into its hollows.

Tsungali watched silently. This was one of many beautiful days he had sat through, awaiting his prey. He had visited the mill, to smell its interior and the purpose and strength of its occupants. He knew their number, colour, and creed. He had hidden his motorbike in the tall bamboo by the side of the river and walked the water road to this place, stepping between the rippling stones. He had traversed the path to the hamlet, five buildings in a ragged line, swirls of scented log smoke rising from two of the dingy houses. The tallness of the land and the multitude of trees had filtered and tamed the savage sunlight into a lukewarm dapple that suggested peace, but a stiff, pale indifference stained the air with trouble.

The hunchbacked cottage grafted to the side of the mill was a public house, with noise broadcasting its presence. He walked to its door and tasted its interior: cooking smells; drink; smoke and loud voices; a company of conflict. Inside was worse; a solid décor of masculine tension, sprawled between loud guffaws and sullen quiet, occasionally diluted by drifts of alcohol.

He took a seat, a black man's seat, against the wall, in the shadows. From there, he watched and gauged the company under hooded eyes. He pretended to drink, rolling orders of deep spirit, spilling each under his hand and beneath the table. He instantly recognised three of the occupants as assassins. One he could name as Tugu Ossenti, a fellow member of the same constabulary, before the Possession Wars. Ossenti had been dismissed after allegations of torture. Since then, it was known, but not proven, that he had murdered for money and sometimes for satisfaction. He would not recognise Tsungali, who had been much younger and clearer skinned then, his teeth unsharpened the last time they were face-to-face.

Ossenti's consorts were twins. Thin, white, and edgy, they had the suddenness of small reptiles, their eyes and hands twitching constantly. Tsungali knew from experience that twins have the ability to think as one, even when they are apart. He had seen it in the village before, observed two working in unison, without a word of discussion or direction. In a fighting situation, such adversaries could be unpredictable and overpowering. The rapid watchfulness of the men worried him much more than their companion's strength and history.

After watching intently, he allowed his gaze to sweep the smoky, irregular room. A solitary drinker sat in the far corner, in shadows that dissolved his features. Even in the gloom, his posture could be read, and Tsungali looked past him. Four men sat loudly around a circular table in the middle of the room. They looked like drovers. Their worn clothes and thick boots propped them up against their slurred conversation. The mud had dried on their leather gaiters and fallen in clumps around their sluggish feet. They had been at this table for hours.

At the bar sat a tall, thin man, erect and pitching indifference. His spine was the straightest thing in the room. Sipping the clear fluid from his glass with a long bamboo shoot, he drank without using his hands, which hung limply at his sides. He gazed before him into the rack of bottles behind the bar, their rears reflected in the mirror that held the slumped room in its cracked, misted eye. His bleached, distorted face floated out of focus in the glass. Apart from him, the only other occupants were the barman, a wheezing old man in the back room, and a gormless youth with a dog. The tension in the stuffy room was congested with human silence and the twitching of the dog's dream.

Sweet pushing inside her pushing pumping the bitch clasped hard by me pushing over and over again held to the ground smelling open pushing sweet the pump of my heart pulsing she tries to move but I hold her fast pumping bending in the middle we turn in the scented dust my teeth on her spine my spine heart-pumping sweet she skidding me going deeper locked inside pushing she flinches against me spins I turn leg slips we spill rolling pushing touching the ground its smell twisted backwards my cock facing out she the other side of me now tail to tail pumping sweet spinning locked snapping. Then the cuts the stones the kids throwing stones double-ended so we can't fight back they know it we circle still sweet pumping locked twisted the stink of kids the hurt snapping pulled both ways fuck bite fuck bite blood from stones my eye pushing spinning stones she yelps I snarl pumping now water over us others touching pulling us apart she runs away full of my spunk I can't stand still bending uncontrollable reflex air fuck bending bending fucking nothing over and over and over again bite fuck bite fuck bending spine still fucking nothing still still the kids laughing but they run from my jaws claws in the ground teeth searching balls empty sweet she still in my nose mouth cock dripping licking sweet.

Tsungali saw there were no weapons propped in the rack by the door, which meant that everyone carried concealed ones. This was no place for nakedness, but Uculipsa was not here with him. The rifle lay in her brass scabbard, high up in the leaves of the bamboo forest, the patina of her metal matching the colour of the whispering foliage, a charm of invisibility attached to the slender rope that held her in place. In these surroundings, he needed close-range companions; a blunt-nosed, hammerless pistol sat in the folds of his lap, and a long-bladed kris hung beneath his armpit; additional weaponry was concealed under the bridge.

The men twitched their sight towards the dreaming dog, shuddering under the table. For a moment, their eyes were dissolved of their previous purpose and shed their watch to partake in the flinch that nipped and shook the sleeping animal, unlatching it from its tension to let it swing in forgetfulness. It awoke with a shudder. The table of assassins dismissed Tsungali's hidden stare and returned to their previous clandestine conversation.

He read the men, then examined the room to measure the dimensions of fight or flight, the exits and angles of possible violence. There was a back door, a window, and an open fireplace. The upper stories were connected only by steps outside. As he sat, he projected killing fields into the room and rotated scenarios of defence and attack. He had no doubt that everybody else had done or was doing the same, except the dog and the old man, who rattled and flinched in other dreams.

One of the twins caught the vibration of his hidden eyes and muttered something to the others. After a suitable but ridiculous pause, Ossenti turned in the pretence of a stretch, tilting his head to look directly into Tsungali's shadow.

➤→

I feel as if I have been asleep, asleep too long. My dreams, if they are dreams, are always in advance of my sleep, awaiting me to continue their tale, to unwind their continuity. In daylight, they ache continuously. I have become bewildered by their closeness and my distance. I have been swallowed to this spot of land, the previous arrows stitching the way to here. I cannot see the bow, which must have fallen beneath me, lying somewhere in this place of contradiction, where it smells of snow and glows humid. My feet had held the ground before, but now I am unattached, and the roots and sinews of my pain nag at my hope in dopey, vague wafts. I am being erased by familiarity, the sense of knowing this journey from before. The arrow's path has made me as vacant as the half-light landscape around me.

There she moves; there in the scrub grass, wire, and rotted paper, she turns towards my hand again. I have been too slow on this journey; the air and sky have seduced me. No blood has been shed, and history cannot move without this. I have to cut the light with blood, let her exhale and twist in my hand. Tonight, I will divide a life and paint the future road glorious. Enough of these shallows: The cities lie on the other side of the great forest, and I will burn my way towards them. She is in my hand, demanding arrows and distance.

I loosen a new, darker arrow into the evening towards the first star, which has risen over the lip of the world and will set among the far-off trees. The arrow I release flies like a whistle, setting my direction for tomorrow.

➤——

Tsungali watched the afternoon arrive. He had moved his camp again. He was becoming familiar with the patch of land that would be his killing ground. The spirit of his victim would be offered to his ancestors, and the ritual of its transmutation would occur here in this valley, the name of which he did not know.

He sat by the fast water, enjoying its speed, its splendid indifference, and its rippling sound, silently observing the wading birds with their shrill curl of beak and voice. He drank deeply of life so that he knew the taste of it here, knew the vibrant wealth of its dominion, knew exactly what he was taking from the man who would die on this ground.

Looking upriver, he tried to remember the great forest that brooded there. It had been a long time since he once saw it. His visual memory was dimmer than its legends and his grandfather's stories of it, which burnt brightly.

But mostly he saw a painted picture of it, one that hovered at the end of the water. A bearded man stood in a cave. Around the cave was the endless forest, its power darkening the sky. In front of the cave ran the river, depicted as a twisting blue stream. A fish swam under its paint and against the flow, so that it could watch the man, who would soon leave the safety of the cave and enter the wilderness, where he would meet his God or his demons. Tsungali was just about to let the image go when, unexpectedly, it became familiar. Something about it shifted into the actuality of his dreams, or a memory of a different world. He closed his eyes and let the sparkling water flicker on his lids; he stared through them, searching. It was the photograph in the museum, the picture of his grandfather sitting at the entrance of the carved trove house. Both images merged, and he looked into the painted shadow behind the old man, expecting to see himself again. But now it was not the lean, grinning boy who hid there. It was the huge, unfolded wings of the man he had remembered as a saint or a prophet. They filled the space inside the cave and were far too large to ever squeeze through the jagged entrance. Tsungali opened his eyes wide, recognising, at last, the expression on the bearded face.

➤—→

Sidrus had slowly prepared himself at the back of the inn, deep in the animal shadow of its primitive architecture. He moved his large hands around his cane and adjusted his hat and the side panels of his green-glass spectacles.

Walking around to the entrance, he stiffly made his way to the bar, seemingly without registering the other occupants and their irritation at his presence. He hissed the name of a drink in a foreign accent, displacing himself even further from the company's sympathy. His back was insultingly square against the faces of the seated clientele; his eyes could not be seen, but they picked every detail out of the mirror. All movement was measured and assessed in its cracked, murky glass.

The twins exchanged a twisted look and approached him, breaking a shaft of light at the back of the room as they sauntered towards him, grinning. He stood three heads taller than they, implacable and deadly calm. The twin with the earring was rehearsing a suitably caustic and insulting address, when Sidrus's left hand crawled around from the side of his body to the small of his black back and stopped suddenly, one outstretched finger pointing menacingly towards them, statue-like in accusation. The pair froze, confused by this unpredictable and peculiar gesture. The other twin started to laugh on the strange side of his previous grin. His brother's mouth was a wobbling slit of anger.

"Who you pointing at, you stick-legged cunt?" he said as he approached the hand. "We'll cut your lungs out, yoooo!"

The rest of the wide body slowly turned to confront him, and he swallowed his voice in a gulp. Both hands were now pointing, a digit at each twin, the cane balanced across the stranger's wrists like a conjuror's wand. The face above the hands was long, broad, white, and totally unnatural, a stretched, boiled egg, with tiny eyes and a flattened, broken nose. It looked unfinished and malleable, as if its shortsighted sculptor had retired midway through its creation. The twins had met and murdered all manner of men and women, but they had never come across an apparition like this before, never stood in the presence of indomitable wrongness.

With a voice like a paper cut, Sidrus hissed, "Divided one, you have died!" He drew the blade slowly from the cane with great deliberation, in the manner of a salesman handling a stock of priceless antiquities. As he brought it to a stop at eye level, the room was reflected in its polished shine. Words, engraved along its length, shimmered in the light for all to see.

It was impossible to tell the span of time that had passed since Sidrus's utterance: It might have been a fraction of a second or a full day. The earringed twin jolted from his torpor, assessed the distance of the blade, and pulled a curved dagger from his coat. His trajectory was certain to maim the stranger before he could turn his blade into a defensive or aggressive posture, and he charged, eyes locked on one of the blade's shining words: TRUTH. With all his strength, he lunged onto the blade that clicked out of the wooden cane's other end and twitched up, across his rushing throat.

The mortally wounded twin dropped his knife, grabbing at his own neck in a hopeless attempt to strangle the flow. His brother rushed to his side, one hand on his pistol, the other hopelessly attending to the ravaged wound, not knowing whether to fight or save his twin. The debate was settled for him by the lightning point of the written sword, which pierced his eye and was pushed to the back of his brain—he caught flashes of text as the words raced past the confusion of his other oculus.

As children, both twins had received some formal education. In their early years, they had been taught the elemental principles of grammar by a country curate. Later, they attended two years at a nearby seminary, where their reading and writing skills were greatly enhanced. They had not come from the gutter, like most of their kind, but from a respected family of seed merchants; the little town where they were born had been mildly affluent. But at the tender age of twelve, they had turned from the upstanding paths of scholar and cloth and wilfully run onto the twisted, bitter road that brought them to this place, where they now danced in their own blood.

The stranger brought his face close to the shuffling man and hissed, "The scripture of the blade says, *the way!*"—he thrust the blade in farther, so that the words were deep inside—"*the truth!*"—the point grated and stopped against the bone of the skull—"*and the life!*" With this, he brought his other hand down, pushing steel through bone, skewering the blade's length through the bobbing head. He twisted the blade, the words vanishing with a crunching sliver, and then pulled it clear of the wobbling rag doll in one swift, smooth stroke. Caught in a moment of rubber balance, his victim briefly looked like a child's toy or a dancing monkey. Still holding the dying man, Sidrus cleaned the blasphemous blade on the lapel of his victim's twitching coat, before letting him drop to the steaming floor.

The dog, inert up to that point, twitched an eye open at the sound. But it had all happened so smoothly, with such minimal movement, that there was almost nothing to be seen, and observing nothing of consequence, he stretched comfortably, laid his head back on the stony floor, and returned to his dreams.

Each action had been focused, precise, and confident. It had been an execution in every meaning of the word, and the power of its malice was pristine in its inexorable certitude. There had been an air of delight about the act.

The perpetrator turned to the innkeeper, who had remained motionless throughout, and placed two heavy coins and a flat wooden sheath on the bar. He opened the sheath and displayed a tablet of hard wood, covered in gold writing, a wax seal at its base and an insignia on the seal. The innkeeper's gaze was fixed on the coins.

"The money is for you to clean this away. Do you know what this is?" The fat man nodded and avoided looking at the stranger's face.

"I am Sidrus, and I have jurisdiction in this sector." He opened his hand to reveal the same wax insignia, tattooed onto the palm of his hand. "How long were these two waiting here?" he demanded.

"Eleven or twelve days now," said the innkeeper, cautiously picking up the coins and holding their weight in his closed paw. "Them and the other one together, the black one."

"And where is he?"

"I don't know, been gone two days now."

Sidrus knew he was telling the truth; he had been watching the inn, entering only after the other man had left. "Have any others passed this way in recent weeks?" he asked.

"Just drifters and strangers, moving on."

Sidrus suspected that there would be many more hunters seeking their prey, more assassins trying to kill the man with the bow, before he got close to the Vorrh. He did not know how many he would have to dispatch to protect the Bowman and allow him to make the impossible journey through the forest to the other side, where he would be waiting for him. He could not enter it at all and had circumnavigated its perimeter to reach him. It had taken him two months to arrive in this shit hole.

The bodies of the twins had stopped twitching. Stepping clear of the lake of their blood, he picked up the wooden tablet he had displayed and made for the door. A dim, gawping youth stood in his way by mistake, frozen to the spot as the incident replayed through his slow brain. "Kippa! Kippa, get out of the way!" barked the innkeeper.

Sidrus stopped moving and brought his sheathed cane into view. He knew there was no danger from this faint one, but he had no intention of showing mercy as the other drinkers watched; even the dog had awakened to the danger and watched him with bared teeth from beneath the table.

Kippa was still rendered immobile, unable to take his eyes away from the approaching demon. The blade made a great, circular arc, an elaborate matador flourish that had none of the surgical precision of its previous use. On its upward swing, it cut between the youth's legs, severing his budding manhood and sending him, toppling and screeching, out of the deliberate path of a living, grinning nightmare.

CHAPTER SEVEN

*H*e was now Edward Muybridge and his focus was sharp. He had caught landscapes and tribes in the darkness of his exposure. He had a reputation and his new name stuck to it like shit to a blanket.

He spent more and more time back in the cities, especially after he captured the great wastes of Alaska. Their cold loneliness prompted unwise warmth in his humanity and he decided to "settle down."

Flora walked into his life like another dimension; it was the only time he lowered his defences and overpowering love had trampled all his apertures, calculations, and timings. It had shaken his terse tree of knowledge to its roots. His young wife, like new blood, warming and radiating every part of his ordered existence, bringing a joy that he could not own and for the first time had not wished to. The birth of his son had overwhelmed him with more feelings than he had been able to understand; a ball of life burnt and writhed inside him whenever he held the child in his bony hands. Then he found the letter proclaiming her love for another man and the whisper that the child might be his. Then Muybridge knew that they had only ever been deceitful diversions—things that were never meant to last, moments of deception to rob him of purpose. He should have stayed with the wilderness, instead of being tempted by the vain hopes of family and wealth: He knew that was what the London doctor would have advised. His love and his money had been squandered; he would never make that mistake again. He justified his weakness with the ill health and puerile wishes that all men have injected into them by their mothers; the belief that finding a good woman and making a home is a solid and resolute accomplishment of maturity. He had never truly felt the draw of that ambition, only its slender side effect of respectability. He had always been aware of his difference, and so had his mother, who doted on his younger brother.

But at least he had tried giving his thin, forlorn heart in trust to a wife, albeit a fat woman who had trampled it in the smeared bedsheets of her adultery. He had survived far worse than heartbreak in the wilderness, going beyond his guide's wisdom, cutting trees away from untouched landscapes to construct the composition he desired. Compiling fierce light in the inverted world that was totally his. In the same cold passion he climbed the hill to the silver mine, calling his adversary out from a card game and into the fragrant landscape, cooling under the setting new moon.

"Good evening, Major Larkyns," he had said to the man squinting in the doorway, trying to see who was speaking against the bright light. "My name is Edward Muybridge, and here is the answer to the letter you sent my wife."

He had levelled the pistol at the philanderer's chest and fired. Quick blood coughed into the bright, moving leaves of that October dusk; the victim staggered through the house and died in the back garden, hugging a tree. Muybridge walked behind him, apologising to the players, whose hands were frozen in disbelief.

He knew now what the good London surgeon already understood; he had warned that his injury would become inflamed by people, and it had. This would even be mentioned in court:

how the lesions in his brain had opened, becoming red raw with her deception; her lies and faithlessness running like lava, hot salt, ammonia, tears; her fecund fluids pissing in his wound. He must close it forever and never let another finger his interior or violate the pristine bone closure of his vision. He was finished with proximity and all the cankers that grew in it.

He had resolved to never again be the person described in that courtroom: a "lost animal, vacant and mad." People he knew—friends, neighbours, even servants—had told of his seizures; of incoherent jabbering, his eyes starting from his head, jaw hanging open; his dreadful appearance, haggard and shivering all over, a terrible paleness swallowing his humanity, while his breathing shrank to gasps and smelt rank and toothy. At one point in the trial, he was said to have sunk into such a fit, his countenance becoming so horrifying, that the clerk of the court had been obliged to restrain his furiously working hands and hide his hideous, contorting features beneath a handkerchief, while the jury left the room, some in tears, and the judge retired for thirty minutes, needing the consolation of a sturdy bourbon. Why they had told these lies he never knew, but it had somehow helped all to see his righteousness.

When he stepped free from the courthouse and into the cheering crowd, it had been a sanctified rebirth. Friends and strangers held him up, helped him walk limply home; after only a few steps, he had heard the white, death-faced voices of the singing circle and begun to understand the significance of the Ghost Dance. He slowed and twisted around, weak in the arms of his helpers, to look back at the crowd at the foot of the courthouse steps—they milled and revelled, picking their hats up from the dusty street where they had landed only moments before, a jubilant and temporary resting place after being cast into the air of his triumph.

Now that his wife was dead, the bastard child given to a

home, he was free once more. Free to continue, and to never again allow such treacherous emotions to poison his will. When friends tried to update him on the growing child or on the striking resemblance to him that it had apparently begun to bear, he had cut them dead, severed them from his righteous mind. He moved again and again, photographing all he could, wandering into the deserts and high mountains without a whiff of Christ or Satan as companions.

Muybridge was becoming famous for his encyclopedic studies of animal movement, but also for his most popular invention, the zoopraxiscope—a mechanical tabletop precursor of cinematic motion. But it and its family of more and more sophisticated devices were mere toys in comparison to the new machine, a brass hydra of lenses, cogs, and light that no one had ever seen. This was not a passive projector of illusion or entertainment, but something far more disturbing and revolutionary, with an engaged conversation with light itself.

He had recognised, many years ago, what had been screaming at him from his archives of movement: His misdirection, up to that point, had been complete. The measured delineation that filled his life was a lie. Observation was *not* the primary function of photography, but a side effect of its true purpose. The constant gathering of pictures of life was only a harvesting of basic material. Deeper meaning lay within the next part of the process, a kernel waiting to give up its flavour after being savagely reworked: The camera was a collector not of light, but of time, and the time it cherished most was in the anticipation of death.

It could look between the seams of existence and sniff out an essence that was missed in the daily continuum. It fed on a spillage between worlds that was denied to common sight and ordinary men. He had first noticed it when making portraits of the defeated Modoc chieftains, all those years ago, though he saw it also in Guatemala and in some of the invalids who graced his movement portfolios. They had stared into life, and his camera, differently from other men. Their portraits sang against the world, their eyes threading through the viewer's gaze.

There was an aura of nonvisible vibration in his glass slides, an effect that shimmered in the emotional eye but not in reality. It somehow transferred to his prints, so that while they depicted the noble or twisted sitter, framed in space, they also hummed a lucid resonance that slivered alongside the viewer's subjective intelligence. Astoundingly, the effect was increased when the image was projected, rather than stained, onto paper.

The twelfth-generation zoopraxiscope was not like the rest. It was certainly not like the first four. He needed another name for it. Gull's peripherscope kept floating to the surface, but he always banished it, not wanting a minor medical instrument to be seen as any kind of influence on his totally original concept.

No one would ever believe what it did, looking at its complex entanglement of lenses and shutters. They would expect more pretty pictures to dance on the wall yet would meet instead a rippled light that sliced the optic nerve into a whip of driving visions . . .

Muybridge was keen in his arrogance, sharp enough to know that such a statement, made publicly, would unbind his esteem and threaten his well-forged place in history. Those little minds that scratched at his achievements would make light work of his undoing, were they privy to such a discovery—but they would never be allowed to snatch away his triumph or his secret. He would let it seep out, after they were all rotted bones. Let others announce his genius, as Huxley had for Darwin, or as Ruskin had for Turner, men not yet born, men of the growing age who would recognise his enlightenment. He would save his strength and maybe live long enough to witness it. He had made the device, found the conclusion. But he had seen others of his age brought to the pillory in the last years of their lives, shredded and broken by their generosity, choked on the crumbs of wisdom they gave, too freely, to the mob. He had better things to roll into the future than explanation. He was too old to debate and be questioned. He was justified and right, so he concealed his knowledge of the brass creature that engineered the invisible.

A long time ago, what now seemed like hundreds of years, he had visited the Isle of Man, a derelict rock in the Irish Sea between England and Ireland, ignored by both antagonistic islands. His parents had taken him there to see the peasants working the thick, dense earth and the violent, ragged sea and to avoid the questions of a smouldering family horror at home. On a rare, blistering afternoon, without shadows or any other form of shade, he had been trusted to explore alone as they wandered the beach and not to move from the place in which he winched and roamed without finding interest.

In a shelter of cupped rock, nailed with white painted cottages to the cliff, he had met a fisherman. His boredom had been like bait to the old seaman, who was hiding his own endless tedium in the morbid actions of work. They had talked intermittently, dribbling sentences into the sand for each to watch without comment. The tide had receded and given a bellowing space to their breath, letting speech occur in salty bubbles. The highlight of the interaction had been in the contents of a battered pail of slopping brine, fetched by the fisherman and dramatically screwed into the sand for his young mind's attention. A clunking, pissing sound had come scratching from the bucket. He was instantly hooked. Walking over to look inside, he saw five crabs of various sizes, struggling against the limited water and the steep tin sides of their containment.

"Are they trying to escape?" he stuttered. "Trying to get out?"

"Aye." The fisherman nodded after a tobacco pause.

"But why can't they do it?" he asked. "There are more of them than the water."

"They be Manx crabs," said the man. "See—every time one crawls up an' nearly escapes, the others drag it back down."

Even as a boy, he had recognised this, known it to be as true as the ocean, and he had been instantly grateful for an adult fact. He had known, even then, that he would use it all his life.

He had never looked back.

CHAPTER EIGHT

*G*hertrude told Mutter to bring the next case up to the third floor. He obeyed with little relish, panting, huffing, and stumbling on each turn of the staircase. At their destination, she instructed him to open the crate and leave. He did so without a word, even as quick, infuriated splinters pierced his hands.

She removed the wooden shavings and other packing and looked into the box. Stenciled on the inside was "Lesson 315: The Songs of Insects." Forty screw-capped jars nestled tightly in the crate; there were no instructions. Ghertrude gingerly lifted one of the containers and held it up to the lamp. Small air holes had been punctured in the lid, and a letter *J* printed across its top. An elegant plant cutting shuddered within, a thick brown cricket gripping its stem. She began to remove all of the jars, placing them in alphabetical order on the dining room table. After *Z*, the letters were doubled: *AA, BB, CC*.

All manner of creatures ticked inside their glassy prisons. Suddenly, as if by some unknown command, they began to chirp and strum as one, their growing voices squeezing through the tin holes and vibrating the glass, until the room shimmered with aural beauty. Ghertrude stood entranced, her hands clasped together in a gesture of spontaneous pleasure. Ishmael watched her, waiting for his lesson to begin. From below, Mutter heard the third floor come alive, shook his head, and lit a cigar.

Ghertrude tried to explain the contents of the jars but soon found she had no idea what to say. She stumbled through the first nine before running out of words. She asked her pupil what he thought. He stared blankly at her.

"How would I think anything?" he asked, incredulous. "What are these things? What is their place?" She blushed in her ignorance and shrank in her failure.

Many of the cases that followed were even more obscure, rendering her speechless before the packing material had left her hands. Salvation came with Ishmael's change of heart. He decided to give up his petulant student status and listen graciously, without the rancour that had previously spilled over with his hunger for knowledge. It was true that she possessed more experience of the world outside, but he had a sharper mind to examine the facts before him, without the hindrance of their known function blinding their potential. He would try to do it her way, to speculate on the contents of the boxes and come to a conclusion based on each of their contributions.

So it was that they began to open the boxes together, with a newfound zeal and what she believed to be a rising tide of intimate respect. It became a pleasure: the anticipation, the piecing together of meaning, the guesswork. He was easier in his movement and speech, the angles and corners of previous mannerisms smoothing into softer, more natural alignments. Weeks passed in this way until, one afternoon, as they excitedly examined the textures and toughness of different kinds of leather, he asked, "When will we practise mating?"

She hoped she had misheard. "What do you mean?" she asked, with caution.

"When can I put my man tube inside your cleft? For pleasure and practice?"

She blushed and became tongue-tied, her hands overgripping the chamois in her clutch. She averted her eyes, looking down and noticing, with surprise, that his trousers were unbuttoned and gaping.

"It's been a long time now, and I miss it."

"We can never do such a thing," she hissed. "It's unnatural and shameful." She was about to explain the moral codes and the potential genetic disasters, when his words finally arrived at her understanding. "When did you do that before?" she asked slowly. "And who with?" Even as the question formed, she knew the answer, a picture of it assembling in the furthest recess of her mind.

"With Luluwa," he said. "Many times before."

The shock hit her in the strangest of ways. An unknown taste entered her mouth; her spine shivered, and she had the overpowering sense of being very far away, of being tiny while her body bloated, expanding to become the size of a continent. A flapping edge of swoon treacled her eyes, making everything peripheral to her speeding distance. And worst of all, in this ocean of disgust, fright, and repulsion, delight quivered, on a far-off island, on the other side of the world: in her womb.

It was two days before she could bring herself to return. She did not know how she had escaped that last afternoon; her memory had been rinsed to make space for her imagination. The image of their unholy coupling had crowded into her skull, the elbows, knees, and heels knocking against the bone. When she opened the door, he was standing by the shutters, picking at paint. He turned and anxiously began to speak. She put her finger to her lips and hushed him.

"Say nothing," she said. "Say nothing."

She crossed the room, taking his raised hand away from the shutters and holding it tightly in hers. Quietly, she led him through the room into the adjoining bedroom, guiding him onto the edge of the bed and unbuttoning her long raincoat. She stood before him, naked and trembling. He undressed quickly, fumbling with the buttons while she sat next to him. His last garment discarded, he placed his hands on her shoulders and felt her shudder. He was startled by her softness and warmth, and she shivered in the excitement of wrongness, the fear of the unknown and her commitment to the untold levels of power she knew she would wield from that point on. He ran his hands along her body, feeling the curves swell against his touch. She had the same contours as Luluwa, but his first teacher's cool hardness had never moved under the pressure of his body, and her rigidity had been the height of his eroticism. Now the heat and pliancy were transferred; she was like him, and they exchanged pressures by exquisite degrees. His fingers touched the inside of her legs, leaving tiny flakes of paint from under his nails. There was a jolt when he brushed against her pubic hair. He lowered his head and looked deep into her nakedness. An unmapped cog turned in the pale engine of his near humanity.

They coupled for two hours, shifting positions and angles until every aspect had been achieved. He fell into sleep while still inside her, his weight balanced across her. She looked down across his back at his breathing. He was drawing out of her, leaving a glistening trail across her thigh, in the shadow of his body. His penis had a counterclockwise spiral and turned as it retracted. In future couplings, she would find herself watching it in fascination, but for now the motion was hidden and proclaimed itself in a tickling sensation that made her squirm, waking him from his total slumber.

It had been Ghertrude's first time with another. She felt tired and exhilarated. There was no blood—she had taken her own virginity many years before. She had learned the conclave joys of auto-satisfaction through hours of practice and used the secret acts to inform her clandestine ways. She was proud of her self-sufficiency, the way it elevated her above common appetite. The day was a fissure in her containment, one that she would monitor with precise care.

Ishmael lay sprawled across the bed, ecstatic and soothed by his own pleasure, feeling his male dominance rise for the first time on the third floor. He reached out for her as she moved away from him, his fingers just touching her hips as she grabbed her coat and prepared to leave. He wanted to say something warm and appreciative but did not have the language. Beneath his heart, there was a subtle and churning bonding, and he wanted to be able to stroke and soothe her with its gentle fire. She left him unrelieved of his thoughts, and hurried downstairs to the bathroom on the second floor, where she had prepared a douche of alkaline salts.

━➤

In the centre of Essenwald, the great cathedral was German in origin—a facsimile of Europe nailed to the core of Africa. It had two towers that should have been twins, but irrational time had delayed one, causing a fluctuation of ideas to warp it. Some shards of fashion and theology had dented its skeletal helix, making the thin needle twist out of symmetry with its sister. A slim silver bridge joined the towers near their apex and highlighted the subtle difference between them: One tower had the clock, the other the bell. Each month, a trumpeter would celebrate the moon from the dizzying heights of the slender walkway. The pagan lunar ceremony, one of many that were the responsibility of Deacon Casius Tulp, had been imported along with the stones, the design, and the meaning of the great church.

(Many of the natives of the area also believed that the freak changes in the weather had been smuggled in with the invaders. It was certainly true that a new cold infested the nights in the winter season. Frost had been seen for the first time after the spires had been made, and different kinds of clouds now lurked above their spikes and tried to swallow the moon. But nothing ever changed in the Vorrh; it seethed in heat and ignored any rumour of ice.)

Deacon Tulp stood in the whistling, circular room with the pallid musician and one of the younger wardens. They were all panting after climbing the forever spiralling stairs, and pointed clouds of silvered air wheezed from them into the cold chamber, two hundred feet above ground. They were like so many arctic fire-eaters: None had the energy to talk, which made their steamy speech plumes all the more vacant. They were giddy, faintly nauseous, and desperately trying not to think about the space below. The inexperienced warden had already opened the arched door onto the frost-covered walkway, which trembled and sang with the wind. The musician was becoming the same colour as the platform from which he would perform tomorrow.

Casius Tulp spoke first. "It's perfectly safe," he said. "This weather is very unusual; never seen the like of it before, just like the old country. Your music will be heard all the better under these conditions; it will sound out across the whole city."

Nobody moved or wanted to think about tomorrow, and everybody had forgotten the old country. Their thoughts were about the grip of their shoes, the strength of the floor, and the little bit of their own personal gravity that enabled them to resist the wind. They clutched the railings, the walls, or anything of a solid nature with a fervent vigour.

Ghertrude's bright head appeared through the floor and startled them with its ease. "Here are the keys and the moon ring, Father." She climbed into the room with a wave of excitement that made the men grip their supports even more firmly. Giving the ancient velvet bag to the older man, she turned into the blast from the open door and, in purposeful joy, walked towards it and out onto the bridge. The men's insides shrank, their spines and stomachs slivering over the threshold and plummeting, with the imagined falling girl, towards the hard, cobbled ground. She was laughing as the wind plucked at the fur of her collar and her hair to make another jealous imitation of fire. "I can almost see to the other side of the Vorrh!" she yelled. "Look at the people, like ants!" Her shoes rattled on the slender metal as she tapped her feet in excitement. She had only one hand on the silver rail; the other waved towards the abyss. Nobody went out, and nobody would have ever dared to look down. It took some effort to get her back into the tower.

She had been fourteen at the time and had begged to be given the job of organising the moon call every year. After ten days of incessant pleading, interspersed with silent, certain haughtiness, the dean had given in and she had been awarded the position: the first woman and the youngest in history.

Now, all these years later, she stood again on the bridge and gazed out over the city. Flocks of birds were wheeling below, their shrill cries caught in the rising chimney smoke. Farther down, a warren of business squirmed in the mud. She looked down onto 4 Kühler Brunnen, lit by the slanted rays of the afternoon sun; into its courtyards and odd-shaped garden; at its shuttered windows and what she knew to be inside. She pictured him, like a flea or a speck of grit, hard and senseless, encrusted into the upper rooms. She thought how tiny his eye would be from here. Looking at the streets that he would never see, she shivered at his growing need to walk in them. A raven crossed her view, circling the roof under which he paced or slept. It landed and looked down into the garden. She grinned at their telescoped comparison, then thought of God peering down at her petty elevation. This was a fancy that she did not care for, and she switched to more practical matters, deciding to go to her parents' house for dinner that night. There were a few more questions to be asked about the old house.

At this moment, the rods under the bridge, which connected the clock to the bell, started to move. She felt their expectancy shift, seconds before the mechanism fell into gear. The weights lurched and the cogs started to gnaw into the allotted time. It was time to go.

Ghertrude turned towards the door and moved a fraction, when something hooked her back to the distant rooftops: There was something below, almost unseen. It pecked at her mind's eye and slid a new dimension into what she thought she knew so well. She moved back, targeting the raven and opening her sight. There it was: a tower. A shrunken, octagonal chimney, rising from the corner of the roof of 4 Kühler Brunnen. The tiled turret was hidden in the patterned complexity of the rooftops, and the raven stood on its brim, his shadow sliding over its edge. This was another secret of the house that she was beginning to think of as her own.

She flew down the spiral stairs into the echoing nave, its booming organ trying to rival the setting sun, which was already stoking up the great windows of the west side. She knew that, if she sped, she would catch Mutter before he returned home that night.

He already had the quiet, hasty key in the lock when she pounced. "Sigmund! Come with me."

She entered the garden gate and hurriedly walked around the side of the house, looking up at the roof. Mutter trailed behind her, his head too tired to stare at the sky.

"There! There!" She pointed upwards. She was crouched, almost sitting in the shrubs, beneath the tall wall at the garden's far end. Only from such an extreme angle could the tower be seen, sheltering in the fractured perspectives of the interlocking roofs. She pointed again. "There! What is that? Look, man, look!"

He lumbered over to her, bent sullenly, and stared upwards.

"There, there! What is it?"

After a few moments of squinting and shifting, while she jabbed rabidly at the air, he said, "It's a raven, ma'am."

Back in the house, they climbed the main stairway. Ghertrude was quiet and intent; Mutter was stiff, formal, and distant. He had become used to her commands, to her shifts of mood and her haughty righteousness. He had come to expect it. But nobody had ever spoken to him in the way that she just had. If it had been a man, he would have cuffed him into submission and apology. No woman had ever dared to call him a fool and worse; it stung his pride and abraded his manhood. And all because of a crow, or a raven, or some invisible chimney! He was saturated in sulk and wore it with a sullen distance.

Ghertrude knew she had been wrong to lose her temper with him; she needed this man, especially now. She stopped on the stairway and turned to face him. "Sigmund, I am very sorry for behaving so badly. You are a good and trusted servant and I have talked to you like an angry child. I must ask your forgiveness; it will not happen again."

He was amazed. Before her outburst, he had been secretly growing to respect her; now it seemed she had proven him right in doing so. He was lost for words, and strong emotions erupted in small spots inside him, like pennies in a cap.

"Do I have your forgiveness?" she asked.

He grunted a nod.

"Good. Now, let's find this tower," she said, turning to resume her climb and lead the way up through the house.

On the third floor, she put her finger to her lips as they crept past Ishmael's suites. They walked the length of the corridor, but no other door could be found there, or in any of the adjacent rooms. Mutter pointed up at the ceiling and whispered, "The attic," the entrance to which was at the other end of the building.

It was the most unused part of the house, not counting the cellars or the well, which were best ignored. Inside a tiny box room, which at one time must have been used for servants, they found the stairway. Its carpentry was different from that in the rest of the house. It was tree-cut wood, still showing forms of branches and organic twists in its length. It suggested that the ladder had been grown, rather than constructed, conjured from the forest for a measured purpose. It was neat and strong and led to a roughly painted hatch in the ceiling.

Mutter lit the bull's-eye oil lamp and started up the stairs. His bulk made the wood creak as he pushed upwards, flipping the door inwards and lifting the light into the dark volume.

"Please wait a moment, mistress," he said, and continued to climb until just his feet were visible, huge on the delicate ladder.

Ghertrude was instantly reminded of the fearful giant following Jack down the beanstalk to terrorise his world. She suppressed a titter and looked up. "What can you see?" she asked.

"Not much," he answered.

She climbed onto the ladder too, intending to ascend, but it objected noisily. She got a whiff of Mutter's rear end, an aroma that was, essentially, peasant: root vegetables and meat, laced with hard work, tobacco, and strong drink, all amplified by a distaste for bathing.

She stepped back onto the solid floor and into more fragrant air, just as he disappeared into the groaning hole.

"My God!" he said, in a voice that rang with sympathetic resonance, like a child calling into a lute.

"What?! What is it?" she cried, hands once more holding the ladder, but this time with firmer intent.

"You better come and see," he called.

The immense attic ran the entire length of the house, with a dramatic, right-angled turn at the far end, suggesting its continuation over an adjoining property. Her eyes slowly became accustomed to the dry gloom and the resonance, which seemed to be tuning itself to her breathing.

Mutter spoke with an unearthly, musical clarity. "Take care; the floor is covered in wires!" The words transmuted into a fluttering choir of angels. If his harsh, guttural voice had been so cleansed and extended, what would she sound like?

Then she saw the taut and gently glinting strings in the light of their lamp. Spider yarns delineating the distance, causing it to resemble the open fields as seen from above. Nitre, she thought, lines of fungi glistening, but it hummed. Yet again, that impossible word leapt into her mouth. It had been ordained that she would forever question strangeness with strangeness in this unpredictable house. She breathed out the call.

"*What!*"

It sang with a liquid vibrancy that coloured the space and made the blood dance in every quivering capillary. A tangible thrill rattled their bones and forced them both to grin like cats. When they drifted back to reality, the attic was ready to show them more.

They saw limp lines of cord hanging from the ceiling, almost touching the strings. Boxes of iron balls and boxes of feathers were interspaced, placed close to the wall. The prone wires were listening to them, accosting and commenting on their movements and distorting Mutter's whispers.

The wires resonated with their every sound. Her word still sang in the air. There was a narrow path across the attic between the strings. Not a straight path, which would have made more sense to the fixed delineations, but a winding track that forced the tense wires to make a more random pattern, or perhaps it was the other way around. Unlike the rest of the house, there was no dust covering these mysteries. Ghertrude stopped to touch and admire the objects as she walked, in a dreamlike glaze, through the hollow room. Mutter was more cautious and thrust his hands deep into his tarry pockets. Then they saw the door, and knew, without words, that it would lead them to the tower.

➤—→

Ishmael was restless. He had explored every crevice and recess in his suite of rooms, and he wished for more. He wanted variety and difference, contrast and resistance. He knew Ghertrude and Mutter were outside; he could smell them through the shutters. He also knew that all the others out there had at least two eyes. He should have known this before. He had once asked Luluwa why all the animals she brought him had many eyes. She had said it was because they were of a lower denomination. The answer had seemed true at the time. Perhaps it was still true now. He saw nothing superior in Ghertrude or Mutter, certainly not in relation to himself or the Kin. But being locked in these rooms, he would never find out. There were many secrets and mysteries. No one knew who sent the boxes or who arranged for Mutter to be paid. He had discovered this by mistake; he was learning guile by watching them, by observing the unsayings and the quick looks. He wanted to train his powerful and undivided sight further into the world, but she would not let him. For his own good, she said. She claimed to be protecting him from the cruelties that would befall him outside the walls of the house. But she could not know that he had already been taught the lessons of cruelty, from the contents of the two crates that had been delivered together, so long ago.

He knew that he was watched. He had heard movement above, heard muffled voices up there when the house was supposed to be empty. He was not meant to have noticed the small hole that had appeared in the plaster scrollwork of the ceiling, the gap that let them peer down into his seclusion. He, in turn, picked at the paintwork around the lock on the shutters, splintering away a shard of wood, which could be set back in place with spit and cunning. He had seen the courtyard and the live animals and sometimes the street beyond, when the gate had been opened.

Some nights, he dreamt of the Kin: the hard brown of their kindness; Luluwa's unflinching touch; the watery hiss in her body. Some nights he pieced together the bits of learning they had given him and strung them on a thread of meaning that was entirely his own. If she would not let him see the world outside, then he would not let her see the one he was constructing within.

➤—→

There was no key for the door to the tower, just a slit, its edges rounded by use and the gnawing of rats. She put her flat hand inside and her fingertips touched the string. She scissor-gripped it between the polished almonds of her nails and pulled it out.

"Let's come back in daylight, mistress," Mutter said.

She heard real concern, not fear, in his voice. The oil lamp was smoking and the night was inking in the volumes around them. What had been magical was beginning to give way to the eerie.

"Yes," she said, letting the string fall back to the other side of the door. "We will return in the morning. With new light, we will see so much more."

They climbed back to the civilised part of the house. Lost in her thoughts, she exited the stairwell brushing cobwebs and dust from the folds in her dress. It took her some moments to realise that her action was purely mechanical, designed to announce her arrival—there was nothing on her clothing to be removed.

The light declared that it would be a glorious day, limply draped in water at first, but with a glowing intensity that would burn off any trace of shadow by noon. They climbed the stairs to the third floor in a saturated brightness that followed their ascent, pencil-thin rays of sun spinning through the singing attic, creating a magnificent landscape of shifting perspective. At the door, she retrieved the string once more and tugged on it eagerly. With a meaty click, the door opened and they stepped into another stairwell.

"I sometimes wonder if this house will ever end," she said, as she began to climb up the wooden, panelled tube. At the apex was a large, circular table, sheltering under the beautiful curves of a domed roof. A brass rod and lever pointed down to the faded silk cloth that covered the disc. She knew instantly what it was, and her heart pounded with glee.

She pulled the cloth from the disc to expose its subtle curve. Reaching up, she drew the lever down, while holding the thick brass knob at the end of the rod. A panel in the ceiling slid open, sending dappled light onto the table. She turned the knob and the juddering blurs cohered into an image of the city below. Mutter was leaning on the white surface when a horse and carriage crossed the back of his hand. He pulled away as if stung.

"It's all right, Sigmund," she said. "It's just a picture."

She twisted the knob and the city spun and turned under her control. Continually adjusting the lever and the rod, she selected and focused on the distant life at her will. She trawled the contours of the horizon and the black shadow of the Vorrh, before focusing tightly on the cathedral door. Marvelling at her perfect detachment, she caught all the faces of those who passed through the great door, their purpose and activity reduced and smeared across the white dish for her inspection and delight.

It was then that she saw another potential rise from the milky whiteness: This camera obscura could be the solution to the cyclops's discontent. From here, he could view the city at a safe distance, saturating his curiosity in its shifting image. She decided to make a surprise of it and bring him up to the attic room without telling him why.

On the morning of the street market in the town square, she dressed him in warm clothes, unlocked the doors, and led him through the house. He had not been outside his rooms since the traumatic day of Ghertrude's arrival and the Kin's demise. He looked at everything and marvelled at the shrinkage that had occurred, relative to his own growth. Mutter led the way up into the attic, as Ishmael, then Ghertrude followed. They stepped into the singing room and she caught his hand in a gentle camouflage of restraint. Against their expectations, he recognised the contrivance in the room instantly.

"How wonderful," he exclaimed. "It's a Goedhart device."

Mutter and Ghertrude were stunned. "A what?" she said.

"A Goedhart device, one of the rare and unique instruments of Joanhus Goedhart."

At the word "Goedhart," the floor chimed with a deeper and more significant resonance. He pulled away to examine the strings. Ghertrude felt an irrational anger begin to grow inside her.

"Let's go to the door," she said, setting off quickly across the room, with Mutter following closely. But Ishmael could not be rushed and made his way slowly towards them, delighting in the wires and their reaction when he murmured into them. He touched them all, pulling at the cords attached to the roof, stroking the feathers and feeling the weight of the metal balls with an increasing pleasure.

"We have not come to see these things," Ghertrude snapped, sensing that the importance of her gift was being diluted by the inconsequential and irrelevant intrusions and his understanding of them. He left his enquiries reluctantly and caught up to them, strumming five of the strings in a discordant slash en route. They climbed into the dark, octagonal chamber and stood around the circular table. She grabbed the controls and, with a dramatic flourish, twisted the projector into life. The narrow parting in the roof sprang open and the market jumped onto the table, shimmering with activity, colour, and bustle. Mutter, sensing the growing emotion, moved back down the stairwell to search in the attic for a window or an opening.

Ghertrude watched the cyclops. He stood very still, slightly bent over the table. His eye was enormous, starting from his head. He was pale, a greasy film of perspiration on his skin reflecting the light of the scene below. Suddenly, her body reinstated the revulsion she had felt when she had first seen him; that moment seemed decades away now. Their intimacy and her growing feelings for him had made his face normal: Wonder and secrecy had repaired his learned abnormalities, while familiarity and desire had stitched up their differences.

She was overpowered by the shock of the old feeling, especially as they stood together, in a moment that could turn in any direction. Had she made a mistake in bringing him here? Why did he look so? A tear splashed onto the glowing disc, briefly creating another tiny lens. He made an indecipherable sound, deep in his chest. She thought, at first, that it was a composite of longing, but as it slid over her array of perception it changed, taking on sharper and more alarming tinctures. The second tear fell, and she was cleaved by the need to go to him—to touch and reassure—and the desire to escape. The table seemed to get brighter as the room blackened around them.

He started to undress as she watched, unable to do or say anything. As he unbuckled his belt, he became aware of her stillness, its perfection denting the air, and angrily pointed at her blouse while yanking at his trousers. When she did nothing, the pointing hand converted into a clenching fist that snatched the docile lace and wrenched her forward. Pearl buttons flew in all directions, and she was about to cover her startled breasts when he shouted, "For me, you for me!" She closed her eyes and slowly removed the wrecked blouse and the thin straps of her chemise beneath. He pulled away the rest of her clothing, trampling it and cracking the fallen buttons under his stiff, impatient feet.

His purple cock was enormous, its spiralled barrel twisting and telescoping back and forth with his heavily beating heart. His eye continued to drip tears, now onto her legs as he braced her across the table. The blurrily focused crowd and the now-clumsy architecture smeared on her naked belly and her torn clothing. Their bodies united in the silent light, and deep inside she gave up, wanting the keys to be taken away. She wanted to be a child again, with no understanding; to rip her guile into a forgetting womb and pamper offspring by a warm hearth, to let milk drown her lime and become inside out, gloving another life that would fold her to a gentle, smiling death, where all spoke of her wisdom and love. In the long time of silence before he withdrew, a ruthless, automatic kindness unfolded in him, its weight matching the shock of excitement that laughed secretly in Ghertrude. The rawness of both expressions bound them together in a shame that was sublime in the depth of its contradiction.

He fell back as she leaked on the polished surface of the porous, inert table. Low on its right-hand side, blind to their panting bodies, a drawer lay open in untraceable measures. It exposed a shallowness in its recess that was gently covered with a curved, articulated piece of polished wood. Had they examined it, they would have found a tiny cleft, oiled by perpetual moisture, concealed beneath the tonguelike flap. It sat, expectant and totally unnoticed by the pair above it. As they unfurled, and only their white breathing filled the room, it slid closed, becoming seamless and invisible again.

He stood, his eye still shut; words existed elsewhere. She

slanted over the table and gazed across herself. Some previous part of her being wanted to adjust the splutter that moved over her body, twist the focus back into detail and rewind the clock. She watched as he returned to the moment; he began to make small, pinching movements with his finger and thumb, trying to capture the Lilliputian figures that bustled in the streets, to pluck them up. She assumed he was jesting but discerned no trace of amusement in his stern and twisted expression.

When they left the tower, they found light and the scent of woodsmoke in the attic. Mutter had found a window and opened it onto the rooftops. He had long since gone, driven away by their animal sounds, which had slid down from above to tantalise the recumbent wires.

They returned to the third floor. At the door of his dwelling, Ishmael held his hand out towards her. She reciprocated, touched by his gesture of affection. The instant their hands met, she knew she had made a mistake. His rigid fingers were eloquent in their distance.

"No," he said, "the keys."

Thus, the cyclops changed his status in the quiet house on Kühler Brunnen; the next episode of their life together had begun.

CHAPTER NINE

Charlotte spent many leaden hours in the hotel room, especially after the turmoil of their arrival. She could still feel the derringer, grasped hard in the palm of her hand; the suffocating crowd of grinning faces, squashed against the car. She had travelled to many places with the Frenchman, but never to such a primitive location. Before, he had always stayed with her, in their interconnecting suite of rooms. He had never walked out into such a street, had never made appointments and plans without her. She was anxious about him, knowing how easily he could become embroiled in trouble. His predilection for the poor and the criminal led him to the most sordid and dangerous parts of town. He had a hunter's nose for those quarters and would find them instantly in the newest, most unfamiliar locations. But he would never wander out alone. They always cruised the streets and alleys in the massive vehicle, often blocking the road and scraping the crumbling walls, causing a sensation. Sometimes, when he was too dissolute to venture out to catch his quarry, he would unfold a map of the place, pour a glass of his favourite Alsace, and ponder it for hours. He would imagine the streets, sniff the alleys, and finally select a site. She and the chauffeur would be dispatched to that place, to collect or trap a partner for his night of pleasure. It was the least favourite of her duties, and the only one that genuinely made her feel unclean. No innocent was ever kidnapped, and no one was taken against his will: Any doubts in the mind of the chosen one were quickly muted by an offering of money. But the journey back in the car embarrassed her, especially when they questioned her about what they had to do and what her part was in those delights. She had never been prudish, but the last five years had stretched her experience into realms of disbelief.

The difficulty was her kindness. She could explain the sexual details and the intricate peccadilloes that sharpened them so for the Frenchman. She could elucidate the manner of their conduct and the level of brutality that was expected of them. But she could not give voice to the instant abandonment of their humanity after the deeds were done. The suddenness of their expulsion, propelled by the total disgust of their existence. This part of the ritual she hid from, closing the doors to all her rooms, leaving the chauffeur to ringmaster the debasing event, which she suspected he enjoyed. Charlotte had no delusions that the abused vermin she had solicited would have been offended by these actions; indeed, most would have been overjoyed to escape the limpet passions of the aesthete's bed, especially after drinking as much as they could, and with the bundle of notes grinning in their pockets. She felt pity for them, but it was the debasement of the Frenchman that so unnerved her.

He was not just a ruined brat, spending his family's wealth on indulgence; she had known many of those. He possessed, or was possessed by, something else: a crippled soul, which might just pucker into genius, if only he allowed his wretched shred of joy to grow. She had seen it and knew it was closer to his vision than the exhaustion of his heart and the poisoning of his body. She knew that, for those who have everything in abundance, there is always a gap, a hollow that will never be filled. Long before she had met the Frenchman, before his mother had even conceived of proposing that Charlotte become the companion of her beloved son, she had known of the hunger and some of the ways of its manifestation. The fruitless mangle of emotions, spurred and strangled by the auto-cannibalism of guilt. The humiliation of being animal, the whipping into cruelty of lost affections. She had accepted his mother's offer out of kindness and the need to provide the possibility of change. They had thought she needed the money and the elevated social position—perhaps she had. Nevertheless, it was a good bargain. The son had a companion whom he would learn to trust and who would give a glint of beauty to all his endeavours. He could wear her proudly in all Parisian society, and she would neither expect nor demand anything from him. The mother could entrust her son to a bright and elegant creature, who would keep him on at least one fixed rail, which was considered respectable and normal in decent society; moreover, she would own the young woman and never have to suffer the machinations and spite of a daughter-in-law.

But these were malign and tragic fantasies; she knew her son's appetites ran in opposite directions. Previous attempts to arouse his masculinity had been woeful disasters. She had supplied him with a comely mistress for his twentieth birthday, but the poor woman was driven to distraction by her supposed lover's endless, limp readings of interminably long poems. So monstrous was the abuse that she had demanded one hundred thousand francs in compensation from the old woman, for the aural and temporal violation. And Charlotte? She could settle and pretend for a while. There was no need for real marriage in her life, certainly not yet. And thus it came to pass that the two strangers became witnesses in a shared life.

But he was still missing. She looked across the colonial-style room at the grandfather clock, emaciated in its light, timbered case. She thought of calling the chauffeur but could not face hearing his monochromatic indifference. Dinner was at seven, and after all the fuss the Frenchman had made about the menu, she dreaded the chef's reaction to a postponement. She went to the window, threw open its juddering glass, and stepped out onto the balcony. This had been the only hotel in Essenwald of sufficient quality to satisfy the Frenchman's fastidious requirements. They had taken the entire upper floor. The balcony extended around the building. She began to walk its rectangular length. Peering into the crowd below and shading her eyes with her long, delicate hand, she looked into the distance.

Far off, the black shadow of the Vorrh could be seen, sealing the city on its northern side. She searched the faces and the gaits of the seething streets beneath her, unable to find him in their constant shift and bustle. She became suddenly aware that one of the crowd was still and facing her. He was tall and motionless, his face hidden by a tightly wrapped *ghutra* of black silk. She could feel his stare, even from the distance of several hundred feet. Coldness plucked at her optic nerves with a bony nail; her sight flickered in distress and she grabbed at the squeaking door. From behind her, there was a sound on the landing outside the room. Approaching footsteps, unfamiliar and ponderous, drew her away from the street and its intruder and back into the room, composed and ready to receive anybody. No one knocked, but the brass door handle slowly turned and the Frenchman quietly entered. So pleased was she to see him that she didn't instantly notice the strangeness of his approach.

She greeted him with lapping warmth. He smiled gently and touched her arm. This was unknown. She was dismayed, overwhelmed, and silenced by it. He deflated into one of the enormous Moroccan armchairs and said, with eyes already shut, "Charlotte, my dear, I am a little tired."

The evening was luxuriously calm. The perfume of the jasmine that twisted through the wrought iron of the balcony fluttered into the room. The fireflies buzzed the dusk in overlapping eclipses, and the frogs and cicadas accelerated a chorus. There was a settled peace in their suite of rooms. He was asleep in the chair where he had collapsed. She had checked that he was well, then taken off his shoes and placed his hat and cane in the hall. The cane felt curiously weightless, her excessive use of muscle giving it an illusion of levitation that made her laugh.

He slept for three hours before waking slowly, creaking in the leather and blinking into the room as she lit the lamps. There was a softness about his eyes that had never been present before. She saw the child in the old man, wonder and contentment where cynicism and greed had been scratched before. This was the man she always knew but hardly ever met.

"Come and sit with me," he said. "I want to tell you about my black friend and his vision of the forest."

They talked for a very long time, pausing the conversation only to fetch wine and delay the dinner. He told her of his new friend, of his kindness and his lessons, of the chapel and the saints and a living Adam, somewhere at the heart of the wilderness of trees. He wanted her to meet "the black prince" and share in his tales of belief and wonder. Quietly, out of nowhere, he asked, "The little silver crucifix that you sometimes wear; is it of great sentimental value to you?" She looked a little confused, and he continued, "It's just that I so want to give my prince a gift; I wondered if I might purchase it from you."

"It's of no real value to me," she lied. "I have several others; please do take it."

He was delighted and crossed the little space between them to kiss her cheek. His mouth was surprisingly cold. His request satisfied, he continued to talk about his day.

They moved into the dining room, without a break in his enthusiasm or a pause in her amazement. It was to be a much lighter dinner than he usually demanded: only sixteen courses that night. At times, during his eloquent nibbling, he would adopt Seil Kor's voice and dash ornate French with a rich Arabic bias and sonorous tones across the tabled landscape of food. She would laugh loudly at his pronunciations and roll against the joy that projected them. He was a genius at imitation. He could copy all voices, whether they belonged to strangers or friends, animals, or even the inanimate. He once held a party of poets spellbound by his portrayal of a collection of old hinges. She loved it when he was playful, when his gift was not soured by malice.

It was almost midnight when he left the table and sat down to the piano with a cigar. She went to the window and walked out into the glittering night. The city was already sleeping, and the heavens took up the sound of the creatures below, the stars making a notation of their trills and bells, which rang in the darkness like glass. Whispers of Satie joined them from the room, and there seemed, in this inimitable moment, to be an agreement between time and the proximity of all things, as if clumsy humans might have a place in all this infinite, perfect darkness, if only they played at the edge. Out of sight, blindfolded, and in agreement.

Charlotte smelt the coffee when she awoke; indeed, it might have been its bitter warmth that quaffed her dreams. She slipped on a yellow robe and opened the door to the Frenchman's room; he was already awake and seated at the breakfast table. He had never been known to stir before noon. Slightly unsettled, she joined him at the table, an empty cup in her hesitant hand, her eyes never leaving his excited expression. He smiled.

"A beautiful morning, Charlotte!"

"Yes," she said, noticing for the first time that thick shafts of light divided the room, motes of dust swimming expressively in their beams, giving the simultaneous impressions of animation and stillness.

"Did I tell you last night that today I go to the Vorrh?" he asked. "Seil Kor is coming for me this morning." It was the first time he had used his new friend's name; previously, he had referred to him as a "native," a "black," or, on occasion, as his "black prince."

She was unmoved by the name and unsurprised he had endowed his young guide with the same moniker as a character from his *Impressions of Africa*. She had never seriously under-taken to read any of his books, poems, or essays, only the letters he addressed to her. It was not part of her duties. She knew that it would ruin their relationship to hold an opinion on his works: She was merely a woman, and they both preferred it that way. However, she had once flipped through the pages of the African book. She had found it confused and obscure. No doubt it was art, for she knew him to be a man of dangerous appetites and total selfishness. That was what made the smiling man before her such a disconcerting sight.

"I have packed my bag for a three-day expedition," he said.

Her shock at discovering that he knew where the luggage was kept was augmented by the revelation that he was capable of packing it. "I shall take the Smith & Wesson, the one with the pearl grips, and leave you the Colt, the Mannlicher, and the Cloverleaf, for your protection. May I borrow your derringer for my little journey?"

"Why, of course," she replied, "anything you wish."

They always travelled with a small armoury, ostensibly for the pleasure of target shooting, but always with the excuse of protection. He was an excellent shot and had enjoyed teaching her how to handle and fire his collection of pistols. The guns also gave her some confidence against the "street visitors" he often brought home or sent the chauffeur to find. His taste ran hard into the criminal and the lower manual labourer. They were easy to find and would fulfil all of his sexual morbidities, but they were tricky to get rid of afterwards, difficult to scrape off the shoe. Countless times, she had returned home to find some half-naked urchin or dockyard worker going through her belongings, ejected from the Frenchman's bedroom after the brutality, so that he might drown and wallow in the true depth of his debasement. Countless times, she had been forced to haggle over the price of flesh. The currency of usury had become part of her vocabulary; she dealt with it efficiently and from a distance. Some small fold of her enjoyed talking to the exotic underclass about the most intimate actions of vice. She felt like an ornithologist, or an entomologist, viewing horrid little wonders through the wrong end of a perfect telescope. But she could not abide the blackmailers, those who went too far and allowed greed to ooze out with the secretions of their bodies. There had been many hushed-up cases, many insidious threats to expose his obsessions. She had brokered them all. Sometimes she was forced to enlist the support of the chauffeur, who liked to wrap metal chains around his fist when dealing with the stubborn.

"Are you going alone with Seil Kor?" she asked cautiously.

"Oh yes," he said, in a theatrically disinterested way. "He is not to be one of my 'paramours,'" he added, a trace of the old acid leaking back into his speech. "He is a friend and noble person of these regions—I would like very much to introduce you."

"Thank you," she replied, "I would like that. Don't forget this." She handed him a tiny, delicate package of folded tissue paper containing the cheap, silver-plated crucifix that her first love had given to her at the age of thirteen.

On the steps of the hotel, the light was blinding. He wore his Eskimo spectacles and pith helmet, with a costume that needed at least fifteen native bearers to maintain it. Childlike, he gripped his suitcase and strained through the brightness to see his friend in the whirling, dusty clouds of passersby. Charlotte stood beside him, arms folded and trepidation rising.

"There!" he cried. "By the tree; he is waving!"

She could barely distinguish a single figure, just a mass of activity in the luminous dust. The Frenchman stepped down the stairs and into the throng, motioning to Charlotte to join him, but the dust was unbearable, and she put her hand over her mouth, averting her face from the onslaught. He reached Seil Kor across the street and tried to explain about meeting Charlotte, but she was lost in the crowd and his guide was anxious to depart. He gave in to the unfolding events and they made their way out of the throng—their journey to the Vorrh had begun.

Seil Kor took the Frenchman to his home, far across town in the old quarter. From there to the station was only ten minutes' walk, he promised.

"Why do we go to your house first?" he asked.

"To change," Seil Kor said, without emphasis.

"But this is my exploring costume," whined the Frenchman, who was beginning to be irritated by the change in plans.

"Trust me, master, it is better for you to melt into the crowd, become one of us. This way you will see more and get closer to the heart of the forest. We have to travel for a whole day on the train, and I want you to be comfortable."

They walked down a high, mud-walled street that changed its curve every fifteen paces or so. Alleyways led off at frequent intervals, and there was a sense of a great populace concealed behind the twisting façade.

They turned again, stepping into a long, straight street with two ancient wooden doors set into its crumbling surface. Seil Kor hammered on the first door and, moments later, the second one opened.

They stepped into a broad, sand-coloured courtyard with a square well and a palm tree dominating its luxurious simplicity. A small, grinning boy stepped from behind the gate and closed them in. Seil Kor clapped his hands loudly above his head, and the doors of the long, low building that occupied one side of the enclosure opened. Vividly dressed women emerged carrying a carpet, a squat folding table, and brass and copper bowls of fruit and sweetmeats. In a quick flurry, it was all set up under the shade of the tree, and the Frenchman was shown to the guest seat at its centre. The women brought piles of native robes and Arabic-style headgear for the dandy to try on. He liked this game and, once he got over his essential stiffness, became completely engaged in his transformation. He loved to dress up and had often donned the national costume of the countries he had visited before. But it had never felt this real before, and his guide had never been so gracious, so encouraging. He tried on many different styles and colours, spinning and giggling as the women and the boy applauded. He bowed. They all bubbled over in this pantomime of innocence. Carefree and conceited, he thought to add a dash to his apparel and dug the pistol out of his case, sticking it jauntily in his belt. The party froze. Seil Kor raised his hands and the women covered their eyes.

"Master, what is this? Why do you bring this?" His bony finger shook as it pointed towards the gun. "Please, leave it in the bag. Where we go is sacred; such a thing is a blasphemy there."

"But what about wild animals and those savage people?" the Frenchman stuttered.

"We will be walking with the Lord God; his angels will guard us."

He dropped the pistol back in the bag and stepped slowly away from it. Seil Kor met him with a grin, and he moved to his friend's side, gripping his arm conciliatorily.

"Oh! One moment," said the Frenchman. "I have something for you." He removed the little tissue-paper package from his person and carefully unwrapped it, holding the gleaming crucifix up for his new friend to admire.

"For me?" asked Seil Kor, genuinely surprised.

The Frenchman nodded and handed him the chain; he fixed it at once around his neck. The cross shone brightly against Seil Kor's jet-black skin and the others applauded the gift all the way to the door as they prepared to depart. By the time they crossed the threshold, the Frenchman was unrecognisable. He was happy and very at ease in his flowing robes. A prince of the desert, he thought—if only he had a photograph for his collection. He resolved to have one taken on their return, on the steps of the hotel, when he and Seil Kor would present themselves to Mademoiselle Charlotte, in celebration of their triumphant expedition.

The moon rose full on that same clear night, bringing with it a wind from the distant sea, a gale that gained force as it swept inland towards the Vorrh. By four o'clock, an hour after the good shepherd Azrael had collected his flock from the world of the living and the night had settled back in the last three fathoms of its darkness, the wind shook Essenwald with a near-tempest velocity. It rattled the old windows in its finest hotel; Charlotte turned over in the warmth of her sleep, untroubled by the gale, tightening the crisp sheet and plaid blanket about her untouched contour. She dreamt of an American who would walk into her forgetfulness and ask about tonight. She was in Belgium, where she slept all day, and a clock without hands said it was an impossible 1961. The young man was telling her that he was a poet. He had a large, kind, soft face, but it was difficult to hear him because of the clattering, glassy sound that emanated from his pencil and notebook.

CHAPTER TEN

*E*dward Muybridge's time in the wilderness was coming to an end. His work and his roaming had turned from gossip into legend. After all these years, his fame was spreading even farther. Rocks and buildings became his subjects and stepping-stones. He used lenses that moved long exposures and denied human presence, paradoxical stairs to the sight traps of movement. New and unusual commissions called to him, and he needed a single address to be reached by them all.

Once more, he moved back into the cities, cleaning his shutters for people. He opened his temple of lenses, and a trickle of curiosity turned into a flood of interest.

His experiments in capturing animal movement caught the public imagination. His great success was founded on a gambler's bet: Leland Stanford, the Prince of Wisconsin, wanted proof that horses flew, that they were suspended in midair as they galloped, jumping through space, all hooves losing contact with the ground. Muybridge's job was to capture that momentous truth, and his wealthy patron was generous with both money and time.

Academic institutions wanted him. Europe called. Triumphantly, he returned to London. He was no longer Muggeridge, the coal seller's son, or Mirebridge, a name to span a bog, the split-headed, hollow man hiding in the colonies, but Muybridge, the scientist and artist. London praised him and he lectured to it. He had, of course, sent invitations to the surgeon, Gull, but never received a reply. He looked for him in the audience and at the countless receptions but was never rewarded with a sighting. He wanted to show the great man that he was healed, successful. The surgeon had seen deep into him; he had predicted the trouble when people became close; he may even have glimpsed the murder in that little whirling instrument of his, and the imbalance of their relationship made the photographer uncomfortable. He wanted to show Gull the man he had become.

One day, when picking up a new batch of specially made lenses from a workshop in Clerkenwell, his impulses led him across the Thames to the expanding hospital at London Bridge. The cab dropped him by the great iron gates and he quickly found a porter.

"Do you know if Dr. Gull still works here?" he asked.

"Sir William?" said the porter, and Muybridge was impressed, though not surprised: All men of excellence are eventually so rewarded. "He's here today, sir. He's lecturing up in the north theatre."

He pointed the way and Muybridge rushed ahead, not wanting to miss the moment. He was out of breath by the time he got to the top of the long flights of stone stairs, jammed with students, who had flocked here from all over the world. The stairs narrowed and changed noisily to wood on the last flight, leading to a high door. He listened for a moment, then opened it quietly and slid in, his tall felt hat already in his hand.

He was at the back of a steep-sided anatomical theatre, its six-tiered auditorium tapering down towards the focused space at its centre. Each of the semicircular tiers was crowded with an attentive audience that stood and leaned forward, looking down towards the voice, which he recognised as Gull's. He squeezed into the back row of students, who moved along to make a space for his dignified presence. Only an iron handrail stopped them all from tumbling forward like a collapsed wedding cake.

Gull had aged. He was heavier and squarer than Muybridge remembered, with a solid authority that was grounded in his sonorous and empathic voice. But perhaps all those qualities were merely accentuated by the creature that stood next to him. Muybridge had seen many human forms, but never one like this—certainly not alive. It was difficult to guess her age—he thought perhaps early to mid-twenties. She was the same height as the sturdy surgeon, but a mere quarter of his girth. She was naked; every bone showed under the surface of her pale, porcelain skin. She was a living skeleton. Not an ounce of fat existed anywhere on her fragile frame; her muscles must have been as thin as paper.

"Alice started her condition sixteen months ago, and she will continue until it reaches its obvious conclusion. Isn't that right, Alice?" said Gull, turning to the waif at his side.

Alice nodded, and her huge eyes blinked in their dark sockets.

"Her condition, which I have recently identified, has never been properly recognised before now. Others like Alice have died without diagnosis. For the most part, they would not have been seen by a physician, and their families have assumed that they had been suffering from a wasting disease.

"Alice is typical of those thus inflicted, coming from the upper and middle classes. While the poor have the problem of finding enough food to survive, this is a sickness that stems from affluence. Starvation is, as we all know, a daily companion to the underclass that throng this vast city, but, gentlemen, this is not a disease of the body; it is an affliction of the mind. Alice chooses not to eat. Her mind holds a picture of herself that is the opposite of the truth; not simply a negative, but a physical, three-dimensional distortion of reality."

He then filled in the case history and more detailed medical observations. Muybridge watched with growing fascination, finding the woman's shrivelled starvation hypnotic at the end of the collapsed perspective of the room. He thought about building a camera like this, of photographing an entire flock, or herd, or harem of these withered beauties.

On the stairs outside, he waited for the last of the hungry students to leave the good doctor alone. Two would not let go and attached themselves to Gull's every movement. He could wait no longer and stepped into the narrow space of focus that had previously displayed Alice. He hoped to be recognised, but Gull looked at him in a blank, friendly way. The student stopped talking and gave in to the strangeness of his agitated intrusion.

"Dr. Gull, eh, I mean Sir William, if I might have a moment?"

Gull, startled at his voice, looked closer. "Mister Mireburn?" he questioned.

"Yes! Muybridge!" the other answered energetically.

The doctor excused himself from the students and led him to an impressive suite of rooms, one much larger than the turret chamber Gull had previously occupied.

"How are you, sir?" Gull asked, indicating a seat.

"Oh, I'm well, thank you. I have done very well."

"And your health?"

"Since last I saw you, I am greatly improved. I have had a few bouts of nerves, but I grow stronger each day. Your advice has held me in great stead."

"Good, good," Gull answered, not really knowing why this man, who now looked like a wild prophet, was here.

Muybridge saw this and responded.

"I have brought you some of my pictures by way of thanks." He lifted the small portfolio by the side of his chair, untied the strings, and opened it out onto the massive desk.

"This is really very kind of you," Gull said, seeming genuinely taken aback.

Muybridge had brought a collection of ten prints, five of which were of the wild places Gull had advised him to seek out all those years ago. He laid them out on the grand mahogany desk and stood back, allowing the doctor a clearer view.

Gull ignored the magnificent views of Yosemite Valley, the panoramas of San Francisco, the ice mountains of Alaska. He even ignored the running horse, Muybridge's most famous work. Instead, he homed in on the four other, more diverse images, pushing the landscape masterworks aside to see them.

"What are these?" he murmured with obvious excitement. On the table lay a picture of an ancient sacrificial stone from his visit to Guatemala, a print of the Ghost Dance, and another, from the same time, of two medicine men of the Shoshone. The final image was his composite of *Phases of the Eclipse of the Sun*. Gull pored and clucked over them, wanting to know their exact history and meaning. It became obvious by his questions that he had not the faintest interest in Muybridge's artistic talent or technical skill; he was interested only in the subject of the photographs. He drew the four images closer to him.

"May I keep these?" he asked.

"They are all for you," answered the dispirited artist.

"Remarkable!" he said to himself. The doctor seemed to have forgotten Muybridge completely. "Look at the intensity of those faces; such men could do anything!" he said, as if speaking to the photographs themselves. "Truly remarkable!"

"I wondered if my photographs might help your patients?" Muybridge said.

"What? Sorry, what did you say?"

"I only wondered, Sir William, if my photographs might be of help to your patients?"

"How?" Gull asked cautiously.

"If patients, like the one we saw today, had an actual image of themselves, then could they, perhaps, compare it to their misconceptions and find a treatment in the photograph's truth?"

Gull thought for a moment. "It would not work. I tried giving them all mirrors; they don't use them the way we do. A picture would be the same," he said dismissively.

Muybridge was deflated by such an obvious comparison; surely his offer was worthy of a little more consideration?

"Have you heard what Charcot is doing in Paris?" Gull asked.

The name was familiar. He ran it through his memory, but Gull was oblivious to his ponderings and proceeded to tell him anyway.

"He is a clinical doctor, like me, good old solid anatomy, body mechanics. But, like me, he is moving into the machinery of the soul, the invisible stuff that doesn't bleed and won't be sewn, perhaps the true centre of malady and health. This year, he will open a new department to investigate that which cannot be seen: the hidden pulses of the body. I envy him that. We both have our private wards, but this is something altogether different. If I were twenty years younger, I, too, would throw away the bone saws and totally engage in the surgery of the mind."

Muybridge was a little confused and said nothing.

"Anyway, the reason I tell you of this is that he is using photography, not just to make pictures of a patient, but as a therapy in itself. I have no idea how it works, but one of our junior doctors was there last year and he saw what they were doing. You should go and see it."

It was all beginning to sound like the kind of spurious fiction Muybridge so thoroughly distrusted, and it being a French innovation only made it worse; his distrust of French claims was long-standing and inherent—he often found them to be greatly exaggerated, and the natural boundary between fact and fiction to be a lot less substantial in France. Even Étienne-Jules Marey, with whom he had exchanged many ideas, had a fanciful turn of mind that was more interested in the aesthetics of his machines than in the result they were supposed to produce.

He suddenly realised where he had heard Charcot's name before. "Yes, Salpêtrière!" he exclaimed with relief, happy to be able to prove his knowledge. "The Parisian teaching hospital." His host looked at him oddly.

"Yes, precisely. You should go," said Gull, closing the subject.

Muybridge realised he was not going to talk his way into Gull's private wards. He understood for the first time that Gull had no real interest in him. It had been the malady that had sparked his interest, not the man who bore it. The surgeon wanted a new set of tools to reach in and adjust, to be able to remake the man. The individual was incidental and expendable to his quest. He glanced at his host as the understanding dawned, but the man in question was looking again at the Ghost Dance photograph.

"Remarkable; the strength of willpower."

"Like that poor woman," Muybridge said.

"Yes! Exactly!" said Gull, the energy of a small, wiry man jumping up and down inside his solid, unmoving frame. "The determination of that pathetic creature to believe in her view, even until death itself. And I have others who show even more voracity." He pointed at the shaman. "If that willpower was focused like these, and sharpened with knowledge, well . . . then we would have an instrument to investigate and repair the soul of any man or woman. I could put my hands into their heads and hearts and change everything."

Muybridge nodded silently.

Outside, the London particular—that noxious, greenish-blackish smog thickened with soot and sulphur dioxide—had arrived, a dense and all-consuming fog that swallowed light and dimension, misplacing the blurred sounds of the city. As he stood in the dim, damp chill, Muybridge realised that Gull had said nothing about the print of the eclipse, although he had touched it repeatedly throughout their conversation.

He tried to find a cab in the confusion of muffled shadows and sounds but failed and realised that he was lost. His only way home was to ask each person he bumped into which way he should go. Stepping-stones again; stepping-stones in a fog. His life was full of them.

CHAPTER ELEVEN

*I*t was the perfect place for Tsungali's planned ambush. The road by the water was narrowest here, and it would force the traveller to slow and watch his footfall.

He did not know how long he would have to wait—there was always the possibility of being taken off guard or of his quarry slipping through while he slept. But white men always told you where they were. They sent out a bow wave, so that the earth and its animals would murmur, well in advance of their arrival. Their wake was immense. Crushed and contaminated, the land was forced to repair itself, even after the gentlest of their journeys.

Farther back down the path, Tsungali had laid traps that would release vapours and spoors into the air when they were trampled. Traps that would tilt the colour of birdsong, or cause insects to stop and listen for too long, giving tiny vibrations of warning to the trained ear. He sat across the river, the tang sight of the rifle raised for a long-distance shot. This would be an easy kill, so he had given himself obstacles to sharpen his craft. The last two men he had killed had been close range and far too quick. He wanted to use the Lee-Enfield again and prove his marksmanship.

He had eaten an early supper of fresh river fish and was standing in the bamboo grove when the whistle passed high over his head; it changed into a light, thin rhythm of exquisite tapping. Poised and dry, it slid, beautifully, down through the leaves towards him, in a constant shift of emphasis and pause. The sight of it stopped him dead: a long, dark arrow with translucent fletching gently dropped before him in the rustling leaves.

He was not alone in the evening. He must have a rival for the blood of the plodding white man, and any being who could place such a flight should not be underestimated. Picking the arrow up, he was stunned by its lack of weight. He examined its point and found a tiny seed head of beaks, each individually joined and locked by a stitch of thread, constructing a hexagonal husk that would let air warble through its delineated contours. He knew its high trajectory meant the arrow had come from afar, but he still looked around hastily and felt a shudder course through him.

The next day, late in the morning, the birds in the low trees a mile away stopped singing for a minute or two. He found his practised place and rested Uculipsa in the slit he'd found at the top of a flat rock. He was ready. He waited for inevitability to cross his sights.

His mind began to drift.

By the time the young Tsungali had returned from his trip abroad, the rumours about Williams had sped well beyond the borders of the True People and reached the coast. Williams had become Oneofthewilliams, and a cult had grown. Tsungali had been horrified to learn, upon entering the village, that the chosen one was the same officer who had given him Uculipsa. The Englishman had shown him kindness and taught him to shoot well, had separated himself from the other whites and shown alliance to the True People almost from the moment he had arrived; he had risked the displeasure of his superiors and made himself an outcast by saving the great prize, the blessed young shaman, Irrinipeste, from the church and from the abominations that the priest of crossed sticks had subjected her to. But still Tsungali had wondered if this man could be trusted, if he would arise against his own kind when it mattered most and help banish these lying intruders forever.

His deliberations had been short-lived. Minutes into his return, his homecoming was interrupted by the news that his brother and two of their friends were being held by one of the sea tribes, who demanded the return of the long-awaited One-ofthewilliams to the coast, where his own people yearned for their messiah.

Tsungali had gone immediately to explain the situation to Williams. He told him of the kidnap and the meeting with the Sea People and asked him to come with the rescue party, for his help in the parley; what he did not mention was that the Englishman was the prize, the desired barter that would ensure the safe release of his fellow tribesmen.

They met on the sands—jungle on one side, sea on the other; six of the Sea People holding the three hostages. Tsungali had brought five men to represent his tribe: three warriors, a policeman, and, of course, Williams, who stood slightly to the side, motionless and cradling a small rucksack in his arms. He had taken off his boots and they hung around his neck by their laces, leaving his white feet bare in the wet, sucking sand. The hostages were tied together and knelt before their captors, all of whom were armed with spears and blades. The Enfield was not present. Instead, Tsungali carried a ceremonial spear with the colours of authority tied on: He was speaking for his people.

The leader of the Sea People barked out his terms, eloquently concluding by tapping the staff of his spear on the back of Tsungali's brother's head; the crouching man's eyes darted back and forth between his bonds, his brother, and the foreigner.

They were finalising the niceties of the exchange when Williams raised his hand and took a step forward. From inside his rucksack, he withdrew a small bundle and threw it between the two parties. He spoke ten words in the language of the True People before pulling the monstrous pistol from his bag, stepping forwards and shooting Tsungali's brother and the Sea People's leader at point-blank range. The wounds plumed in the dazzling fresh light, and the force threw the bodies back into the sand. Nobody moved. Williams picked up the barbed spear of the dead leader and walked over to Tsungali, taking the bound spear from his tight grip. He uttered two more words, then turned and paced back towards the camp, the sound of his feet matching the heartbeat of the stationary warriors.

The prisoners were untied from the dead man, who had thrashed against them and tightened their bonds as his blood darkened the beach. Nobody spoke; they just dispersed, going their own way towards jungle and seashore.

The bundle thrown between them had been a shamanistic truce of great potency; no man would argue with it. The fact that it was his proved the truth of what he said, as well as his purpose. His words had confirmed that he was indeed Oneofthewilliams. But their betrayal and wrong actions meant that, from then on, he would belong to no one. Sacrifices would have to be made, to appease his anger and hold the tribes in constant balance.

Tsungali had guessed where the bundle had come from, who had made it and given him the words. The whole incident had been overseen by Irrinipeste; she had warned Williams and given him the power to triumph.

The tide had begun to turn inwards, water filling the impressions in the sand where he stood. He thought about her opal eyes watching him at that moment, thought of her astonishing eminence. She would be the key to the uprising, a key Williams had just turned.

Tsungali did not have anger or sadness. The bundle had

smoothed it away; rightness had been performed. He picked up the pieces of his brother and returned home. Home, where the wrath of his tribe was already boiling over.

In his wake, the sea came in and removed the blood. The brilliant red swirled with the yellow sand beneath the crystal-green water. The bundle was lifted and carried out, far beyond the land, where it dissolved in the millions of pulsing waves. When the sea retreated and the endless sun turned the mud back into glittering powder, there would be no trace of the men or the consequences of their actions.

By the time they returned, the atmosphere in the camp was taut. A commanding officer was scarlet as he spat abuse into Williams's face in front of the entire company. They were standing in uniform, a small, tidy, geometric rank, before the fidgeting avalanche of True People, a momentum seething with rage and betrayal. They had been thinking and sleeping on all the wrongs Tsungali had told them, the duplicity and the evil of all these whites. All except one.

The commanding officer tightened their insistence with each pompous word. Just before the snapping point, a quiet movement slid from the centre of the clutching warriors, slipping softly between the stiff uniforms as they secretly revelled in Williams's humiliation.

Irrinipeste drifted next to the accused like a vapour and touched his hand. He looked down at the beloved shaman and into her impossible eyes. The officer raged above them and then saw their indifference. He stumbled down from his small pedestal and snatched at the girl. Grabbing at her throat, he tried to pull her aside, but it was like yanking on a granite column: Nothing moved, and his fingers screamed. He snatched at her but fell to the floor, still barking his orders, with only her torn amulet and part of her dress in his hands. His raging never ceased. He barked orders from the dirt; he barked orders as he scrambled to his feet. He was still barking orders when the .303 round from the Enfield burnt through his rib cage and skewered his loud, bulging heart. Chaos ensued.

Irrinipeste guided Oneofthewilliams past the clashing wave of hacking men and out; out of the beginnings of the Possession Wars and into the Vorrh to heal the wounds of yesterday, today, and tomorrow.

Now, years later, his prey was edging along the river as predicted. Tsungali heard him coming half an hour before he appeared and watched through his binoculars as he entered the light: just another ignorant white man carrying too much equipment on his back. Then Tsungali spotted the bow. The sight jolted him, and his instincts kicked hard against his better judgment. He set the glasses down and adjusted the rifle; his entire attention was drawn along the barrel, anticipating the sights: an elemental flaw in marksmanship, and a lethal practice for a sniper. His mind stopped; there was only the rifle.

The white man pressed himself against the rock, inadvertently presenting his greatest area of target as he nimbly sidestepped the path. Tsungali squeezed the trigger. The Enfield barked deeply into the gorge and the man fell from the path. Tsungali worked the bolt and recocked the gun, then searched the bank with his glasses to locate the body. It was not there. He stood to see if it had fallen behind a rock or somehow slipped into the water, but there was no sign of the dead man or his equipment. He had vanished.

He gathered his things together quickly and started wading across the river, the rifle held across his chest. At the halfway point, his eye flickered between the distant bank and the fast water speeding over the smooth, irregular pebbles. As he stopped to pull his twisted boot free from a stone, the first arrow struck. He saw nothing until the flaring blue pain. The arrow went through his hand, piercing the stock of the Enfield and coming out the other side, its broken head digging into his ribs. He bit hard and flailed in the water, trying in vain to locate his adversary. The second arrow hit him in the teeth, smashing through his mouth and breaking his clenched jaw. It fractured the hinge and severed the strings of muscle that held it in place, exiting close to his pulsing jugular vein, where the shaft pointed behind, like a bent quill. His ruined mouth was full of blood and blue feathers. The fletchings pushed against his cut tongue and throat, choking him as globs of blood splashed into the pure waters. The third arrow would have killed him, but he spun wildly and slipped, falling into the tide, which mercifully carried him away from the attack. He kept his head above the wash, swallowing air, blood, and river in equal measures.

An hour later, he bumped ashore and crawled onto a gravel bank. Even in his pain and failure, he knew he had travelled a lot faster than the white man and that the path he'd been on was now many miles away; he had time to hide and regain himself before the battle continued. The shafts of the arrows had broken off, and the river had washed the feathers out of his wrecked mouth. His hand was loose from its pinning, but he had managed to keep hold of the Enfield and his pack, which had swung round his body and partially emptied itself in the raging river. Flinching, he put his hand tentatively to his hanging jaw and crawled through the gravel into the reeds, dragging the split Uculipsa behind him.

He lay down in the grasses, breathing deeply and trying not to suck the cold air past his loose nerve endings. He was drying and coagulating, staring at the growing evening sky. The pain welled and throbbed; every time he swallowed he felt sick, imagining that he had ingested another part of himself. He had no teeth in the front of his face and no voice in the back of it. Using ripped lengths of fabric, he tied his jaw hard against his head, for fear of it falling away completely.

He was furious at having missed such an easy shot, for not killing him point-blank, like the others. How had he so underestimated the powers of this strangest white man? What kind of force was he up against? The man's arrows had not only found him with ease, but passed through all his levels of protective charm without a single deflection; no white man could do this. He knew he had to escape the Bowman's intent. With great difficulty, he swallowed a root that was in his pack and felt some of the pain diminish. He watched the sky turn to a rich darkness and, as he passed out into its embrace, his heart sank with the acceptance that he was no longer the hunter. Their roles had been reversed: Now he was the quarry.

➤→

I feel its energy course hungrily through my body. My gentle years are over. A long-forgotten hunger has been rekindled by my unexpected adventure. The murderer across the water has awoken a coiled reaction—I can taste his blood, even at this distance. Why anyone would find cause to shoot at me remains a mystery. My dealings with other humans are decades past, and all before that is erased. Only my wife keeps the memories in her flesh and moisture, both of which live in my bow. We will find the assassin and dig the answers out of him; my foes in this unfamiliar and treacherous world will not remain hidden.

I will rest and make an evening camp. In the coming morning, I will make new arrows and use them to sign my passage and sweep all enemies aside. The man in the water will be in no hurry to meet me again, and the next time he does, the first shot will be mine.

CHAPTER TWELVE

*M*utter liked things in their places, with clear delineations between them, but everything in the house was changing. All of the rituals, hierarchies, and conventions were sliding over one another to find new settling places; Ishmael moved freely between the third floor and the attic, and the camera obscura had become a focal point for them all, even Ghertrude. Mutter's collection of the crates was the only thing that continued, unchanged, twice a week.

Through Ishmael's constant use, the spaces were becoming his own, his domain. Each place had its own sound, and Ghertrude and Mutter were able to track his movements from any part of the house. He could often be heard pacing and moving about in his rooms, rearranging furniture and adjusting the layout. In the attic, the strings would sing his presence, often for hours at a time. It was no longer an access space; he was making it important in its own right.

The tower of the obscura was marked by silence, quieter than sleep itself when he was there. His commitment held the house still, lifting it by its scruff, so that it could be felt in its roots. But that was the one place he did not go: where she most feared he would be drawn, where he might betray her more easily. She left nothing to chance and had Mutter double-check the padlocks and barriers to the cellars almost daily. She told him clearly that it was forbidden to all, and that was the only rule of the house. He did not answer but nodded in intelligent approval. Even so, she instructed Mutter to keep an eye on him and on the cellar door.

Being in the house now made Mutter uncomfortable. He did not know when or where the cyclops might turn up, and he was still a little startled by his appearance. Furthermore, Ishmael was becoming more familiar: He sought interaction, asking him questions about his employment, his family, the outside world. Mutter had never been a great conversationalist, and with this weird creature he found it easier to scurry away or hide in the yard, with the horses. He enjoyed their dumbness; the rich smell of their bodies and the perfume of the hay soothed him, and he would often take his lunch out to where they grazed. He smoked his bitter cigars in their mute company and watched the seasons turn, unhurried, and mostly safe. Sometimes, he felt keenly that he was being watched from above. He imagined his likeness, smeared on the circular table of that ungodly machine, the gloating eye tasting it like some terrible fish. The idea chilled him and made him move farther back into the stable, reassured by its shared warmth and temporary concealment.

Returning to the house late one day, he found the cyclops standing near the stairs of the ground floor, looking in the direction of the prohibited door. It worried him; he knew that he should say something or take some action, but it was a position he was neither designed nor equipped for, and he could find no frame of reference with which to begin the necessary conversation. He stood, jaw open, vaguely moving his limp arms in unison, like a broken gate in the wind, or a disused pump, trying to raise a spoonful of water from some immeasurable distance.

"Herr Mutter, where are the old crates?" Ishmael asked,

stepping into the doubt and reversing it, making the question his own. "I wanted to check something before you return them tomorrow."

"They are in the tack room, next to the stables," the yeoman replied thinly.

"Show me," demanded the cyclops as he walked towards the door. Mutter opened the door for the young master and pointed, expecting his honest direction to be noted and the matter closed.

Instead, Ishmael strode out of the door and across the yard, leaving Mutter without words or action. The cyclops slid back the bolt on the tack room door and walked briskly inside. Mutter blinked hard, hoping that the rapid movement would return all things to their proper place, that this impossible thing would rewind and he would be exonerated of the stupid mistake he had just made. But alas, that was not the case. He dashed across the cobbles and erupted himself at the side of the escapee, who was casually examining the side of a long, thin crate. Showing no sign of agitation, the cyclops asked, "At what time will you take these away tomorrow?"

"At eleven o'clock, sir," answered Mutter automatically.

The word "sir" had entered Mutter's mouth out of habit and because there was no alternative. It was the first time Ishmael had been given status, and it marked a further shift in their dynamics—he knew now that the old man could be easily bent.

"And where will you take them?"

"To the warehouse."

"Good. I would like to go with you."

Mutter's heart ceased its beating and leapfrogged into his mouth. The cyclops walked past him into the yard and stopped and looked up to the rooftops, then beyond them to the fleeting clouds.

"But, sir," Mutter stammered, "it's impossible, the mistress . . ."

". . . will never know," finished Ishmael. "It's not the mistress who pays your wages or cares for your family, is it? It's not the mistress who cares for me, not really. The person or persons who look after this house are responsible for our well-being, Mutter. It's my family that employs yours. And now I wish to make a brief visit to them, to see, for a moment, the one other place that I know to be connected to me."

"But, sir! I was told to take nobody there. Not even my sons may visit before they are ready to be trained in my job."

"Sigmund," said the cyclops in curved, enduring tones. "Don't you see that everything is changed now? I am no longer a child. I have the house. Soon enough, it will be me who employs you. Ghertrude need never know about our little trip."

Mutter was silent and horribly perplexed. He looked from his scuffed boots into the pleading eye, then back again.

"Unless you'd prefer that I go by myself?"

Mutter followed his gaze towards the gate and saw that it was held on a draw bolt, not double-locked as he had been instructed. He knew that the cyclops was agile and could reach the gate long before him; the only way to stop him would be to cuff him or tackle him to the ground. He assumed that such an act would not be looked upon favourably by his unseen masters. He was beginning to panic, when Ishmael smiled and inflicted the coup de grâce.

"I have no desire to get you into trouble, Sigmund. And I'm sure neither of us want Ghertrude to know about this afternoon's little mistake; she is scared of me running away, and it makes her overreact. So I shall say nothing tonight when she visits, and in the morning we will make a brief, discreet visit to the warehouse, yes? What do you think? Can we make our little adventure together and return without anybody knowing?"

Mutter gave in; there was no alternative. The delighted cyclops clapped his hands together in satisfaction.

"Excellent! Come, then; let us go over my plan," he said, propelling the deflated old man towards the stables and telling him to pick up his tools on the way.

The next day, they waited in different parts of the old property for Ghertrude to leave. Mutter stayed in the stables, with the crates loaded onto the carriage, while she and Ishmael ate breakfast together. When it was over, she left by the front door, calling to announce that she would be back by seven that evening. Ishmael waited impatiently for her nippy steps to vanish from the lane outside, then sprang to his feet and unlocked the front door. He hurried over to the stables, slipped quietly inside, and stepped onto the waiting carriage.

The long, thin crate that had been "Lesson 318: Spears & Bows (Old Kingdoms)" was securely strapped into the open rig. Its contents had been removed and now lay hidden behind a dusty old curtain in the far corner of the stables; their replacement crouched expectantly in his hiding place. A hole had been drilled in the side of the box, about a foot from the closed end, and Mutter saw the glimmer of an eye as he fastened the gates behind them. He hadn't said a word that morning; his instinct had been to obey in a stoic, inert manner, while desperately wishing for it to be over and done with as soon as possible.

The crazed and rattled fragments of the outside that Ishmael saw amazed and excited him. The confusion of scale and the smells of the factories unleashed sensory responses that he did not know existed. The colours were much brighter than the tower projections, and he felt the enormity of everything as the town burst with unbridled life. He had been right about their eyes; Ghertrude had told him the truth, and soon he would find out if Luluwa had too.

By the time they reached the warehouse, he was brimming

with questions and choking with answers. Mutter unfastened the gates and led the horse through into the courtyard, tying the steaming beast to the front of the loading-bay banisters and returning to the entrance to seal them within. He pulled a huge bunch of keys from under the driving seat of the carriage before knocking brusquely on the cyclops's crate. Ishmael emerged, his one eye squinting as it adjusted to the light.

They entered the warehouse. Mutter went about his usual business, seeking notes and collecting the details of the next batch of crates. He turned to explain the importance of this function to the cyclops, but he was not there. The old man finished his tasks and waited for Ishmael to return to help him lift the boxes, but the minutes passed and he became impatient and angry and decided to load the carriage himself. The two new crates were different from the rest, their labels no longer stencilled red, but now painted a regal blue.

As he loaded the wagon with his cargo, Mutter was desperately trying to construct a feasible story about how he had found himself in this position. His lies were monstrous and each more ridiculous than the last; even he could see they were totally unbelievable. By the time the escapee returned, he had decided that the truth was the only option.

"Shall we go?" said Ishmael.

The slim crate had remained on the carriage, and the cyclops squeezed back in, pulling the lid tight after him. His coffin journey home, though still eventful, was overshadowed by the stranger things in the warehouse; his mind raced with them. When the bumpy ride was at an end and they were enclosed in the stables once more, he slowly pushed his way out of his confinement with theatrical vigour.

"Thank you, Herr Mutter," he said. "Our secret will stay intact. No one will ever know of our time together today."

The servant opened the door to let him in. The sense of relief was wonderful, and he locked him in place at once, returning home before Mistress Tulp arrived; he had no intention of dealing with her as well that evening, or of letting her look into his far-too-honest eyes.

The next day, with a great lightness in his heart, he returned. He planned to tend to the horses, to spend the day in their magnificent, uncomplicated company and let the intricacies in the house take care of themselves.

He was beginning to feel at home again, the busy muck fork in his hands, when the voice of the warehouse boomed suddenly and gravely in his ear:

"Herr Mutter, you have disappointed us and grievously betrayed our confidence. For this, you will be punished. If this should happen again, the punishments will be amplified, and our blessings on you and your family will cease and turn against all. The hands of your first son, Thaddeus, have this day been removed. They have been crossed over and sewn on backwards, right to left and left to right. His palms will always face outwards. He will receive the best medical care until he is healed. His hands will be useless for work, but perfect for begging. You may save him from such a future, but not from the operation. That is the price you owe to us. Be calm, Herr Mutter, and remember our care and protection of your family over all these years. Accept your wrongdoing, repent, and return to our favour."

When Mutter ventured home that night, he dreaded the reality that the voice had promised but hoped that it might have been a delusion, a befuddlement. He entered his home with permafrost rotting his heart. The rolling wave of warmth and the hug of coiled noise did nothing to thaw him. His wife took his heavy topcoat and seated him at the solid table as his daughter, Meta, brought him a mug of thick, black beer. He watched them flurry back and forth with steaming pots and clanking plates. The sumptuous energy of home, rich and seamless, stirred the glow of continuity out of the shards of necessity. The food was served, and everybody ate enthusiastically. But Thaddeus's chair was empty, and Mutter stared dumbly at his meaningless dish, its smell arousing nothing within him.

"Where is Thaddeus?" he choked.

"Oh! Wonderful!" his wife chirped. "A letter came with the possibility of employment, so he went to the eastern quarter; he should be home soon." The table fell away, and sharp, inward tears fell to make a razor chain of slow constrictions inside his throat; it tightened with every joyous mouthful his family ate. No one noticed the change, not even his lifetime wife, and he swamped his horror and guilt in thick, heavy beer that stung with each strangled gulp.

Thaddeus did not return that evening. Nor was he seen the next day, or the one after that. Mutter went to the warehouse and knelt in his son's absence; he gave his word to the building that he was, forever, a loyal and unflinching servant. He returned to his duties, weighed down by despair.

Early the next day, Thaddeus stood outside the family home, a worn exhaustion in his confused but settled eyes. He was immaculately dressed in a silk suit, his hair elegantly styled like that of a prince, his beautiful new shoes shining in the dusty sunlight, his wrists bandaged, his hands open at his parents' door.

The wind groaned and bellowed around the tiny rooms where Mutter's family slept. The yeoman heard it rise and fall, gasping against the corridors and the empty kitchen, where mice, smaller than blurs, darted like needles trying to stitch the gusts. He watched his wife sleeping fitfully, her judders in and out of time with her breathing. He knew that the next day she would tell him that she did not get a wink of sleep that night. He would not remember if he did. He tossed in a thorny bed of guilt and vengeance, anger and defeat. He did not know how he would face his family or the world, or how he would continue in the employment he could never end. His hollow home sighed, and he tried not to think about the coming day or the creature he now loathed.

From Mutter's hunchback dwelling, the wind curved upwards to the gleaming mansion of the Tulps. Ghertrude slept in the enforced lie of her childhood room, facedown on her soggy pillow, her duvet pulled over her head to diminish the tapping that she hoped was only the sound of the trees lashing against the windows.

There was less turbulence in 4 Kühler Brunnen. The doors there were firmly shut, the craftsmanship precise and tight; the wind could be heard only where damage had occurred. It snarled in the locked lower floors and whispered perilously near the stairs above the ancient well. It droned in the attic but remained ethereally quiet in the room with the cyclops's empty bed. In the tower, it watched the occupant focusing on the moonlight, examining the dim glow from the miniature maze of the desolate streets. Ishmael was naked, goose pimples shifting over his pale body, as if offering an index, or a rarefied notation, to the observations of the table. His eye was very close to the surface; like a spoon, it glided among the streets.

The dry storm could have reached the moon that night; such was its magnitude. But a stronger force was demanding its attention, and it billowed northwards, under the influence of a far greater, more dominant presence: It was being swallowed forever into the Vorrh.

>→

Ishmael had only Ghertrude to talk to now. Since their adventure together, Mutter had avoided him entirely; no matter how hard he tried to initiate conversation, the old man refused to be drawn. He barely made eye contact, and when he did it was baleful and suspicious. Ishmael thought it a dramatic and surly way to behave over such a small breaking of the rules. However, he would not be diverted by a servant's bad humour. He had noticed the market square changing over the last two days, its simple frame being decorated between its daily functions. Something was being prepared. He cornered Ghertrude when she arrived to change his bed linen.

Her visits had become less frequent recently, and she seemed remote and uninterested in his questions. She had certainly lost her appetite for mating, having nothing new to show or explain to him. He still possessed an active interest in the subject, but when he suggested that they might try other ways of doing it, she became defensive and limp. Not wishing to disturb his comfortable position within the house, he chose to let his desires go untended.

Besides, his need to be outside again and explore the city in detail was of greater importance. She had told him of the perils, explained that a rarity such as he would be in danger from the mob. She told him the story of a small, ornate bird she had owned as a child. Its plumage was vermilion, with a trim of yellow. Its voice was exquisite, and she often put it in her window so that it might sing to the sun. Local, indigenous birds would flock to the areas nearby to listen to it and admire its splendid colours. One day she sat, with the bird tamely on her finger, talking to the brightness of its attention. She did not notice the window's slight opening, and as the curtain swayed, the bird smelt the air and flew to freedom. In horror, she ran to the window and watched it flutter and swoop in poor, close circles. She called to it and it turned in her direction; she saw the excitement in its eyes, just before it was torn to pieces by the same grey flock that had watched it before.

That would be his fate, she had explained. His exotic originality would be seen as a threat; they would call him a monster. But he knew he was superior to the double eyes, and he had proved it. She did not know this, and the time to tell her had not yet dawned.

"Ghertrude?" he said, as she worked with her back to him, "why are the streets below being decorated?"

"Oh!" she exclaimed happily. "That's for the carnival!"

"And what is 'carnival' in this place?" he asked.

"Well, every year, the people have a party to thank the forest for its gifts. It lasts for three days and nights, everybody stops work, and the streets are alive with music, food, and dancing. Everything is decorated, even the cathedral. The people dress in costumes that they have spent all year making. Lords and ladies mix with peasants and rogues, not knowing each other's rank or status."

"How is that possible, when everybody recognises each other here?"

"Because of the masks!" she whooped, carried away in the joyful momentum.

"Masks?" he queried.

"Yes! Fanciful, mysterious masks of every description, angels and demons, animals and mons—"

"Monsters?" he ventured slowly.

She had become suddenly quiet and unsure of where to look.

"Could it be," he pressed, "that on such an occasion, a 'rarity' might hide its strangeness, that an exotic bird might conceal its beauty, and that a *monster* would be safe among so many others?"

And so it came to pass that the beast went to the ball.

They stood just inside the gate of 4 Kühler Brunnen. They

made a fine pair, plumed and bejewelled, masked and covered, loose and sensuous silks flashing provocatively beneath their cloaks.

"Will it be like the story you read me, the one you liked so much? With the clock and the coloured rooms, the one that gave me nightmules?" he asked.

"Nightmares," she corrected. "Yes, but not so solemn. It will be much ruder. Everybody is drunk and behaves badly."

"How badly?" he asked, apprehensively.

"Behind a mask you can be anybody, do anything. No one is found guilty, no one is innocent; there are more children sired during these three days than the rest of the year. And no one looks too closely for family resemblance, nine months later, when the babes are born."

"And nobody is ever unmasked?"

"Never!" she said, with more certitude than she felt. It was true that one felt a certain freedom under the protection of disguise, and she had committed petty crimes and minor malices before under the mask. But she had never possessed the nerve to engage in open debauchery. Until now.

They peeped through the gap and plucked at the springboard of their nerves, readying to be jettisoned into the whirling throng of dreams that bustled and shoved in the streets outside. The noise was colossal. Hurdy-gurdies and pipers roamed the streets, confusing the vast steam organ that played from the heart of the market square. There were fireworks and pistol shots, trumpets and singing, screaming and laughter.

Suddenly, the gate was open and they were gone. Mutter locked it hard behind them and spat on the wet cobblestones.

➡

Ishmael was intoxicated with the number of people he had touched and seen in the first two hours of his freedom. His entire body was becoming luminous beneath the costume. Was it the same for everybody that thronged the streets, opened their doors, and gave themselves up for molestation? He had lost Ghertrude somewhere after the third house and had no idea where he was, which made him even more excited. He entered a grand house full of music and laughter. Women and men held him and felt beneath his robe, making joyous sounds of pleasure at what they found there. He wanted to explore the rooms more, so he pulled away and slunk close to the lushly carpeted floor.

In a magnificent room lit by flickering torchlight, he felt a different perfume and crawled across the floor towards it—an animal of his own making, his long, white proboscis sniffing, his whiskers quivering, as he nodded from side to side. His rangy, pale legs seemed to both tiptoe and slide on the polished wooden floor. The top part of his body was clothed in a silken green skin, which caught the garish light from the blazing flambeaux on the balcony outside the windows. The lower half of his body was naked, its huge, swollen phallus swaying like an independent entity as he approached his next engagement like a creature possessed.

The last bed was in great disarray, the covers pulled messily around the softly snoring body of its spent occupant. The room was full of whispers and laughter; small, animal noises of hunger and fulfilment rippled the landscape of opulence. Sighs gilded the tangled scent of incense, musk, and intoxication.

He reached the next bed and slid his gloved hands beneath the sheet. They were instantly gripped by the smooth, trembling grasp of the woman who waited there. She pulled the beast inside and drew the covers over them both. Her form was older, large, and voluptuous, and she was dressed like an owl, black feathers accentuating the ivory wideness of her eyes. He slipped a catch on his beak and pulled it backwards, leaving the lower half of his face exposed, so that his mouth was visible and active in their lovemaking. Pulling him close, she kissed him passionately. He jumped back, startled, almost falling from the bed. Neither Luluwa nor Ghertrude had ever done such a thing; it had never been explained to him, and Ghertrude had always looked away when they mated.

"Don't be shy," she said.

He let her suck his mouth again, and it was sweet and arousing. He kissed back, and his manhood surpassed previous dimensions and expectations.

Even in the overpopulated room of revellers, the sounds of the Owl and her new companion rose above all others. Their bedding thrashed wildly, and something else wallowed out from their conjunctures; other couples and trios found their attention hooked and pulled across the pulsing darkness, away from their own compacted intimacies, peering towards an unnameable eminence that was outside and beyond their own little shudders and sighs.

It was almost dawn when he crept from her bed to search the rooms for his black velvet cloak.

When the Owl awoke, she began to cry. She pulled her mask away and started to shout. She stumbled to the window, her hands on her face, and began to scream.

➤→

The Owl was Cyrena Lohr. She was thirty-three years old and had been blind since birth. In the early light of post-carnival, with anxious friends and strangers standing by her side, she shivered, naked and overpowered, at the window, watching the brilliant sunrise, yellow and crisp on her first visual day.

How had he done this? Who was this miracle worker who had entered her bed and given her sight? She had to find him. The moment she could be sure she was not dreaming, she would find him and thank him on her knees.

The remaining revellers in her mansion were dressing quickly. One brought a dressing gown and wrapped Cyrena in its warm folds, while attempting to steer the emotional woman away from the window and back to the bed. But she would not be moved, so they brought her a high-backed armchair and seated her safely within it. Most of the crowd that had occupied her many rooms had disappeared; the combination of unmasking and being a witness was too much for their frail identities to bear, and they had fled as the whisper slithered through the house. Miracles are never comfortable; for the hungover, the debauched, and the anonymous, they are intolerable.

Four weeks later, she had settled with her sight. All available tests had been completed, and it was unanimously agreed: She had excellent and enduring vision.

With the help of various companions, she spent two of those weeks visiting the city she knew so intimately, adding colour, shape, and tone to its sound and texture. She stared for hours at the faces of her friends and the few of her family who were left. The new details were catching up and beginning to make sense. Only her dreams remained slow and auditory; the pictures came but would not attach properly, flopping and draping over the hard skeletons of sound and becoming transparent. It would take a year for them to solidify into trust.

She redecorated her splendid house. She gave all her old clothes to the poor and went on a lavish spending spree to dress her body in the rich colour and sumptuous design of her wildest imaginings. She burnt her white sticks, unceremoniously, in the gardener's fire, the sweet scent of leaf smoke disguising their brittle stink of anguish. And then she focused her zeal on finding him—to become his devoted acolyte, or to make him her own.

■—→

Ghertrude had returned to 4 Kühler Brunnen first. She'd expected him to be there already and climbed the stairs to listen at the doors, but he was still out, even though the carnival had ended the night before. Fleetingly, she thought that perhaps he might never return, and the idea bounced far too blissfully for a while. Then she became anxious for him, anxious for them both, and, finally, scared of being found out.

They had stayed together for the first three hours, coupling deeply in the first room of the first house that the party had surged through. He had pinned her to the silk wall, as she looked over his shoulder at another pair, who drank ferociously from each other's cups as they lounged on the sable carpet. Their hands had gripped tightly in the excitement of wrongdoing, before sliding apart in the grounds of one of the great houses, where the throng of dancing fantasies surged and bumped, entangling and repartnering at will. She had been whisked away by a small, bubbling party of young people dressed in shimmering foliage. The Green Man theme was rife that year. She spent the first night with a willow, whose languid courtliness extended into all of his surprising attributes. Her time with Ishmael had paid off; the last of her inhibitions had fled. She relished the contrast she had discovered; the willow and the cyclops had little in common, and she marked and compared the difference, trying to decide where her true taste lay. She balanced passion against technique, hunger against restraint, and dominance against submission. By the morning, she knew she needed even more comparison. The carnival would accommodate her experimentation. She would rise to the challenge of expanding her knowledge of the hidden intimacies of manipulation and the breadth of her own sensual appetite.

She thought that she had seen him the next evening at a tableau vivant in the hall of the De Selbys'. He, or someone dressed like him, stood as motionless as the naked figures that formed

the classic scene of Mars disarmed by Venus and the Three
Graces. The room was packed and concentrated. New arrivals
were hushed as they spluttered into the hall, and she saw him
whisper to the woman standing next to him, saw her squeeze
his arm and quietly laugh, her hand covering the serrated teeth
of her beak. Ghertrude assumed the woman to be one of the
countless numbers of whores and courtesans who gate-crashed
the homes of the wealthy. She had an urge to confront them and
reveal the truth behind the mask but decided that she preferred
the lasting prospect of her secret to a quick demonstration of
her power. Besides, some of the company there may well have
relished his deformity; many of those women may have found
it perverse enough to arouse their jaded and cankered passions.

▶→

Ishmael had arrived back at 4 Kühler Brunnen in the midaft-
ernoon. He had been lost in the empty streets, exposed in his
costume. He was not the only one to be walking dazed, or sleeping in the parks or back alleys: Many denizens of the revels still
staggered in their grotesque outfits, now stained and wet from
nights of rain or morning dew. But, unlike him, they were all
unmasked, to share in their embarrassment and have it forgiven.
Anyone who wore his disguise past the magic hour of unveiling
was prey for abuse, or even attack. The same crowd who crossed
so many boundaries, who permitted so many exchanges of lies,
fluids, and dreams, instantly returned to the stiff rigour of the
other three hundred and sixty-two days of the year. Everything
of those three nights was forgotten forever; it was mutually
agreed by all, and strictly enforced. Masked strangers, continuing into the fourth day, were renegades and a threat to the
contract. Worse, they blatantly challenged the anonymity of
the group with their audacious arrogance and became a target
for all, from lords to dogs. He would be unveiled and disclosed

by any who crossed his path; he would be beaten and driven through the humiliated streets.

Ishmael had not been aware of the rules as he'd left the Owl's bed earlier that day. As he walked across one of the circular arteries of streets, his efforts had gone into trying to retain his bearings against the combined effects of alcohol and lack of sleep, not to mention the stalwart attentions he had paid his companions. Bunting and strings of paper flowers were hanging wet and wild in the air, the wind giving them a disturbing sense of animation; they flapped against what should have been normal gravity with an insolent abandonment. Just as he walked past them, he heard voices calling out to him:

"You're late, friend; there's nothing to hide now; the hour has sounded!"

He ignored the two men and the woman, who had turned into the road from a narrow alley, just ahead of him.

"Did you hear me?" barked the taller man, stepping away from the other two, who seemed to be propping each other up, interlocking against inevitability. "I said take it off, show yourself!"

He stood in Ishmael's way, but the cyclops was quick and deftly stepped around the big man, who was dressed as a penguin. His movement incensed the man, who shouted a warning to his friends. Ishmael was caught between them when the first man turned, growling. "What gives you the right?" he spat. "Better than us, eh?"

Ishmael leapt, but the second man stuck a foot out into his stride and he tripped badly, falling into the leaves and hard cobblestones and banging his knee and the side of his head with great force. Some of the paste jewellery he was wearing broke in the fall and lay strewn across the gutter. The big man was laughing as he dragged him up onto his good knee and tore away his mask; a string of fake emeralds, with which he had been garlanded, snapped and spluttered down, skidding into hiding in the cracks of the murky road.

"That's better." He leered. "Now you're one of us." Then his eyes focused on what he was so firmly gripping. He let go instantly, his fingers splaying out, as if he had been scolded or electrocuted. Ishmael remembered a sound the Kin had some-times made, and he screamed it out across his rolling tongue. Both men ran, leaving the woman to slide down the wall. She had not seen his face when she hit the pavement. On impact, her yelp turned into giggles.

"Now you havta carry me!" she squealed.

He bent down close to her face and grinned with the exag-gerated gusto of a demon prince. She looked up at point-blank range and screamed. He punched her over into the gutter and kicked her in the head until his shoe broke and she had stopped crying out. She lay, quietly sobbing, as he limped away, calcu-lating a safer route home. He picked up his crushed muzzle and skullcap from where the coward had dropped it, and refitted it onto his face. Most of its whiskers had fallen out, and its dam-aged length now gave him a new comic appearance, not unlike toys that become misshapen by too much love; squeezed and hugged into character, remodelled by the damp affections of their owners until they are abandoned.

He had found his way eventually and hobbled back, bruised, wet, and tired, with a rising feeling of nausea. The day was dis-tilling his triumphs of the nights and converting his prowess and conquests into a hollow gruel of cold disgust. He desperately wanted a hot bath and a long, dreamless sleep, so that he might unwind himself from all those sticky, desperate bodies that had embalmed his light with the thickness of their embraces. He wanted to remove every last atom of the tastes and scents that he had so recently cherished; to comb out all their rotted sighs and smiles and never touch a human being again.

It was three days before he would speak, locking himself away in his rooms and refusing to acknowledge Ghertrude's pleas. On the fourth day, when she let herself into the house, she heard the music. She followed its source, climbing the stairs as she listened, spellbound by its eerie resonance. By the time she reached the attic, its volume and complexity had increased. The Goedhart device had been tuned and set in motion. The lead balls with their attached quills had been tied to the ends of the cords that hung down vertically from the ceiling. They swung in long, pendulum arcs, each of the feathers strumming one of the horizontal piano wires with every passing, sending the shivering strands of metal into melodic voice. Thirty or so such strings played in the dusk, each of a different length and pitch. Plucked harmonies echoed back and forth; the light from the open window shimmered on the pendulums' movements. Everything sang.

Ishmael sat in the far corner, his back against the wall, hands folded in his lap. Ghertrude found her place and also sat; she knew better than to attempt to open a conversation now. Over the next hour, the pendulums lost their momentum, the pulses changing and the volume dropping, each feather only lightly scraping against the strings, eventually coming to a rest against them. Towards the end, their hearing strained into the attic to fetch each little tremor of the heart-stopping sensitivity. When the concert was over, they sat in silence for a long, intuited amount of time.

"It's getting cold," he said at last.

"Yes," she answered, "hot days and cold nights."

"I am going to leave, Ghertrude," he said, finally. "For good."

She got colder and hugged herself. Her eyes flickered to the floor; she knew it was useless to argue.

"Where will you go?" she murmured in half of her voice.

"To the wilderness," he replied. "Away from all people. To the Vorrh."

➤

Cyrena Lohr combed the city and caught three names, which now wriggled in her teeth. Two had been regular partygoers, inconsequential gentry of deplorable reputation, the kind of creatures whose very existence is antagonistic to miracle. The third had no name. He was said to be the companion of a young woman whose family Cyrena knew. She made more enquiries, buying information and paying street eyes to unwrap small morsels of sight or whisper.

She found out that the man she so desperately sought had arrived at the carnival with the affluent heiress Ghertrude Tulp and that, whatever their relationship was, it allowed them to slip separately into many different beds over those three spectacular days, which had been such travesties of life. She discovered that, some time after he left her bedchamber, he had been involved in a street altercation, in which an aging doxy had received permanent damage to her saturated brain. She knew that Ghertrude and the man lived at 4 Kühler Brunnen and that he had never been outside in public. She could not be sure but suspected that the Tulp girl held some power over him; that she imprisoned him there, her prize, her possession, which she bitterly hoarded.

She stood before the double gate, magnificent in her knowledge and the certain triumph of her discovery. Taking a quick, deep breath through her feline nostrils, she stepped forward and hammered on the shaking wood.

In her heart, she felt sure that he would open the door to her love; that she would see him, beautiful and beaming, moved by her persistence in finding him. As the scene played in her mind, she saw Ghertrude unlock the great secret and give in to her overpowering enquiry and rightful passion. What she did not expect was the hump and shuffle of Mutter, whose sour response did not even seem to recognise her grandeur.

"Is your master at home?" she asked, unprepared for the sound and need of her stilted formality.

Mutter gawped at her through bleary eyes. He removed the dead cigar stub from his wet mouth and said, "I have none here!"

She jittered slightly. "Your mistress, then?"

"Out!" he said, as he started to shut the gate.

"Where is he?" she demanded, her hand against the gate, equalising Mutter's pressure from the other side.

"Who?" he said, genuinely unaware of whom she meant.

"The man," she said softly, through a nervous smile. "The mysterious young man who lives here."

There was a long pause while Mutter came to, looking into her working, expectant eyes. "Gone," he said. "He's gone. The monster has left." And with that, he shoved the gate shut.

→ *Part Two*

Listen to me. The worlds swarm with an infinity of
creatures. Those we see, those we never see: Naga snakes,
who live in the depths of the earth. Rakshasas, monsters of
the forest's night, who live off human flesh. Gandavas, frail
creatures who glide between us and the sky. Apsovahs,
Danavas, Yakshas and the long glittering chain of gods,
who live like all beings in the shadow of death.

The Mahabharata (1989)

So he drove out the man; and he placed at the east of the
garden of Eden Cherubims, and a flaming sword which
turned every way, to keep the way of the tree of life.

GENESIS 3:24

CHAPTER THIRTEEN

*D*awn, like the first time. The lead-grey clouds are armoured hands with the weak sun moist and limp inside them. The night still sits in the high branches, huge and muscular, rain and dew dripping to the pungent floor. It is the hour when night's memory goes, and with it the gravity that keeps its shawl spun over everything in the forest. The crescent-eyed hunters sense the shift, feeling the glory of darkness being leeched and, ultimately, robbed of its purity. The vulgar gate of day gives no quarter, and its insistent brightness will tell lies about all, forcing the subtlety back into the interiors of trees and the other side of the sky.

The brightness lets the humans out and all those who are like them, as well as those who walk in their stead. The trees breathe and accept it all again. Unnatural greens cuckoo the sensible blacks, where all the great forests live. Men, and other, weaker beasts, grow in confidence and dare to believe that the place is theirs. For a few hours they stride and hack at the rim, shouting to match the sunlight. Twilight will soon shush them away and return the forest to its true condition. The sap still rises in the dark; the sun's pump sucks in the veins, long after the fire is hidden. It is this squeezing, from root to leaf, that finds sympathy in the stenotic memory of men. It is this force field, like magnetism or pressure, that influences all similar structures inside it. The effect on modern men could be explained thus, the persistent rumours of subspecies, living comfortably inside the rings of trees, could find a foothold.

Herodotus and Sir John Mandeville had already written of the unthinkable: "the anthropophagi" and "men whose heads do grow beneath their shoulders." Beings such as they would thrive in this environment, where evolution was robbed of memory, hope, and purpose, and distortion was not ironed out by the Darwinian uniformity of blind greed.

The Frenchman and Seil Kor stood on the platform. It was painted grey. It had always been painted grey. The layers of its skins had boiled every summer, sleeping when the sun set and freezing in the freak, imported winters, waking in fear in the uncertain times that many called spring. They stood in the flapping colours of their robes, in the weird entanglement of midday wind and pulsing steam. The engine was at the back of the train, its heartbeat reverberating through the wooden ribs of the nameless station. The trio of carriages were next, followed by three simple boxcars with SLAVES stencilled on their sides. The words had been painted over, but their message bled through, making them all the more conspicuous. Far beyond them and the boundaries of the station extended the flatbeds, each gently hungry for their cargo of tons of bleeding wood, some still wet from their previous journey. Like a perspective drawing, they pointed towards the lush darkness of the Vorrh.

There were four other passengers on the platform, but it was the solid bunch of men standing in a compacted block next to the boxcars that held their attention. These were the core workers, the ones who had made the trip many times. They no longer had homes or families, but only work and sleep. They stood shoulder to shoulder to resist the cold, facing predators en masse, like the legendary musk ox. Here, it was not the freezing arctic wind or the wolves, but some other external agency that seemed to threaten them. The Frenchman could not take his eyes from their expressions of agitated blankness, and he spoke without moving.

"Who are they?"

Seil Kor was pretending not to see them, and it took him some time to answer, which he did by turning his back on them and speaking through his teeth. "They are the Limboia, some call them 'Die Verlorenen'—the lost."

"But what has happened to them?" the Frenchman asked.

"They have been to the Vorrh too many times. Some part of them has been erased, forgotten. It can happen if you go too often or too deep."

"Are we in danger of this, Seil Kor?" he asked worriedly.

"No, effendi. These men have been hungry for work, or have hidden themselves in the forest, disobeying the scriptures and offending the angels. We make only one return journey and will stay close to the rails."

They turned, instinctively, to look more intently at the Limboia, who instantly stopped moving and turned into their enquiry, staring back. Then, in unison, the workers unbent the index fingers of their left hands, raised their arms, and pointed to their own hearts. The Frenchman was amazed and embarrassed at such a poignant answer to the question that he had been about to speak, a question that had formed between his mouth and his mind, in the vapour of his heart, and evaporated in exact proportion to the intensity of their physical response.

The doors of the slave carriages opened. The huddle of men dropped their hands and eyes to the ground, turning from their unified gaze to move forward into the train. There were no seats in the boxcars, just racks of narrow bunks. The Frenchman watched as they climbed into their shelves and fastened wide leather straps over their prone bodies. His melancholic curiosity was violently bleached by the engine's whistle, its shrill steam sounding departure. They climbed into their carriage and prepared for the long, slow journey away from the reluctant city. The Frenchman fussed in the wooden luggage rack over his head, moving and adjusting his wrapped possessions against the elaborately carved scrolls of ivy and oak leaves that decorated the shelf. He was still rearranging when the train began to move. Seil Kor touched his arm and guided him back to his seat, where he could cool down and stop his breathy mutterings.

After the first hour, the Frenchman had stopped looking out of the windows. The view was of trees, only trees, passing by in incessant uniformity. The track had been cut in a straight line through the density of the forest, forming a tunnel within the living mass. The train was built for power and the movement of great weight, not speed, and they travelled at an unhurried pace, gently rattling along the tracks. The driver sat at the back, reversing them forward into the forest. The long line of clattering flatbeds had no human guard or observer at their head, no one to look out for obstacles or problems, because there would be none. The sharp wedge at the front of the train would push aside any twigs or debris that might have drifted onto the track, but nothing would. The dull, insistent velocity never changed.

"How many times have you been here?" the Frenchman asked Seil Kor.

"This will be my second complete journey. I made the first pilgrimage when I was a child, with my father. I was twelve years old then. It was the week before my confirmation."

"Oh. I thought you had been many times," the Frenchman said, unconcealed disappointment stealing his volume.

"No, a man may only visit the heart of the Vorrh three times in his life. I have told you, more is forbidden."

"But you said that it is forbidden to go beyond a certain point in the forest, not the number of times you visit."

"It is the same thing."

"How is it the same thing? How can trespass into a sacred place be the same as the time a man spends arriving?"

"It is the same because all of the Vorrh is sacred, from its outer rings into its core. The time and the space are an intrusion: all will offend."

"Then how can all this industry survive? Surely it intrudes more than a single man could, and takes far more from this sacred place?" The Frenchman was becoming increasingly perplexed.

"What the city takes is material," Seil Kor answered. "Lone men enter the Vorrh for more than trees; they seek something else. This track and the eastern lung, where the trees are cut at the moment, are a given. They are a balance between the Vorrh and the world of men, between those who dwell here and those who dwell in the city."

"But how can there be a balance, when the forest and its gods don't need the city to exist?"

A vertical furrow appeared on Seil Kor's forehead. He did not like "gods" in the plural; he had explained all this before. "Essenwald is a library to the forest, an appendage. It was attracted here when the Vorrh was already ancient. The physical closeness of so many people gives God a direct index to the current ways of mankind; his angels can learn there. It is an open shelf."

The Frenchman frowned back at Seil Kor. There was another question, and he let his gaze drift to the window to formulate it, but the shifting trees shredded it, like the movement of the Limboia.

He sat back in his seat and imagined a silent giant, walking in a clearing, one hand stroking his long, white beard in deep thought. He saw angels in flowing robes, walking the noonday streets of the city; standing in a public garden, staring up at his hotel, where a woman stood on the balcony. He jarred out of the stupidity of the picture, amazed at its naïveté.

He looked back to Seil Kor for a whiff of reassurance, but he, too, had relaxed back into the journey; he had lost his frown and was watching the movement outside. His eyes flickered with the trees and a mesmeric calm filled his body and radiated in his face. The Frenchman felt his power and his resolve, saw how it illuminated his presence and made him shine in an untouchable perfection. He could watch this man for hours. Every nuance of his poise and expression fed his delight; in his company, he could forget his clawing anger and the spiteful visions in his head.

Seil Kor turned to look at the white man dressed in a pantomime of coloured robes. He saw a change in the eyes of his friend, and a look of uncertainty crossed his face. The Frenchman responded with a faint, unguarded smile.

They were asleep before twilight as the carriage rattled forward at its constant speed. There were no lanterns in their compartment or in any other. All were sleeping before the ultimate darkness arrived, and would remain in their slumber to a far-off dawn. Nothing could be seen of the train but a few sparks and a blush around the smoke as it left the chimney. The trees ignored its dark progress; the animals were too busy to notice it. Some of the nocturnal tribes of the rim stopped briefly to listen to its rhythmic, linear voice. Most knew it to be part of the Vorrh's day-to-day business and kept their distance. Once, in its early history, a few of the unspeakable ones had tried to kill it, standing on the track with spears to confront the monster's speed. Their time was short-lived and messy, and the legend had bled back into the future generations, keeping them away.

Thus, unassailed by plants, beasts, or anthropoids, the train was almost automatic in its continual shuttle back and forth. There was only the trouble with the engineers and firemen, who took shifts to be awake over the rattling miles. Something objected to their vigil, something that made its presence felt on the confined space of a footplate. It stared between the shovelled coals, stoking the fire, spitting embers. It leaned, annoyed, against the burning oil and steam. Voices worried the pipes and handrails; voices from the rushing night, which could not be heard over the thunder of the engine. Some said it was the angels becoming anxious about consciousness trespassing the Vorrh. Others said it was the ghosts of the Limboia, looking for their hosts. Those who worked the engine said less and less, as they heard more and more.

They did not wake the next day. Nobody ever did. The next day was always dimmer, maybe because the forest grew thicker the deeper the train travelled, its huge canopy thrust up against the sky by greater and greater trees. Or it could have been the murmuring speed that never changed pulse or velocity, the rhythmic, chanting tracks sending the passengers into a haze of hypnotic coma, much like the metronome of a piano is said to do. Or perhaps, in this strangest of places, the natural laws of the world, which were known and trusted, came unbound and bent. Night here might have a different saturation, so that the dawn, which had begun to fragment onto the leaves, had taken forty hours to arrive.

They blinked and rubbed their eyes against the new light, standing and stretching as the train whistled. There was a strange smell in the compartment, one that goes unnoticed in normal life. He knew the scent from his younger days, when he had attempted caving in Switzerland. He and his athletic guide had been forced to enter a shallow crawl space, deep in the arteries of the Nidlenloch. It had taken them an hour to crawl through its pinching tunnel. That was when he had first noticed it.

"What is that stench?" he had asked his guide at the time.

"It is us, *mein herr*. Humans."

The young Frenchman had recognised the truth in those words almost before they had been spoken. It was the smell of something inherent, innate.

Yet this was a scent that was altogether new; another, higher note, complex and thrillingly shrill; he thought it might be the breath of the Vorrh itself. As he turned to his guide, intent on asking more about it, his eyes alighted on the luggage rack, and his query was lost. He stepped onto the plush seat like a fretful lapdog and reached up, yanking at his case. It did not move. The fears of his first sight had proved correct: The rack had grown tendrils and stems, delicate branches, which extended from its hand-carved foliage and gripped his possessions, entangling themselves about the leather in licentious affection. The same thing had happened along the entire length of the rack, and the few other passengers present, noticing his reaction, realised that they were in the same predicament. They joined him, pulling and worrying their belongings away from the lustful new shoots. The Frenchman would have hacked at the foliage if he could have found a suitable tool, but Seil Kor stepped in to help him, bending back the stems and unwinding the tendrils, before lifting the unnecessary luggage and setting it down at the little man's feet.

The train slowed to a standstill, the hissing brakes dragging against the dreary momentum with a squeal that made singular ears turn, in the impenetrable distance of trees. There was a raised wooden platform for the passengers and a ramp for the slave carriage. The low flatbeds continued, into a distance of scarred tracks and rutted furrows. The station had no name; none was needed. A small wooden house lay beyond the platform. They gathered themselves and walked towards it, legs stiff from the carriage, their heads still dazed from sleep; a wooden hangover, badly nailed together by amnesia.

The house was a waiting room, barren and empty. It contained only benches and a flyblown map of the Vorrh, pinned to one wall. They peered at the large, simple paper, which was wrinkled and made frail by sun and rain. It showed the city and the forest, balanced in ridiculous, improper proportions; the railway was delineated, as was the house, and there were a few lines leading away from it that faded into nothing. The course of a river was suggested by an uncertain, faded blue contour; there was a shaded area, labelled "Forestry," and a vague dotted line that roamed about near the middle of the paper, accompanied by the word "Forbidden."

The map should have been informative and authoritarian, but its poor execution ensured that it had the opposite effect. It looked like a lost insect had fallen into the cartographer's inkpot, crawled out, and made its bedraggled route across the paper.

Seil Kor put his finger on the largest of the lines that faded away to blankness and said, "This will be our way."

His finger rested in a small grey crater, almost a hole in the map, where countless other pilgrims had indicated their journey in the same manner. They stepped outside and smelt the air, looking at the clear, even sky before turning onto the track. Behind them, three of their fellow passengers, insignificant until now, stood staring at the map, one with his finger on the same indentation identified by Seil Kor. The Frenchman saw this and increased their pace into the waiting forest.

After three hours Seil Kor slowed and began to sniff the air and move his hands in all directions, as if feeling the textures of the space around him.

Seil Kor raised his right hand.

"We must turn here," he said. "Either back, or to the right."

His body strained towards the right, one foot already on the track.

The Frenchman looked up into his friend's gleeful face. "I think we are going right," he said.

They headed down the narrow path, wanting more of the wonders they had already seen. The day was unpredictable, but the allure was worth a dark return. They had witnessed the flowing winds of the Vorrh, long, singing currents of turbulence that flew and rippled between the contoured ground and the vast canopy of still leaves. Its profound, limited hurricane was still in their lungs, the cleanest air ever breathed; as sharp as lime, as soft as new snow. It bore youth and purity in its rushing particles, setting the eye clean and level. When it first hit the Frenchman, he choked as the corruptions of the cities and his own store of malice were dredged from his tarry crux. Scales fell from his cemented being, and he gave up all in a cough. There were no words to glue the two friends' experience together; it was all shared, in moments that existed forever.

They entered a small clearing that felt virgin, untouched— the animals and plants seemed surprised to see them and dropped their normal attention, their continuum, to acknowledge the presence of the strangers, before vanishing into the sound of parting leaves. Seil Kor walked ahead and into the middle of the clearing, looking intently at the ground.

The Frenchman examined the perimeter and was amazed to find dozens of tracks leading away from the space. They were regular but overgrown, like paths leading out from the centre of a clock face. The path at four o'clock was the widest, as if made by a beast much larger than the others. He assumed the assortment of animals had come from various directions to drink or eat at the clearing, but he could find no trace of water or food, nothing that might obviously attract them. He turned to his friend and found him standing in the middle of the space, a yellow book in his hand: Here was the answer. He walked over to the black man, who was gleaming blue in the mottled light and wore an expression of agitation tinged with magnitude.

"Seil Kor?" he asked. "What is it?"

"This is the place," the black man said quietly. "I was here before. This is where he lived."

"Who?"

"Saint Antonius," he said, barely whispering. "See the ground, look! There is still a scar of his shelter."

The Frenchman's eyes examined the space, which did seem to have an indentation, or a scar. It looked like the rectangular footprint of a hut or small house, drawn in the plant growth of discolouration, faint and without significance. He might have walked straight across it without noticing anything was there.

"This is where he lived, centuries ago; his simple home was in this place."

"How do you know?" questioned the Frenchman uneasily.

"This is the place I told you about, that my father brought me to, when I was young; he told me the story, showed me the signs, just before I was confirmed into the true faith. We prayed here together that day." Seil Kor looked at his friend. "This is why I agreed to come with you here, so that you might touch this sacred place and see the way. We can pray together here. That is why I brought you."

The Frenchman was astonished with this outburst. He felt a shiver of anger against his friend, an emotion he thought he had shed, something that felt most out of key in this place. The moment was a towering mistake that shuddered louder than the trees and longer than the metal rail that brought them here, to the centre of nowhere.

"I came to see the forest," he said with controlled limpness.

Far too quickly, Seil Kor answered: "This is not a place for seeing, for curiosity! Nor is it a place to be observed and then forgotten. It is sacred and all-knowing; men must give themselves here, sacrifice some part or all of themselves. You cannot walk in and out as you please; it is not a park or a city garden."

There was a pause, when only the ringing in their ears was present, sounding the sudden iron in their distance. The jaw locks at such moments, as if waiting for the noise and hurt to stop resounding. The animals and birds that first held the clearing had long since departed, the rising tidal wave of conflict driving them out through the trees. Seil Kor's next words were far too loud, but they snapped the tension.

"I told you, journeys here are limited; this will be my last and I give it to you. I have never met a more needy man. I bring you for salvation; it is your only chance."

He then knelt, opened the book, and began to read out loud; the book was of vellum and loosely bound. He read about Eden after the expulsion; it was a different version of Genesis, one the Frenchman had not heard, dense with local details and obscure references. His patience waned; he was disappointed by his friend's motivations. Their expedition had been spoiled for him, turned into a grotesque, evangelical ruse, a trick to convert him to a gibbering Christianity of Old Testament nonsense. He turned his back and walked out of the clearing, leaving the droning voice to recite the names of angels. He would wait for him at the station and there explain his inbuilt resistance to this kind of thing.

He marched down the track, talking under his breath, rehearsing all the lessons he would have to teach Seil Kor if their friendship was to last. Low vines and abundant foliage dragged at his ankles as he stormed through, and he faltered on pebbles and flat stones that had gone unnoticed on their smooth, leisurely walk here. He pushed harder against the path and its growing resistance, all the while muttering his embarrassment of the situation. The dialogue stopped when the track ran out.

He stood, silent, eyes wide open, staring at the blank wall of vegetation before him, at the end of this, the wrong track. A tiny trickle of panic sped coldly through his blood. Looking around, he heard his own laboured breathing. He struggled to see the track he had just walked, though he had not deviated from it and stood on it still. He knew he must control the moment. Closing his eyes, he tried to remain calm, laying his hand on his heart and letting his blood flood the fear away. He opened his eyes to an impenetrable jungle. Slowly, he began to walk back the way he thought he had come, expecting at any moment that the path would clear and become smooth and straight like before, that it would blossom out onto the chanting Seil Kor and the way home. But his footsteps led him to the trunk of a vast, dark tree, the path ending in the way that paths never do. He turned with his back to the tree and stared into the tangled forest, dread now rising like fumes from its pathless floor.

Over the next tangled hours, which felt like a decade, he shouted and called until his voice ran out. He had walked in all directions, seeking a path or a sign, but there were only trees and the growing wind. Surely his wise friend or one of the workers would find him? Even the Limboia would be a welcome sight. He thought he heard calling and had hurried towards it, but it had faded back into the other sounds, leaving him no closer to an escape.

He was irretrievably lost, with very few provisions, the main bag being in Seil Kor's possession. He stopped to ferret in his shoulder bag, expecting to find hope, along with solution, in its cramped interior. Instead, he found the secreted derringer, loaded, and with two extra bullets in the snug of its holster. He could afford only one to signal his position; the others he would need for protection. God knew what horrors lived in this matted place; he had seen the paintings, had heard the tales.

He took the little gun out, carefully cocked it, and held it above his head. He fired into the sky, or where the sky must be, on the other side of tons of leaves. The sound stopped the quiet and gave him silence back for a moment. He bellowed *"Seil Kor!"* with the last cracked and serrated edges of his voice. Then the quiet gushed back in, carrying the small foam of a sound: the long-distance whistle of the train. It seemed miles away and unfocused, without direction. For a few moments, he thought it must be in response to his signal, that they had heard the report of his gun from this dismal patch, determined his whereabouts, and begun their search. Then it sounded again, and in its reverberation he heard movement—it was leaving the forest, laden with wood and a few exhausted passengers, and he had been left behind, forgotten, maybe never seen at all. All those who cared and knew he existed were in another time and place, all except the one he had walked away from and would now never find. His legs buckled and he slumped against the ancient tree, sliding down into the hard, veined nest of its serpentine roots.

CHAPTER FOURTEEN

I have truly left the sanctuary of our home behind, as I wade back into the ways of men.

Este is strong and forthright at my side. When I carry her, slung against my back, I feel her touch, ebbing through the rocking bow, feel her fingers on my spine, her palm between my shoulder blades. She whispers continually and spots my foes, hiding in the trees or across the river. Together, we have seen the one who follows; a tall, dark-clad man, who looks like a shadow. He keeps his distance but is in some way attached. She says he is the most dangerous, but we will be safe in the Vorrh: He will not dare to enter the great forest.

I begin to recognise this country where I have never been: small corners, tricks of light and sound; odours that find recess in me, a cup to sit in for a second or two; enough to weigh down an indentation, an impression; the echo of a memory that is not there, or should not be.

I have stayed close to the river and found a boat to take me into the trees. The boatman is called Paulus. He is of unknown age, haggard by travel and nightmares, worn out by strong drink and imagination. He tells me stories of gins he has made, complex mechanisms that try to mimic the sounds he has heard while sleeping on the water in the Vorrh. He is an easy companion because he asks nothing of me; I must only be his sounding board.

He is the only one who navigates these waters, taking his boat, the *Leo*, alternately powered by wind, muscle, and steam, farther and farther into the core and farther from the voices and ears of men. In this, we have much in common, and the small, objective part of his racing brain that still exists knows it, and thinks it well. I ask him how far the river will take us and whether it is possible to pass through to the other side. He does not know but thinks he has been deeper and stayed longer than any other could claim to.

He explains that he suffered from narcolepsy from an early age but that it ceased when he first entered the Vorrh. Now he stays here and makes continual trips to balance his malady. He says that the water is in sympathy with renegade sleep; it protects him from being rubbed out and made transparent by the voices of the beings that he hears. This is not reassuring, but his commitment is. He promises to go with me until the river runs out, to the place where it is swallowed back into the earth or climbs the mountains. He says there will always be new sounds for him, that they have become his food. I do believe this is true. In the four days that we have travelled, he has eaten almost nothing, only picking at the fish I have caught and cooked from the vast abundance that lives here. He drinks much. "To dream," he says, "to fold at the bottom of the well and listen." He drinks until he cannot speak. His scarlet-veined eyelids work independently, like slow spoons attempting to sagely wink and taste the passing night. Yet each morning, when I awake, he is already at the engine, preening it into life.

I discover that "the cooling system," a tangle of brass and copper pipes that sits above the boiler, is in fact a still. His fastidious care of it suddenly makes more sense, and I am left to wonder whether the boat's engine is as reliably maintained as his alcohol supply. Paulus had come here from the lowlands of Europe, the depression where Germany meets Holland and Belgium. He had been a *Kahnführer* on the mighty Maas, an industrious bargeman, pushing every cargo through the then neutral, neighbourly lands, before the Great War. But that was half a century ago. He never says why he left and becomes vague when his motives for being here are questioned.

Paulus only once asks me about the bow and why I do not use it to hunt or fish. I explain that it is not for use, being frail and of unsure design. He accepts this, and we change the subject back to his inventions. He tells me of another mechanical gin he once saw; not his invention this time, but a gin that projected light, chopped into pieces to coincide with blinks, so that an impression of movement was achieved. Always the same movement, endless. The same woman on the same stairwell, taking the same three steps, continuously; a horse running to nowhere; a naked patriarch swinging an axe. He says the more one watches, the more their time becomes real and the watcher's time leaks out, becoming insignificant, the same as watching the water for too long.

I can see that shadow play written on a wall. It matches our movement as we edgily drift on this monotonous tide. I feel my body recognise the spaces between the significant throbs of life, as if it has been cut into sections and rejoined in a crooked line, cut on a rough surface with a dull blade, and spliced together with the wrong glue.

By the fifth day, I am detached from the boat. Discorporate, I can see him, her, and us from the trees, as if a bird has framed the boat's path between branches, high in the wooden trellis, close to the sky.

Paulus is no longer talking and spends more time watching the river ahead. His loose expectation is infectious, and we both look at the tiny horizon, guillotined in the moving trees. She holds my hand from the end of passage, as the "I" of me is shaken loose, absorbed by meeting the other, who was born here.

Unexpectedly, the river straightens, making a long, unflinching channel, without bends or turns. He says it is like the canals of the Maas, that he has never been this far in before. The engine chugs and propels us just above the speed of the water; the surface is clear and highly reflective. As evening unfolds, we become mesmerised by the forest, which grows from the water and rises to the clouds, ploughing down into its depths in absolute sameness; a perfect symmetry, unwound in perfect perspective. Nothing changes for hours; the dusk moves slower than our eyes, and we are pulled into the glimmering reflection without any sense of self. We are dissolved.

➤→

Such is the price of all trespass: Clever men and dolts give it up with joy; others struggle and claw against it, burning their hand bones to hooks, until fatigued or abased to nothing.

The boat turned grey and the men glowed in the vespertine current. The Bowman gave his voice to the waters as his name floated into the branches, and his brain tree turned to match those in the inverted sky, which was brimming with shy stars. The boatman thought of a new type of gin, a kind of water weaver, a loom for folding the sea. His imaginings brought the angels in. They awoke to the density of such trespass, to the vibration of the mechanism of thought, even when the idea it produced was of little consequence.

They came in with awareness and observed with caution, seeing the selves float against the stream, away from the men. The angels kept their distance, for fear of being caught in the amber of the human auras. Sticky sunlight stuff, not made for here, and shedding profusely.

The Bowman and Paulus were entering fast-running shallows at a place where the land rose out of the thin water in broken blades of stone, vertical, resolute, and overwhelming. They stepped out of the boat into three feet of water, wading the vessel aground on a long shingle beach and letting its weight wallow into the glinting pebbles. The Bowman walked up onto firmer land and looked about him: He had been here before. The gravity of the place spoke of an entwining outside of his memory. He looked around for visual signs but found none: The place spoke to him through another vein.

They sat for a while and talked about their separate journeys, before and beyond, in a way that helped them arrive and depart. The Bowman was going inland; the boatman was returning to the mouth of the river. He would collect his self on the way back. Paulus explained that their landing place was the origin of both the river and the forest and that it was a difficult place to walk; its ruggedness was not made for people, its steep ascents being full of declivities and unpredictable impasses. According to the unknown sources of history, the very name of the Vorrh came from its description.

They continued to talk for a few hours, letting their experiences waft and disperse until the moment came. It crept in during a pause, announcing itself bodily with the stretching of cramped legs. The bow, quiver, and other possessions were unloaded and placed safely away from the water. They rocked the boat gently out of the shallows and into deeper water; Paulus clambered on and punted it farther out with the boathook, while the Bowman waded back to shore and watched the *Leo* join the stream, diminishing with its waving captain, beyond the range of sight. As it vanished, a light ripple dazed the air, a rhythmic shudder of ambience. He smiled to himself, realising that it was a farewell from his friend; a short, percussive riff, played on the rim of the boat's wooden hull, as it returned its captain to another world.

➡

Tsungali's jaw now worked in a sideways motion. The wise man who had performed the repair was a healer named Nebsuel, who lived in the outcast isles, just inside the mouth of the great river. Tsungali had visited him on his way into the Vorrh.

Nebsuel possessed a great knowledge of the body, of its fluids and lights. His services could be bought but were better given. He was not a kind man; he did not apply his knowledge for the well-being of others. He performed surgery and operated the chemistry of plants to see further inside the workings of the human animal. His true ambition was to isolate the gum that joins flesh to mind and mind to spirit. His tools and procedures for such work were simple. He would divide and subtract, add and multiply, the pain and its relief, while probing the interior of structure and sensation. He was not a man to be taken lightly, and Tsungali knew he might be killed or rearranged by his practices. He also knew that if he did not get help soon, his jaw might never heal. Starvation and blood poisoning seemed a far worse conclusion than Nebsuel's intrusions.

The isle of outcast had been a leper colony. Nebsuel's family had lived there and suffered the relentless disease, but he had not. Some potent resistance in him had kept him "clean," while he watched all around him suffer. He had seen how the outsiders had treated his family and friends; on trading expeditions to the outside world, he had witnessed open disgust and cruelty against his loved ones.

How he became a wise man was not known, but the legends were thick and terrible. Some said he cut open all the dead of the isle and read the complex tales of their mechanisms; others said he travelled away, to collect the wisdom from many tribes, some from beyond the sea. He was rumoured to commune with forbidden spirits and unspeakable creatures that came to trade knowledge for the souls of men he kept in jars. None of the reports could be confirmed, and they grew more fantastical in their ambiguity. But his powers of healing were not so unclear. They were the only thing about him that was certain, and they were worth the risk of contamination and agony.

Tsungali had sat in a large chair made of sturdy wood, a strap holding his arms tight to his body and firm against the chair. He had laboriously drunk the mixture of stewed leaves that Nebsuel had given him, and now his face drooped numb and cold. His broken teeth had been removed and dropped to the earthen floor, where ants flocked to harvest them, swarming in collective shoves to nudge the prize along their conveyor-belt lines of frenzied black bodies. Metal and wooden probes extended his jaw, giving access to the glistening muscles, unnaturally exposed inside. Nebsuel worked from both sides, one finger in the exterior wound, which he had unstitched, the other hand teasing and adjusting the tools inside Tsungali's mouth. His arm, already treated, lay throbbing under the strap. An hour later, he lay in a sweat of recovery, beaming in pain.

"Tell me of this Bowman," Nebsuel said as they sat around a smouldering fire, three days later. Tsungali spoke through gurgles and splutters, as though a wet sock were stuffed in his mouth. He explained his quest and how it had been foiled on both attempts. He told of the white man with black-man skills, of his cunning and excessive knowledge. He did not tell of what he feared, of what he had seen for those few minutes at close range: the shock of recognition; a face he knew from years before, unchanged by time while his own grew old and his body, slow. It must have been a mistake, a trick of the mind—the man's son, perhaps, grown identical in form. The alternative, though it would have explained his power and his automatic place in Tsungali's memory, was impossible.

"I will kill him in the Vorrh," concluded Tsungali.

"Or he will kill you," Nebsuel stated blankly. "Why do you think he heads for the Vorrh?"

"Because he has a destiny there, something unfinished. Something the white soldiers don't want to happen." Tsungali prodded the glowing embers with a stick, making a new citadel within their flickering hearth. "Perhaps he means to meet the angels or the demons that dwell there."

"Ah!" said Nebsuel. "I know nothing of demons, but the Erstwhile you call angels are another matter; they have a presence everywhere."

"You have seen them?" asked Tsungali.

"I have sensed them, felt them near, watching, when a soul shudders on my knives. Some are attracted to the extreme action of men, wanting to see deeper and understand, and maybe become part of man. Have you never known their presence amid your actions of war and butchery?"

There was no answer, so Nebsuel continued.

"The Erstwhile in the Vorrh could be different, older; a residue, like something left in a closed pipe or one of my test tubes; concealed and contained, too viscous to climb the sides. At least, that would match the stories that are told of that region."

He made a brief sign over his head, as if stroking some invisible coiffure above his shining, bald scalp. He knew Tsungali had seen more, that there was an understanding that had not been mentioned. For that little act of selfishness, he would give him weak, inexpensive balm to close his wounds. Had he shared all his knowledge and fears, he would be leaving with an ointment that would have healed the wounds in two days.

For the wrongness of his quest and his inability to alter or change his purpose, Tsungali would have to pay dearly, but not yet, and not to this doctor. Nebsuel attached a trace scent to the scarred warrior; he would be trackable for up to a year; trained beasts could be used to carry messages of his whereabouts; it could be used to find him if he never returned—the state of his body, intact or otherwise, would not hinder its efficacy.

The next day, Tsungali gave his thanks and said goodbye. For his treatment and recuperation, he had traded three dozen safety pins, twelve blue shells collected by the coastal tribes, and five ampoules of adrenaline stolen from army medical supplies. He had also, unknowingly, traded a week of his life and all possibility of the fulfilment of his commission.

After his patient's departure, Nebsuel opened a slanted box and removed a tiny piece of pungent, scrolled cloth, designed for the purpose, stretching it between intricate brass flaps. He took a delicately nibbed pen and scratched a musical, Arabic tracery into its waiting. When it was dry, he unpinned it and rolled it into a tiny tube, which he screwed into a weightless tin cylinder, not much bigger than the curved nail of his little finger. He cooed and hummed to the black pigeon he cupped in his hands as he attached the cylinder to one of the bird's legs. He stepped outside and cast it to the skies, towards a flutter of rising stars, whistling after it to increase its speed.

➤→

Sidrus sat at a circular table in his house, close to the forest. The black pigeon arrived out of the sun and flew to its familiar perch and food tray in the tower above him. Its weight set a light silver bell in motion, which called the gaunt man to attend. He peeled the message from the bird and straightened the scroll:

The assassin goes on into the Vorrh to kill the Bowman.
He is spoored. Act with speed or be lost.

Sidrus put the slip of cloth into a glass phial and locked it in
a steel box. It was impossible for him to enter the forest, but he
needed to prevent the Bowman from dying within it. He would
have to send another in his stead, someone to wipe out the fearsome warrior on the Bowman's trail. There was only one: the
Orm.

The Orm lived and worked within the Limboia. It was at
home in their blankness; it hid in their absence. In fact, no one
knew what the Orm was: If it was to be used, a message was
given to the lost core of them all. Something of them, something or other, stepped out; no one knew what, and most did
not care to. It was said that its brain was black and as hard as
granite, unlike the limp mush that swilled in the walnut skulls
of the Limboia. The process and the price of contact chilled
even Sidrus's contaminated heart. But it had to be done, so
he went to the slave house near the station, where the Limboia were kept when not toiling in the forest's interior. The
slave house was isolated from all other buildings, three sto-
reys high and surrounded by a fenced enclosure. It had been
a prison, constructed to hold slaves in one part and criminals
in another. Most of the criminals were simply escaped slaves,
and eventually the two parts of the grim building had merged.
The uncomfortable history of slavery was far too close; even
in these more civilised times, its scars were far from healed. In
other parts of the world, the abolition was a matter of growing
moral rightness. Here, it changed by evolution, some said to a
state of increased degradation. The slaves had been superseded
by a deformed generation that developed inside them, replacing the stolen workforce with another that had been hidden all
along. Continual, forced exposure to the Vorrh bred an alter-

native clan of beings, and within the original slave army grew another: the seed of the Limboia.

Most of their number were black and of local origin, some were white, and a very few had strayed from Asia. Getting them to work was easy: They all longed to be in the Vorrh, and their addiction was easily exploited by controlled, rotating shifts. The train carried a continual exchange of those whose week's containment in the slave house left them desperate to return to the swallowing forest, and those whose fatigue left them too dazed to know they were leaving it.

The slave house and its upkeep were the collective responsibility of the Timber Guild, a society made up of the larger factories and exporters that fed richly from the forest's abundance. The Limboia were far more difficult to control and explain than their abducted predecessors. There was something so terrible in their collective presence that most normal humans could not abide their company. Overseers lasted only a few weeks; even the most callous and brutal of souls found that, within a few days, they were questioning their own existence and the meaning of mortality. Those who could previously whip a man to death without rage or guilt found themselves waking at night, sobbing, as questions about eternity bubbled in their ill-shaped minds. In the early days, it appeared as though it would never be possible to organise and focus this mass of free labour. Then the stillborn came, to offer a tool of control.

There were some ragged legends and a few squalid myths, but the truth was even more bizarre. Sidrus knew that truth and how to use it. He knew that it began with William Maclish, a former Black Watch sergeant, once a hard-drinking, no-nonsense kind of man, with a muscular personality and a wiry, red-haired temper. He had obtained the position of senior keeper to the slave house and moved in to the keeper's house with his pregnant wife and their few possessions. It had been a new beginning. He had changed his ways, his job, and his country, and there was a bright, gruff optimism in the teetotal air. Three weeks later, beset by Limboia-induced depression, he was thinking of suicide. But his desperate plans were abruptly halted, and the course of his life forever altered, by the death of his firstborn child.

CHAPTER FIFTEEN

William Maclish had sat by his wife's bed while the doctor wrapped the lifeless bundle tightly and put it into a canvas bag. A noise had come from outside, a growing song mixed with broken glass. His first thoughts were of riot, and he had hurried the half-finished doctor out of his house, unable to face the possible collision of these two parts of his life while in the man's melancholy presence.

His departure secured, Maclish had listened more carefully. One hundred and nineteen lost souls—the entire population of the locked house—had broken the windows of their dormitories and were singing out into the night. It was a call of loss—discordant, pure, and hair-raisingly eerie. His head cocked to the song of the Limboia, he heard pibroch woven inside the wail, Highland dirges that uprooted his nerve and stitched him to a childhood that had been so gapingly forgotten. He stood at the door of his squat home and stared at the slave house, its every window filled with mooncalf faces, all calling to him.

The next day he walked slowly from his sobbing home to the slave house. They were still singing. He unlocked the door and they fell still, remaining silent as he walked among them, each pointing at his or her own heart. He returned to reassure his wife that all was well, but she was sleeping at last, so he walked instinctively to where the doctor had left the bundle, picked it up, and tucked it under his coat. He did not know why he was doing this; he could have given no man a sensible answer. He carried the concealment out of their home and into the hushed, glacial silence of the slave house. On the table that stood at the centre of the recreational hall, he placed the treasure, unwrapping it and arranging the tiny, stiff corpse for all of them to see.

The response was astonishing. They became galvanised, moving as one, forming a queue from all parts of the three-storied jail that tapered to the hall and its table of focus. The first of the Limboia brought a piece of broken mirror, which he held close to his head. A tension was rising in the space between understanding and fear. When his bony legs touched the table, he looked away, holding the mirror with both hands. His body and head contoured so that he could hold the glass in a difficult position, to the side of his face. He squinted into the mirror, at the backwards-peripheral reflection of the dead infant. He looked there for a few granite-solid minutes, then passed the mirror to the next man, who imitated him exactly.

Hours later, they had all made the same ritual, all seen his child in a squint, all shown respect. Maclish was exhausted and could not explain what had happened, except in the way of the tongue: Deep inside, he knew that they had all taken something, not from the dead infant, but from the world that it would never walk in. He also knew that all of them were now his. He wrapped the little body up tight and took it back to his home, hidden in the dark, silky lining of his winter coat, next to his rapidly beating heart.

Obedience had been bought or given that strange day, and with it a protection against the Limboia's unconscious but pernicious influence: Maclish had become master of the workforce of the Vorrh. He had done it without violence or force, and the Timber Guild was amazed. Nobody knew how it had been achieved, but all who were engaged in the commerce of the forest talked about it, and he was marked as a man of consequence. It changed every aspect of his life and gave him the position of respect he had always desperately craved.

It took the company doctor several days to return and collect the tiny body. He had been detained on the other side of the city and apologised profusely for his tardiness in completing the prescribed task. They were walking through the scullery as they talked.

"I haven't told my wife that the child's body is still here," Maclish said. "She assumed that ye took it with ye on that night."

"Oh, I see," Dr. Hoffman said. "Well, I can only apologise again for placing you in such a position. I will take it with me now and spare you both any further upset."

Maclish thumbed the noisy metal latch of the pantry door and they both entered. From its shadowy seclusion at the back of the narrow room, he produced a circular old biscuit tin. He opened it clumsily and offered the contents to the doctor, who, with a flicker of hesitation, reached in and removed the bundle. There was an instant response. He frowned deeply and started to manipulate the cloth-bound form in his wise hands, taking it out of the room and placing it on a low table surrounded by cooking utensils. He unfolded the fabric gently to examine its contents.

"I am very sorry to have to do this in your presence," he apologised, "but something here is not quite right."

Maclish was indifferent to the incident but intrigued by the doctor's response.

"Extraordinary!" muttered the practitioner, touching the tiny body on the table and examining it closely.

"What is it?" asked Maclish.

"It has been three days since the child's passing, and there is not the slightest trace of decomposition. It's quite remarkable." He turned to the keeper in obvious awe, then remembered the nature of his visit and brought his excitement under scientific control. "I don't want to sound callous, but would you permit me to conduct some slight tests before the burial?"

"What, cutting?" the startled father answered.

"Not as such, no; more observation."

"The poor wee bairn has gone. Do what ye must. But not too long, mind! I don't want my wife upset any more than is necessary."

The doctor agreed and gathered up his prize. As he left the house, an excited air graced his expression, one that had never before been seen about his usually dour countenance.

It was a week before Dr. Hoffman again knocked at Maclish's door, to be answered by the less-than-civil warden.

"Where is my child?" he demanded. "Why have ye kept him this long?"

"I must apologise for the delay, but the fact is this is a most remarkable incident, I think unique."

Maclish looked at the pink, grinning face, screwed into its pinching celluloid collar; at the pink, overwashed hands, restrained in their celluloid cuffs. White and pink, pink and white. He had heard rumours about this man, rumours that suggested his services, his skills, and his oath could be bent at a price. Pink and white, white and pink.

"Come in, man!" he said sharply, his abruptness scratching a warning in the air between them. The doctor stepped hurriedly over the threshold and into the dim hallway.

"The truth is," the doctor continued, turning to face the keeper, "your poor child has been untouched by the process of corruption: He is the same today as when he was born."

"Aye, dead!" growled Maclish.

"Well, yes, dead, of course. But perfect! In all my years as a physician I have never seen the like. Pray, please tell me, did anything unusual happen while I was away, between the birth and my retrieval of the remains?"

Maclish did not like the question and asked one of his own. "How many have ye seen?"

The doctor looked confused. "Born-dead bairns? Oh, perhaps thirty a year. It varies."

"And what normally happens to the bodies?" asked the keeper.

"Normally? They are buried within three days. I don't usually keep them; as I said, this is a very unusual case. I can assure you that the greatest care is—"

"Does anyone else see 'em?" Maclish cut in.

"Er, no." Hoffman frowned.

Maclish took the man's arm and led him through to a small sitting room, the kind that is never used; overfurnished, smelling of wax and stale lace. He seated the puzzled doctor and quietly closed the door. The conversation that was to follow was not one to be exchanged loosely, especially beneath the floorboards of the pale bedroom above their heads.

They talked a knot of meaning and purpose, closing in on a subject that neither of them understood.

"Can ye make a profit from this?" he asked the doctor.

"Not in financial terms, no. But I can find benefit in knowledge," he said, sounding more earnest than he had for years. He was beginning to believe his own prescriptions.

"Supposing it never goes off?"

The doctor blinked in silence. "Goes off?"

"Aye, never rots: Wouldn't the mother want to keep it with her, keep it close and quiet?"

"That's not really what I had in mind," said Hoffman uncomfortably.

"My focus would be on medical research; on discovering a new understanding of mortality; finding the distinction between the quick and the dead!"

"Aye, and that," said Maclish.

Two days later, the doctor gave in. He arrived at the warden's house in a purple dusk that made all things shine, bringing another small bundle with him.

They took it, together, to the house of the Limboia. Something more than silence greeted them on the other side of the door. On echoing shoes, they took their prize to the table, and the ritual of the mirror slanting began again. Of the time that passed, little can be said. The Limboia shuffled back and forth, their breath becoming even and untroubled. The doctor and the warden hid in silence and tobacco at the other end of the building.

"What do ye think?" asked Maclish on their way back to his house.

"I have no idea what it is, what it means to them, or why they do it." The doctor shrugged, confounded. "How it can affect tissue is completely beyond my understanding."

His understanding of it, however, did not impact its effects, and the bundle he carried away stayed fresh and flexible forever, far beyond the doctor's own questionable life. A month later they tried again, with exactly the same result. Meanwhile, the Limboia worked harder and obeyed all the commands that Maclish gave them. They continued their experiment for a year, with great success. Until the doctor made his most grievous mistake . . .

As Maclish had anticipated, some of the heartbroken parents paid to have their preserved children back, keeping them in quiet parts of the house, holding and talking to them until the next child came. One couple never conceived again and secretly enjoyed the fictional infancy of their little corpse all their life.

It was during the days of the long rains, when even the Limboia could not work, that Hoffman brought the fateful bundle to the prison. They were all there that afternoon, the rotations halted by the torrent that lashed and hammered the narrow windows and the slate roof. The old prison was crowded and choked by the silent mass. The doctor and Maclish spluttered into it from the puddles outside, noisy raincoats flapping over their heads, shuddering off water like dogs in a hall.

They put their prize on the table and uncovered it. They had become used to the process, made immune by the dependency of the ritual and its cleansing aftereffects. But the sound that flew through the tall building on this occasion was like the slap of a single wave hitting a cave: a quick intake of breath from all the Limboia, all at once, all together. The warden and the doctor froze and the hair on the backs of their necks bristled uncontrollably. The doctor turned white and looked between Maclish and the wet door. Nothing happened, and the Limboia started to make their usual line towards the table, the first with the mirror in its hand. This time, the scrying was different. There was the same action, the same impassive hunger-quiet queue, but it had altered utterly in another basic way, as if its temperature had shifted or its scent or colour had changed, and whatever this abnormality was, it was growing with each participant. The rain roared outside, its dampness seeping through the entire building.

After every one of the inmates had visited the table and returned to their beds, a new sensation joined the sound of the water: breathing, at first barely audible, then growing, more in rhythm than in volume. The two men looked at each other as the suction and blow increased. It was one breath. One breath, made by all the inmates in perfect unison. It was, at the same time, disarmingly unnatural and absolutely understandable.

Then, out of the corner of their eyes, they saw something move. They watched, aghast and openmouthed, as the curled cadaver opened its eyes.

Maclish paled. "Holy fuck," he stammered. "Oh God, no!"

The doctor said nothing, one hand covering his mouth in horror. The tiny eyes moved, turning in their dead sockets to look directly at him. He stepped towards it, the wind of the breathing echoing in every part of the room. He stretched out a tremulous hand, the spectre's gaze now focused into a question. The breath whistled in his ears, and he leaned closer to the abomination, finally touching its leg with the tips of his fingers. The eyes closed and the breath stopped, silence descending with such rapidity that both men flinched, but the momentum of the phenomena continuing to roll in their bodies and souls.

Maclish drew his pistol from its holster and looked around uneasily, peering up the flights of metal stairs, which dominated the building. Nothing stirred; even the rain outside was beginning to ease.

"Bring that," he commanded the doctor, jerking his head towards the table. Hoffman wrapped the bundle and lifted it tentatively into his large Gladstone bag. They left the slaves to their silence and made their way out into the puddles and fresh air, the warden walking backwards, his gun pointing a warning back into the empty space, like a child's torchlight prying into infinity.

Back at the house, he stood panting while the doctor stared

limply at the bag on the kitchen table. Maclish needed a drink like never before, but there was none in the house, and it had been more than a year since he had taken the pledge. Not to anyone else—he would have broken that—but to himself. The contradiction and the lack of choice fuelled his anger.

"What the fuck went wrong in there?!" he shouted at the doctor, who shrugged and struggled to speak. "Is that thing dead or alive?!" Maclish demanded, waving his gun towards the bag.

"It's dead!" said Hoffman.

"Then why did its fucking eyes move?"

"I think . . . it was just a reflex action."

"For God's sake, man! It looked at me!" choked Maclish.

"Yes." The doctor nodded unhappily.

"What made this happen? What's wrong with it?" Maclish pointed at the carrier again with his gun.

In a distant and strangled voice, the doctor said, "It wasn't stillborn; it was aborted."

Maclish glared at Hoffman and very carefully put his revolver back into its holster, buttoning the flap tightly down.

"You fuck," he said flatly. "Get it out; get rid of it."

He snatched open the door to the backyard with such brutality that it jolted, spraying water into the tension between them. The doctor left and Maclish shut him out, slamming his retreating figure out of sight.

The amassed eyes watched in silence, through the broken glass, as the figures parted; construction of the Orm had begun, and all would understand its consequences before the year was over.

➤

The uncanny should be no match against scientific curiosity, thought Dr. Hoffman on his way home. He thought it like a mantra in an attempt to drown out the horrific, impending prospect of unwrapping the bundle again when he got to the house. He imagined movement inside his bag. He thought about it opening its eyes in there, looking out at the darkness, trying to see him.

He knew it was dead. He had seen the dead open their eyes before, had even heard them sigh. He had once seen an arm rise to noisily dislodge an unsecured coffin lid. He had even heard the case of a body sitting up, under its mortuary sheet, causing such dismay to the autopsy assistant that he spilt an entire jar of pickled onions over his lunch and a week's worth of medical notes. Hoffman had handled the papers months later; the distinctive reek of vinegar had persisted, even then.

But this was different. Those tiny eyes had conscience. Or was it just a moment of nerves? Dread brought on by that unnatural breathing, a suggestive illusion to make the blood run cold?

The uncanny should be no match against scientific curiosity.

At the back of his consulting room was a conservatory. Its windows were painted white to just above head height, which gave the room a bright concealment. He called it his laboratory. No real experiments were ever conducted there, but he pottered about among its specimens and chemicals, test tubes and retorts, in a delighted pretence of scientific enquiry; it gave him status among the uneducated elders of this prosperous backwater. The most functional thing in the laboratory was its incinerator, which squatted at the far end of the rectilinear space. A lot of uncertainties and embarrassments had vanished in it, along with the usual quota of malign and discarded tissue.

He entered the conservatory that evening in a daze, immediately turning on the incinerator's gas supply and igniting its glowing hum. A few straddles of passing storm gave spasmodic bursts of rain, which ran across the glass roof; rivulet shadows knotted and crawled zebra patterns on the stainless steel table below. The bundle sat in the middle of their flow like an isolated island, devoid of life. Hoffman slipped on maroon rubber gloves and brought a wrapped set of surgical tools to the table. It would have been easier to throw the spectre straight into the flames, but he was curious, and at that moment, in the stronghold of his laboratory, his pride beat stronger than his fear.

He teased the wrapping away from the still body and, with great trepidation, turned it onto its back.

He put a stethoscope to its chest: nothing. He moved the polished end to its tiny lips: No breath clouded the shining steel. He took a scalpel and nicked a vein: No blood flowed out of the black, static body. His relief compounded into certainty, and with one cupped hand, he lifted the limp thing up and crossed the room, wrenching open the roaring door of the incinerator. He hesitated a moment, readying to advance it towards the flames, when the eyes opened and stared at him with undoubtable sentience. He gasped and dropped the thing to the floor, running to the other end of the room and holding his carrying hand away from the rest of his body, as if it were a separate and contaminated entity.

He waited an hour, watching the shadows of rain snake, mate, and dance on the gleaming metal table and smelling the singeing heat pour out of the incinerator. He tiptoed slowly towards it, its door still open, the interior fires raging. He looked warily at the curled body on the floor: It had not changed position since it had fallen. The cloth wrapping was still on the table and he picked it up in passing, standing over the body and dropping it, so that it covered the dead thing entirely. He snatched up its hidden contents and tightened the rags, so no part of the head was visible. His skin crawled; he half expected movement or bony pressure to struggle in his grip. But it remained limp and passive, as if waiting to receive its fate.

➻

Six weeks later, Maclish contacted him and asked him to call by on the pretence of visiting his wife, to check her over and see if she might be fit enough to continue with his plans for a family. After a cursory examination, the doctor joined him for a pipe of tobacco in the garden.

"How are they?" asked Hoffman.

"Restless and slow," answered the keeper.

"Are there any more side effects since last time?"

"No, they are back to their normal cheery selves."

Maclish's attempt at gallows humour eased the tension between them, and the doctor smiled.

"I think they need another one," said Maclish.

The doctor stopped in his tracks, unable to believe his ears.

"You want to do it again? After the last time and what you called me?"

As he spoke, the doctor became flushed and agitated.

"I did not mean to insult ye. I was shaken by that horrible thing," said Maclish, while fiddling with the bowl of his pipe. "It rattled me, man; I did not mean to speak out of turn."

The doctor knew that this was the closest thing to an apology that he would ever get from the sullen Scot. They stopped to relight their pipes, then walked on in silence for a few moments.

"It will all work out fine if we stick to bairns that are naturally born dead." Maclish raised his brows at the doctor, who hesitated before slowly nodding his agreement.

So the ritual began again and the Limboia were once more satisfied. A greater bond grew between the keeper and the doctor; their secret remained hidden and effective; Mrs. Maclish was pregnant again.

In the spring, an intake of new lost men joined the throng, some younger than ever before. One was a runaway who had hidden in the Vorrh for two years, living wild until he was erased and then found by others cutting trees nearby. He still had a remnant of language but never used it—until the day he told Maclish about the Orm.

It had happened after his first scrying session, when all the others had returned to their dormitories. He stood alone on the metal staircase as Maclish and the doctor, who hadn't noticed him loitering, wrapped the bundle and prepared to leave. He started knocking on the iron banister, and they turned to see him waiting for them. Surprised, the keeper strode over to him and was about to bark an order when the young man pointed at his own heart and spoke. The voice was sluggish, without emphasis or effort.

"From the shallow place, we have say. Say is bout the one who lives inside us, say came not with the fleyber, but with the one that looks back." Maclish was about to stop the gibberish when the word "fleyber" rang a long, distant bell. It was a Scottish word; his mother had used it. He could not remember its meaning. How in God's name would this native have it on his tongue?

"Bring back that one again so Orm walk on. Or we cease. All cease."

"What do ye mean 'cease'? Ye think ye can just stop work when ye want?" barked Maclish.

"All cease," said the herald of the Limboia. "Cease live."

"What are we going to do about this?" groaned the keeper, his head in his hands, elbows on the kitchen table. The doctor sat opposite him, saying nothing. "Have ye any idea what in hell that idiot was gabbling about? Was that a threat?"

"I think so, yes," said the doctor, reluctantly. "Some part of them wants the aborted child brought back, some part that calls itself Orm."

"That's ridiculous; they can't ask for anything!"

"They mean it," said Hoffman.

"Anyway, it's impossible: ye burnt it." He looked indignantly at the doctor, whose eyes met his only briefly before sliding back to the table.

"Not exactly," said Hoffman.

Maclish's family were from Glasgow, his wife's from Inverness: It was possible that she would know the word, be able to dredge a meaning for it out of her memory.

She was watering some newly planted vegetables in a corner of their garden when he came upon her.

"Marie," he said, approaching her, and the subject, cautiously. "Do ye recall hearing the word 'fleyber' before? I remember my mother using it, but I cannae for the life of me recall its meaning. Is it Gaelic, do ye know?"

Marie was a strong, neat woman, her thick, dark hair pulled back from her broad face in a bun. "Fleyber," she repeated, her neck and her ears blushing a deep blood red under her fair skin. He nodded eagerly, not noticing her discomfort or her backwards step onto one of the thin shoots she had just watered. "William, why do you ask this of me? What do you want? Haven't we been through enough?"

He was instantly irritated by her irrational response. "I only asked the meaning of a word," he blustered.

She drew in a deep breath, resting her weight on the hoe at her side and looking him square in the eyes. "It's from the Highlands. The fleyber is the spirit of one that died in childbirth; they say its soul wanders the moors as a ghost light, a will-o'-the-wisp."

Her voice quavered as she said it, but her eyes never left her husband's. "Is *that* what you wanted to know?" she said, blinking hard before returning to her plants, ignoring the one crushed under her foot.

>—→

Dr. Hoffman had kept the cadaver in a polished wooden box, a kind of substitute coffin that originally held a small, portable microscope. Since that day at the incinerator, he had peeked into the box several times. The eyes were always closed, except for yesterday, when he returned with the request from the Limboia; then the eyes had stared out at him from the rigid interior.

He was preparing to pack the creature when his servant announced that Mrs. Klausen had arrived for her appointment. He had completely forgotten about the wretched woman and her insistence on being examined again for yet another of her imaginary illnesses. He went through to his consulting room, where the plump Frau sat, smiling like a bird.

"Dear Dr. Hoffman, so nice to see you again, even if it is because of my poor, ailing body."

The doctor smiled and prepared to charm the pestilential woman, hoping to send her on her way quickly.

"These are for you," she said, offering a richly embroidered silk bag containing an ornate box. "They are Chanteuse bonbons," she gushed, "all the way from Stuttgart."

He thanked her and began the consultation, probing and questioning the woman's hypochondriac needs for almost an hour. When he finally got rid of her, he rushed back into the laboratory to pack the bundle. Late, and desperate to be on the road, he bustled about, his curiosity running in a lapse. The new voice in the Limboia meant that he could gauge his experiments. He hoped to see again the response of the lost ones, this time without fear clouding his perceptions.

In his distracted panic, he mislaid the creature's carrying bag and spent ten minutes crawling under the furniture, looking behind the books, and spinning around like a giddy dog. Time was running out, and he knew Maclish would be chewing his claws and growing ill-tempered. Perhaps he had taken it next door when he'd gone to examine that dreary woman? He sprinted across the hall and scanned the examination room. The bag was not there, but her silk pouch was. He quickly threw the repulsive sweets in a trash can. The bundle fitted perfectly in its elegant new conveyor.

Maclish was standing outside the prison house, chafing and irritable. The doctor gave him a limp wave from the fence door while hurrying towards him.

"Sorry to be so late; I had a patient."

Maclish said nothing but stared at the bright, noisy sack that Hoffman pulled out of his Gladstone bag like a garish conjuror. With a slur of incongruity, he said, "Is that it?" Hoffman nodded, and they entered the anticipant building.

Inside the stillness, the herald stood waiting at the table. "The one that looks back," he said, staring at the embroidered bag.

Maclish and Hoffman said nothing, setting their prize down on the table.

"You leave; we need lone this day."

"Now, wait a minute . . . ," bristled Maclish.

"It's all right," said the doctor with a certainty that sounded believable. "Let's do it their way this time."

"One hour!" barked the keeper. "One hour only; then we come back." They did not turn around as they left the building, the hallway reverberating with the sound of the multitude descending the clanking stairs behind them.

Exactly one hour later, they returned. The hall was empty and quiet. The thing's eyes were mercifully closed.

"It's all right," said Hoffman. "They are content. Let's take the child and lock up."

Maclish conceded but looked puzzled. "Where's the bag?" he said, his eyes scanning the room.

"Oh God, not again!" groaned Hoffman, stooping to look under the table.

"They've taken it, haven't they?!" Maclish exclaimed. "The stupid fuckers have taken the bag!" He was not a man famous for laughing, and it sounded odd somehow, solid and unused, as it erupted from him, the hallways listening to it in concentrated surprise.

There was a scrap of cloth left on the table, and the doctor used part of it to cover the face of the tiny form, fashioning the remainder into a weak sling to carry it away. The idea of the Limboia cherishing such a garish, effeminate bag was unbelievably comic, and they left in a mild hysteria, the keeper still smirking uncontrollably.

The doctor had been right. The Limboia were contented, working in the forest with an even greater vigour than before. All seemed to return to normal, in the most abnormal of situations. And then Mrs. Klausen was reported missing.

The rumours arrived just ahead of the police. Her hypochondriacal visit to the doctor had occurred two days before she disappeared, leaving her home and servants without money or explanation. The Die Kripo officers told the doctor all the details, and he told them even more: cysts, headaches, womb pains, night perspirations; varicose veins, haemorrhoids, allergic distress; breast lumps, vapours, and all of the other symptoms he had been invited to probe over the years. He showed them files and medical records and they left, satisfied, but with no new directions. He sat down in the consulting room, a blackness flapping in the pit of his stomach. The beating fear had a shape, and it was brightly embroidered.

———

"We must ask him," he pleaded of the Scotsman.

"Ask him what?"

"What they did with the bag."

Maclish no longer found the Limboia's appropriation of the bag so amusing. The herald was brought down into the central hall, where he stood vacantly, like one hanging on the thickness of the air. His speech had deteriorated since the last time they met; he was not reluctant to answer their questions, but his replies were slow and suspended.

"You give Orm scent from looking, looking inside. After Orm wear it, went out, hollowed for you, all gone."

Maclish and Hoffman looked at each other, desperately hoping they had misunderstood. They whispered to each other and Hoffman asked, "Was the scent that of a female?"

"Scent is spoor, is animal trail for looking out."

"Where did it go to?" cried Maclish.

"Vorrh."

"That's impossible," the doctor said incredulously. "Mrs. Klausen would never go there—I don't think she's ever left Essenwald!"

"Orm hollowed out for you and looking one. Hollow to nothing, nothing left inside, only the rind walked into Vorrh to nothing," the herald said, smiling. He bowed to the startled men as the understanding of what they had done began to seep into them, their eyes meeting in the fearful perception of what they had released and how its hunger could end up devouring them all.

As they left the building, the herald remained in his stooped pose, head bent obsequiously and the smile fixed to his unwavering face.

CHAPTER SIXTEEN

*M*uybridge was ecstatic. Gull had changed his mind. Three months after he declined him at his offices a letter arrived.

DEAR MR. MUYBRIDGE,

I pen this hasty note as a disclaimer to my previously false assumption about photography and my special patients. I now think you were right in your belief about their response to images of them.

Please, the next time you are back in London, let us put your suggestion to a clinical test.

W. W. GULL

Muybridge stood in the leafy suburbs of London, having been redirected from Sir Thomas Guy's hospital by another note, this time held by a surly porter. He was in Forest Hill. The southern railway from London Bridge had deposited him there, where Gull had said his private clinic was situated. He stepped out of the station and into the overly green trees; a coachman waited for him at the roadside. Ten minutes and dozens of green turns later, they pulled in through high metal gates and stopped. He was taken inside by a custodian, or a warder, he thought, a rhino of a man dressed in a long apron over a dark uniform, with a peaked cap that accentuated the man's hornlike nose and low, sloping forehead.

"Thank you, Crane," Gull said to the departing shadow.

"Mr. Muybridge, welcome." He put out his square hand for his visitor to shake, looking about as if to greet another guest. "But where is your equipment?" He looked towards the door; the coachman shook his head.

"I did not bring any," said Muybridge. "I presumed our first preliminary meeting would be more theoretical than practical?"

Gull was mystified and twitched his mouth in a small movement that looked like a rehearsal for a larger one—irritation in advance of anger—before it was quickly gathered back. "Quite right!" he blurted, in a boisterous and obvious lie. "Let me show you the business at hand, and then you can make your professional assessment."

The good doctor took him by the arm and amiably propelled him along the corridors in Crane's wake. Muybridge was instantly ill at ease; being touched was repugnant to him, and not something he tolerated well. He had never understood why so many people, common people, derived such pleasure from pawing one another, even in public. His treacherous wife had demanded these suffocating duties from him. She used to grab at his arm while walking, hanging from the speed of his sprightly gait, complaining about his pace, telling him to slow down, and hanging on even harder if he failed to comply. It had been embarrassing. But when they were alone, she had demanded much worse. He had never refused his husbandly duties. In fact, he quietly enjoyed them in moderation, and practice had improved him in the rigours of their physical exertions. He fulfilled all that might have been expected of him, but she always wanted more: to cling, to kiss, for him to linger inside her, long after his business was done. Some of her requests had been downright offensive, and against all modern notions of hygiene. The worst of it was that she even pawed him in front of the neighbours or the servants, and at social functions to which she had forced him to take her. It had been uncomfortable, unnatural, and thoroughly time-consuming.

Shaking off the horrid recollections, he returned to the present and found that Gull had removed his hand to denote waiting. They stood outside a long, ward-like corridor. The walls were painted in a thick, heavy yellow, more marrow than flower. The same apron-clad guard stood in contrast by the doors. Gull gestured, and the guard pulled an elaborate bolt that slid levers and greased phalanges to open to the ward beyond. It all seemed highly theatrical, more like one of the new zoological gardens than a sanctum of health.

Gull caught the scent of his thoughts and began to explain. "Some of the women here are very unstable, a danger to themselves and others. Their tides of mania and excessive will are beyond discipline or control. Therefore we contain them, and for good reason."

Muybridge felt his excitement grow at the proximity of these demented creatures. The pair walked the corridor and stopped at another door, where Crane stood waiting. Gull nodded and the assistant unlocked it.

"First," said Gull, "I will show you Abigail. She is the one I gave the picture to. She was picked up off the streets, where she was working the Penny Finger trade; she has been here now for nearly eight months."

"But you said this was an affliction of the affluent, not of the poor, not of street women?"

"Quite right!" said Gull. "But to understand a disease you have to find its root. To instigate it from the beginning. So we collect test subjects and create the malady in them. This is the same protocol that grew from vaccine research, but here we apply it to the mind. Those already suffering are only useful to study symptoms—not the cause, effect, and cure: You can't grow a plant from a leaf."

"So the subject of your lecture at Guy's was different from this one?"

Gull looked at him in the way strangers do when they are trying to politely judge the age of a friend's child. "On the surface they are different, yes, but fundamentally they are the same. The one you saw at the lecture hall came into my care with her malady already fully formed. Her family were glad to see the back of her. They would have willingly packed her off to the bedlam, to die in the filth with all those other patients who have caused grievous embarrassment to their parents and siblings. This one came here undernourished but in good spirits— I saved her from a life of rotting on the streets. She will take part in the experiments and then eventually be released, if she is well enough." Muybridge watched the doctor as he spoke, glancing at the guard every so often to gauge a reaction, but both their expressions remained impassive.

"When she first arrived, we treated her like royalty, spoiling her with food, compliments, and fine clothing. She grew fat and weak, and she was soon ready for her first encounter with the Lark Mirror."

"The Lark Mirror?"

"Yes. It's a tool we use in our hypnotic process, not unlike the peripherscope I used for your treatment."

Muybridge did not care for the comparison.

"Anyway, as I was saying, the problem started when we gave Abigail here the picture."

"What was the picture of?" asked Muybridge.

"It was a picture of her, taken three weeks ago. I took your advice and photographed all my special cases."

The news took Muybridge aback. He had offered his services

and been flatly turned down, and now, a few years later, Gull had taken the idea and instigated his own photographic enquiries? He tried to hide his disdain as Gull continued.

"When I gave her the print, she just stared at it. I had to tell her it was her likeness. And then she ate it. Before I could stop her, she stuffed it into her mouth and refused to take it out. By the time Crane arrived to part her jaws, it was gone."

Before the words had time to settle and sting, he opened the door. She was on the far side of the room, standing in the corner. She was skeletal and absent. Only the top part of her body was clothed. A thick blouse that looked many sizes too large was wrapped about her torso. The lower part of her body, from her sternum down, was swathed in bandages, ending in a small, dangling flap for decency.

Her sticklike legs were naked and shivering. Her feet turned inwards and were blue with cold.

"She's undressed again," said Crane, exposing the reality of his below-average intelligence.

"Yes," said Gull calmly. "Cover her up."

A blanket was wrenched from her thin mattress and wrapped around her waist. The guard seated her on the equally skeletal bed.

"Her wounds are healing slowly; it takes a long time when the body has so little to draw from."

"What happened to her?" asked Muybridge.

Gull turned and directed his gaze with withering force into the photographer's unsuspecting eyes.

"She tried to get the picture back. She clawed herself open to find it."

Muybridge yanked his gaze away from the surgeon to look at the frail creature again: her distant, vacant stare; the bandages; her birdlike hands with some of the fingernails broken off. He felt queasy and somehow aroused, one sensation cancelling the other out, making him impassive, becoming for a moment like her.

"If we had not found her in time, she would have bled to death. She ripped her abdominal wall, lost part of her lower intestine, and nicked her fallopian tubes without screaming or making any other sound." Gull was obviously impressed. "Imagine the willpower that would take!"

"Did she use a weapon?" asked Muybridge, already fearing he knew the answer.

"No, sir, that's what I am telling you: She used her bare hands."

"Is that possible?"

"Not to you or I. We would hesitate. The hand would lose its power and only scratch and bruise at our weakness. The human hand is a potent and massively strong mechanism. It is a series of fulcrums and levers worked by tough and dominant muscles. Its sinews and bones are tensile and capable of bearing colossal strain. We barely use a fraction of its potential strength, developing its agile pliancy and delicate touch instead. The hand, without doubt, is an awesome tool. Did you know it is one of the most difficult parts of the human body to destroy? You have to crush and mangle it just to get it to break into smaller parts."

Muybridge was not sure he wanted to know all this, but clearly he had no choice, and Gull galloped on.

"There is an ancient funeral practice in Tibet called 'sky burial.' Deceased monks are carried to a high platform, where their bodies are dissected—butchered, really—into small, devourable pieces. The surgeon-priest then leaves the platform so that a flock of vultures may descend onto the meat table. They then eat every scrap and depart, taking the body of the holy man into the clouds. In this procedure, the hands require the most work. All else is child's play in comparison. To get them shredded enough for the birds to eat takes great effort, heavy, sharp tools, and time." He paused for a breath. "Yes, sir, the hand is a ferocious weapon when sent forth, without doubt."

All four of them fell silent, with not an ounce of communication floating between them. They all looked in different directions, into different worlds, and waited for theirs to begin again.

Muybridge stood with his hands behind his back watching Gull speak.

"I am now working on making direct contact with that ferocious willpower, trying to set aside the starvation obsession, to cleave it from the unique determination it engenders. I am gaining remarkable results: It has been possible to map its mechanism in the brain and produce its exact responses under experimental rigour."

They were walking the corridor again, Gull finally keeping his hands to himself. He had his thumbs hooked into the pockets of his breeches as he strolled past the locked metal doors. There was something unstoppable about his confident posture.

"There is one side effect, however, that does not make clinical sense," the doctor was saying. "There appears to develop a taint of violence in all I have treated or experimented with, as if there is some fundamental correlation between the activation of peripheral sight and the loosening of the moral codes that keep us all in check."

Muybridge was about to ask a question, when the implication of the words hit home.

"There is also some distortion of the libido," Gull continued. "The peripherscope and the Lark Mirror seem to call something wild out of otherwise docile patients; the continual application of the devices seems to heighten these effects in a cumulative manner. In fact, I have some more hypno-optical instruments that I would very much like you to see while you're here."

As he looked at Muybridge's troubled and knotted face, which was again taking on the countenance of a vengeful God crossed with a scolded child, he was interrupted by a long, mournful wailing, a sound so unusual that it arrested all other sounds around it. Muybridge, his own thoughts disturbed, recognised it as a savage animal, exotic and lethal; he had heard such things before and instantly knew it was not native to these shores. On his extensive travels, he had heard the calls of many such feral beasts—perhaps these bolted corridors really did contain a zoo?

Again it sang out, and this time he caught the tincture of its humanity. He had taught himself to listen carefully to many peculiar tongues, to hear and trust his instinct to decode their meaning. This one had the same extreme edges he had heard in the mountain tribes of Guatemala or the Eskimo shudders of the high Alaskan plains; the songs of the nomads of the fallen land bridges to Greenland and the North Pole. It was totally out of place.

"Ah, this will interest you!" Gull pointed to the source of the eerie noise and Crane knocked on the metal door. A few moments later, it was opened by a small bald man wearing a white apron and stiff, red, gutta-percha gloves.

"Good day, Sir William. She is restless again."

"Good morning, Rice. Let's have a look at her, shall we?"

The howling stopped when she saw Gull. Her huge eyes widened and she covered them with her ornate, scarred hands. She had luminous black skin that had been polished into blues and purples by the smooth, uninterrupted breeding of thousands of years. She was slight, but not emaciated like the others, and had a head of statuesque beauty, more horizontal than vertical, like a long lozenge of graceful stone balanced midway on the poised, slender plinth of her neck. Muybridge had seen and met Negroes in America, had seen their plight and their strength. But she was quite a different species.

"Allow me to introduce you to Abungu. We call her Josephine here. Josephine, this is Mr. Muybridge. He is the man who made the picture you so love."

She put her hands down and looked into the photographer's mystified face.

"Show him what you have done with it!"

Crane grabbed at her clothing, trying to pull her into action.

"Leave her, Crane; she will do it herself."

Josephine crossed the room, leaving a trail of water, which seemed to be coming from her underskirts. The men pretended not to notice. She went to a small trunk that had been painted the same colour as the cream cell. She opened it and stood aside; it was full of neatly stacked pieces of paper, all the same size, and all with one rough edge, as if they had been torn from notebooks. The men crossed the room to the trunk and its owner.

"Show him, Josephine," encouraged Gull. She dipped down to retrieve the top sheet and lifted it in front of Muybridge.

"Take it!" said the doctor, using much the same tone as he had with the black woman. Muybridge felt he should say something about being patronised in such a way, but curiosity reigned and he followed the command. He glanced at what he was holding, then looked again in surprise: It was a perfect copy of his print *Phases of the Eclipse of the Sun*. Staring at it more closely, he saw that it was not a photographic print at all, but a drawing made on paper with black ink, identical to the one he had left with Gull years before. Only the five lines of text, which explained its provenance and gave the times of the exposures, had been left out. Each drawing had a hastily scratched "A" in its corner: her signature. Every "A" missed its middle, joining stroke, so that it appeared closer to an inverted "V."

Muybridge looked from Gull, who was stroking his jaw and partially concealing a smile, to the sleek radiance of the woman, whose huge eyes looked right through him, then back at the box full of paper.

"Go ahead, help yourself. She won't mind," said Gull.

He picked up a small wad of paper and examined it. Each image was exactly the same. She had made hundreds of copies of his picture, all signed the same way. Gull saw the question and answered it before it became sound.

"Josephine is remarkable. She constantly surprises us. I once showed her your picture. She could not have looked at it for more than a minute. Some weeks later, after a session with one of my new instruments, she was given some paper, pens, pencils, and ink. She is allowed those; she is one of our passive patients, the only one not showing the disturbing side effects I told you of before. Anyway, she sat down and started making these copies. From the first to the last, they have all been precisely the same. If I gave her paper and ink now she would make another."

Muybridge wanted to ask dozens of questions, but none of them could be answered by Gull, and possibly not by the woman. Feebly, he settled for the easiest.

"Does she know what it is?"

"It's impossible to say; she never speaks."

"But I heard her. Those strange sounds."

"Yes, she makes strange sounds, but never speech. Sometimes she cries like an animal, or sings like a bird: Her cell sounds like a veritable menagerie! But never words, no matter what insistence or inducement is applied."

The man called Rice steered her back to the bed, from where steam was gently rising. Three bowls of water, a towel, and a rubber Higginson tube were under the bed, hastily stowed there when they had arrived midtreatment. Gull gripped Muybridge's cringing arm again and propelled him jovially from the room. They resumed their conversation in Gull's office, which was small and surprisingly sparse.

"It's Josephine I had in mind for your photographic studies. She has an astonishing range of facial expressions. Each of them can be summoned with the aid of a mirror and a bell. I would love to have a record of her before she is gone forever."

"Where is she going?" asked Muybridge blankly.

"She has been here for two years and has been wonderfully responsive to my experiments. She can produce demonstrations of willpower that would stagger you, and there is no trace of any side effects. But I think it is time to stop. I don't want to push her any further. Surgeons have instinct about such matters; it's an unteachable aspect of our profession. It only grows out of experience. I feel that if she went further, she might turn, and that implacable strength might curdle and turn inwards or even worse. But she is stable and healthy now; you saw that for yourself."

"She refuses to speak?"

"Yes. That won't change. It's from her childhood. Deeply rooted. Her parents were brought over here in the last batches of slave cargoes. She was born some years after abolition was finally enforced. She must have experienced some appalling poverty, possibly depravity. Enough to remove her from conversation entirely. But she understands everything. It could be seen as a blessing, having such a beauty graced with silence. None of that endless female prattle that most of us have to put up with." Gull chuckled without mirth. "Anyway, what I want is a series of photographs over the next few years."

"But, sir, I am far too busy to give up so much time on one study. My work in America and beyond demands my constant attention. And I'm not sure a portfolio of medical portraits would sit well with the rest of my oeuvre."

"Quite right. Indeed, I would not ask such a thing of you. You are a busy and important man—I can see that, though I know nothing of your oeuvre or any artistic matter. These pictures would be for my attention and mine alone, a special commission. Let me explain: I am a wealthy man with few expenses except for this little folly. I intend to observe some of my special cases for the rest of their or my life, to see what long-term effects my treatments can have, and maybe adjust them every so often. The laws are changing, and private clinics like this are falling under the same bureaucratic, maternal dogmas that now so blight our major hospitals."

Gull had again fixed him with his demanding stare; it was clear he was determined to have his way.

"So, to the point: I intend to release Josephine and some others. Set them up in their own rooms and keep them fed and well and off the streets. I will do this close to London Bridge, so that I might have easy access to them. In her case, I will rent an extra room and furnish it with photographic equipment to your specification. This means that you may visit her and achieve the portraits whenever you are passing through the city."

Muybridge was tempted. He liked the secrecy of the process: It appealed to his natural and tuned acclivities. He found the woman striking, remarkable even, and he could see that pictures of her would indeed be very fine. But wasn't he being treated like a mere hireling? There was nothing in it to increase his esteem or proffer greater awareness of his talents, and the good surgeon obviously had his own motivation in all of this, though that meant they would surely be protected against any public and malicious rumour. He, too, was a man of position and standing, all of which must remain unassailable and worthy.

"If I were to consider your most singular offer, then I would also need a lockable, secure space for my other optical equipment and inventions. This will enable me to spend more time in London and, consequently, more time with your protégée."

"Quite so!" Gull was delighted at the ease of the transaction. "You shall have a workshop, or a laboratory, or whatever you fellows call it. I can help with the expense of your inventions."

The photographer had taken the bait and was becoming excited. "They are very costly to manufacture and maintain. My current work even runs parallel to your own; there might be overlapping areas of interest."

Gull stood up, misjudging the moment.

"Yes, good, of course. Most interesting. Now, tell me of your whereabouts for the next six months."

Gull's obvious indifference and implied doubt of the value of the photographer's inventions prickled at his guest. They were both men driven entirely by self-interest. Their flywheels had been spinning in separate, but firm, unison, until this slip. Muybridge was coming off the surgeon's hook.

"Before I accept, Sir William, I must say that I have some misgivings about how a project like this might affect my status in society. If I may be so blunt, spending a considerable time alone in the presence of this damaged Negress could be compromising. I have had difficulties with women before, and I normally eschew their company. Not in an unnatural way of course!" he quickly added.

Gull's incredulity unfurled—he was beginning to think his guest a complete ninny. Thousands of men had their mistresses stashed away, all over the good old city; the borough of Walworth was created simply to contain the overflow! And yet, here was this photographer: no position in society, a technician, an artisan. So why was he worrying about his feeble reputation? Gull pulled his thoughts up short. Ninny or not, he needed this man. He was the only one for the job.

"My dear fellow, there is no question of you being compromised. I will make all the arrangements to be certain that our little transaction is utterly clandestine. Your part in this scientific study will be entirely honourable."

His words seemed to smooth the gaunt man's ruffled feathers, and Gull moved to execute a perfect coup de grâce.

"My position in society will protect us both. Since Her Majesty so graciously endowed me with my knighthood, many things have become much easier to obtain and operate. I am fortunate enough to be in constant touch with her and the royal highnesses. They view me as a friend and confidant, as well as their humble physician. In fact"—he leaned towards his guest with implications of confidential undertones—"they have more than once consulted me on the delicate matter of the selection of future peers. Her Majesty has a great interest in the arts and sciences; it will be only a matter of time before a man with such a distinctive reputation as your own is proposed. Who knows? We may both meet in the Upper House before too long." His approach was perfect and placated Muybridge completely. They shook hands on the steps outside and went their separate ways, both men departing in gleeful anticipation of the future.

CHAPTER SEVENTEEN

*T*he Frenchman knew there was something wrong with the food. He had tasted it in the second course. He was now on the ninth, and it was getting worse. The *crème de testicule* had a bitter tang, astringent and disconcerting. The kidneys had been swollen and leathery, and now the foie gras had a sulphurous aftertaste. He dined with one of his urchinous, casual companions. This alone was unheard of: He always had them removed before he bathed and dressed for a solitary dinner. The boy shovelled the food into his emaciation, washing it down with brimming glasses of the Frenchman's favourite wine. He spat while talking, laughing out great gobfuls of exquisite cuisine, which now looked like chewed cud as they flew ungraciously across the shining tablecloth.

The next course smelt like the crystals that the servants used to clean the water-chamber porcelain. He started to gag. The movement roused him and he awoke in the damp mulch of leaves and the naked surface roots of the tree that signified his despair. The glowing table and the gentle candles were gone; twilight had begun to exhale from the trees. Dread swamped him as he bolted into the understanding that this was not the dream.

He stood up and tried to collect himself, tears filling his eyes and choking his swallowing breath. He walked aimlessly away, needing to escape this immediate place that had been the site of declaration, the horrible trees that had witnessed the realisation of his sentence; he had to rid himself of their mocking indifference.

The aftertaste of the acrid food lingered as he pushed through the cool, damp leaves. He found a hollow in one of the long-dead oaks and crawled inside its stiff embrace, the hard fungi breaking off against his shoulders. He scrabbled around to face the outside, the derringer in one hand and a small camping knife in the other. By the time night finally arrived, he had steeled himself for its attack.

The forest grew dim as the shadows lengthened into one continuous form. The world outside of the tree was beyond dark but constantly moving; blue blurs matted with the dense blackness of distance. Things slid and rustled, crawled and flapped, in the infinite depth of closeness. He held his hand before his face to test the old adage. It was true—he could not see it—yet the ebony fluid in his eyes sensed all manner of things swirling within a terrifying proximity. A prayer almost found its way to his lips. It began in the icy fear of his heart, the ventricles white with the frost of anticipation, and travelled outwards to become a pressure, like wind against the meat sails of his lungs. Funnelling up, it passed like a shadow through the rehearsal of his vocal cords, up into his mouth, tongue, and lips, before being garrotted by the thin, taut wire of his mind. No heart word would ever pass that frontier unchecked; not even a hollow, sapless tree was allowed to hear that hypocrisy.

Towards what might be dawn, he slept. By the morning, no creature had worried him, and a vague sense of hope had begun to return. Perhaps he could survive? Maybe he had some deep, inspired understanding of the wilderness. Many great explorers underestimated their gift until confronted by extreme adversity; his inventive mind might be capable of transcending these base afflictions. Other, lesser beings had triumphed before when tested thus.

He was beginning to feel the warm flood of confidence, when he saw his boots. They had been handmade in Marseille, adventure boots, worn to confound and conquer the savage lands. The straps that held them in place had been eaten through, gnawed away, so that only stubs remained on either side of the nibbled leather tongue. He sat bolt upright to observe the outrage, wiping the morning dew from his eyes and face. It was sticky and pungent. He looked at what he had removed and sank with the realisation that it wasn't dew: It was saliva. He was soaked in it. He scrabbled to his feet, banging his head and knees against the rough interior of the gnarled oak, causing a shower of dry fungi to crumble and snow about his departure. He lurched out of the tree's vertical enclosure, flailing at his wet clothes and his soggy hair in a pathetic attempt to wipe the mess away. His indifferent boots became loose and vacant, twisting away from his agitated feet, so that he stumbled over them on the wet, thorny ground, which grabbed at his socks and bare ankles. He yelped, hopped, and slid, falling facedown into a gully full of mud and harsh stones, the derringer firing a deafening, burning blast.

He lay there, hoping he was dead. Nothing had ever been as bad as this; his Paris apartment seemed like a dream he had never had. Then, with the pistol's fire still ringing in his ears, he heard Seil Kor's voice, far off but distinct.

"Seil Kor!" he bellowed frantically. "Seil Kor!" He called again and again and then got a clear reply.

"Do not move, effendi! Just call; I will come to you."

This they did for hours, without success. Sometimes his voice seemed farther away, lost in the depths and twists of the vast, impenetrable forest's endless animal trails. Two or three times, the Frenchman heard something move in the thickets of trunks and leaves, but it was not his salvation; more likely, it was his demise stalking him, the recent taste of his body on its breath. He plucked the reloaded derringer from his pocket and turned a full circle. Then he saw it. Far back in the trees, a hunched, grey creature was watching him. He could not make out its form; it might even have been human. A twig snapped behind the Frenchman and he spun in the opposite direction.

"Effendi!"

Seil Kor was coming towards him, parting the leaves with a purposeful grace.

He rushed to the tall figure and flung his arms around him, bursting into tears, his diminutive, brightly robed body shaking against the protection of the quiet black man. He was saved. Then he remembered the thing watching him, and he untangled himself, looking back to see if it was still there. It had moved to a point a little farther away, shadowed but still watching. He clutched Seil Kor with one hand and pointed with the other.

"Do you see it?" he asked.

"Yes, but I wish I did not."

"What is it?"

There was a long pause while Seil Kor again made the gesture of moving his hand above his head. The creature moved into a patch of bright light. It was a kind of human. Its skin was grey and wrinkled, like that of a primate deprived of fur. It was motionless in their observation.

"What is it?" he asked again.

"I fear it is Adam," answered Seil Kor.

The Frenchman coughed out a single, uncontrollable laugh. Its nervous splutter startled the creature, who loped into the foliage.

"Adam?" said the Frenchman, the sound of the laugh still wet in his mouth.

There was no sound from Seil Kor, whose drooped eyes were full of remorse.

"Seil Kor?"

There was still no answer.

"Seil Kor, that animal is barely human. How can it be Adam? He would be thousands of years old by now."

"The Bible says that Adam died," said Seil Kor. "It even says that the tree planted on his grave grew into the wood that became the true cross." He looked out into the trees and started to walk away from the place of the sighting. "We must go. We have come too far."

The Frenchman tried to follow but had to stop to retrieve his gnawed shoes, slipping them on loosely and trying to hold them in place with his bunched toes.

"Please, wait!" he called ahead.

Seil Kor stopped walking, his back towards the shuffling dandy. As the Frenchman drew near, he began to walk on, without a word or any indication that they were travelling together. His pace was slow to allow the Frenchman to follow. He seemed to know where they were and where he was going. After many awkward moments and several turns, they reached a broader path. The widening space vented some of the tension between them, and the Frenchman's queries bubbled uncontrollably to the surface.

"Please, Seil Kor, tell me more," he implored. "I assure you I will listen this time." He looked beseechingly at his guide, who considered him evenly before slowly beginning to speak.

"There are different Bibles, with different tales," said Seil Kor. "In these regions, the truth is told. Adam was never completely forgiven; his sons and daughter left this place and occupied the world. He waited for God, waited for forgiveness and for his rib to grow back. But he became tired of waiting and walked back into the forest. The angels that protected the tree let him pass because there was nothing else for him to do in that sacred place. But in his absence, God forgot him, and so he has remained. Each century he loses a skin of humanity, peeling back through the animals to dust. This is what I was reading to you when you went away."

There was real upset in Seil Kor's voice, and for the first time the Frenchman realised that his affections for the young man were reciprocated. All that nonsense about Eden had been his way of bringing them closer.

"I did not understand before," he said. "Will you forgive me and tell me more of your wondrous book?"

Seil Kor turned, looking deep into his companion. "You have much to learn," he said, smiling slowly, "and I will teach you. But we must leave this place quickly."

The Frenchman took his outstretched hand and they walked together through the flickering foliage.

They were still talking about Adam when he thought he recognised the broader track as the one that would lead towards the station and, hopefully, the waiting train. He had endured quite enough of this. Even with Seil Kor's fanciful stories and his warming presence, he wanted to be back in the hotel with hot water and cold wine. His ankles and toes hurt from the exertions needed to keep his ruined shoes intact. The bruises, cuts, and insect bites rubbed incessantly against his stained robes, the texture of which now expressed itself as irritant and rough. Dried saliva still covered him and had turned rank and sticky under the humid heat of the forest, its persistent odour seeming to have gained access to every pore of his exhausted body.

"Adam will never leave now," Seil Kor was musing. "The angels have grown old and weary in the forest; perhaps they have forgotten their purpose. Perhaps God has forgotten them all."

"How much farther do we have to walk?" asked the Frenchman, realising that he had recognised the wrong track and that there was no sign of the rail line.

"Two more hours," answered Seil Kor.

➡

Tsungali's hand guided Uculipsa out in a long, slow motion, the gleaming bolt pulled back and forth to load one of the charmed, .303 rounds into the breech. The nose of the rifle poked through the bushes, sniffing at the voices that were approaching.

Tsungali pulled the eager rifle back; it was not his prey. He slid the bolt open and removed the cartridge, placing it in one of the charm pouches he wore on a bandolier. He did not see the thin trace of string escape from the flap of the pouch, the low, damp air catching it in a gust of heated breath. Every bird in the immediate vicinity took off in a startlingly discordant flapping of wings. Tsungali's gaze twisted up sharply and he observed them in keen suspicion, as they filled all the spaces in the sky between the leaves of the canopy.

➡

Seil Kor and the Frenchman also stopped in their tracks to look towards the shudder in the trees.

The string drifted, kneading the atmosphere, eager to find its host. It possessed an astonishing longevity and was capable of lying dormant, but sprung, for years, until the heat or scent of a passerby triggered its urgent jump and vampire attachment. On this day, it would have only a few minutes to wait.

CHAPTER EIGHTEEN

Ghertrude was feeling lonely and out of step with her life. Since the end of the carnival and Ishmael's departure, everything had seemed dimmer and without flavour. She felt flat and unexcited by the city and her diminishing secret in it.

She turned the corner into Kühler Brunnen and was nearing the house, head down and mind elsewhere, when she almost collided with a figure standing at the gate. The woman was taller and older than Ghertrude, with eyes she would never forget. They looked down at her, absorbing every particle of sight, every ounce of meaning. She had obviously been waiting for her.

"Mistress Tulp!" She beamed in a triumph that seemed without reason. "Please allow me to introduce myself. I am Cyrena Lohr," she said, holding out her hand. "I believe our families are already acquainted? May I call you Ghertrude?"

She had heard of this woman: Everybody had; if not before the miracle of the carnival, then certainly after. She suddenly knew that they had met once before, when she was a child and the beautiful blind stranger was put in her care at one of the grand parties of the city's gentry. Or perhaps it had been the other way around? But there was certainly a memory of vast rooms and music, of being separate and in the company of an elegant blind woman. She remembered being able to stare at her, to examine her without politeness, and to think about what blindness meant for the first time. Her sight then had probed the blackness of the beautiful, dead eyes, which were now more than alive and staring down at her.

"Of course, Mistress Lohr," she answered to the barely remembered question.

"Then you must call me Cyrena, if we are to be friends."

Ghertrude was taken aback by the speed of this assumption and was about to answer when she realised that Cyrena was staring at the locked door.

"Oh, I am sorry. Please do come in," she said, fumbling for the keys in her pockets.

Inside, they sat at the kitchen table and talked about their mutual acquaintances, their memories and experiences of being the city's chosen daughters. Ghertrude's uncertainty at their introduction was beginning to pass when, without warning, Cyrena smiled and broke all the rules.

"Forgive me, my dear, for asking such a taboo question, but I simply must know: Who did escort you to the beginning of the carnival frivolities?" Ghertrude fluttered and flushed while trying to remain calm and indifferent. The hungry eyes saw all and pressed harder.

"I am not asking you to be indiscreet or break a confidence, but I owe something to the gentleman concerned and I am anxious to pay."

"Are you sure we are talking about the same person?" questioned Ghertrude, clutching at straws and finding it impossible to conceive of any situation where the unlikely pair may have met.

"I do hope so," said Cyrena. She described the costume without ever having seen it. She described it well, and Ghertrude's blush turned to an anxious pale. Cyrena saw the truth behind her blanching and knew her game had been cornered.

"His name is Ishmael," Ghertrude said reluctantly. "He was my friend; he lived in this house."

"Lived?" repeated Cyrena. "Where is he now?"

"He left weeks ago; I don't know where for," she lied.

The older woman stood abruptly, obviously agitated. Ghertrude approached her and touched her shivering arm.

"Why do you need to find him?" she asked.

The unwavering eyes locked on hers with an indescribable eeriness. "It was he who gave me my sight," she said.

The sharp, rank electricity stung her nose and slapped her brain. She instinctively tried to push the glass bottle away from her airway, but Cyrena held it there firmly until the smelling salts had proved to work. Ghertrude gasped for breath as the older woman held her firmly in the upright chair, one hand on Ghertrude's forehead and her other arm hugging the woozy younger lady across her back.

"It's all right, my dear. You have only fainted," she said.

The nauseous zebra vision ceased and Ghertrude bounced back to the dazed reality of Cyrena's revelation. "Ishmael did that?" she whispered. "But how?"

Reseating herself at the table, Cyrena began to explain the situation of that amazing night. She explained it frankly and perhaps with too much detail. This time, they both blushed, but she continued with the extraordinary story, and Ghertrude's mind slowly accustomed itself to the depth of Ishmael's festive experiences. As Cyrena related the exquisite interactions of their encounter, Ghertrude began to realise the terrible truth of the event, the one feature that couldn't have been exchanged by their actions alone. She wished she could undo her involvement, but it was too late; nothing should be held back now. There was no place for deception or half-truths between them.

"Did . . ." Ghertrude hesitated, throwing a sidelong glance at her new friend. "I only wondered . . . did you never see his face?"

The younger woman took charge of the smelling salts. Cyrena had not fainted, but the news had sent her reeling back, like a short, sharp punch to the chest.

"You mean he was born with only one eye?" She gaped.

"Yes. It is here, in the centre of his face." Ghertrude pointed to the area just above her nose. "It takes time," she said gently, "but you get used to it. After a while, you only see him."

"But, there was no sign that he was so deformed; I had no idea! The mask, the mask . . . it . . . He felt normal!" Cyrena ran out of words as she remembered the events of that night and struggled to hold back tears.

"He is not like us," Ghertrude said, shaking her head. "Not like us at all."

The day passed. Ghertrude fetched a bottle of Madeira and two glasses. They sat by a window as they drank, watching the sun set over the Vorrh. She told the stranger, fast becoming a friend, much about their life together in 4 Kühler Brunnen, but not about the beginning. Though she ached to tell somebody of the abnormalities in the basement, to share that impossible truth, she knew that, without any evidence, she would sound deranged, incredible. Who would ever believe such a story? She looked at Cyrena: Might it be her? Might this strong, clever woman, who made her feel childlike again and curiously protected, be understanding of such a tale?

"I must still find him," Cyrena was saying. "Whatever he is, wherever he has gone, he has changed my life completely."

Ghertrude sighed and let the last crumbs of denial fall to the kitchen floor. "He said he was going to the Vorrh," she declared. It sounded like a pact.

➤—→

Later, Cyrena sat in her favourite room, the one with the wrought-iron balcony outside. She used to spend hours there, over-sensing the city, its aromas and sounds shaping a landscape of poignant, knitted contentment and longing. One of her favourite times was the evening, when the city's sounds folded down to allow the distant forest its full voice. She loved to feel the exchange, the tides of human and animal sounds passing each other in the growing dominance of night.

Her sighted friends (and all were) had always said that she had marvellous perception of the world they shared. Over the years, they had learned not to lead their conversations with descriptions of sight. Cyrena had never minded, but she could always sense their embarrassment when they inadvertently referred to appearance or invited her to look at something; little words that created errors in their shared reality, small slips in perceptual reciprocation.

High above, the swallows turned into bats, foraging the sky for its shoals of insects. The birds' tiny, sharp cries were like single stars, calling for a fraction of a second out of a constellation of glittering darkness; they became the stars she had never seen. Her first sightings of the swifts in the bright air had delighted her. Their spinning and darting were faster than anything she could have ever imagined, their spatial acrobatics instantly displacing her previous image of pinprick chirps echoing from a vast distance. At first, it had been a more-than-adequate barter, but over the weeks their sky weaving had become predictable; dismally, unimaginatively attached to the food chain. Other things in her eyes were also beginning to flatten and become commonplace. The colours of her furnishings had started to pall. They had invigorated her in the beginning, their richness accentuated by their textures, which had once been their greatest appeal. Now they seemed to jump unpredictably, or daze the depth of the room; with sight, things seemed smaller and somehow pinching.

Perhaps it was the recent meeting that had so depressed her. The Tulp girl had given a little friendship, but it had been a very slight compensation for the greater loss. Her expectations had been single-minded: Their reunion that day had been the only option she had considered; she had pictured every detail of the moment. If "pictured" is the right word; in truth, her anticipation had not been shaped by her visual imagination at all. It had been carefully sculpted out of touch and sound, his presence bolder in the contours of those memories than anything she had seen since the miracle. Ghertrude's descriptions had made it worse. How could she accommodate this ugly portrait with the sweeping clarity of the beauty of that night? Her new eyes were bringing more disappointment to her than she could have ever anticipated. They shunted in a continuous torrent of irrelevant detail for her to respond to and process; she feared that the profundity and articulation of her previous world was being frittered away, erased by an endless low tide of brightness and an infinite shingle of pictures.

And yet, it must be sacrilege to think such things. Everybody gave such enraptured sermons about "the prime sense" and how wonderful it was that she had gained it—how could she be so ungrateful? How could she secretly long for the uninterrupted, dark containment of the world she had always known as reality? But sight made her lonely, and she had never been that before. The indifference of the world was jarringly apparent, and its knotted, adamant distance had begun to shrink everything she had ever achieved. It dwindled all she understood, and the intimacy where she once dreamt was engulfed by loud and vulgar light that always spoke of the space between things.

The doubts suddenly ignited an obvious omission in her celebrations. She had shared the miracle with all around her, but she had forgotten one, the only one who really understood her sightless world. The one who had asked her to imagine sight and had changed her childhood in a way she had never understood. Uncle Eugene. How could she have been so thoughtless? She did not strain at the question, because the answer was a shadow, a sourness; it was her doubt, her anxiety, that made her remember him, because those were the tones of his being. He would understand. She would write and try to explain, to describe the bouts of sadness that came from nowhere, and he would advise her, tell her why light felt like treachery.

The evening light drifted towards her, licking at her little resolve; it tugged at her need but she shook it off and sat down to compose the earnest letter in its sulking wake.

Many minutes had passed since her moment of insight. As she wrote, a glass vase of fresh flowers billowed between her and the evening outside. The swifts were darting and spinning in the cooling air, their squeaks and dizzying speed calling her. She wanted to go out onto the balcony and listen to them, but the vase and its contents blocked her way. The colours held her at bay, their breath growing violent and unfurled. Plants had held little meaning in her life until now; she had never before understood the insistence of their horrid pressure and omnipresent existence.

This bunch had been a gift. A well-meant but unnecessary mob of growth and vibrancy, just one of the many visual feasts bestowed on her with an overgenerous zeal by friends and strangers eager to celebrate her new sense, her new affinity with their ranks.

The vase was crowned by a bloated roar of colour. She decided to really look at the uncompromising entities within; she thought her maid had called them peonies, but she could not be sure. They had straight, confident stems that bristled with hairs and spikes, presumably to keep the subtle mouths of beasts and the nimble beaks of birds at bay. The leaves were long and pointed, catching every shudder of breeze from the balcony and giving the obstacle a faint animation, a lure just large enough to trap the casual eye into looking. At the end of the stalk gloated the flower. There were two varieties here, scarlet and pink, and they both shared the same salacious contours. Each head was like a bowl of crushed silk, opening out to reveal its dense, heavy layers and display the complex folds of its interior with a powerful relish. The petals curled and ruffled to catch any saccade and pull it in, so that a maximum density of viewing was folded in on itself. All human sight was sucked towards a central concentration, a habitual, swollen funnel, like the mouth at the centre of an octopus's beak, demanding to be fed by all its arms. The blooms seemed designed for the eye, matching their own craving to humanity's visual gluttony; they even mimicked its anatomy, once the external ball was peeled away. A dozen or so of the bright, rumpled orbs moved at a speed concealed from her hectic eyes. Others stirred more positively, picking up the passing breeze, nodding in what seemed like a smug, taciturn agreement among themselves. Their vanity appalled; she could see the strain of opening as they demanded to be seen, the hinge at the base of each petal bending under the pressure, stressing until they fatigued and fell loose, leaving a swollen, pregnant ovary. That was the extent of their purpose: to gush colour and expose the wrinkles of their complexities;

to attract admiration and excited insects and perpetuate the fertilisation of their kind.

The more she looked, the more she saw the extravagant blooms as an insolent, mimicking raid on her eyes and a mocking sham of her womanhood. Their heads nodded in agreement, grinning in a pretence that lay between frailty and obese saturation, and her indignance overflowed. She could have rung the bell and called the maid to take the odious creations away, but that would have been too easy. She clenched her teeth at the thought of being defeated by these wretched weeds that shouted denial at her sensibilities. Then, without plan or agreement, she snapped shut the lids of her perfect eyes, walked forward, and picked up the vase; it slopped water onto her dress and all over the floor. She clasped it to her bosom like a troublesome child and walked purposefully across the room to the open door of the balcony, stepping out into the evening air as the peonies slid sideways in their vase, clinging together in an unordered, clammy sheath. At the far end of the balcony, she opened her eyes briefly and looked down into the corner of the enclosed garden. It was deserted. Closing off her vision once again, she lifted the swilling weight up and over the iron balustrade. The immense weight pulled at her joints, almost levering apart the clamped lids of her eyes. Then she let go, and a great gulp rose from the earth beneath, to meet the vase as it plunged through a long and delicious time before smashing, in glorious auditory technicolour, on the patio below. She remained there for a long, luxurious moment, arms stretched out, her eyes still shut, looking like an enchanted sleepwalker, smiling triumphantly on the edge of a precipice.

Rumours tend to spread like ripples, circular waves moving out from a point of incident. In cities, they stop for a moment when they reach the outer walls, especially when the city in question is circular. Against those arcs of fact and protection, they are questioned, the hard litmus of stone, straw, and lime interrogating their origin and validity, in the same way as those who camp outside, dreaming of entrance and stability, are made to prove their origins. If the story stands, it is filtered to the outside world in muted or fragmented form.

When the miracle of the carnival reached the dispossessed and the injured who sulked in the shadow of the walls, a great stench of hope rose, its heat cooking the story and causing a bubbling at the gates. That was when they started to arrive at Cyrena's home. Not having the nerve to knock at the lofty door, they loitered outside her garden walls, hoping for a sight, if sight was in them, of the blessed lady, believing that proximity might affect their damaged condition, that radiance might mend.

Chalky and his sister had found their way there hand in hand, begging their path to the ivy-covered wall. They carried white sticks, but, unlike those that Cyrena had so recently burnt, theirs had been cut each year from the forest and painted white by their father. Chalky's eyes had been taken by flies when he was a child. They had crawled over him from the moment he'd left the womb, suckering and sweeping his sweaty skin, before leaving their eggs buried in his pupils at the age of three. It was not a rare occurrence in the village where he was born, but outside, on the road to the city, it prompted pity from passing travellers, and a slight income appeared in his father's life.

Exactly how his sister had gone blind was unknown. It had been sudden, having taken place in the middle of the night; all she remembered was the pain and the feeling that she was being held down, tangled in her gripping, sleeping sheet. Since then they had travelled the viable road together, bringing in an even larger revenue for the insatiable old man. The picture of them hand in hand, foraging by the busy track, would melt the hearts

of travellers and prise open their usually reluctant purses. Their
father did not know they were here; he assumed they were stopping the traffic outside the city with their tragic appearance, not
in it, standing at the door of miracle.

The story they had heard told of a grand lady who invited
blind people to her home during carnival. The house had been
bursting with them; the rattle and tap of their sticks could be
heard outside, like the beaks of storks sounding from the rooftops. Perhaps she might make an exception outside of carnival
time for two so young and needy?

They arrived to find others lurking below the wall, sense
depleted and seeking supernatural intervention in their grubby,
alienated lives. Chalky, filled with the courage of lost hope,
tapped gently on the garden door. His approach was answered by
a deafening explosion of glass, as if some terrible, angry weapon
of water and crystal had erupted on the other side of the wall.
His sister clutched his hand and they staggered quickly from the
scene, in fear of such a reply, or of being blamed for the calamity
that had just so violently transpired. Most of the crowd ran with
them, leaving only a few behind to watch the sudden exodus in
surprise. They were the deaf ones.

➤──→

Ishmael was thirsty. He had finished his supply of water the day
before and was following a track that seemed straighter than the
others but was, in truth, identical to the rest. He had walked so
many since turning his back on the city and pointing himself
into the depth of the forest. He had resolved to never take a fork-
ing path that curved to the right or the left, and instead sought
only straight paths, knowing that even they could be deceptive
and capable of making him walk in circles.

This was a truth he had learned in one of his lessons with the
Kin; something about navigation and sense of direction. What

at the time of its telling seemed difficult and abstract now hovered over his will like a halo or a beacon in the night. "Humans always walk in circles"—this is what Seth had said, adding that human beings were faulty in their alignment; they were off balance, permanently tilted from birth. Even placing one foot in front of another and staring straight ahead was not a remedy.

But he was now sure that he was not human. Maybe some part of him had been gleaned from there, but not his whole. He was unique, and his dealings with the women had proven that. He would not be sullied by their fears or crippled by their imperfection. All their ailments and stupidity meant nothing to him, and here, in the midst of the Vorrh, they all seemed petty and trivial. None of the hurt and shame had lasted past his fifth hour among the trees. He was unbridled, and the yoke of his previous emotions lay in discarded ruins at the entrance of his new life.

He had slept in patches throughout the days and the nights, always facing towards the inner direction of the forest. He had spent nights in sandy hollows or in a trampled nest of undergrowth. Once, he had tried sleeping in a tree but found that it attracted attention from the things that dwelt there.

He and the Vorrh were beginning to converse, and he was finding a pleasure in its growing strangeness. He knew he would have to hunt and forage it soon. The loaf of bread, water, and wine he had hastily brought were gone, and his body was starting to complain, the pangs of hunger and thirst and his aching feet confirming his corporeality. Perhaps, as he got deeper, these too would burn off and he would change, evolve into a different being. He would have tasted and spoken the possible names of such an original entity if his tongue were not encrusted to the wall of his mouth and his throat blocked with sand and emptiness.

As he tramped forwards, he noticed a stone blocking the slender path ahead of him. He approached it, and the rock focused its smooth contours from a supposed stone to an earthenware bowl, containing pure, fresh water. He marvelled at the miracle, seemingly conjured by his thirst, and sniffed at its cool freshness. In only a few seconds, he had swallowed every drop, drinking it with relish. His thirst quenched, he took a closer look at the mysterious bowl. Its shell was that of unfired nut, packed rigid with mud and still showing evidence of the finger marks of its maker. The prints were tiny; the hands of a child, he thought absently, his brain still soaking up the fluid and its function. He put the bowl in the sack that he carried over his shoulder and resumed his journey through the trees.

The animals in the forest seemed tamer than those he had passed on his way out of the city, indifferent to him, as if they carried none of the natural fear that most creatures have of the earth's most bloodthirsty predator. Or perhaps it was his differences that affected them; perhaps only double eyes carried that taint? He had seen a snake lift its head at the side of the track, its flickering tongue tasting the molecules of his being. Several times, small, deer-like creatures calmly watched him pass without starting in the slightest. He was beginning to feel that he was continuously under surveillance, that the trees and their occupants were watching him; it made him feel safer, somehow, protected from afar.

Several hours passed, and he stopped to rest, pulling the final chunk of hard, stale bread from his pack. He longed for something more substantial, remembering the dishes prepared for him in the secret basement so very long ago. The memory suddenly seemed so close to him, as though the aroma of cooked potatoes was wafting through the air at that precise moment. Then he realised: This was no mirage—he could smell food!

Startled, he clambered to his feet and looked around. A few feet behind his resting place was another bowl, filled with steaming-hot food. He laughed at it, astonished, then plucked the dish out of the grass and held it to his nose, savouring the luscious scent of potatoes cooked in a rich sauce and gladdened with sage.

"Is there somebody here?" he called out. No answer came back.

He prodded the warm food and tasted his finger. Within minutes he had devoured every scrap. It was excellent, so similar to the dishes the Kin had made for him. Could they be there with him, in the dense foliage? The thought brought back a great and unexpected wave of emotion, one he had never allowed himself before, not since the day of their desertion. The delayed comprehension of his loss overpowered him, and he started to weep in the forest clearing, the warm, earthen bowl in his hand and the taste of his innocence in his mouth. He choked back the unexpected tears and called out again, this time with hope.

"Who is here?!"

Nothing came back, but he sensed a different kind of stirring in the undergrowth and spun to face it.

"Please, if anyone is there . . . !"

Nothing met his ears but the sound of birds. For the first time, he thought about returning to the city. He had been foolish to believe that some remnant of the Kin might be here. If he had really wanted to find them, he would have done so before, in the house where they had lived, not in this twisted wilderness of plants and miracles. In frustration, he packed his meagre belongings and stalked deeper into the trees, watching the bends of the narrow path curl and curve with his changing moods.

An hour later, he found another bowl of water, placed neatly and noticeably in the centre of his route, and he guessed they might be leading him safely towards the forest's interior. He felt energised and protected, reassured that his path was cared for and significant. Again, he thought of the Kin skulking around him, the bright, dappled light camouflaging their shiny brown bodies with ocelot intensity.

➤

Cyrena left her house at noon for another meeting with Ghertrude Tulp, intent on forging a plan of campaign to find Ishmael before he became irrevocably lost. As she walked through her garden to leave by the side gate, she slowed under the balcony to look up for a moment, then back down at the hard ground where the vase had smashed. Naturally, there was no trace of it: Her enduring kindness to her servants kept them diligent and discreet. She felt a brief shudder of satisfaction before exiting into the narrow street that ran parallel to her garden wall. Her mind, indulging in the private pleasures of rebellion, barely registered the shabby figures that loomed outside her wall, and she would have missed their presence entirely if one of them had not addressed her directly.

"Pardon, lady. Pardon us being here so."

She blinked and stopped and found herself without speech. There were six of them—all of different ages and sizes—standing together beneath the shadow of her wall. The young man closest to her spoke again, and the juxtaposition of his polite tone and his undeniable poverty amazed her; yet again, sight had given too much information and poisoned his sad voice.

"We've come here to you, lady, to be healed. It is said that you make blind people see and deaf people hear; that's why we've come."

She looked into his milky eyes to ease the shock of his words; then her own eyes darted to find the lame and diseased parts of them all. "I am truly very sorry"—she faltered—"for you all. But I am afraid you are mistaken. I can help nobody. It was I who was healed by another."

A sinking silence ensued, and those who were able exchanged

suspicious glances. The spokesman sensed the unrest and pressed further. "Who was it who healed you? Are they here? Are they inside?" He pressed his hand against the wall, some loose stone crumbling beneath his touch. Her pity transformed to annoyance at the thought of them dogging poor Ishmael.

"He left weeks ago," she said, hearing the flutter in her voice.

"Where's 'e gawn, then?" said another, this time without a trace of politeness.

"I don't know. He did not tell me; he just left."

They moved forward into the gap she had created, to hear her voice more carefully. "Why did 'e go then? What made 'im? Did you chuck 'im out? Chuck somthink at 'im?"

Terror crawled in her sight; she had never known intimidation before. Her fears had always been internal and speculative, only walking in the cloisters of her imagined future. This was very real, and she was losing authority over its direction.

"I don't know what you mean and have had quite enough of this!" she said curtly. "Now, I must be going. I'm already late. Please do not loiter around my door any longer!"

She turned to leave, but a figure stepped out from behind her, blocking her path. He had been born without eyes or nose; smooth planes of skin covered the areas where the sockets and nostrils should have been. He reeked of vomit and gastric juices and was laughing in astonishing proximity to her face.

"Well, now, m'lady, that's no way to talk to folk who have come a long way to see ya, is it? Especially when you bin one of us!" He lurched and grabbed her by the arm, his roughness too quick for her coddled reflexes. She struggled but he gripped harder, leering and laughing uncontrollably. "What's wrong, miss, don't ya fancy me?"

Incensed, she drew back her right hand and slapped him across his featureless face. He bellowed with laughter. "You'll 'ave to do a lot better than that!"

They scuffled in a tight circle in the dirt of the road, her skin bruising and burning as he tried to pull her down, the others closing in to watch or listen to the fray, when suddenly he stopped, his hands covering his face. Everything became stationary; only the dust still moved in swirls around their ankles, beginning to swoop and settle about their feet. He let his hands drop to his sides, and a gasp rippled through the sighted members of the crowd.

"What is it?" bleated one of the blind. "What's happened?"

The question was greeted with silence. The scene before them was impossible, a blackly comedic spectacle of ugliness. Two slits had appeared beneath the brow of the man's face, small incisions that seemed to be deepening, like cuts in fresh pastry. A clear fluid flowed out, something nameless and unfamiliar. A terrible awe fell upon the crowd.

Cyrena was frozen to the spot, eyes fixed to the horror as her thumbs probed her fingers, checking for ornate rings and plausible explanations, anything that could have split his flesh so swiftly. The man was probing his face repeatedly, pressing his fingers into the slits, making them gape in wide, uneven "O's." They gave him an expression of imbecilic amazement, as if he had been drawn by a child, his eyes rendered as two irregular, hastily penciled dots. "I got eyes," he said, the crowd too gobsmacked to correct him. He waved his wet fingers in the air, seeming not to notice as all around him shrank away. "Eyes! I got *eyes!*"

Cyrena jolted out of her shock and rushed at the gate, her keys still miraculously secure in her other hand. Nobody tried to stop her, and those nearest to her cowered away from the power of her speeding presence. She was inside before sense restored itself to them, and swiftly locked the gate as the cries of "Eyes! Eyes! Eyes!" yelped behind her. She ran to the house and slammed the door behind her, hoping to shut out the noise of her spiralling life.

As she attempted to calm herself with a pot of exotic tea, Cyrena sat and reflected on what had just passed. There was no way that her hands could have inflicted those wounds—if wounds were what they were. She examined the flat of her hand again. There was nothing there to cause more than a slap. So how could she have made that happen? There was only one explanation, and it was not one she considered easily. She regarded the balcony warily, then crossed to the doors, opening one just enough for the faint breeze to edge its way in and catch the fine hairs on her neck. Beyond the wall, a rise of discordant voices still made jagged sounds; cries of ecstasy and abuse, amplified by passion. She called her servant to her side with feigned ignorance.

"Myra, why is there such a commotion outside the gate?" she asked, with suitable distance.

"I'm not sure, ma'am," the girl said in surprise. "I'll send Guixpax to see." She left and Cyrena sat in the plush window seat, sipping at her tea and trying to appear ambivalent, while secretly straining to catch a shard of word from beyond the muffling wall. Down below, Guixpax, the gatekeeper and gardener, had been outside, and Myra returned with news from the street.

"It's rather unusual, ma'am," said Myra nervously.

"Go on, girl. I want to know!"

"Well, it seems there is a poor, deformed madman outside; the crowd are calling him a miracle worker!"

"A miracle worker?" Cyrena asked nervously.

"Yes, ma'am! Apparently he walked straight up to a blind man and . . ."

The girl hesitated, her excitement faltering.

"And?" demanded her mistress.

Myra bit her lip. "His sight came back, ma'am!" she exclaimed, her eyes examining the carpet. "It's a miracle, just like yours!"

Cyrena's eyes cooled knowingly on the waiting servant. The girl had crossed an unforgivable line, and even the kindest of mistresses could never accept such impertinence; it was the final straw after the disgusting incident outside her gate. With her head still full of the hideous language and the stink of peasants, she turned her hard back against Myra and made her voice ten degrees colder than her eyes. "Dismissed," she said.

Later that night, she could not meet her own eyes as she brushed her hair before the bedroom mirror. She had always done it there, ever since she was a child; her mother had taught her so, in the warm greyness of her daughter's sightless space. She closed her eyes tight against this moment and tried to grasp something positive in all that had happened. Perhaps she had been too harsh towards her servant, too quick in her response? But it had been *her* miracle, and not the property of others. It was not something to be shared, begged, or taken.

In her bed, she was sure she could still hear the crippled mob whispering down in the street, their blind eyes seeking her like darting fireflies in the hot darkness.

Over breakfast the next morning, Cyrena learned that the newly sighted man who had insulted her had touched a lame girl, who was then able to crawl off without pain. This rumour confirmed her fears that the miraculous gift had been passed on and was now turning into a kind of wondrous game of tag, a contagious gift of healing. The news made her feel hollow and deepened her isolation. She stayed in the house and gave orders only to Guixpax.

Soon after, she was informed that the healed girl had gone blind while cleansing a leper, and something akin to gratification passed through her shrunken soul. The purity and originality of her own miracle had not been taken. In the sick hands of those who had been cruel to her, the benediction had turned septic and been passed on, a blessing defiled into a curse.

CHAPTER NINETEEN

*T*sungali was closing. His canoe was loaded with everything he needed: He did not trust this country to sustain him, and he wanted nothing to do with its people. He felt healed and strong, and the paddlings had refreshed him. He could feel the river knot and buckle around the slender boat, its muscle and his balance taut, as one. He could steer it by his chakra alone, turning his hips at its fulcrum, snug below the waterline, only a thin skin between it and his centre.

The *Leo* appeared ahead, and he quickly estimated his distance from his target. As the two vessels passed, each man watched the other through slanted eyes, looks that held each other across the sliver of their crossing. Each guessed the other's identity, and the suspicion polished their eyes to steel. They were no more than forty feet apart, and passing fast.

Tsungali's Enfield, like the boatman's shotgun, stayed cocked and flush against its master's leg, turning with him to secure their continued passage upstream. Only when the men were out of each other's sight did they turn away and face their own direction. Tsungali's hackles had been raised, but he was more worried about the birds. They had watched him in silence throughout his journey, whistling and squawking and fluttering their colours before he arrived, and then falling quiet, hunched and watching, small beak whirrs and clicks flinting their treacherous eyes. It was affected, unnatural, and he sensed an omen or a spell buried in their intentions that chilled him.

By dusk, he reached the place where the self must be given; he felt it being tugged loose in the tranquillity. He pulled the boat ashore, not wanting to travel in the dark with the dizzying sensation as his companion, and made a simple camp, deciding not to eat or sleep, but to stay alert and face anything that might want to shave or dissect him with hungry guile. He tied amulets over his ears and plugged his nose with scrolls; he put a yellow pin through his tongue and, below the waist, he hung sealants against entry. Last of all, after he had looked around and placed his back against a sturdy rock, he covered his eyes with sight amulets that locked all out and allowed him to see into other worlds. With Uculipsa on one side and a short, engraved spear on the other, he was ready for anything that dared to approach.

The Erstwhile watched on, dismayed by the hunter's barbarous arrogance. He was an imposter. His disconnection of self, for such a short time, was a small price to pay for entrance to these sacred lands, and they stayed afar, wanting no contact with the trespassing stranger. If they could have hoped, then it would have been for beasts to devour him, or for lesser men to emerge and gnaw on his godless, selfish bones. But morning found him safe and intact, and when the first warmth touched his face, he peeled his protections away, pushed the canoe back into the water, and headed upstream.

Dusk and the benediction of shadow were coming back, but not for the Erstwhile, who had become too old. When the sun went away, they creaked and cracked, crawling on the forest floor and hanging sloth-like from the trees. There was no cave or simple dwelling for them. They did not have the pleasures of men or the ability to make and change what was around them.

They had each forgotten their purpose and the details of their design, how they had come to roam the ancient wood. But they all had longing, and it was attached to the actions of humans.

Their lightweight skeletons of spun coral and honey had absorbed the densities of water and time; now, heavier than bone, they filled their sluggish bodies with despair. Where feathers and light might once have been, there now grew vines and rough, scarred bark. Some had assumed coverings of fur or scales to keep their endless life forces protected.

Their unions with women had occurred thousands of years earlier, the resonant orgasm bleaching their voices and their sense of direction. Those that had mated were the ones that had been left behind with Adam, and with those that had been called the Watchers. Now derelict, their purpose and their application had washed away to rumour and ache. They roamed, pilfered, and scratched a life in utter, total materiality. Their ambition was to become invisible, to waste away into mist and breeze. But that, too, had been lost. Their given task was to protect the tree of knowledge, and so they remained in the forest, slowly becoming a forgotten part of it.

In previous times, a few had crept out, making short, scavenging journeys to the city. Fewer still had stayed away, to sleep with the Rumour, the name that they had given all those humans and semihumans after Adam, to twin with them in attempts to understand. They were chosen for the task, to go to places full of the Rumours, where land and time had been cultivated in scratched, straight lines and chopped, mean patches.

Aside from the chosen few, it was forbidden for any others to trespass the places of Rumour and false gods; the species carried such a virulent contagion and misunderstanding of knowledge that even God's name was slutted by it. No one knew of the Erstwhile's journeys to Essenwald until they pillaged the Chapel of the Desert Fathers. They should have been pitied, or sympathised with, but that was not the nature of men turned Rumour, who could not be blamed for following their own righteous teachings.

The Erstwhile had broken into the little church to look at the paintings. Without strength or tools, they had rubbed repeatedly at a patch in the wall, gradually wearing it away a little more each night, until eventually they were able to squeeze through and crawl about in the clean, closed darkness. Such an enclosure was beyond their understanding; its straight lines and solid walls confused them with wonder and fear. They were like insects at a glass window; everything there contradicted the laws and form of their existence.

They crept and flapped through the mystifying unity of out and in. When they came to the paintings, they froze. They stood, whimpering, before the framed print and the thick, black icon, shuddering and shaking in great swathes of moment, until they were stumbled upon the next morning by the young priest. They paid no attention to his presence, and he was oblivious to theirs, until he walked directly into them at the far side of the church. He dropped his box of waxy candle ends in shock, and yelped as he fell to the floor under the draft of their exit.

"It was a kind of wind, Father," he jittered. "A kind of bumpy wind, like being pushed about in the market, but there was nobody there."

He was standing outside in the sun an hour later, his breathing almost returned to normal, talking animatedly to the old priest and one of the city's watchmen. The old man was watching him intently, while the other puffed knowingly on a curved briar pipe. As he described his extraordinary experience of that morning, it suddenly became much, much stranger.

As the images appeared before his eyes, the young priest fell off his chair, screaming and scrambling a pointless retreat.

"Oh God, oh Jesus!" He flailed in fright. "It's them! They've come back!"

It took them a long time to calm him down. All the while, he looked about him fearfully, gripping the elder priest's arm with a strength that had almost become painful.

"It was them, Father. I saw them; they were here! Running at me. Terrible things. Oh Jesus, protect me!"

"Be calm, my son, be calm; God is with you."

"But, Father, it was them; I know it was. It was everything I felt them to be this morning; it was as if their visual form appeared to me from an hour before. How could that be?!"

Father Lutchen was very concerned but tried hard not to show it. "They have gone now; they won't come back," he said, and the words sounded like they had been said before. "Tell me one thing, my son."

"Yes, Father?"

"Were they frightened?"

The young man pulled himself up the older man's arm in small grabs, until their faces were almost touching. "They were terrified," he said.

The priest sent the boy home with the watchman and made his way back into the chapel. He was in little doubt as to what he would find. He went to where the visitation had occurred, taking in the knocked print hanging askew on the wall. He looked at the floor and, slipping his shoes off, he walked carefully in tight, quiet little circles, a small, solemn dance in threadbare stocking feet. Occasionally, he flinched or abruptly lifted his foot, as if from the piercing of an invisible sharpness; his expressions flickered, wavering between a grimace and a smile, the bare environment seeming to send a message that he alone could interpret. Eventually, his circles locked into a shuffle, and he moved intuitively across the room, where he discovered the rubbed-away slot in the chapel's sidewall. He had found their entry place.

He walked slowly back to the print, brushing his socks with his hand before slipping his shoes back on. The crooked picture caught his eye and he felt compelled to level it before he left. He reached out to straighten it, and his touch jolted it from the wall and he felt its weight drop into his hands. With a start, he pushed his hands up to return it to its nail, but it resisted, and as he drew slowly away, it remained in place, an inch away from the wall, unattached.

Though his instinct was to recoil, he had seen much stranger than this, and he refused to be shaken by it. He lifted the dusty string from the back of the frame and rehung the picture, its weight shifting again to the accepted limitations of gravity. He considered the image for a moment, a rendering of the angelic host from Gustave Doré's most revered work. And then he turned and left, deep in thought, the illustration hanging limply in his wake.

➤→

Sidrus regarded Father Lutchen contemplatively.

"Twigs," said the old priest to the forest guardian. "Twigs and leaves. A path of them, from the lesion in the wall to the point where they stood. All invisible, which means they came out of the Vorrh again."

Sidrus and his tribe—all named Sidrus after the centurion who had saved the Sefer haYashar from extinction in the ruins of Jerusalem—had started as a scholastic branch growing out of the split tree of the Tubal-Cain. Somewhere in its tangled history, it had bred with the testaments of Enoch and Lilithian blasphemies to produce the hieratic order that Sidrus now fervently represented. The warrant he carried was of the Boundary

Holders of the Forest, a position of responsible fanaticism that suited him well.

Their relationship was not a comfortable one: Many of the things the guardian and the priest believed and stood for were in opposition. Then there was the problem with Sidrus's face: The old priest had tried to avoid direct confrontation with it for years. However, in the working business of policing the sanctity of the forest, they were united.

"Surely 'invisible' is a contradiction?" said Sidrus, in response to the old man's comment. "I prefer to refer to them as 'visually elsewhere.'"

"The elsewhere of the Erstwhile," the priest mused, without the faintest sign of humour.

"It's the same old problem of resemblance," Sidrus said in a weary tone. "Not holding their form away from the forest's time, which is the very substance that bonds them; the delays of similitude slicing them into separation outside of its boundaries."

"Well, their dislocation must not be witnessed here," said Lutchen, "and they cannot be allowed to take our cause and effect back into the Vorrh." He looked resignedly at the forest guardian. There was nothing more to be done: life had to be preserved in its current state, and for that to happen, action had to be taken.

They set about constructing the deceptively simple trap. A square section was cut out of the panelled wall where the Doré print hung. It was then set on a long, vertical spindle, so that it could rotate freely, and a small wooden wheel was attached to the top of the spindle, just above one of the U-shaped brackets that kept it in place. Strong, thin string was wound around the wheel, then looped out into the yard at the back. Sidrus had small, crude paper copies made of the print. He trailed them back to the forest, to the point where the Erstwhile had first escaped. The damp and sun would exhaust the pictures in three days, but hopefully not before one of them caught hold of the scent and was reminded of the larger, more vivid version. Now it was just a question of waiting.

They sat in the stillness for four nights, the young priest trying to keep his eyes open and away from the white, distorted countenance of the heretic at his side. The old priest had warned him of the night's requirements—he had assured his young apprentice that it would be a test of his strength and of his faith. As he shivered in the moonlight, trying not to stare at the abnormality standing next to him, the young man could not be sure if the priest had referred to the trapping of the Erstwhile or the malign warden himself.

On the fifth night of waiting, the young priest spotted movement between the trees and hurried to tell Sidrus and the priest, who quickly made their way into the yard to take hold of the string.

In moments, there was a scraping sound around the worn-away slit in the wall, a rustling of entrance. They waited ten minutes, and then, very gently, the guardian pulled on the string. After a pause and a little tug, the wooden panel with the picture hanging on it spun around to face the outside of the church. There was an immediate shuffling inside the wooden building, like animals running through a stormy forest. After a while, it quietened. The three men held their breath: A faint movement could be heard outside, and they correctly assumed that the Erstwhile were very close. The picture frame swayed a little, touched by an unseeable force. Lutchen nodded to Sidrus, who again pulled the string. The panel turned back on itself, the picture again facing the inside of the chapel. The rustling grew frantic, but without the hollow resonance of size or weight. It distanced itself from the three men, as its creators returned to the chapel's interior. The process was repeated for the next hour. At one point, when the ethereal beings were once more inside, the young priest began to giggle. Lutchen hushed him severely.

"This is not a game," he said. The youngster returned to his imperceptible orchestrations, solemn faced in his superior's rebuke.

On the final turn, with the image facing out, Sidrus leapt forward and retrieved it from its nail. He ran silently to the far end of the yard and placed the framed print at the top of a pyre of old wood. When he returned to his companions, his clothes reeked of kerosene.

The Erstwhile emerged more quickly than they had previously; perhaps they were learning. It was unlikely, their minds being that same, impenetrable substance as saturated sponge, but they did seem to find the panel in less time. Its emptiness sent them into convulsions. They rattled in circles as they looked for it; the men heard one go back inside. Lutchen knew that he and Sidrus would see all this in an hour or two, see this and worse. He would have to remember to warn the boy and not let him witness the burning, the detachment of visual existence; its delay in time was an unsettling phenomenon, especially when attached to such an act as today's cleansing.

There was a commotion in the woodpile.

"They have found it," whispered Lutchen.

The noise became louder as more and more wood slipped down, falling aside under their clandestine weight.

"They are climbing—do it now!"

Sidrus took a bottle out from the shadows and lit the rag that was stuffed into its neck. He rushed towards the pyre and threw it with all his might into the heaped wood. A great, explosive blaze bellowed up the dry wood. The whole yard was lit by its roar.

"Look away! Do not turn back!" demanded Lutchen of the young priest.

Inside the fast flames, there were slower movements, lumbering, slow-motion flailing. The wood was collapsing onto the thick smoke; the framed picture had fallen, shrunken into a crisp ball.

They watched in awe as a greater brightness grew inside the heart of the fire; oxygen being sucked into its vortex was turning the screaming core white. Many minutes later, it all collapsed into a tall heap of vivid coal and gleaming ashes. The smoke smelt strange: choking ammonia mixed with sweet cinnamon, sandalwood with briar and oranges, with bitter edges like the smell of roasting seashells.

"Is it done?" asked Lutchen.

Sidrus moved carefully forward. The pyre was now half his height. It twitched and cracked with loud retorts, a slow turning emanating from its core. He looked back at Lutchen and shook his head. He made a shooing gesture with his right hand, and Lutchen leant over to the young man still turned away from the flames, and whispered in his ear. He got up and the old priest pointed him away from the hot, moving embers. A steamy, bluish haze seemed to be condensing above the heat.

"Look, the animation, the halos," said Sidrus with an excitement that made his face even more malformed. "The gas of their life escaping."

An hour later, both men picked up the long-handled tools that they had concealed nearby. They probed the coals and the white, charred wood for anything that might be larger or living. They found only one part, its ash covering giving it the appearance of presence. It appeared to be a section of hip and upper thigh; the ball and socket joint was exposed and working, swivelling in the gritty charcoal, its stump pointing aimlessly towards the sky. There were other, smaller suggestions of form, but it was difficult to be sure exactly what they saw, because the heat from the fire was still so intense; their eyes smarted with it, causing them to shield their faces and continually turn away from the ripples of temperature.

As the flames slowly began to lose their power, they started to rake through the cooling embers, breaking up anything larger than a fist and reducing the wood and the Erstwhile to a low, smouldering carpet of ashes.

The job done, they quickly parted, not wanting to be together when the visual record of the incineration played in their heads. It would be an inescapable nightmare to watch this, to see the writhing and the screaming projected onto the inside of their eyelids; inflicting it on strangers or fellow brothers would only amplify the terror and demand a nauseous response that no other should witness: They chose to contain that horror in solitude.

The young priest, returned from his boundary of exclusion, was quiet and cold by the old man, who was white-lipped and tense.

"Father," he said, with great care. "Father, is it not a sin, what we have done?"

The question helped Lutchen, giving him a substance to resist, a grit to stand firm on: "Those wrong creatures brought madness and fear into our world. They were never meant to share the time of men. Our work here is God's work, and the pain of the experience of it will be written in scars that I shall wear with fulfilment and modest pride until the Day of Judgment."

The young priest remained silent and still, moving only to comply with Lutchen's orders. He tied the older man to a chair in the vestry of the church, laying cassocks and a few old prayer cushions on the wooden floor, to soften the blows in case the old man became convulsive. When all was set up, he left, under strict instructions not to return before midnight, and not to enter the room, no matter what noises he heard coming from it.

———

Sidrus drank six glasses of absinthe and descended to the basement of his dwellings. In the pitch-black cellar, he would face the
seeing on its own terms and wrench some power from its horror
to use to his advantage. No act or crime could ever debase him.
It was the way and the duty of his clan to milk cruelty and terror of their own benefaction, and some part of him relished the
disgust that was about to erupt in his head. He gripped an iron
ring in the wall and braced himself for the visions. He would not
have long to wait.

➤→

The sun was fierce, and the bald cliff stood clear of the great
mass of the forest; like a hermitage in a mythical painting, it
shone pale gold against the greens and blacks of the trees. The
sky was heroically blue, with vast, rolling white clouds that
seemed to move in all directions in the light breeze.

The Bowman had scrabbled over the broken terrain for
two days before finding the cave, though the notion of having
"found" it seemed inaccurate, somehow; he had felt drawn to
it by an ungovernable magnetism that seemed to turn his every
step; that weak force, which holds every star and cell in check,
had tilted him towards the crack in the rock.

He pulled himself over the last ledge and surveyed the landscape in all directions; the Vorrh seemed to go on forever. He
wiped the sweat from his eyes and moved into the mouth of the
cave, its coolness overwhelming. Light, shafting in through fis-
sures in the high ceiling, gave it a church-like atmosphere that
suggested sanctum and calm. The sense of having been here
before overcame him; he knew this place. Then the bow moved
in his hand. At first he thought a gust of wind had caught it, but
it moved again, twitching like a divining rod sniffing at water.

He dropped all his other possessions and held the bow firmly
between his two hands. The inexplicable movement steered

him with tiny twitches along its length, twitches that united to make a pull. He went with it farther into the cave. It guided his growing excitement to a point at the back of the third chamber. There, a rock seemed to mark the spot the bow was pointing to. He brushed dust and wind-flung twigs off the stone and gasped at the pictograph inscribed crudely onto its surface, a semicircle, struck through its middle by a slender, pointed dart: a bow and arrow.

He rolled the stone aside and started to dig, scraping at the compacted earth with his hands and the large knife he carried at his side. After twenty minutes and a forearm's depth of excavation, he struck something solid. He swept the earth around it to reveal a heavy wooden box. With some difficulty, he freed it from the tight, stony earth, stopping to take several deep breaths before forcing the lid off. It prised free to reveal a heavy parcel and a scrawled note. The words were written in a familiar hand. It read:

> You and I are Peter Williams. I already have little
> memory, so I am writing these words from Este's dictation.
> You will find this after she has died and become the bow of
> your arm. You are returning to whence you came, from the
> other side of the Vorrh. You are now midway. Many will
> try to stop you; some will attempt to take your life. You
> must be vigilant and sly. Este is the only one to travel with
> us, the only one you can trust. She led me out of the lands
> of struggle when blood poured. We lived here in this cave
> for a year, and then moved on to start a new life. It was
> heaven, but it was waiting for hell. She saw it all and our
> place in it. Your returning is to balance the dead that will
> follow. Este sends all her love from our time, to you, and
> her present. I leave you a little something from before, a
> dragon that will stop some of the monsters, and a memory

*from the village that will let you hear us and the others
from afar.*

GOD SPEED.

YOU.

He stared at the paper for a long while, and then started to
shake. The air in the cave seemed to adopt his agitation, so that
all things except the letter trembled into a blur. Something like
fury and torpor were wrestling inside his shock, and his eyes
closed to watch his opposites tear and scratch at each other. His
body was in spasm, the muscles clenching hard, as if to defy the
turbulence around and inside him. It was reaching the point of
fracture when the sound came: a terse, dry report, like the toll-
ing of a cracked bell. It echoed once in the cave and grounded
his unrest. Perfect calm swallowed all the ruptured time. He
turned in the milky stillness to look at the split box that was
now nothing but a nest of splinters.

He let the letter fall and walked over to the origin of the
sound, stooping to retrieve the contents of the box. He lifted
a heavy package of brown oiled paper from the wreckage, and
something caught on the parcel and fell to his feet, like a dead
bird. He set the package aside and picked up the two halves of
coconut shell, joined together by a fractured, curved twig and a
string of twisted vine. One of the shells had split; he lifted the
other to his ear, the vine dangling around his wrist. A hollow
wash of the ultimate, distant sea filled the cave; in its shell-like
whiteness, voices whispered.

He carefully laid the contraption aside and lifted the heavy
parcel. Unfolding the paper, he felt the reassuring weight of the
Gabbett-Fairfax Mars in his hand; without memory or reason,
he felt the heavy presence of the pistol ground him to another
time and place.

He slept the night in the cave, unnerved but warm. He hoped some part of them might seep out of the stone, to embrace their current incarnation. He slept with Este in one hand and the letter in the other, the gun and the shell on either side of his head. He slept knowing that everything in his life was a mystery and that his only purpose seemed to be to travel through the Vorrh. There was a reservoir of memory that twitched towards the letter, but its cup was smaller than a synapse, and it held a single word: Oneofthewilliams.

CHAPTER TWENTY

*M*uybridge stood alone. The rooms on the first floor had been squalid; now their interior was simple and immaculate. The surrounding streets and alleyways teemed with the shiftless poor, the dispossessed and representatives of every tribe on earth, trying to scratch an existence outside the livid ghost of the old city wall. It was perfect. No one was known, and no one wanted to be. The seething carapace kept the clean, anonymous rooms shielded and safe.

The flat was carefully divided. The bedroom and parlour were Josephine's; a small kitchen joined them to the long, open room beyond. A huge window jutted out of its centre into a blind courtyard. It worked as a skylight and made the room light and airy, even when it was full of gloomy machines and boxes. This was Muybridge's studio and workshop; his darkroom was built in at the far end.

He had been there three times already, initially to meet Gull and one of his men, to be given the keys and instructions about the rooms, but also, more important, to be given a file on Josephine, as well as a small mirror and a handbell.

The next visit had been to supervise the arrival, unpacking, and assemblage of his equipment. Gull had been as good as his word and provided for everything; he had not baulked at the sets of expensive lenses or the intricate, handmade brass gear-ing systems. Muybridge now had all he needed; the secret in the shadow and atmosphere, which somehow lived and thrived in his photographs, was within probing distance. The new zoo-praxiscope would be a very different machine from its forebears.

Muybridge's third visit had focused on the most delicate element of the plan: the installation of Josephine. She had arrived in the middle of a spring downpour, with a companion and one of Gull's servants. Muybridge had been irritated by the surgeon's absence; surely such a crucial moment should be overseen by its instigator, especially in a case such as this? But it wasn't to be. The servant had explained that the companion would be staying for a week or so, until Josephine "got to know the ropes of the place." The servant introduced her to Muybridge and she curtsied, holding herself in a modest way, which he appreciated, but from a professional distance. He certainly had no intention of visiting the rooms while two females lived there, even if they did know their place.

The servant showed him that the rooms were well stocked, with every possible comfort provided for. "You'll be snug as bugs in a rug," the man said amiably. Muybridge gave him a withering stare, privately wondering if Gull recruited all of his staff from his list of ex-inmates. The impertinent fellow talked him through the basic details of the house, the most intriguing of which was a small, concealed compartment in the wall to the right of the kitchen door. Hanging inside was a thick, flat cosh made of leather. Its short but significant weight was achieved by the lead shot that filled its interior.

"Just in case, sir—we all 'ave 'em."

"Is there a chance I'll need to use it?" asked the alarmed Muybridge, who was beginning to have serious doubts about the whole business.

"No chance, sir. Some of 'em cut up rough, but not Josie; she's good as gold."

Nevertheless, the photographer resolved to always be careful. He would carry his trusty Colt pocket revolver with him at all times; who knew when it might be needed for protection, outside of the rooms or in?

Their first sittings began a little awkwardly. He found her silence uncanny and her eyes unnerving. Whenever he arrived and quietly let himself in, he would find the rooms full of birdsong, as if dozens of bright and active creatures were whistling with great joy. This would stop abruptly the moment she sensed his presence.

She had been alone in the rooms for the last three weeks and seemed calm and happy. She made him tea and he drank it in silence, stealing glances at her when she was not aware. Her savage beauty still amazed him. He had seen such perfection occasionally flare in the many primitive peoples he had visited and lived with; he had photographed an Aztec woman of magnificent sensuality in Mexico; he remembered two Modoc women whose striking appearances had remained with him long after his meeting with them had passed, their balanced symmetry accentuated inside their broad, flat faces.

But Josephine had something more. There was a glow of strength and dignity inside her ideal proportions, which made her every movement hypnotic to him. It soon dawned on him that this was attraction: His masculinity was being nudged awake by her, roused from a slumber he had been hitherto oblivious to; the part of his life he had long considered dead and shrivelled was wakened in her presence. How fat and stupid Flora had been in comparison to this demented vision, and how petty her vanities now revealed themselves to be. But still, it was better to put such thoughts out of his head; they could lead only to pain and confusion, as history had so deftly proven. Better to work, to trust the life he had invented, the one that paid him so handsomely and seemed to ask no price in return.

"I am going *next door* to *set up* the *camera* for your *photograph*," he said, overpronouncing each slow syllable as if talking to a deaf person or a foreigner. "It will take *one hour;* then I will *come for you,* do you *understand?*"

She nodded and allowed a small smile to grace her lips. Muybridge felt the snag of it in his lungs, as if it were a slow shutter of great precision, catching a fast and out-of-focus world. He left the room in a daze and shut the door behind him, the room ricocheting with the chirps, whirrs, and clicks of the fast, invisible bats held apart from his company.

After the slightly jerky start, their first session had been brilliantly successful. She was one of the best sitters he had ever had, possessing the same stillness and distant focus that had made the Plains Indians such perfect subjects, but with a vibrancy that shone and showed the camera the great battery of power stored inside her. She sat without any guile of expression or artifice of intent: The camera simply loved her.

He did not think it proper or necessary to use any of the posthypnotic responses; the bell and the mirror stayed in their box. He processed the negatives before departing and was amazed at the clarity of her white face and black teeth. He said he would be back soon and she nodded. In truth, neither could be sure when he would return; his diary was stuffed with appointments, lectures, demonstrations, and meetings, and their moments at the studio would have to be stolen ones; she would be just another jigsaw piece in the multifaced puzzle of his identity. The principle of this arrangement appealed to him as much as the participation, but he suspected he would soon seek more time to truly appreciate and savour the theatre of it.

The second session was as successful as the first, but their third session was remarkable. He arrived at three in the afternoon, fitting her in between an important lunch and an evening lecture at the Royal Academy. When he arrived, he was mildly dismayed to find her in his studio, already preparing for the sitting. He had not known that she had been given keys to his room and felt uneasy about her open access to his possessions and most valuable instruments. But she instantly disarmed his vexation by curtsying and smiling, pointing questioningly to the framing chair where she would be fastened.

"Yes, just give me a moment to gather my thoughts and we shall begin," he said distractedly.

She turned away to allow his mind free roam of the studio. She wore a simple white blouse, buttoned up to the neck, and a long, layered skirt of muted turquoise and greens. Her hair was pinned back and exclaimed the dynamic contours of her skull, neck, and face.

He prepared the plates and returned. She was seated in the chair, the box of unused instruments already lying next to her. Had he done this in the last sitting? Placed it so in rushing departure to remind himself of their usage? Or had she made the decision for him? He pondered this as he adjusted her head and tightened the head clamps, seeing her smooth skin dimple under the pressure. He framed the camera, focused it, and loaded the film.

"Josephine, the first image will be a static reference to the poses that come after it."

Her eyes blinked in understanding, and he took the first photograph, observing her implacable exterior before changing the plates. He returned to the camera and paused for a moment, holding the pneumatic shutter bulb in his right hand and the bell in his left. He rang it twice.

Instantly, she contorted into a position of wretched exhaustion, as if frozen mid-nightmare. Her head twisted sideways, straining against the brace, and her mouth lolled open, eyes turned upwards under heavy, almost closed lids. The rest of her body slumped, sack-like, into the chair.

Muybridge was shocked by the speed of the transformation: So utterly different was the person before him, it was almost impossible to recognise her. Gone was the inner dynamo, with the outer beauty and gentle sanity he had begun to so enjoy. He quickly took the picture and rang the bell to return her, but to his horror, the ringing only heightened the pose. Her body twisted farther away from itself, as if a great rope had been wound around her and connected to a cruel windlass, which had been tightened against normality. There was a spiteful crack, and for a horrifying moment he thought one of her bones had shattered; his astonishment augmented as he realised it was the sound of the metal head brace snapping behind her neck. Not knowing what to do next, he did the only thing he could: He reloaded the camera and made the exposure. Her head was now loose and driven back, as if by a mighty force. He changed the plates again and picked up the bell. He had forgotten every instruction he had read about this procedure; he couldn't be sure if another ringing would release her or turn her invisible winch more severely; opportunity and curiosity lay across from pity and aid, in equal measures on the other side of the turn. With an uncertain exhilaration that he did not care to name, he rang the bell again. She slumped forward like a dead weight against the leather belt of the seat; it pressed up under her breast, forcing out a great exclamation of air. She was totally inert. Muybridge stepped towards her, disappointment congealing into concern. He lifted her weight back into the vertical and was stunned at its solidity; she seemed to have changed density. Her subtle bones and gentle curves were cast in lead and granite, and when she opened her eyes, he saw a space in the universe he had never dreamt of. He distanced himself, stepping back as one of his long, shivering arms held her in place.

"Josephine, are you all right? Can you hear me?"

The eyelids mercifully closed, and she seemed to soften into normal weight, falling into a detached slumber. He returned to the camera and collected his things, deciding against wakening her—it seemed safer to leave her undisturbed.

He gathered the plates and made his way to the darkroom. He processed them in an immersed daze, totally engaged by the images produced. He was beginning to understand what Gull had wanted from these sessions; tomorrow he would use the mirror.

Suddenly, he remembered his scheduled lecture at the academy. His memory jolted, and he rapidly put away the chemicals and set the glass negatives to drain, returning to the studio to help Josephine out of her confinement. But she was gone.

He walked quickly and quietly through the kitchen to her rooms. Her bedroom door was ajar, and he softly pushed it open. She lay diagonally across the small bed, a blanket draped from her knees to the floor. Her breath told him that she was deeply asleep, and he crept a little closer. The restraining belt had wrenched away some of the buttons of her blouse; it fell to one side as she slept, exposing the rich upper curve of her right breast. Her hair comb had fallen out and was on the pillow, precariously close to her eyes. He moved it to the bedside table and picked up the blanket, lingering for a moment to savour the view of her exposed shoulders and chest.

He gathered his things and quietly left the studio, the warm glow of self-sanctified chivalry brightening his view of the grubby streets outside.

The mirror session was less alarming than the bell sitting. Her body remained calm throughout, though her face went through a colourful dictionary of rictus. It spasmed into unbelievable contortions, each time returning to its natural beauty. Muybridge was fascinated; he had never seen anything like it before. His daily demonstrations and meetings began to bore him, and he felt himself yearning for more time with the exotic creature in front of his camera. He revelled in the seclusion, where nobody knew him or what he was doing; it was so utterly different from the hoards of ill-informed on whom he had spent so much precious time. Squirreled away with Josephine and his inventions, he was becoming happy again.

The zoopraxiscope had changed beyond recognition. He soon realised that the earlier models had been little more than clumsy toys to entertain a gawping crowd. True, they had demonstrated the possibility of movement being projected into the unsuspecting eye, the mechanical delusions of leaping horses and running figures, paintings becoming alive. But the new machines sought a very different quarry, one that entered the brain directly, through the spinning mirrors and measured, shuttered light, which bent and warped via the array of lenses. Peripheral sight was the causeway around the picture, flicking the optic nerve to erection.

He had tried it on himself repeatedly and felt the shadows infiltrate and pulse. They sought absorption in some part of the brain, and while they danced so, the uncanny was released. Every time he tilted the sunlight or lit the lamps or changed the lenses, he came a little closer; every time he put his head in the machine and cranked the brass gears, he felt the movement try to coalesce; every time his eyes were licked by crooked light, he felt the ghosts arrive.

After his first seizure, alone in the back of their small studio, he was more cautious. He had come out of the machine with a jolt, his legs going in and out of spasm. He remembered nothing, but when he awoke he was on the floor, with a split lip, a bleeding nose, and a torn shirt. He must have looked the way those villains had described him in courtrooms, all those years ago: dislocated, unwell, and raving. He had always felt sure that it was not the *morbus comitialis* that had ravaged him, but some other, sensitive, higher function of the brain that portrayed a similar effect. And now he had proved it, by finding a way to manufacture it from light.

When he had found his way out of the studio and into the kitchen, he must have been quite a sight; Josephine made a silent scream upon seeing him. His long, greying beard and white shirt were covered in blood, spread everywhere by his excessive perspiration. He tried to reassure her that he was all right, just a small accident. He poured water into the sink to wash, and she went back to her room and locked the door. Locked doors were good things, he thought, as he rinsed his chest. When not in the wilderness, he preferred to live and work behind them, constructing his instruments and carrying out his experiments behind their infallible security.

He resolved to be more careful in the future; he did not want Josephine to be alarmed again. He could not risk her inquisitiveness drawing her fingers to the workings of his delicate optics. The process of logging each variation of light, each arrangement of lens and shutter, and all the effects they subsequently produced in him was a protracted and systematic one. The large, heavy ledger sat in the desk in the corner of the room, a sturdy clasp keeping it shut. Soon, he would visit Gull with his findings, and he was looking forward to seeing the doctor's expression when confronted with such significant research.

But he was not ready yet. America and Stanford were calling. His two years in England had flown by, and he still needed more time, but that was not an option—he had to return to his adopted homeland as soon as possible. He was musing on this when Josephine knocked on the door. He unlocked it and invited her in. She walked to the chair in front of the camera, touched it, and looked at him. He checked his watch.

"Yes. I do have time for a short sitting this afternoon."

She actually seemed to enjoy these displays of malady. Even the cruellest of contortions only ever left her tired, and she was always ready for more. He admired this in her. She showed no fear or remorse, never complained or even tried to find a way to; she was so different from the scheming, selfish oaf he had married. He enjoyed her silent company and felt dismal at having to leave so soon with no return date set. He sighed and began to prepare for the exposure, clearing a few things from his workbench and putting them on shelves. He moved his version of the peripher-scope from the back of the shelf to make room for a box of nega-tives. He felt her start behind him and turned to see her reaction.

"What's wrong, Josephine?"

She pointed to his hand.

"What, this?" he said, holding the clockwork halo of glass and metal towards her.

Her eyes widened and she produced an expression she had not yet demonstrated, a cross between sexual hunger and short-sightedness, as if she was drawing the object towards her; he felt a little awkward. She approached, holding out her hands. He gave her the halo, and she placed it on her head, imitating the sound of its small clockwork motors while placing her flat right hand over her head and making a series of circles with it. Her actions reminded him of one half of a children's game, one hand circling in front of the solar plexus, the other above the head, to demonstrate the pull of unity between separate coordination of the left and right brain. But this was not a game: She wanted him to operate it for her.

He saw no obvious difficulty in her request. Gull had evi-dently used it in her previous treatment, and its desirable consequences seemed to have given her pleasure. He took the peripherscope from her and wound the motors. Checking that the mirrors were not loose, he arranged it securely on her head. She returned to the chair with sauntering pleasure. The brass and glass shone in the sun from the bright window, against the darkness of her uplifted head. She was a crowned princess, awaiting her cloak of gold on some distant shore; he, her intrepid provider, the carrier of her inner riches.

They were both smiling when he pressed the tiny levers and set the machine in motion. The effect was instantaneous. Her body tightened and rippled into a firm contour of readiness, as if the nondescript clothing that she wore had somehow become magically tailored to cling to every line of her body. Her posture was catlike, with a salacious stealth that screamed her sexuality. Muybridge was frozen. She closed her heavy lids over smouldering eyes as wave upon wave of orgasm rushed through her body. Every guard, defence, and restraint was swept away from him. His erection was beyond his wildest memories, and it bayed in the constraint of his Scottish woollen trousers. Her sighs turned into mews, then roars. The chair broke, split apart by the energy being driven down through it and into the cringing floor. She stood, fists clenched and head thrown back, panting as the clockwork ran out and the photographer exploded with unbelievable pleasure inside the embarrassed dignity of his thick darkroom underwear.

They went to their own rooms without a word. He waited until he thought she must be asleep, and then he escaped, into an outside world blissfully ignorant of his appalling indiscretion, though he couldn't help but think that some of the passing mob gave him looks that were all too knowing.

The three or four sessions that followed had been very formal and brief. He spent much of his time shut in the studio, working on the new device, which he had not yet named. Somehow, "zoopraxiscope" did not do his little miracle of reflection justice.

Josephine behaved with her usual decorum, as if the incident had never occurred; their formal and professional friendship seemed unaffected by the nameless incident. However, he had noticed with some disquiet that his version of the peripherscope had been moved from its exact place in his studio. Each time he had gone away she must have taken it, presumably to her room. It had always been returned before he came back, but he noticed the slight differences in its meticulous setting down. Nobody else would have spotted the variation: It takes a trained and scientific eye to observe the unmentioned. At first, he thought of scolding her, but that would mean admittance and knowledge of all, and he had no desire to tread that path again. He could have locked it away or taken it apart. In the end, he did nothing. It was easier to ignore her animal appetites and pretend that he did not know about the daily pilfering. At times, he even congratulated himself in letting her use it; another of his acts of uncalled-for kindness. Anyway, the instrument was no longer of much value to him. He had surpassed Gull's little plaything; she could have it.

Yet he could not so easily ignore the image of her that afternoon; it tugged at his consciousness each time they met, and it always had the same physical effect on him. After a while, he stopped trying to restrain the memory and its attendant arousal, choosing instead to reclassify it as the normal reaction of a particularly healthy and virile fifty-two-year-old man.

He had begun the process of packing away his things. Josephine knew that he was leaving but that he would visit again upon his return. She had seemed genuinely downhearted at the news of his departure, but perhaps that was just her reaction to the prospect of being separated from the peripherscope.

He had contacted Gull, telling the doctor of his progress and sending the previous batches of pictures to him; the last batch would be picked up the next day by one of his men. But he was hesitant—he could not find it in himself to pack his new invention away, to stop testing it; he certainly did not want to leave it behind. He had had another fit while operating it and was getting butterflies about using it again; he was so close, it was madness to stop now, but he couldn't continue alone—he needed a guinea pig. Then he heard movement next door and the idea came full circle. Gull would be delighted.

He cleared all appointments for two days and brought provisions to the rooms so that he would not have to go out. In the corner of the studio he set up the camp bed the maid had previously used. All he had to do now was convince Josephine to help.

He arrived very early the first day; she was still sleeping while he made tea and toast in the kitchen. She heard the early kettle boil and came to see what was happening at this time of day. Her hair was tousled, and she wore a heavy hospital dressing gown over her nightdress.

"Good morning, Josephine!" he said to the blinking ex-slave yawning before him. "I have made you some toast and brought us some excellent marmalade."

Such hospitality was alien to her, and the gaiety of his breakfast making was beyond expectation; she regarded him, and his culinary efforts, with a wary delight.

"These are my last few days before I go away. I have only one important piece of work to finish and I wanted to show it to you later, because I think you might like it. Now, come and sit down."

He drew a chair out for her to sit, then went to his side of the table and started buttering the toast. "You will like this marmalade; it's come all the way from Oxford. Some people, myself included, believe it to be the only thing of any value that has been produced by that city!"

The joke was beyond her, and she sipped her tea. He pushed the toast towards her as she looked blankly at him, his scruffy beard full of sharp crumbs that caught her eye.

"I have a gift for you!" he said suddenly, bounding across to the wide-open studio as she looked from him to the food and back again. She was not fully awake, and the marmalade and gifts were causing her the exact amount of confusion he had been aiming for. He returned, grinning, with one arm behind his back.

"I want to give you this; I know you like it."

He thrust the brown paper parcel in her face and she frowned as she accepted it. Two days before, he had taken the peripherscope from its normal place, wrapped it up in thick brown paper, and placed it in a drawer. Now she held it in both hands, turning it, feeling its obvious form. She immediately knew what it was and started to pick at the string.

"Oh no, not here—it's yours now. Take it to your room; you can open it there."

She was suspicious, delighted, and confused. Unable to convey all three emotions at once, she beamed at him and crunched into her toast.

"After breakfast, I will show you my new machine; it's a bit like that one, only better," he said, jabbing a prurient finger at the parcel.

She finished her breakfast and went to dress, while he prepared his nameless device. He had moved its component parts around so that she might lie down on the table with her head between the reflecting mechanisms. He had brought the sunlight to the machine with the aid of three parabolic mirrors. It was less smelly and irksome than using the oil lamps, and the day was very much brighter than had been the case in recent weeks.

She was at the door, observing his joyful demonstration. "See? It works just like the other device; these little mirrors spin around, cupping the light from over there. There are lenses all over, look!" He was pointing and fluttering his hands over the polished wood and brass; the sunlight glinted in the lenses. "There are two disc shutters and a rotating drum shutter back here. It's all controlled by this crank, which I shall turn for a few moments. So what do you think? Are you ready?"

She hesitated a moment, then nodded and sat on the table, swinging her legs up to lie flat. He positioned her head and put a simple, thin restraining band across her forehead.

"Excellent! Let's begin. Ready?" Her eyes blinked "yes."

He pushed against the crank and the machine spun into motion. By the third turn, he had found his rhythm. The lenses turned into glowing, spinning spheres, stretching, chewing, sphinctering, and splitting the now invented light, which drilled into the sides of the black, responsive eyes, as the shutters chopped and shaved pulses of shadow, brilliance, and darkness. For the first time, the machine hummed. He looked back and forth from it to her face and body, which remained motionless, and to his half-hunter pocket watch, propped up on the shelf nearby. After three minutes, he began to slow down, eventually bringing the machine to a stop. He removed the head strap and helped her to sit up. She was breathing normally, her eyes looked normal, and there wasn't the faintest trace of any effect. He gave her some water and asked her to walk around the room, which she did while drinking. He was mildly perplexed; there should have been some effect. He consulted his logbook, made a few minor adjustments, and said, "Could we try again, please?"

She nodded with a shrug and climbed back into the device. He cranked it into action again, this time for five minutes. He was perspiring under his tight, itching collar and cuffs. He sat her up again. Nothing. He asked her to lie down and close her eyes, expecting at least dizziness to manifest. She fell asleep. He gently but irritably shook her awake. "One last try, please. Just one."

They went back to the table. He fastened the strap and cranked again. Eight minutes later, he stopped: The machine was a failure. It worked only for him; she was totally impervious to its influence. It did nothing. He dismissed her with great irritation and sat, gloomily staring at the ridiculous hand-built tangle of disappointment.

He sat until it started to get dark; then he dragged himself together, snatched up his topcoat and hat, and left, slamming the door and waking her again in his exit. He stomped the gritty and dissolute streets for hours, walking in circles, trying to exhaust his rage and fathom what had gone wrong. He stopped at a public house and quietened it for a long moment with his wrong, brooding entrance. He made his way to the bar and ordered Nelson's Blood from the surprised barman; men of Muybridge's class were never seen in such neighbourhoods, and certainly not drinking concoctions as potent as the admiral's blood. Of course, unbeknownst to his unwilling bar fellows, he had been in much rougher establishments than theirs: from the shabby beer halls of the Arctic to the decrepit ratholes of Guatemala, to the gambling house of the Yukon, decorated with icicles of human blood. But he had never drunk alone in a public house in England. Here it was improper; the chronic barriers of position and wealth forbade the fluidity he found everywhere else.

The second drink hit, stirring some mirth out of the sediment of his gloom. Everybody in the cramped, overvarnished rooms of the pub was intensely aware of the gaunt, scraggly-bearded man with crazed prophet's eyes, who had started talking to himself and grinning into his drink. He was oblivious to them all.

His mind wandered to an earlier time and place, where he had consumed a weighty amount of the potent black-rum-and-port mixture, with a man who had since become an infamous figure, even to those on this miserable rock. They had been in Cheyenne, in the wild Dakota Territories, distinguishing themselves by making loud toasts to the Bard and to Scholarly Conduct, to the Fine Arts and Chivalry. The saloon had been full of armed riffraff; many there with a price on their heads had ignored them and refused to be stirred by their conduct. Muybridge's drinking companion that day had been John Henry Holliday, the notorious gambler and gunfighter who had made the London newspapers a year earlier, when he and the Earp brothers had staged a magnificently theatrical gunfight in the little-known and appropriately named town of Tombstone. Muybridge was sure that "Doc" Holliday had done most of the killing and maiming on that day, and he wished he had been there to see it, maybe photograph the heroes afterwards.

He shoved his hand into his topcoat's inside pocket, looking for more money but finding instead the loaded Colt pistol. It was getting like the old days, he slurred to himself. He now had the appetite for a bit of gunplay. Then, with all the rhyme and reason of an amateur drinker, his thought switched to Josephine, to her passive and inert reaction today, to her electric performance with his copy of Gull's device. Her pliant and sensual magnetism seemed a much better option than shooting the worthless clientele of the Roebuck.

He pulled himself up and made for the door. No one caught his eye, and the pub breathed out when he was gone. He sobered on his way back, getting lost twice and deciding never to drink publicly again, especially with a charged revolver. He stopped over a gurgling drain and emptied the bullets out of the gun; they fell like brass comets into the speeding firmament below.

He turned the key very slowly and entered the apartment without a whisper. He crept back towards his camp bed, trying not to make a sound. He did not want to wake her, to let her see him tipsy after she had seen him in defeat.

As he dragged off his coat and unlaced his boots, he heard a noise that made the hair stand up all over his body. Something was scratching in the rooms. This was no faint animal, no rat or mouse scrabbling for figments of foods; something else was clawing nearby. He patted the walls, finding his way to the shelves. He found the simple tin candelabra and matches, lit its three stubs of candles, and peered through the rooms. The scratching stopped. He was totally sober, with an icy wire inside his spine. He waited, and the clawing began again. He heard wood splinter and rip, and he pushed the hushed light towards it. It stopped again, but he saw a mass on the kitchen floor. It was Josephine's dark body against the black floor. She was naked and lay very still, staring with unblinking eyes at the flaking ceiling. He brought his light close to her to ward off the unseen creature that scraped in the room. He knelt and touched her arm; it felt very cool, as if she had been out of bed for hours. He held the light high above his head to scan the room and keep the thing at bay; hot wax spilt and splashed across her face. There was no reaction.

"Josephine?" he whispered urgently. "Josephine!"

He touched her neck and felt no pulse. He bent over and put his hairy, impudent ear between her breasts: There was no heartbeat. She was dead. He sank back like a sullen, wet sack, into the collapsed quiet of the rooms and the world. Then the clawing started again. He spun the candles towards it and saw her left hand, frantically digging a pit in the floorboards. The nails were broken and the fingertips bloodied, but the old wood yielded under their insistence. He looked again at her set, dead face; she was elsewhere, but the floor was being eaten away by the live hand's independent labour. Then silence fell again. He dared not breathe, waiting for the hellish tattoo to start again, wondering fearfully at the life force that sustained its momentum.

As he watched, he realised that her body was slowly coming out of its coma. It warmed and connected to the arm that was still working, the hand continuing to scratch with a violent motion, as if it contained her entire will. Its furious work had lasted for only a few minutes, but they had been the longest he had ever endured. Gull's words about the hand's strength came back to him, as did the insane, frail woman who had gutted herself, and the fact that the doctor had named Josephine as his most successful patient. The context of her success brought a sudden, inexplicable chill to his skin.

Gull's questionable ethics were in the half-lit kitchen with them, two slumped figures caged in a night of fear and guilt. Had his machine produced this? What would he tell Sir William about his prized patient?

She was sleeping normally now, the black curves of her body glistening in a thin layer of sweat. He decided not to move or wake her and instead crept towards her bedroom on all fours, pushing the light before him and trying to keep it away from his beard, which brushed the floor; he intended to fetch a blanket to cover her modesty. It briefly occurred to him that it would be more natural for him to be naked too: His animal posture would then complement hers; if nothing else, it would make an excellent series of photographs, two beasts crawling in one small enclosure. All manner of naked people could be caught thus, in fragments of motion; a zoo of measured humanity.

He was about to stand when he heard movement behind him. She was across the room in a moment, standing over him, her scent overpowering, a purple musk of mammalian heat. Her eyes were luminous and locked on his. She suddenly lashed out at the candles, kicking them across the room. Now it was only her eyes that illuminated the shrunken space. She pushed her face into his, grabbing his hair and throat with massive force. He gasped but was powerless to react. Her strength had become superhuman, and all his instincts told him that, if she decided to, she could snap his neck in a moment. Their noses were crushed together, the glowing eyes staring point-blank into his. He could see nothing but the unfocused light; he felt nauseous and terrified. He tried to close his eyes, but it made him feel worse; the thin skin shrivelled under the intensity, and the glow passed straight through.

They remained meshed together in the hideous coupling for only a few minutes, but for him it felt like suffocating hours. Suddenly, she fell away, peeling off into sleep on the cold, barren floor.

He pawed at his eyes, which felt bruised inside. He was drained and trembling; it had all happened so quickly, each incident taking only moments, enormous quantities of focused energy burning for a few minutes. A few minutes. The spell of clawing had been shorter than the intense staring of her eyes . . . a few minutes! The sequence of minutes she spent in his machine: three, five, eight. It had worked, but it had been delayed! The flash of understanding and triumph was instantly snatched away by the thought of the next attack: He had only a few moments to escape or defend himself before she woke again and launched a full eight-minute strike.

He scrambled to get up, his legs sliding wildly from under him. Dragging himself to his feet, he collided into the sink, sending a small wooden dryer of crockery crashing to the floor next to the prone sleeper. Cups and plates shattered and spun as he grabbed the door handle to the outside stairs and his escape. It was locked. The keys were in his discarded coat, somewhere in the studio, but where? Where had he dropped them on his drunken return? There was some moonlight, and he stumbled about in it, frantically searching. He heard her stir in her proximate sleep but did not dare to stop and look. He found the coat and thrust his hands into the pockets, fingers rattling for the keys. He was at the door when he found the empty gun. He had twisted the coat inside out, and it clung to his arms. He savagely pulled at it and made it worse. No keys could be found, and his hands were trapped inside the knotted lining. Then she moved.

He screamed as she flung herself at him. Her eyes had dimmed to beyond darkness; no whites could be seen at all. She was a pure, muscular shadow. He tried to cover his throat, but she had no interest in that; it would not be the focus of her prolonged assault. She clawed at his trousers and dragged him to the floor by the ripping waistband, tearing the thick cloth and sturdy undergarments away. He kicked his legs and feebly half-punched at her head with the hand that was not entangled in the coat. She brought one fist pistoning up into his face, and his head snapped back from the sickening force, blood and stars hurtling in all directions. She dashed back to her target. He dared not strike her again: Another such blow would finish him. He waited for her to slash through his abdomen wall, but that was not her target either. She grasped his skulking manhood and threw the last remnants of its covering across the room. Gripping its base with the thumb and forefinger of her right hand, cradling his balls with the others, her left hand worked underneath him, and she violently pushed her index finger deep into his anus. Now he was struggling involuntarily. She pushed her finger against his prostate and squeezed with her other hand. His erection reared up, startled and automatic from its cringing sleep. He stopped fighting and fell back, realising what her true target was. She twisted round without loosening her grip. She was over him and lowered the power of her glistening body onto his triumphant, astonished cock. Her hands leapt upwards and grabbed his throat and squeezed while she pumped violently against him. He felt himself continue to grow inside her, expanding to colossal proportions. The pleasure was beating back the outrage and he gave in. He felt the brittle china edge of the broken saucer cut into his rump just before he erupted for the first time. She did not let go, but rode him into the floor, cracking cuts and welts into his skin until the full eight minutes were exhausted. Then she stood up, dripping slowly across the kitchen to her room, quietly shutting the door. He heard the key turn softly in the lock. He tried to get up again, scooping what was left of his pride and his clothing to cover his genitals, which still looked surprised, though this time by the abrupt interruption. He finally peeled the ball of cloth from his arm and found the key to escape. Shaking, he turned his topcoat the right way out, put it on, and limped away.

Making a charge against her was completely impossible; he would be a laughingstock. It was bad enough trying to tell Gull, who looked at him as if he was an idiot. He gave the incredulous doctor an edited account of her violent, mad, animal behavior. Gull calmed him condescendingly and had his wounds tended to by one of the male nurses. Six hours later, when Muybridge was rested and recovered, Gull sent him back to the rooms with two of the hospital's stoutest men. His crossing was in forty-eight hours and he had to retrieve his property and get it to Liverpool in time to make the boat. He had reloaded the Colt, and he gripped it firmly in his pocket as they entered the scene of the crime, but Josephine had gone, and she had taken all the expensive cameras and everything else that was portable and of any value. His machine was the only item left untouched; it stood in exactly the same position as when she had last been inside it. He did not have time to dismantle it now.

"Please, take great care in crating that up for me."

"Yes, of course, sir. But Sir William said you were to keep the rooms for your next visit."

Was he mad? Did Gull seriously imagine that he would take on another of his monsters? He could not wait to see the back of these rooms of deceit and pain. He collected what was left of his possessions and put the logbook with them in the trunk that the men carried away. The long sea crossing suddenly began to seem like a blessing after this. He could rest and heal in its progress, removing the dismal and nightmarish memories of the last twenty-four hours. They left and he locked up behind them. He kept the keys. The stitches in his buttocks and back pulled and twinged as they walked towards the waiting carriage. His instrument had worked; now he had to find a function for its genius.

CHAPTER TWENTY-ONE

*T*he shrill steam slid through the trees: The train, ready to leave, was calling for passengers. Had his footwear been more stable, the Frenchman would have jumped for joy. Instead, he squeezed his friend's hand with a mighty happiness, especially for one so small, and they moved on towards the sound, the Frenchman leading and pulling the long frame of his laughing, stooping companion through the leaves and high grass.

He saw the stillness set before his eyes, heard everything stop, just before he was yanked off his feet by Seil Kor coming to a sudden halt. Everything was arrested: the birdsong, the rustle of leaves, the shudder of life's continued existence. He scrambled up, preparing to ask his friend for explanation, when he saw his guide hollow. The electricity and moisture, the pulse and the thought, the tension and the memory—all had drained out of him, into the ground. Seil Kor crashed to his knees, breaking some of his straight fingers in their vertical collision with the earth; they snapped like dry twigs, but he did not notice. The Frenchman broke out of his shock and rushed to embrace his friend, who toppled into his arms. There was no weight; he had become a wildly staring husk. His eyes, which darted to and fro, were the only sign of life.

"Help! Help! For God's sake, help!" he screamed towards the

trains. He found the derringer with its last cartridge and fired into the air. *"Help, please, help!"*

Then, just as he heard people running to their aid, the sound of something else reached his ears, turning his blood to water: a laugh, so close that, for a moment, he thought it was Seil Kor himself. It hung in the air around his dying friend.

"Hello?! Hello! What is wrong?" bellowed an approaching stranger. "Where are you?"

The Frenchman retrieved his voice from a sickly, viscous shell beneath his stomach and called again for help, in the feeblest of tones.

They carried Seil Kor to the wooden hut station and laid him on one of the hard pews. Nobody knew what to do. He was cold and stiff, with not the faintest sign of breathing, but his eyes worked frantically, seeking the faces of all in the room. They sent for the overseer from the workforce on the train. The Frenchman held his friend's damaged hand, two of the fingers pointing comically at the ceiling. He thought about straightening them in an attempt to change the reality of the moment, to tidy the discordant and form a splint to normality by fussily adjusting the details. Maclish arrived and was confused by the tableau.

"Please help my friend!" pleaded the Frenchman.

Maclish came closer, putting his hand on Seil Kor's chest and touching his fingers to Seil Kor's throat. He saw the darting eyes and recognised the condition, quickly realising that the intended recipient was not the man lying prone before him: The Orm had taken the wrong man.

"Your friend?" he said, his anxiety inappropriate and incongruous but lost on the flapping state of the Frenchman.

The Frenchman agitatedly explained their journey and what

had just taken place. Maclish's culpability turned him stern and distant. "He can't stay here; we have to get him back to the city," he said brusquely, stepping outside and shouting commands along the platform. Two of the workers looked up and loped towards him. He pointed at Seil Kor and barked out more instructions, in a tongue that nobody else present understood. They lifted him from the pew and started carrying him along the platform, past the hissing train and its waiting carriages. There was no urgency in their actions, and the Frenchman was enraged to see that both of the Limboia were grinning.

"What are they laughing at?" he demanded of the Scotsman.

"It's just their way; they are not all there," he said, tapping his forehead with his index finger.

The Frenchman suspected at once that this was true and was convinced of it when he saw the vacant men carry his friend past the carriages and off into the perspective distance drawn by the flatbed trucks, which now bristled with stacked trees. "Where are those idiots taking him?" he squealed, rushing after them.

Maclish groaned and stomped after his loping run.

"Stop! Stop, take him back!" the Frenchman shouted at the grinning workers, as they carted his friend into the distance like a piece of game. They ignored him and plodded on, getting farther and farther from the passenger carriages and the Frenchman's comprehension. Maclish barked again and they slowly halted, like clockwork winding a slow release. The Frenchman tugged at his friend, but he was held firm between the workmen, who looked down at the small man without interest or recognition, the smiles never leaving their greasy, blank faces.

"Tell them to take him back to the compartment!" demanded the Frenchman of the Scot.

"He is not going back on the train," said Maclish; "he is going back on a flatbed with the trees."

For a few moments, the Frenchman was lost for words, panting and twitching on the other side of speech. Then he let fly with a tirade of demands and abuse while the Scotsman became red and even more stoic, as if his growing colour was a swelling gauge of his inflexibility.

"He's dead, man!" said the Scot emphatically, as if talking to a child. "He is *not* going in any of the carriages!"

The Frenchman was stamping with rage, so much so that his left shoe finally gave up the ghost and sprang from his foot with a flourish of something like embarrassment. The Limboia ignored the growing argument as the hanging body, slung limply between them, swayed slightly, its eyes paying fierce attention to the discarded shoe.

"He is not dead! You will be made to pay for this outrage!" the Frenchman bellowed at Maclish's back as the Scotsman resumed his walk towards the back of the train.

Maclish shouted a command over his shoulder and wound the Limboia into walking mode again, the deflated Frenchman hobbling slowly behind. They halted at the last flatbed and deposited the body on the hefty wooden floor, securing it with heavy metal chains. A wall of equally lashed trees lay steeply next to Seil Kor, their sap oozing everywhere. Maclish pulled on the chain to test its fastening. He spoke again to the Limboia, who lost their smiles and ran back to their compartment. On his way back to the head of the train he passed the Frenchman, who spoke first.

"Where shall I go?"

Maclish bit his tongue and directed his gaze away from the Frenchman's eyes. "Wherever you damn well please," he said.

The small man took in the length of the train, trying to conjure a decision from his confusion. The whistle jolted him, but it was suddenly too late: With much clanking, the train started to move, the engine's iron wheels shrieking on the sap-wet iron rails, its massive load teetering forward. He ran to Seil Kor and threw himself on the flatbed as it gained momentum, the other shoe flying off and disappearing into the undergrowth.

As the train gathered speed, its load shifted, shaking the flatbeds with bone-jarring regularity. Seil Kor showed no signs of life; his body trembled with the bumps of the track, but all else was inert. The Frenchman held on tightly, one arm covering his friend protectively, the other hooked around the chain. He had closed his friend's eyes: The intensity of them staring out of the handsome, expressionless face had been too much for him to bear. It had taken four attempts to shut them; he eventually resorted to smearing the thick tree juice over his friend's lids. It broke his heart to treat those once-beautiful eyes so roughly, but it felt necessary. He still believed that the energy they showed was a sign of survival and that his friend's present condition might be a form of coma or sleeping sickness; similar things, seen before in his lifetime, allowed him to retain a little optimism. He would find a doctor the moment they arrived in Essenwald, with enough knowledge to awaken his beloved friend and restore him to brimming health. This was his best hope as they sped through the darkening forest, rattling and slipping together.

Seil Kor's eyes opened and flashed at the speeding trees as they hurtled past. The Frenchman could not remember his name or why he was clinging to his cold, hard body. He knew he loved him, but not why. The terrifying situation was exacerbated by the stranger's mad eyes. He tried to look away, but the movement made him slip again. He was sliding in a black, sticky pool that was blood or sap, viscous and sickening. Thin rain had made it spread and stretch, the darkness taking away its identifying colour. He had been shaken to the side of the prone man; he wanted to reach out and close the lids of the snatching eyes, but the train jolted and he grabbed hard at the chain instead, scared of being thrown clear. The flatbed juddered and swayed more violently, its cargo of butchered trees shifting and straining against its fetters. He knew if the chains came loose they would both be crushed, or swept over into the racing night to be broken like kindling against the tracks.

He gripped the staring man and began to sob. His heart hung like a pendulum in a long, hollow case of hopelessness, abrupt shudders discordantly jangling the weights and coiled chimes, which whimpered and knocked, while the other man's eyes ticked away all life.

Sleep was farther away than the city, and he dared not let fatigue cajole him. The trees grunted and struggled, shifting the weight of their enormous carcasses again. He tried to focus on the stars, but the engine's smoke and the vibrations made them bleary and out of focus. He knew he was lost if he could not anchor his mind. He thought of his mother and of Charlotte; he must not let their memory be erased. He even conjured some of the faces and bodies of the street boys, but they would not stay, and his purchase slipped away. He looked for God and was considering Satan, when his genius spoke up to save him. His books! Those unique works of fiction, and the one he would write next: The very thing that made him significant had almost been forgotten in the wrath and momentum of this, his mad time in exile from them. He should not have been in this dismal forest, putting his life at risk with ignorant savages. All he needed was a locked room, ink, and sheets of virgin paper. This was his anchor, and he embedded it with the few scraps of energy he had left. He instinctively knew that memory and imagination share the same ghost quarters of the brain, that they are like impressions in loose sand, footfalls in snow. Memory normally weighed more, but not here, where the forest washed it away, smoothing out every contour of its vital meaning. Here, he would use imagination to stamp out a lasting foundation that refused the insidious erosions buffeting around him. He would dream his way back to life with impossible facts. He gripped the man and the chain harder as they thundered towards dawn, the chapters unpeeling across the wet miles.

He came out of the nightmare into the nightmare. The scream of the whistle and the blistering sun illuminated worse than he had dreamt. He had no idea why the floor shuddered, why he held on to a dead man who stank of vegetation, or why he could not wake out of it. The train was slowing, the first signs of civilisation beginning to show. Fences and enclosures appeared by the side of the track, cut into the edge of the forest, which seemed to be loosening its grip on the land. Slower still, and the huts began to cluster and swarm around the track, gradually gaining height and culture. The shrill train braked, piercing its arrival to the approaching city. The corpse's head jolted to one side, its marble black eyes staring at nothing. The Frenchman looked away with a regret that he could not explain, as the train slouched to a halt in the steaming station. He did not see that the wet, black orbs were still moving, still actively flinching to grab at any motes of light or meaning.

Loose, weird men arrived at the side of his flatbed and immediately started to tear and jostle at the chained trees. A man with red hair and a stiff uniform walked down the platform towards him. "Get off!" he demanded.

The words had a magical effect. He slithered away from the trees and the corpse, off the flatbed, and onto the station's hard, steady ground. The red-haired man pointed him to the exit, down towards the engine, where well-dressed people in clean attire milled about.

His legs buckled and shook, refusing to forget the agitations of the journey; indeed, they insisted on continuing them, acting them out on the motionless platform. His upright carriage reinstated itself outside the station, but he dithered in small, clotted circles. Hadn't he forgotten something back there? Was he supposed to be alone? Wasn't there somebody he was waiting for? Had he a bag, or a stick, or . . . ?

An hour later, unclear and unreminded, he was on the road leading into the centre of the city. He was sunburnt and ragged, his robes besmirched in all manner of filth, and the hurrying citizens eyed him in disgust and gave him a wide berth as he stumbled on.

Charlotte was drinking tea on their balcony when she saw him. She had been vacantly gazing across the crowd for days, trying to distract her worried mind, when the source of her anxieties teetered into her vision. She dismissed the possibility at first, for the man zigzagging below was dressed in some kind of native clown costume; a ludicrous beggar, overdressed to draw attention to his serious mental plight. Then she recognised something in his trampled gait. She stood up, retrieving the binoculars that sat on the table beside her and pressing them to her hope. The haze and the dirt attempted to dull the lenses, but beneath them, his features still showed: the eyes, lost and trawling the street, seeking something familiar, something concrete. She rushed downstairs and ran through reception, calling out to the concierge: "Bring help, it is monsieur, he is hurt, bring help!"

When she reached him, he came to the end of his abilities. He stared at her for a second more, then fainted.

Three days later, he awoke, cool and clean, floating in the still, starched whiteness of fragrant sheets. The smell of their fresh, laundered brilliance painted the inside of his mind with perfectly chilled milk. One of his hands began to search under the blanket for a forgotten thing beside him.

"You are safe now, Raymond." The voice was soft and confident, radiant and restful. It seemed to come from the entire room. "The doctor has given you something. Now you must rest. I will bring you some more beef tea shortly."

The words made no sense but soothed him back into slumber. A huge brown cow stood next to the bed. It wobbled, balanced comically on train tracks made of meat jelly, as the doctor sat below it, pulling at its udders, streams of hissing tea jetting into his white enamel pail. He filled his syringe from the steaming fluid. It misted the glass tube of the instrument, filling the room with its moist bovine vapour. The cow smiled through the fog with the most natural expression of quiet delight.

When he awoke, the cow was gone and Charlotte was sitting by his bed. It took a few minutes to remember her name. She brought tea and talked quietly, while he nodded and frowned at her version of the last few days.

The drug that the doctor administered to him was Soneryl; he would use it, and others, for the next thirteen barren years of his life. As its effects wore off, a great, hollow pain opened out inside him. He stopped nodding, and Charlotte's words lost their meaning. Her voice was like a song, a chanter that made tears rise and fill his flickering eyes. She stopped when she saw her companion's growing distress. Moving to his side, she held his small body in her arms. He sat forward, and she saw that his pillow was blotched pink with perspiration and blood. Beneath his silk pyjamas, his wounds and abrasions had been bandaged and covered in lint.

"It's all right," she said, "you are safe now. You are tired and bruised, but without any real injuries. Do you remember what happened to you and your friend?"

"Friend?" he said, in a voice that surprised him. "What friend?"

Charlotte explained that he had left to meet a man who was taking him into the Vorrh. They had planned to be there for only one day, but in fact, he had been gone for four. She told him of her growing panic and the plans she had been ready to put into place, before she had seen him on the street.

"What was his name?" he asked weakly.

"I don't know, my dear. You called him many things. I think you said 'Silka' or something like that?"

"Silka," he repeated, shaking his head. "Well, what did he look like?" he murmured.

"I am sorry, but I did not see him. You said he was young and black."

"Did I?"

Charlotte nodded and he thought hard, but there was nothing there.

Not a single trace of the last seven days existed between this stained pillow and the previous one, which had been bloodied by dream; not even a rind of memory clung to the empty space in his skull. What boiled and hollowed him was below, in his heart: a vast, pleading hurt that sucked at his being, a loss beyond all other feelings, an overpowering sadness that should have been an overpowering joy.

"Charlotte, I think I am in love," he said, tears streaming down his face as his body shook and wheezed in her frightened arms. They stayed like that until he sobbed himself asleep. Charlotte tucked him back into the bed and lowered the blinds against the late, slanting afternoon sunlight.

She tiptoed about the room, silently packing their belongings back into the suitcases, trying not to think of what he had just said. The warm, dim quiet was hushed and measured by his rhythmic breathing.

Three days later, he was standing in the lobby of the hotel, dressed in one of his immaculate white suits. Charlotte had booked the ship to carry them home. The monstrous black mobile caravan chugged outside, waiting, brimming with their possessions. He dithered as he clung to her arm, looking out into the blinding light of the street. His bone Eskimo spectacles had been changed for a much larger, more contemporary pair, which wrapped around his pinched face, making him appear insect-like.

"Shall we go?" she asked, squeezing his arm affectionately.

He gulped and nodded, and she guided him through the warm glass doors and down the faltering steps. Just before he entered the massive vehicle, he looked up and into the milling crowd, through the little island of trees that sat across the road. He looked hopelessly for someone he did not know, somebody who might know him; a last chance to repair the tearing wound that was devouring him. He looked for recognition in a wave or a touch or a smile. Nobody in the crowd stood out. Nobody saw him in the brightness and swirling dust. He stepped into the car, and it lumbered out of the city, across the arid landscape, towards the coast. In the passenger wing mirror, which had been adjusted for his view, the dark line of the Vorrh receded until it was erased by haze, dust, and vibration. His eyes never left the reflection until they reached the sea.

➤→

After his duties at the train station were finished, Maclish had rushed to find the doctor, his expression grave and urgent.

"It went terribly wrong. We must find Sidrus at once."

"What went wrong?" said the doctor, obtusely.

"The Orm, man, the Orm! It hollowed the wrong man, some other poor black who was guiding a stranger through the forest. Not a hunter, anyway, and not Tsungali," said Maclish.

"But how could that be?" said the doctor, finally relinquishing the remnants of his peaceful day. "He was spoored; he had the trace string . . ."

Maclish shrugged. "Don't ask me, man—I don't have the answers. It didn't work this time."

Sidrus fumed, his head shaking in dismay; its soft, bald surface rippled and wriggled his disturbing face, looking even more unreal in the pallid light of Hoffman's laboratory.

"He had the string worm and you had the description of the prey; how could this happen?" he said ominously.

The doctor looked at the floor and Maclish tried not to look at the articulation of the face, as anger slid beneath its baby-smooth skin and wrinkled between its wide-set, piggish eyes. He had seen many things, worked with all kinds of freaks and barrack life, but this man gave him the horrors, made his flesh creep.

"You have wasted my time and my money, and the one opportunity I had of stopping that animal from killing Williams in the Vorrh," he snarled.

"It worked with Cornelius and the Silver Man," mumbled Maclish, his words barely escaping before Sidrus turned on him, crossing the room and looming into his face.

"Then what fucked up this time?" he shouted, his breath hot and fast on Maclish's face, forcing him to close his eyes. No one had ever dared try this before; the consequences of insulting the fire-headed Scotsman were broadly known. But on this occasion, he looked away. The deepest levels of his well-sprung instinct locked down his hands and his rage, quelling it beside his opponent's ferocious power.

"We will give the money back," said the doctor, trying to defuse the situation. Sidrus sent him a withering gaze, as if to silence him forever; alum for the tongue. The stringent moment lengthened. Sidrus stormed out of the pale room, snapping the atmosphere's tensile thinness with his stomping feet.

Anger was not the most useful tool in his armoury. He had achieved everything without its obvious help, could reach the far points of expression and action without the adrenaline other men required to achieve half as much. So he marched through the streets, wanting to dissipate his rage and think more clearly, but he could only contemplate the dismal outcome of what should have been a foolproof plan—what had those idiots done to ruin such a perfect solution? Now he had to find another way of stopping the wretched Englishman from being butchered in the Vorrh as he tried to pass through it for a second time. Nobody had ever accomplished such a thing; the great forest protected itself by draining and erasing the souls of all men; all except this one, apparently, who walked through it with impunity, even appearing to gain benefit from it. Sidrus did not know how or why this unique possibility had manifested itself, although he guessed that the witch child of the True People had worked some blasphemous magic with her protégé. What he did know was that if the Englishman passed through the forest again, he alone would have the opportunity to understand its balance, its future, and maybe even its past. Not since Adam had such a single being altered the purpose and the meaning of the Vorrh, and now he was being hunted by a barbaric mercenary, one these fools had let slip through their grasp.

Sidrus was faced again with the impossibility of his task—he could not go into the forest, and there was nobody else who could prevent catastrophe. It had been easier dispatching the

Erstwhile than trying to protect the straying man from afar. The twins had been easy enough, but he knew there would be others sniffing out the bounty attached to Williams's desertion and the murders he had committed that had sparked the tinder of the Possession Wars.

His only hope now was that Tsungali would be lost in the tangled depth or that one of the creatures of the core would permanently interrupt his travels. But Sidrus had little faith in these hopes, and he prayed again for a darker shadow to cross the hunter's path, something that would give the Englishman a chance to fulfil his evolution.

CHAPTER TWENTY-TWO

*G*hertrude and Cyrena had heard rumours about the work-force of the Vorrh. Their parents and grandparents and generations of their relatives in all directions had depended on the forest for their living and, eventually, their wealth. They knew that the Limboia were said to be becoming less than human, a condition brought about by prolonged contact with the Vorrh; that only one man could control and manipulate them; and that he was becoming rich and respected by holding the reins of their talent. It was said that his communication with them had made it possible to discover more about the forest and its inhabitants, something that had been forbidden for all known memory. Ghertrude's father occasionally consulted with one of the city's most prominent doctors, a known associate of Maclish, the talented Limboia keeper. So they journeyed to the doctor's house with the great hope of finding Ishmael before all chance had passed.

They travelled in Cyrena's lilac Hudson Phaeton. There had been a light rain that morning, and the chauffeur had raised the roof on the noble convertible. They talked excitedly about the cyclops and his possible adventures, watching the city slip past as they glided by at a handsome seven miles per hour. Large numbers of people milled about on the streets, and occasionally little groups would shout or scream out in some boisterous play. They came close to a curb where four young people tussled together in a noisy sport. Their appearance was odd and caught Ghertrude's attention. As the car drew closer, the two young men grabbed the smaller girl with rather too much force, seeming oafish and common, although their clothing suggested taste and education. They held the young woman by the arms, pinning her forward so she could not turn. The fourth member of their spinning group, a powerful young woman, pointed at her trapped companion, laughing and peeling off her gloves. In the brief glimpse from the passing car, it was suddenly obvious that the younger girl was in terror; the men's game had become earnest under the gaze of the other woman, who was obviously poised to attack. Ghertrude tugged at Cyrena's attention, and they craned their heads back towards the tableau in time to see the woman grab the other's face, much in the same way that peasant women squeeze melons to test their ripeness. There was a horrible scream from the girl, who fell to her knees while the others happily fled.

"Stop the car!" cried Cyrena to her driver. "Rupert, go and see what has happened and if we can be of any help!"

The chauffeur mumbled something and left the purring limousine, walking back towards the crowd of people, who now stood in a circle around the fallen girl. None had gone near or offered assistance. The chauffeur bent down to look at her and then stiffened and stepped back. The girl sobbed, "I can't see, I can't see!"

He stared for a moment then looked away, walking back to the car with his eyes fixed firmly on the pavement.

"Well?" demanded Cyrena, leaning out of her open window. "What's happened? What can we do?"

The chauffeur spoke quietly without looking at them, his hand already opening the driver's door. "It's nothing, ma'am. Just horseplay got a bit out of hand. She's just a bit ruffled; that's all."

"Ruffled?" repeated Cyrena incongruously. Her next question was staunched by the chauffeur, who quickly got in and closed his door, releasing the handbrake immediately and pulling away from the carnage. She looked back out of the car's rear window, but both the crowd and the girl had gone. Bypassers already cut fleeing trajectories through the static where the circle of theatre had been. Rupert must have been right; it had been nothing but her inflamed imagination.

"Go on," she said with a twitch of her dismissive hand.

The car gathered speed, yet something nagged at her. The incident had curdled her day and left her with an ill-determined ache of responsibility. Ghertrude tried to lighten her friend's obvious anxiety by changing the subject and pointing outside to more delightful features of their journey. Cyrena nodded, but her unconscious remained continuously aware of the small groups of people that sped past the corner of her eye.

Ten minutes later, they arrived at the doctor's house. The journey had frustrated Cyrena: Her taciturn chauffeur still refused to meet her gaze; she wished she had learned to drive herself.

They were immediately shown through the spacious house to the doctor's consulting rooms, where he waited to greet them with warm handshakes and a beaming smile. They sat and drank tea, passing pleasantries until Cyrena decided to broach their need.

"Dr. Hoffman, one hears that you are a good friend of the keeper of the Limboia."

"Yes, Mistress Lohr, that is true. We have worked together to oversee and tend to the workers' health."

"Please, call me Cyrena. Everybody does, and my family have known yours for a good many years now," she said, casually adjusting her beauty for the old man's appreciation.

He smiled and said, "Cyrena! Why do you ask about Maclish?"

"It is a delicate matter of great importance to me; to us," she said, looking at Ghertrude. "A dear friend of ours has gone into the Vorrh and we fear for his safety and well-being."

The doctor nodded, presenting his professional face of concern for their benefit.

"It is said that you and the keeper should be consulted in all practical matters relating to the forest, that your knowledge and experience would prove invaluable."

The old man received the compliment with relish, giving a side-slanted nod of gratitude, which also formally agreed with her assumption. "How can I help?" he said.

"We want to go in and fetch him out."

Hoffman's features shifted into stern-father mode. "My dear, I am afraid that would be quite impossible. It is no place for a woman, especially one of your sensibilities and background."

As soon as he said it, he realised he had accidentally excluded Ghertrude from the same description. He half turned towards her, making a feeble scooping motion with his hand to suggest inclusion. Ghertrude frowned.

"You may know that I am a woman of some wealth and that Mistress Tulp's family have great influence among the various guilds. I say this merely to emphasise the fact that both of us have a certitude of purpose and the means to make it happen, and that our backgrounds have given us confidence and aptitude quite beyond the average woman."

Ghertrude was struck by Cyrena's eloquence and strength and was again certain that they had met many years ago. The taste of that time leant on another hinge, which opened on the memory of this doctor attending her when she was fevered. She had disliked him the moment she had entered this room: Now she knew why, and she watched him more carefully.

Hoffman rolled small, soundless words around his mouth until, finally, they fell out. "I . . . I was only anxious for your safety, Mistress Lohr. There are real and extremely dangerous hazards in the forest, that I hope you"—he turned belatedly towards Ghertrude—"both would never have to face. For example, there is the dissipation of the memory brought about by the exposure to the forest's noxious atmosphere. I have made some experiments in this matter, and it is my firm belief that the intake of air damages the brain, even after a few days. It would be very unwise to subject such sensitive constitutions to these harmful effects." He was gaining speed, hoping to impress them with his wisdom. "Imagine the effect of an enduring time in there, what perilous and irreversible injury your health would suffer. Mistress Lohr, you have already had a major traumatic incident this year. What you are suggesting is out of the question."

"Dr. Hoffman, we do appreciate your concern, but you must understand that your descriptions only make me more determined," said Cyrena, her eyes glowing a steady resistance. "Everything about that accursed place makes me fear for my friend even more, and my own recent incident is nothing compared to the horrors you have just described. I must find him and return him to safety, and I will do so with or without your assistance."

The mood in the room had swivelled. Hoffman was irritated by Cyrena's implacable confidence, and she, in return, did not care for his attitude; the patronising tang of defeat was repellent to her. After a long, wooden silence, the doctor cleared his throat and started again. "The problem is . . . ," he started.

"The problem is the problem," she butted in. "But very well," she continued, sensing a loss of ground. "If we can't go, maybe we can pay for someone else to search for him in our place? The Limboia, perhaps?"

The doctor sniggered and tried to hide it with a cough. "My dear, the Limboia cannot find themselves, let alone anybody else; they are a vague, undisciplined mob, who can only be made to work in tight units, doing simple tasks. They cannot be let free in the Vorrh: They would never come back!" He chortled at such a ridiculous prospect.

"Then what about the Orm?" said Ghertrude.

Since the return of her youthful memory, her eyes had not once left the doctor's face. She had seen his dismissal, noted his disinterest in Cyrena's pain and all they had spoken of. Now the smugness disappeared. His face shook as if it had been hit by a gravedigger's frozen spade. Gone were the arrogance and the guile, the oily charm and condescending grandeur. In their place stood a small, washed-out man with nothing to say, only fear and anger flickering in the saggy folds of his dazed expression.

"The what?" he said in a voice that was barely audible.

"The Orm," said Ghertrude, her dagger gaze missing none of the telltale signs that were filling the room.

"I don't know what you mean," he obviously lied.

Cyrena, whose attention had been momentarily caught by the Gladstone bag that dominated the table before her, suddenly realised that the swivel was shifting again and returned her focus to the exchange.

"The thing that lives with the Limboia, that you have use of."

He was completely speechless. How dare this ninny of a girl stroll into his home, claiming to know of the Orm? What if her father found out?

"I'm not sure what you think you know . . . ," he began, sitting back and forcing a chuckle.

"What I know is not important here. It's what you know that will help us in this matter."

Cyrena sensed the needs of the conversation and joined in to construct a pincer movement. "As I have said before, Doctor, this is a delicate matter that I intend to have resolved, at any cost." She watched Hoffman absorb the threat and continued, coating it in the honey of temptation. "I will pay dearly for this to happen, and if you and your 'Orm' are part of it, then we shall all profit from finding him."

The doctor shifted his position on the chair, avoiding Ghertrude's attentive direction. "I will have to talk to Maclish," he said tentatively. "I don't know if it's possible, but . . . I will try to help you find your friend."

Cyrena instantly brightened at the subtle triumph. They were getting closer to Ishmael. She felt an immediate desire to plan and anticipate for his return.

"Excellent! However, there is one other detail of great importance," she said, smiling graciously at Hoffman. She glanced at Ghertrude, then tipped into the doctor's confidence, warning him back into the excitement. "Our friend is severely deformed."

She explained Ishmael's very particular problem, almost forgetting that she had never seen it. But it was better this way; she made it sound brave and heroic. Ghertrude said nothing; she did not trust this man with any detail and was nervous about involving him in such intimacies.

"The whole thing must remain entirely private, you understand," said Cyrena.

"I am sure we are all more than capable of keeping a secret," the doctor replied, his eyebrows raised.

The agreement was made that he would talk to Maclish about setting the Orm loose in the forest to find their wandering friend. A certain sum of money would be paid up front, and the rest exchanged when Ishmael was brought to them. They stood to leave, on fairly good terms, shaking hands in the doorway and agreeing to speak again in a few days. Then, while Ghertrude's hand was still in his, and Cyrena had turned towards the street, Hoffman looked down at Ghertrude's waist and quietly said, "I am here to help you with the other problem, if you so want."

He slowly patted the back of her hand, then uncoiled his fingers and let go of her frozen form, grinning inside his mouth as he gently closed the door.

➤——

Ghertrude had been spending less and less time at 4 Kühler Brunnen. She found it lonely and unexciting without Ishmael. She had stopped expecting the promised letter from the invisible master of the house. It had said she would be contacted again in a year, but almost two had passed and no communication of any kind had been received. She did not know whether she was being scolded or ignored; either way it made her feel powerless. So she retreated to her old rooms in her family home; her parents paid no attention to her comings and goings, being far too occupied with the business of the city, and she increasingly felt as though she had become entirely invisible. Even Mutter looked through her most of the time; only Cyrena seemed to enjoy her company and her mind.

Today, though, she was back at the old house, pottering blindly about on a rainy morning, waiting for her friend to arrive. The message had come through: The cyclops had been found and taken to the old slave house.

"What a terrible place to take the poor man," said Cyrena to Ghertrude when she came to collect her with her car. Mutter had opened the gate, showing even fewer manners than last time, guiding her through to the reception room with a grunt and slouch.

"Why do you keep that ghastly man on?" she said, as he sloped away.

"He has his uses," said Ghertrude, who seemed distracted and focused elsewhere. "It was he who told me of the Orm," she said absently.

"How did he know of such a thing?" asked Cyrena, bemused.

"The lower people are closer to the ground; they exchange

stories about it. They are always talking about base actions or ghosts as things without speculation. They don't have the space for philosophy. They work in the pinching enclosure of fact. So odd details and stories become important, like ideas do with us. It's never been the educated classes that tell stories, carry legend, or invent mythologies."

"Oh?" said Cyrena, surprised and not quite understanding why the girl cared or understood. "But what about the Greeks?" she asked, pulling a wisp of forgotten education to the aid of her feigned interest.

"Exactly the same. The Titans started as no more than tribesmen covered in white mud, circling their huts, shouting stories under bull-roarers, to keep the women and children inside."

"Mm," said Cyrena.

"I'll tell you another thing: Mutter distrusts Dr. Hoffman more than I do, something to do with his son, I think."

Cyrena had lost focus entirely and was fidgeting to leave. The moment had come: She could finally thank Ishmael and begin their friendship together. At the gate, Cyrena looked at Mutter again; he was watching the purring limousine outside and ignored her interest. Ghertrude turned to him as they were about to leave, a look of pleasant companionship on her face. "We are bringing Ishmael home today," she said inclusively.

She turned to get into the car, missing his expression, which suddenly turned ugly. Cyrena knew that her friend was utterly wrong to have any belief in this insolent oaf, and she resolved to monitor his future involvement more carefully.

In the car, she found Ghertrude's distance annoying. She was there to share this moment, not ignore it. She asked, "Do you think he will be all right? Do you think his memory will be affected? He's been in there a long time. He might not even remember me. How will I tell him all, explain everything?"

Ghertrude had a genuine affection for her new friend and

greatly admired her vivacious energy, but now she was sounding like a piping adolescent, fantasising over someone she had never met. She tried not to say it, but perversity was such a willing adviser. "He can be very difficult, you know; he is not like us, not at all."

Cyrena stopped talking, waiting to hear more, but that was all her friend said, and it sounded like a warning. They drove the last few miles to the slave house in silence.

"He was bloody difficult to bring in. Are ye sure ye know this thing?" Maclish's charm had been left with all the empty bottles a long time ago, and the women flinched at his abrupt and coarse manner. The doctor interceded, literally stepping between them, grinning and blocking his partner's impertinence.

"What William means is that your friend did not want to leave the Vorrh. He struggled a great deal and we had to use much force to get him here."

"You did not hurt him?" flared Cyrena.

"No, mistress, he is safe and sound, as far as I can make out," said Hoffman.

Cyrena did not understand what he meant but felt reassured.

"He scared my men," joined in Maclish. "Ye said he was deformed, but none of us were prepared for this!" He banged his hand on the metal door of the holding cell. A shuffling sound came from within. "We hope your presence will calm him down. I'm sure when he sees ye and hears your voice he will settle."

Cyrena was already pawing at the door in expectation; Ghertrude held back uncertainly.

"It's dark in there," growled Maclish.

"Yes, he likes it like that," said the doctor, watching Ghertrude's eyes. Maclish pulled the keys from his belt, put one in the lock, and turned it. In his other hand he held a stock whip. The door creaked on its weight, and a huddled movement rippled under the straw and rags in the dark far side of the cell. They all came in and stood together. Cyrena hesitated, then walked forward.

"Ishmael?" she said quietly, and an attention was sensed in the far side of the room. "Ishmael, we have come to take you home. Ghertrude is here with me."

There was a distinct movement from under the straw, and everybody strained their eyes to make out the crouching figure. Maclish changed the whip from one hand to the other.

"Ishmael, we have missed you; you will be safe with us when we return home," said Ghertrude, his proximity oiling the mechanisms of her voice.

"Yes, we can leave now. Please come with us," said Cyrena. "Do you recognise me? I am the Owl. I am the one that you spent a night with during the carnival."

Maclish curled his lip, and he and the doctor exchanged an astonished glance. The figure moved out of the shadows towards them.

"Yes, that's it; come to us," said Cyrena and turned to Ghertrude, beaming and shaking. "He knows me!"

Smiling with tears in her eyes, she turned back as the figure moved forward into the ray of light, which came in through the barred windows and divided the room. He looked up at them, and both women started to scream.

Ghertrude was holding Cyrena, one arm around her sobbing shoulders. She was glaring at Hoffman and holding back her own tears, which were slowly distilling from shock to rage. Maclish had dragged them out of the cell and into the small office, where they now sat.

"What's wrong with ye?" he snarled. "We got your cyclops, and now ye scream at it?!"

"That thing is not Ishmael," said Ghertrude, gritting her teeth and pushing away from her distressed friend, standing to match Maclish's aggression.

The doctor moved towards her and, in a puzzled voice, said, "Not Ishmael?"

"But ye said ye slept with it," said Maclish, pointing at Cyrena.

She looked up and out of her tears. "Slept with *that*?" she said, each word turning from disbelief into anger, so that the questioned inflection at the end of "that" sounded like a blacksmith's hammer striking a flame from a frozen anvil. She was on her feet: Her eyes had become terrible. Every part of her previous pain and her immediate disappointment was hurtling in a tornado of fury. She was ready to fight, and her stance—her eyes, teeth, and nails—was sprung for the next word; even Maclish took a step back. Ghertrude had never seen a human being like this, let alone a close friend.

The doctor shrank. Maclish recognised the sudden animal; he had seen it in the war. It had been rare and lethal, and he held it in respect.

"I am sorry, miss," he said in clear, cold words, lowering his arms to his sides. She panted for a few moments, and her humanity and her colour flooded back. Ghertrude moved to her side and guided her towards the door.

After they left, the shaken doctor sat on one of the creaking chairs and mopped the perspiration from his forehead with a large handkerchief. Maclish came back in. "She said we can keep the money, but we aren't getting any more."

The doctor just nodded and said, "What are we going to do with that thing?"

"Take it back or kill it. Nobody wants Loverboy here," said Maclish, guffawing at his own joke.

Dr. Hoffman saw nothing to be amused about.

Loverboy stood naked, four feet high, in the straw at the back of the cell. His skin was deathly pale, with a yellowish tinge. He had long, thin limbs, and his torso was squat and square. His head grew out from his chest, so that his forehead sloped into his shoulders, putting his tiny mouth level to where human nipples should be. His single eye was level with his armpits, and it blinked, sphincter-like, in the gloom. He did not think much of humans; their only value was in terms of food. He had eaten one two years ago, and their sweet flesh was greatly prized among his people. But they were dangerous to hunt, and many of his tribe had died in the process.

He knew he was the first of his kind to be taken bodily out of the forest, and he did not understand how it had happened. Unseen from the dense undergrowth, they had watched the humans devouring the forest year after year; nothing had ever entered and dragged one of his kind out before. He feared what he had seen so far and did not understand the cave they kept him in. He did not understand the actions of these tall, ugly creatures; they seemed to use all their emotions at once. He hated the one with red fur: It was known to be cleverer and faster than the herd that it kept for work and food. The screaming ones intrigued him; females, he thought, with hideous, extended heads. He became erect thinking about them, and it surprised him. He would have liked to undress one and play with it before he cooked and ate it. But that was for another time. Now he must escape and get back into the Vorrh.

➤

The two women travelled home together in silence. Cyrena dropped Ghertrude off at 4 Kühler Brunnen, and the pair quietly said goodbye as Ghertrude was admitted by a gleeful Mutter.

In the back of the lilac car, Cyrena's tide ebbed between

wrath and frustration, after the shock of seeing that abomination step into the light and look directly at her. She doubted all her memories, and the strands of tensile fibres that normally made her invincible unwound and came apart for a fraction of a second. In that blink of time, she mistrusted all of her pre-sight experience: What if that disgusting creature actually was the person she had slept with in the carnival night? What if it had been his gropings, suckings, and penetrations that she had accepted with pleasure and gratitude? What if, worst of all, it had been that thing that had healed her before creeping off into the night?

Yet again, sight had trampled everything else, and she had been lessened by it. Doubt nicked the circulation of her energy and bled her internally, so that now she did not understand why she had been so enthusiastic about seeing Ishmael again. Why had that become the centre of her life? How had she managed to expose her hunger and show her will to these foolish men? What was really in it for her? Had Ghertrude not warned her? Well, perhaps she had, but it had come too late and too weak.

By the time she arrived home, she was exhausted. She wanted to wrap herself in the darkness of the bedsheets and banish all visual memory, to remember only the luxurious depth of her stored library of touch, sound, and scent.

Mutter began to fuss around Ghertrude. It was out of character and grotesque, and she could see straight through it. He was delighted that she had come home alone and did not even want to know why.

Her annoyance quickly turned to indifference as she felt a tickling movement in her abdomen; something tiny, not a kick—it was far too early for that—but something uncurling, becoming awake after a long period of hibernation.

She left Mutter fluttering in the hall, like a heavy, damp moth without a flame. She went to her bedroom to rest, to hold herself tight and to pray that this was not really happening.

CHAPTER TWENTY-THREE

*D*r. Hoffman was walking across the city. He had been called to the house of August Daren, one of Essenwald's richest businessmen, who had demanded his presence immediately. Daren's wife had been attacked in the street by a mob of delinquents, who had pulled her from her carriage. He was furious, demanding the criminals be brought to a rough, instant, and painful justice. He ranted so much about the perpetrators that he forgot to mention any of his wife's injuries, and Hoffman had no idea which instruments and medications to bring. Hurriedly, he had shoved a handful of this and a handful of that into his stoutest Gladstone bag. It would not do for him to get on the wrong side of August Daren, especially now that his life had taken such a turn towards prosperity.

The Touch, or "Fang-dick-krank" as it had become known, was sweeping the city. It was said that it first came from the touch of miracle: the laying on of hands, the purification of the unclean and the malformed. Then it turned malevolent, eccentric, and dangerous. Qualities of kindness were exchanged for vengeance. Some who had been outcast because of their disability had turned malicious after they were healed, and their magic touch was passed on as a curse. They fingered the healthy, and the healthy became impaired; they then carried the taint, not knowing if their touch would injure or aid. It cut them off from their families and friends, making it their turn to become outcasts. A terrible fear of contact spread through the city, locking its inhabitants into themselves, hands in pockets, walking quickly away from all others.

The Touch had become so random that it reached fanatic proportions, causing a plague of the injured and the healed to spread chaotically throughout all of Essenwald. It wreaked havoc among the promiscuous, ruined families and made treatment virtually impossible. It changed social decorum on all levels, and in a city based on commerce, where guilds and classes were firmly demarcated by etiquette and formal social meetings, things started to fray when the niceties were removed. The shaking of hands was no longer a reasonable form of greeting; more arcane forms of meeting were now fashionable: Bowing and heel clicking had returned, as had arm crossing the chest with a clenched fist, which had not been seen in civilised communities since the Roman Empire. A Teutonic rigidity had returned to this far-flung outpost of a long-dead empire, one that had until then prided itself in stepping away from stiff ancestral history and revelled in its "modern" outlook.

The blacks and the poor were devastated by the Touch. Their ranks exchanged overnight, the sick becoming bright, the clean becoming ill. A great madness rose out of the confusion, and the growing wave of paranoiac fear was far greater than the actual number of those genuinely injured.

Hoffman had become quite the authority on the Touch, the causes and possible treatments. He told his patients, the Timber Guild, and other municipal authorities that he had carried out extensive research in his private laboratory and was making steady progress towards a cure of the dreadful blight. In truth, he had carried out a few botched autopsies, treated some of the afflicted with prodigious doses of barbiturates, and questioned some chained prisoners that the police—whom he was now working closely with—brought to him to be examined. His major discovery was that the phenomenon was in decline. This he told nobody, but doubled his extensive efforts to find a cure. He even injected some of the "carriers" with a serum of his own design and had them released into the community to help stave off the flow of the malicious disorder. With his usual cunning, he would ride his unexpected nag home to a glorious victory of science over evil. He had always been lucky with outsiders, and this one was made of gold.

His status in the community was growing steadily, and he no longer needed to practise the little bits of unorthodoxy that used to perk up his income. In fact, the less said about those, the better. They, and his business with Maclish, nagged at him. Such practices were yawning bear pits along his successful path of achievement, and he wished they could be spirited away or else be filled in with some amnesiac aggregate. The Tulp girl's knowledge of the Orm had rattled him; it was a step too close to downfall. The subsequent fiasco with the wretched creature they had mistakenly dragged out of the Vorrh had made the whole situation even worse. The Lohr woman was very well connected: A word in the right place could dislodge all his achievements. He knew it was only the concealment of their one-eyed friend that kept those words from being spoken. His knowledge of the cyclops's existence protected him.

His association with Maclish was proving troublesome, and it worried at his confidence; the irascible Scot was far beneath him now and unpredictable in his mood swings. Moreover, the thug always blamed him when something went wrong. And wrong was an understatement: They had now used the Orm nine times, and two of those had gone seriously awry. He still believed that the savaging of the Klausen hag had been the Orm's first outing, and it had led the police straight to his door. All these troubles gnawed at him as he strode purposefully on, towards his undiagnosed patient. His priorities needed to be refocused, and he made his mind up to rid himself of this handful of anxieties as soon as the opportunity presented itself. He was clever enough to silence the women with guile and threat, but the keeper was another matter. That cat would have to be skinned another way.

➤→

Maclish was going to be honoured. The guild had invited him and his wife to a special dinner, to mark the company's increase in productivity; his workforce was the greatest contributor to it, and it was cheaper to give an honour than to award a raise.

Mrs. Maclish hadn't been to anything quite so formal for a long time, and she was feeling apprehensive. The bulge of new life was just beginning to show, and she was mildly troubled that it made her look plump, rather than pregnant. They were dressing in the bedroom: he, fumbling and cursing with a collar stud; she, turning and glancing at herself in the full-length mirror of the wardrobe.

"William, which do you think: the blue or the green?"

"I only just bought ye the blue one; wear that."

"Yes, but which do you think is best for tonight? The green is more my colour."

"Then why did we buy the blue?" he said crossly, as the stud sprang from his fingers and disappeared under the bed. He cursed and crawled after it, his shiny black dress trousers ruffling up the small carpet. She ignored his response.

"It's a choice between them, though; I only have the two."

"Thank Christ for that, or we would be here all night!" he said from under the bed, his voice humming strangely in the resonance of the china chamberpot. He found the stud and crawled out to start pulling at his collar again.

Marie Maclish was not normally a woman to engage with

such coquettish uncertainty; the rest of her stern life was run on simple facts and basic commodities, but she was enjoying herself. This little charade of choice took her back to the Highlands, to her grandmother's house and the girls' play of dressing up in women's lives.

He had finished with the collar but his twisted tie looked limp and apologetic. He was admiring it, when she laughed.

"What?" he demanded.

"What? Oh, William, look at the state of it!"

"The state of what?"

She put the dresses down and went over to adjust the tie, smiling playfully. He bristled at her touch. The more she pulled, the more he stiffened. As her smile fizzled out, his warmth drained away.

"It was perfectly fine, woman; now it's a mess," he said, pushing her fingers away. "We haven't got time for this—we can't be late."

She said nothing and went back to her dresses; they seemed shrunken and indifferent. He looked over his shoulder.

"Where's the blue?" he said, against the fret of disappointment that was filling the room. "I don't know what all the fuss is about; it's not you they will all be watching tonight," he concluded, grabbing his coat and yanking the door open.

She watched him disappear out of the room. After a few static moments, she dressed and went down to wait beside him for the arrival of the car to take them to the celebration. She looked graceful and quiet, standing in front of the house, her hair and eyes accentuated by the green of the dress, her husband too caught up and curt to notice.

The doctor waited for ten long minutes after the headlights of the car had vanished from the road. Then he made his way to the reinforced door of the slave house, letting himself in with a set of keys that nobody knew he had. He put his bag down on the central table and lifted the bundle out. He was just about to strike the gong when he heard a footfall on the metal stair. He turned to see the herald of the Limboia descending slowly, a vacant grin on his face.

"For Orm?" said the herald in flat, dead tones.

"Yes," said the doctor nervously. He had never been here without Maclish, and the place and these creatures unnerved him. His skin crawled every time he came close to the herald.

"What to do?" it asked.

The doctor explained the specific requirements of the task and how it must be done. "You won't need a scent or a trace this time," he insisted, and the herald seemed to agree.

"This time seeing one stays, stays till after."

The doctor thought for a moment, nodded, picked up his bag, and left. The herald tenderly picked up the bundle and held it to his chest.

That was that. Now he would talk to the insolent Tulp girl and hush her defiance; she was in no position to argue, not in her condition. He made an appointment to call on her and was surprised at the address. He had never been to 4 Kühler Brunnen but knew of it; he had conducted business by association and at a distance with it. Why did she live there? Surely it was not a property owned by her father or some other member of her significant family?

He had mentioned the Tulps, and indeed the Lohr family, while treating August Daren's wife, who, it transpired, was a victim of the Touch, the right side of her body being mildly paralysed, as if by electric shock. It was then that he had the idea of treating the afflicted with generated bursts of galvanic energy. It had worked for Mesmer; why not for him? A combination of shock and barbiturates would have them flapping their pocketbooks at him like performing birds; all that wonderful equipment he would be able to buy to furnish his experiments: Van de Graaff generators; spinning wheels; sparks and the scent of ozone; copper wires, glass wires; porcelain resistors like giant shining pearls. His laboratory would look magnificent. As soon as he got these distasteful matters out of the way, he could begin.

"The Tulps are new blood, second-generation merchants made good," Daren had told him. "Lowlanders from Leiden, or maybe Delft originally. Good businessmen with an ambition to become burghers. Three generations away from gentry, if we let 'em. Now, the Lohrs are quite different; here before mine, they were; old wealth. Comparable to emperors, they were; unlimited funds." Daren sat back in his chair in awe of that amount of worldly ownership, believing that the Tulps probably viewed him with a similar reverence. He roused himself at the thought of the Lohr family demise. "A bit gone to seed now, though," he added, with the tiniest relish of spite. "Just that strange daughter to run all that wealth and influence here in the old country."

The doctor was absorbing every word, weighing every gram of possibility.

"Did you know she was born blind?" asked Daren.

"I have had some knowledge of her case, but I am unable to speak of it, you understand," lied the doctor.

"Oh yes, of course!" said Daren, without a moment's doubt, his finger coming to rest on his closed lips.

➤→

Maclish had relaxed his strict social rules and accepted some wine in the name of self-congratulation. After many dry, disciplined years, he drank it in toasts to various companions, who stood and drank to him in return, with words of extreme gratitude. Nobody had ever said such things, and he had no defence. He swam in the flood stream of it, basking after the third glass and hugging his wife ferociously after the fifth; at least he thought it was his wife. By brandy, he was slipping back into his origins, where all sorts of vermin and jokers waited to greet him. Marie had been escorted to a seat four rooms away and sat in the middle of her worst nightmare, with the herd of directors' wives. She had nothing in common with the women and nothing to say, and they all knew it. What was more, she feared William was on a steep decline, and she was not with him to steer the outcome. She hoped he might collapse, that he might pass out before his long-sleeping fangs came out. The prospect snapped her to sense and she acted without stopping to think, cleverly approaching the most senior Frauen.

"I do apologise, but I am afraid that my husband has not taken his medicine," she announced in such a strong, music-hall Scottish accent that it surprised even her. "Please, I must go to him."

Allowing a wife to intrude on the gentlemen's part of the evening was unheard of, but it seemed a matter of severe need, so a maid was called and told to take Mrs. Maclish to the hall of the gentlemen's room. Marie bowed, fluttering and thanking those present until she was outside the room. Then she clicked into action, running through the corridors with the astonished maid in tow. Outside the smoky door, she told the maid what to do and made herself scarce. The lowly accomplice waited for her to leave, then knocked at the heavy door. Eventually, a bleary man opened it, seeming surprised to find anybody there.

"Please, sir!" the maid said. "Mrs. Maclish has been taken poorly; she needs to talk to her husband about her pills."

"Missus who?" spluttered the man.

"Mrs. Maclish, the guest wife."

"Oh, oh, of course," said the man, vanishing back into the room. After a prolonged time, during which the sound of moving furniture and broken glass fanfared his arrival, the soggy head of Maclish came around the door. There were no fangs, just a stupid grin. His concealed wife peered around the corner to make sure the coast was clear; then, at her command, they both pounced and dragged him out of the door and across the hall. Mercifully, there was no resistance, and the three of them staggered towards the entrance and the waiting automobile.

➤

The door to the courtyard was curiously open. With no servant to show him in, Hoffman walked himself to the front steps of the house and rang the bell. Almost instantly, Ghertrude was there, shaking his hand and inviting him to enter. The interior was blank, without sign of individual arrangement, yet the proportions were pleasant and well kept.

"Is this your house, Mistress Tulp?" he asked.

"No, Doctor, it belongs to a friend," she answered, with a modest smile.

She took him through to a reception room that smelt a little musty and unused. He stood in the centre of it, smiling uncomfortably.

"May I offer you a sherry?" she asked.

"That would be delightful!" he said, tucking his Gladstone behind the chair while she went to the cabinet. It was in his best interests to keep the bag and its contents out of her way.

"Please, take a seat," she said, returning with the brimming glasses.

He settled himself and enthusiastically took the sherry. "I have often walked past this house and wondered who lived here," he fished. "It must be one of the oldest houses in the city." He sipped his sherry and looked around admiringly.

"Yes, it is one of the older properties," she answered, without much interest. "The basement is even older; it still has the old well."

"Hence its name," he said.

"Yes, hence its name."

There was a pause of silence, while she fingered her delicate pearl necklace and he stared into his diminished glass. She poured him another and sat back.

"What may I do for you, Dr. Hoffman?"

Her directness pleased him: He could have this matter cleared up in time for dinner.

"Firstly, my dear, I wanted to apologise for that distasteful business at the slave house. I am afraid my colleagues are not the brightest of men." He paused for a moment to truly engage her eyes. "And your description of your curious friend was a little, shall we say, vague?"

She showed no expression and sipped from her glass. He drained his in a single gulp and set it noisily on the glass top of a small side table.

"Anyway, it's all taken care of now, and we can begin again to look for . . . Ishmael, was it?"

"Thank you, Doctor, but that's not necessary. Mistress Lohr and I no longer wish to engage your services."

Hoffman bristled. How dare she speak to him like a common tradesperson? He was just about to comment when she continued.

"We no longer feel it necessary to go searching for him; he will surely make his way out of the Vorrh in his own time." The doctor was speechless, and she decided to use his silence to press the point. "We were curious, though, Doctor: How did you manage to get such a monster out in the first place?"

"We went to a lot of trouble for you, some more specialist lengths," he said, his neck beginning to flush.

"Using the Orm, Dr. Hoffman?" she asked. "What is that, exactly?"

This was all going extremely wrong. It was meant to be he

who had the upper hand. "Well, Mistress Tulp, why don't you tell me? You seem to know all about it," he said in a churlish tone.

"I know that you and the keeper have some power over the Limboia and that you sell it as a service to anyone who can pay; I know that Cyrena paid you a great deal of money to be confronted by that creature."

"Wait a minute," he said. "We did our best to help you. It was you who came to us."

"Best?" she asked, her lip curling sceptically.

There was a silence, as if the air itself had been chopped short, a segment of it removed from the room. After a shallow, gasping time, the doctor sidestepped and said, "How is Cyrena?"

Hearing her friend's name spoken in such casual terms inflamed Ghertrude even more. "Mistress Lohr is still recovering from the humiliation that you and that brute put her through."

Hoffman had had enough and snapped back. "I did not come here to be insulted by you, young woman!"

"Then why did you come here?" she said, as quick as a flash. He was caught off guard again and searched fruitlessly for the right words.

"I . . . came here . . . to . . ."

"Yes?" she quizzed insolently.

"I came here to encourage your silence about our business together." It was Ghertrude's turn to be disarmed.

"I came to advise you that our assistance was given as a favour, out of respect for you and your families, and that it would greatly benefit you if the whole business were immediately forgotten." She took in his thinly veiled threat and countered with her own.

"I think our families would be very interested to know about your favours, don't you, Doctor?"

He had been flushing near to scarlet, but a livid whiteness

began to creep through his broken veins. He took a step towards her, his voice rising. "*You dare?* You dare to threaten me?! If you utter one word to implicate me or my associate in this matter, I will not hesitate to spread the truth about your secret friend; about him fucking you and that Lohr slut, and about everything else! The house, everything!"

"Good! Do it. Say whatever you please; you know nothing about this house, and our indiscretions are nothing to your crimes."

He was astonished; this should not have been happening. He had never met a woman as impertinent and disrespectful as this. "I warn you . . . ," he growled fiercely.

"With what?!" She laughed, challenging the last reserves of his restraint.

"With your life!" he snarled, grabbing her throat and tilting her face painfully up towards his. "You open your mouth and I will shut it permanently; I will have the Orm hollow out your soul and deposit it on my dissecting table, and I will cut that bastard out of your cunt. I will . . ."

His words tailed off as he found himself moving up and out of the room, weightless and undirected. His ring caught on her necklace, breaking it as he flew away from her, the pearls shot-gunning in all directions. She grabbed at her throat and the remnants of the string, her eyes wide and staring at something behind him. He watched, oddly detached, as the girl's shivering figure diminished and he moved towards the door, the tiny white orbs bouncing and dancing around her feet. He had no idea what was happening and was still thinking of what to say when the door opened and he was catapulted out into the cold night air and down onto the shining black cobblestones.

He looked up to see Mutter standing over him. He attempted to stand, but the old man kicked his legs away from under him.

"All right, all right," he said angrily, waving his hands in the air. "Your point is made. I have calmed down now; I won't hurt her."

The next blow totally confused him; he did not see it coming and it felt like he had run headlong into a wall. He remembered doing that as a child; the shock of the solidity against the speed of his intention. But he was not running now.

A light came into the courtyard: Ghertrude was at the door, the beam from the house streaming across the standing and kneeling figures. Hoffman squinted and saw that Mutter had a manuscript in his hand, a tight scroll of paper, some kind of accusation. He would have this peasant crucified for this outrage. He might even do it himself, maim him, as he had once maimed his son.

The servant went to the door and held up a protective hand, gesturing to the girl to go back into the corridor, before shutting her and the light firmly inside. Mutter returned and took a short run with his second blow. The scroll was not paper, but a two-foot length of lead pipe. With the anticipation of its impact, the doctor understood everything.

"No! *No!*" he cried.

The third blow cracked his skull; he heard it go, or it might have been his teeth shattering against each other. He tried to protect his head with a flailing hand, but Mutter kicked him over and stamped on it, his solid weight and hobnailed boot crushing the bones and mangling the gold ring flat and into the flesh. The next blow fell across his ear, sending him rolling across the yard, screaming. To stop the noise, Mutter swung the heavy, inert pipe up under his jaw, flipping him over and making him bite through his tongue. He was on his hands and knees, whining like a lost dog as he vomited part of his tongue, along with the recent sherry and the remains of his lunch.

"*Pleth fof jodds sek sthup!*" he choked pitifully.

He bled and gagged onto the cobbles. The next blow crunched

down into his head and removed the top of his fractured skull, which hung to the side of his head by a few long strands of wet hair. His bright laboratory with all its new electrical equipment splashed out, his triumph and genius trickling onto the night-black cobbles, where vivid sparks bounced like white pearls. Mutter hit him once more, and his eyes rasped and split over the broken bones of his collapsed face.

Mutter dragged the body to the stables and loaded it into the smaller cart. Hosing down the yard, he swept the bits of memory and hope into the sewer.

Ghertrude was cold, numb, and uncertain. She had heard the sounds straining through the thick oak door, as the broken string from her necklace hung in her hand. Mutter had not wanted her to witness the conversion of a man to waste, but she had heard every part of the process, and what she had done to that puppet in the basement swiftly paled to insignificance in comparison. She rested her back against the door and felt the weight of the future gather on her shoulders: It would be a long time before she could fall asleep.

→

The iron hooves of the tin clock stampeded into his dense and sweated dream. He fisted the shrillness into silence and swung his aching legs out of the bed. He fought against an odd, familiar sensation, trying to plan the day ahead, when he realised what was wrong: He was drunk. He had not been like this for more than two years, and he cursed his stupidity at sliding back. It was all so familiar: the dizziness, the smell, the pain in his head; the feeling of utter failure and that smug, crouching, "fuck 'em all" version of himself, poised deep inside, looking up and out of his face.

He glanced at his wife, who seemed to have avoided the screeching siren of the alarm clock, and lifted the bedsheets to observe the growing ripeness of her belly, which accentuated the strong curve of her hips. He dearly wanted this child, and he hoped for a son. At last, he would have something to pass on—and not just the alcoholic temper and selfishness his father had bestowed on him: He was the first Maclish in history to be looked up to, to have done something worthy of others' praise.

It was then that he saw the bruises on her arm and tasted bile in his mouth. He steadied himself and quickly pulled the sheet up, so he could not see her at all. Floundering into the bathroom, he washed in cold water. He hoped the shock of it would cut away the blunt, grey weight that he was carrying so awkwardly. He knocked the cup of toothbrushes and combs into the noisy, skidding sink while trying to retrieve his razor and stared at their spiky divination contrasted against the porcelain. What had he done and said last night? How could he have let this happen? Why had she not stopped him? He leant against the cold wall and pissed wearily in the general direction of the toilet.

Today, he would oversee the exchange of the Limboia, the exhausted ones for the eager, the train loaded with their stupid bodies. They would travel with one extra this time, and the idea of spending the journey with Loverboy, crated up so that he might be returned and set loose, made the keeper's head pound harder. At least he would find a place to sleep: That was inevitable. He wanted to crawl back into bed there and then, back to his wife's warmth and the lingering perfume from last night, but he dared not. Without him, there would be no exchange, no train ride, and the horror would stay hidden in the slave house for another day.

They had moved Loverboy into the basement of the building after the Limboia's interest in his shouting and barking had reached dangerous levels. Admittedly, it might have been his acrid stench: Even after they had hosed him down, it still permeated everything around, and Maclish was even beginning to think that he might be bringing it home; he could smell it on himself, and it would explain why his wife had become so distant again.

His thoughts turned again to Loverboy; his captive was definitely getting thinner. His colour had changed, the old ivory, creamy yellow of his skin having faded to a sallow grey. Maclish couldn't understand it; he had been given the same food as the others, and they had never complained. The kitchen staff always prepared the rich, nutritional mix of dried beans, cornstarch, and ground meat the same way. Maclish had done a particularly good deal with the local knacker's yard, getting almost-fresh meat delivered every week. The workforce needed to keep their strength up, and he had argued it well with the Timber Guild, who now paid a substantial amount for their sustenance. Good meat, of course, would have been wasted on them—they were unable to tell the difference—so he managed to feed them well and make a tidy profit on the side, thus keeping everyone happy; everyone, that was, except Loverboy, who repeatedly threw the bowls of steaming gruel back at his captors. The Chinese cook who ran the kitchen had refused to go back into the cellar after the third ungrateful attack.

"Let the fucker starve!" Maclish had said to his men after the third abortive attempt at the monster; and he would have, but the effect it might have had on the Limboia was unknown, and he could not afford any unhappy impacts on his production rate. "Keep 'em happy, keep 'em keen" was his motto, and it kept everybody else's prying snouts out of his business. For that reason, Loverboy was going back today, hangover or no hangover.

After his third cup of coffee, he began to feel more alert. He buttoned his uniform and pulled on his shining boots in the quiet kitchen, leaving by the back door and walking up the narrow hill towards the slave house. It was just before seven o'clock, and his wife listened to the kitchen door being closed and the sound of his steps on the gravel outside. She opened her eyes and allowed a small sigh to escape from her lips, relieved to finally be released from her feigned sleep and the suffocation of his presence.

They got the crate and the Limboia to the station without much incident. The horses had shied a couple of times when Loverboy had gotten frisky, but Maclish's hammering on the crate with the metal base of his whip had soon subdued the monster's cavorting. After placing the crate on a flatbed near the passengers' coach, they loaded the eager, empty men into the train. The keeper gave the signal and they steamed off to be absorbed into the Vorrh.

As predicted, the train took his wakefulness after twenty minutes. He sank into a dreamless sleep that curdled and fell, amplifying rather than soothing his hangover. Large, abstract masses bumped against him, rubbing at his extremities and dampening his elementals. The train seemed to be crawling at a sluggish pace, and the voice of the crated horror grew louder and louder in his semiconscious skull.

He was woken by a jolting stop and shook his head to try to gather his senses and possessions. His whip was strangled by the vines growing out of the luggage rack and would not come loose when he tugged at it. He knew this kind of thing happened, but this time he was unprepared; unable to dislodge it, he decided to get a knife from one of the others.

He put his head out of the window to yell and was shocked to find no platform. The train had not reached its destination, and it stood at a standstill in the middle of the forest. Looking down its length, he saw smoke and steam rising from the stationary, panting engine. He called out, expecting one of his men to report information on the holdup, but nobody came.

His headache had intensified and he rubbed the back of his neck before opening the carriage door and jumping down onto the gravel of the track.

He walked along to the Limboia slave carriage—it was empty. So were the next three. He unbuttoned the flap of his holster as his boots crunched loudly on the stones. His steps and the engine's puffing heart were the only sounds in the forest; even the birds were hushed. When he came to the flatbed truck and saw that the crate was open, he pulled out his revolver and looked around warily. Nothing moved, and the trees seemed to have lost their motion, their leaves hanging outside of any breeze or growth.

"Engineer!" he bellowed towards the back of the train. It felt reassuring to shout such a matter-of-fact word amid the absence and stillness. "Engineer!" He heard a titter from behind the passenger carriage. He swung round and climbed up onto a flatbed to reach the other side. There was a small clearing at the edge of the forest, as if a straight line had been shaved out, and the Limboia were all there, side by side in a line, looking, he thought, like a ragged regimental parade, waiting to be inspected. He spat and jumped down to their side, his pistol alert and ready. There was more girlish tittering from the line. With a pounding head and a growing nausea, which he could only put down to the previous motion of the train, he approached them, trying to hold back his rage.

"What the fuck are ye doing out of the train? *Get back in!*" he bellowed.

The tittering stopped and they closed their eyes in a slow, simultaneous movement. Then the breathing started: the same unified breathing that he and Hoffman had heard that first night.

"Stop that! Stop that, *right now!*" he yelled.

The breathing doubled in volume. He was suddenly lost and

obviously outnumbered. The Limboia were stationary, while their chests moved in unison. The only individual movement came from the centre of the line. There stood the herald, holding something to his chest, stroking it with slow, intense gestures. Maclish made a beeline for him, closing on him, the pistol held level with the man's face.

"Tell them to get back on the train," he demanded, seeing a way to retake control.

Then he saw what the herald had in his hands. The loose strips of cloth had been peeled away, and the near-naked thing rolled in the manipulating hands, its lifeless limbs flopping back and forth with the movements. Maclish wanted to pull the trigger and end this, but he knew it was already over.

The eyes of the dead, aborted child opened and stared into his. The breathing stopped, and something else rustled between the Limboia. Something was weaving itself between their ranks, rattling their place on the earth with no speed, but a vast momentum. It nudged him like the movement on the train, and he passed out; in a second, every organ in his body had halted, as if they had never moved at all. Every cell gave up in the presence of the Orm. Only his mad eyes flashed in the dead head, as his body slid to the ground.

The Limboia pointed at their hearts and dispersed into the depth of the forest with their prize. An hour later, the engine would give its last sigh, and its firebox would run down to cold ashes.

The frantic, moving eyes in what had been Maclish stared at Loverboy, who had been standing behind the Limboia all along, patiently waiting. He had been busy. Even in his weakened condition he had retained enough purpose, energy, and skill to gather some small branches and vines and construct a basic sledge. He dragged his creation towards the corpse: He was taking Red Fur home to meet his people, and one of his stomachs was already rumbling.

CHAPTER TWENTY-FOUR

*I*t would have been foolish to think that the life of the arrows was inert or incidental. The truth was that each of the Bowman's handmade shafts of wood, feather, bone, and steel was an extension of nerve, breath, and skill. The arrows' continuance was like the nerve fibres outside the brain, which hold memory in a twined conflict of disbelief and certainty; fibres found in the spine and muscles, sometimes even in the hands, that remembered past places, past movements. As it was with trees, whose delicately calligraphic postures waved and shredded the communicating winds with their stencilling semaphores. The arrows were made of all their elements, bound together with intent.

Peter Williams lifted the gleaming bow into the sun of the early morning. He had cleaned and polished it in the dawn, and now he stood outside the cave, on the summit of the outcrop. The bow felt like Este in his hand: eager, lithe, and determined. He nocked one of the whistling arrows and pulled back the bowstring, the sensuous power locking into his entire body. He closed his eyes and rotated, pointing the arrow in a full circle. He stopped when he did not know which direction he faced. He loosened the arrow and opened his eyes. It sang through the clear distance above the forest, before curving to fall into the trees. He looked carefully at the landscape, picked up his pack, and climbed down towards the place where the arrow would wait for him.

Two hours later, he had reached the forest floor, again relishing its scent and shade. He faced northwest, and his intention was clear: to forge a straight line until the Vorrh was left behind him. It was a journey that would take him directly through the centre of the forbidden territory.

➤

Tsungali tripped over the pot. He had not seen it sitting clearly on the path. How could that be? He was an experienced hunter who normally missed nothing. Then he realised it was because his attention was focused on the movements and sounds around him, drawn by the trees to identify who or what was watching him. He had been doing it subconsciously; now he was aware.

He cocked the Enfield and stood stock-still. The shards of the flimsy pot cracked beneath his boots. Something was here with him; there was no doubt. He said a spell and spat into the undergrowth. There were all kinds of beings here; everybody knew that. He hated this place and never dreamt of pursuing a quarry here. The circumstances had changed and the spirits moved against him; his twitching wounds continually reminded him of that. He should have been able to kill the white man before now, should have been able to stop him from entering this haunted realm. But he was no ordinary white man. Tsungali thought he might even be a ghost, or one of the creatures that steals the bodies of the dead to wear, or takes their faces. He had recognised Williams as soon as he'd seen him but could not believe it possible. He should have died with all his company of lying invaders in the first days of the Possession Wars. Even if he had escaped, he should be older than this, not exactly the same age as he had been the day he returned from the beach. Tsungali looked for a moment at his gnarled, knotted hands. He felt his years ache in the hinges of his joints.

Was it the Bowman he felt watching him beyond the trees? Was it he who left this dish in his path, to spook him? He spoke another charm, whistled, and spat. There were worse things than the Englishman, even if he was a ghost.

He continued to tread slowly forward, and after some hours he saw another pot. It was full of steaming, fragrant food. He savagely kicked it off the path and moved on. He was going to tear the throat out of this enemy who played games with his hunger and his fear. The Erstwhile and the demons entered his thoughts, but he knew that they did not prepare food, not even as a sick joke to mock him. No, it was something else, something with human tendencies, which, of course, made it terrible in a different way. He was becoming more and more unnerved, when he suddenly heard the faint whistling in the sky. He had heard it before and it made his blood run cold. Then it came down through the leaves and branches directly above; he dropped Uculipsa and clasped his hands over his head, not daring to look up. The arrow shrieked and trembled to a halt, piercing the path six feet before him.

➤→

Ishmael had come to a place where a mighty oak had fallen, its prone bulk drawing a horizon in the world of verticals. It must have been of considerable age; he could easily have hidden in its girth. A wonderful aroma of leaf mulch and sap exuded from the place, one of dampness spun with age. He walked across the narrow path, under the bridge formed by the oak, before stopping to look up again at the fallen tree, which blotted out the dappled sunshine. New shoots were growing from its old, dead body, and a lacework of vines still thrived on its bark.

He was beginning to enjoy the depth of this place, to feel a sense of belonging in its mysterious interior. Perhaps this was where he was from; perhaps his kind really had lived here, among the peace of the great trees. He imagined a primitive life in simple huts, with a gentle and ancient race that had hidden successfully from barbaric humans for centuries.

The Kin had shown him pictures and models of such places, and he remembered stories of them. Adam's house in Paradise had been drawn on scrolls in the teaching crates, alongside images of strange, manlike creatures living in harmony with lions and other wild beasts. He and Seth had made a miniature shelter of mud, sticks, and stones. He had been proud of it and would sit staring into its rough interior, imagining what a life within it would entail; he saw, in his mind, the hearth and the trickle of smoke from the roof, rising into the motionless air.

He was there again, expecting to turn a corner and find that unique village. So lost was he in the conjecture of that place that he did not immediately notice that he was no longer alone. It took him a few moments to realise that somebody was walking to the side of him, just out of the periphery of his view. He spun around to confront the creature, his heart in his throat. The other stopped and ducked, but he now knew for sure that he was being observed. He wondered if these were the people who had been giving him food and water. He called out to where the figure had disappeared, expecting a response this time. None came. Then there was a sound behind him, a sound to the side, a plethora of sounds from every direction. The creatures stood up, and he turned in horror to look at them all, their faces growing out of their chests.

He pushed back the fear and repulsion that came from being in close and unknown proximity with something that was utterly different. Their squat, square bodies were pale yellow, blotched with a pink mottle; they had no discernible head. Their mouth, jaw, nose, and ears grew out of their sternum, and a single eye stared out from their flat chests with the blinking wit of a farm animal. Pale lashes shading one-dimensional thoughts flicked vacantly between fight and flee.

Then he saw the squint of cunning and knew that this was his end. These were things he had seen in a picture: horror cyclops that could have nothing to do with him. This was a sub-species, not a kindred race. They had been giving him food and direction, not out of aid and sympathy, but to guide him home. They had been fattening and luring him, and he had willingly followed their trails of food straight into their trap and right into the heartland of the anthropophagi.

They moved towards him to look closer and started to communicate in a series of high, ragged bleats, sounds that seemed to be razored out of their small, teeth-filled mouths with a great deal of effort. Theirs were not the mouths of eloquent debate; the holes and their contents were constructed purely for the sake of biting, sucking, nibbling, and guzzling.

They were all naked, and Ishmael, whose interest in genitalia had always been intense, gazed in amazement at their diversity and proportion. Unlike other species he had examined, no two seemed to be alike: Some were shrunken and inverted, while others hung or coiled out of their bodies with wasteful abandon. He was reminded of "Lesson 93: Invertebrates of the Oceans (Certain Soft-Bodied Sea Creatures)" and wondered if their sex organs might indeed be a separate species that shared a symbiotic relationship with their host. How they used them to mate was beyond even his conjecture.

These far-off speculations stopped him from running or fainting with fear, which he knew would be an instant trigger to his demise. They moved closer, and he froze. They touched him, held his legs, and looked up into his eye, their proximity betraying a violent odour that matched their speech patterns. Suddenly, without warning, a searing pain made Ishmael scream out into the trees. A thin hardwood blade had been pushed into the Achilles tendon of his right leg; they were making sure he would not run away. The pain made him fall, and the others pinned him down while a second hobble was stabbed in. He yelled and thrashed, but there were too many of them. Their strength, smell, arms, legs, and genitals flapped and fastened him, while others unsheathed more pointed sticks.

Suddenly, there was an almighty explosion, and the creature holding his leg split apart, the two halves of its upper body flying in opposite directions, leaving the tottering legs standing comically for a second or two. The arms remained connected to each piece of raw meat, spurting mud-coloured blood as they tried to hold on to the ground or crawl off. A second creature was hit in the back, and the great sound pushed his splintered rib cage out through his puzzled face; this one did not even twitch.

The creatures fled the ambush, vanishing into the undergrowth with a practised speed and agility. Ishmael rolled on the ground in agony, straining to see who or what the weapon belonged to—was it better or worse than the horrors he had just been saved from?

"What kind of thing are you?" barked a voice that was out of sight. "Don't look around; lie still or you will bleed to death. Now, answer my question, or I will destroy you like I destroyed your little brothers."

"They are no brothers of mine," said Ishmael through clenched teeth.

"Then what are you?" said the booming voice, the Gabbett-Fairfax Mars pointing at Ishmael's spine from behind an old oak tree.

"I am a man with one eye."

It seemed like a reasonable answer: That was indeed what the writhing creature appeared to be.

"I can help you, if I trust you," said the voice. "Keep still and put your hands in front of your face where I can see them."

"What are you?" Ishmael grimaced.

"I am Williams," said the voice at last, "and I am a man with four eyes."

➤—→

Tsungali was drinking from the earthen bowl when he heard the shots. He thought he was the only one who dared fire a gun in the forest. Perhaps other hunters shared his pursuit? The sound was foreign, not like any gun he had heard before, but it had given him a clear direction, and his stalking took on a more purposeful intent.

The stinking brown blood was still drying on his arm where the thing had bled to death, his kris driven along its shoulder blade to find its heart, or its brain, or whatever else it was that had once powered the yellow demon. It had been tracking him for days; Tsungali had allowed himself the water and thrown the food away, preferring his own dried supplies. Then he had circled back on the demon and killed it from behind. It was one that his grandfather had told him of, the demons that eat hunted human flesh. Any doubts he might have had were quickly dispersed when he saw what his victim wore over its swollen cock and balls: a makeshift bowl, which on closer examination proved to be the skullcap of a man, the skin and bright-red hair still attached.

Tsungali gathered some vines and tied them around the large, pointed feet of his fallen hunter, hoisting the demon up to swing in the trees and show its unseen herd that fear had entered their lives. As he did so, he saw a small movement in the creature's armpit. He grabbed the body to stop it swinging and took a closer look. Under each armpit was hidden a small, delicately woven sphere of grass. It was attached to the skin by curved thorns that hooked it in place. Each sphere contained a human eye.

He cut the little cages out of their hiding place and examined them, one in each hand. Then he saw it, and the shock made him drop them: He had seen many wondrous and terrible sights and was not easily surprised by unnatural phenomena, but this place bred things beyond the nightmares of devils.

He bent and rummaged in the low bush where the spheres had fallen, found them, and again inspected them. Yes, there it was: stronger in one, but apparent in both. The irises were moving, dilating back and forth, adjusting their sights: The eyes were still alive. This was magic beyond the powers of his comprehension.

His hand was wet; he examined it and realised that one of the eyes was leaking. Placing the good one in the deepest pouch of his spell belt, he cut open the grass cage around the damaged eye and saw that one of the thorns had hooked inwards, piercing it deeply. More fluid was escaping, and the eye had started to lose its shape.

He found a flat stone and brushed it clean. Holding the eye between the forefingers of his left hand, he laid it on the rock and, taking his razor-sharp knife in his right hand, carefully slit it open, causing the rest of the fluid to soak away into the stone. Tsungali bent close enough to see the tiny muscles, working to focus the lens, and the iris, still trying to shutter the overbearing light. Their minute energies were independent and self-willed. He probed the interior with his hungry vision; he thought he saw the stub of the optic nerve twitch but could not be sure. The fluid and the movement attracted the attentions of other watchers, bringing the hungry curiosity of a stream of black ants to the rock. Without hesitation, they continued the dissection that Tsungali had started. He watched the eye being nibbled apart and ferried away, its muscles still alive and contracting as the insects held it aloft like a great prize, dragging it backwards along the glistening black chain of their frantic bodies. A few minutes later, there was nothing left—even the stain was fought over and diminished by the porous stone and the cooking sun.

Tsungali put his hand protectively over the closed pouch; whatever its origins, he knew that he had in his possession a most valuable prize.

➤→

"I was born this way," Ishmael answered with a wince.

They were on a high rock in the sun. Williams had carried him there, away from the killing fields of the anthropophagi. They talked and questioned each other as the white man worked on Ishmael's wounds.

"I came here from the city."

"Why?" asked Williams, without looking up from his work.

"I wanted to escape from the people and see if my origins were here."

"What, with those things down there?"

"No, not them, something else. I don't know," the cyclops said, catching a small movement out of the corner of his eye.

"How long have you been here?" Williams asked.

Ishmael noticed the bow at the same time it noticed him. It moved again. Small, muscular adjustments inside its taut form caused it to stir against the warm rocks. He barely heard his companion's repeated question.

"I said, how long?" came the murmured reiteration, from somewhere below his left knee.

It must have been the sun warming it, or his pain and shock knitting together to create the illusion.

"Answer me!" demanded a frustrated Williams. "How long have you been here?!"

"Sorry?! What?" spluttered Ishmael.

Williams moved to the other side of the prone cyclops. "I said, how long have you been in the Vorrh?"

"I don't know. Six days? Maybe more. I have lost count."

"You nearly lost your life," said Williams.

The cyclops said nothing but shuffled himself into a sitting position.

The pain was fading and he was beginning to trust this stranger and his bag of healing plants.

"How long have you been here?" asked Ishmael.

"Now, that is a difficult question to answer," Williams answered. "Maybe a week. Maybe a year. Maybe much longer. I have little memory of the life I led before I entered this fearsome place. But I have been here before; of that I am certain. What lies ahead is only destiny."

Ishmael started to see him in a different way and said, "They say that the forest lives on memory, that it devours the memory of men."

"Do they?" said Williams, handing the cyclops a cup of tinctured water.

"Yes!" said Ishmael earnestly, not sensing the irony in the other's question.

The bow trembled again. Its twitch displaced it, and it slid down across the rock, like the big hand of a clock. Its clatter startled the cyclops, who jerked around to look at it.

"She's getting restless," said her owner. "She wants to move on."

"She?" asked Ishmael nervously.

"It's a long story," answered Williams, walking over to the bow and bringing it back to his side to rest between them.

Ishmael looked at its long, narrow form and felt a radiance exude from its maroon-black surface. He touched it gingerly with the tips of his closest fingers; it was warm and moist.

"Don't do that," said Williams with a sharp, empathic correctness. "I am the only one who touches her."

Ishmael's hand flinched back. "Forgive me!"

"No need. But you must understand: I have had that bow a long time. She is my only real possession."

Ishmael murmured an understanding. Distracted, he asked, "Does it have a name?"

"She did once; I think it was Este." As he spoke, a profound change came over the Bowman's face. He looked shocked at the name in his mouth and appeared to be searching for something; the next word, or the next moment.

"What does it mean?" asked Ishmael.

Williams changed again, staring oddly at the cyclops with an expression that made Ishmael feel anxious and unsafe. He decided to say nothing more about the bow and lowered his head out of the stranger's disturbing gaze. He looked down at his hands; the skin where the tips of his fingers had traced the surface of the daunting object was wet and stained.

"I don't know," said Williams, in answer to a question that Ishmael could not remember asking. "I don't know!"

Ishmael discreetly wiped his fingers in the dust of the rock and changed the subject quickly. "I meant to thank you, for saving me from those savages."

There was no response from the distant man.

"It is said that all manner of creatures live in these trees. I think those must have been the worst; if it was not for you, they would certainly have hurt me again."

"They would have eaten you!" Williams announced, clicking back into the unease of the moment. Ishmael stared at him, suddenly feeling very queasy and tired. He slipped slightly in a disjointed, groggy movement.

"That will be the tincture I gave you," said Williams. "It will heal you and help you to sleep."

Ishmael touched the palm of his hand against his face, seeking some basic, instinctive reassurance. He smelt the liquid of the bow on his fingers; it took his softening mind very far away. He turned to look at Williams, to ask him what it meant, but the words turned to jelly and gas, and he faded into the growing gravity beneath him. His eye closed; somewhere in its narrow slit rested the dark bow, whose name he had already forgotten.

➤→

Tsungali found the remains of the slaughtered demons. He kicked them over and examined the wounds. He had never seen flesh and bone torn apart like this. It impressed him, and he longed to be the owner of a weapon that could cause such utter devastation.

He had tracked the two men from the place with the fallen tree, up to a rocky outcrop. It was getting dark, which placed him in a quandary: He did not like the idea of climbing the rock in the failing light, of coming across the owners of the powerful gun from a point beneath them; however, he did not know what still lived below—the demons might well be nocturnal.

His options were few, and he eventually decided to spend the night perched on the fallen tree; it gave him the best vantage point and better options of defence or attack. He climbed up and onto the vast, fallen giant and walked its length, looking down onto the forest floor for signs of activity or seclusion. All was quiet. He knew the other two waited above. He would find them tomorrow and decide then whether they should live or die. The weapon they carried made him favour the latter—it would be cleaner that way. Then he could move on to find the Bowman; perhaps his first use of the novel firearm would enable him to watch its effects on his wandering prey.

He found a cleft in the tree where he would sleep and set watching charms along the length of the trunk before settling in for the night.

Nocturnal creatures began to wake, climbing and slithering

through the trees, rustling in the undergrowth. He knew their sounds and found them comforting: It meant that neither man nor demon lingered nearby. He set his hearing for silence or flutter and drifted into sleep.

He dreamt of his grandfather and his carved house. He was a boy again, in the time before the outsiders came; in that house, no foreigner would ever tread. They sat together, his grandfather humming while braiding a cover for his sacrificial spear; they would sit like this forever, because the outside world, with all its dangers and strangers, was sealed off by an invisible sheet of magic; those who stared into their space could never get past its tense, crystal barrier. He and his grandfather would ignore them and go on with the business of their day, or else stare through them as though their faces were shadows, lost reflections of a remote and meaningless fiction.

The dream was a good one, rich and secure. It must have lasted all night long; he awoke in the morning with it washing warmly around in the waters of his head.

As dawn broke through the foliage, he found their tracks under the dew and followed up behind them. It was only then that he sensed it, saw the signs in their very footfalls—the earth and the broken twigs in his passing left no doubt: One of them was his target, and he was finally certain of who it was that he followed. It was not a descendant, or a memory, or a ghost of another time; it was the same man, the same physical being who had first placed the rifle in his hands and trusted him to use it so many years ago; the only outsider who had ever understood some part of the True People; the one who was just, in blood and words. He had been with Irrinipeste all this time: That was why he had been so difficult to kill. At last he understood how this man had overcome him.

➤—→

They exchanged names the next morning and set about travelling on together. Theirs were the first conversations Ishmael had conducted with a human man, other than Mutter and a few carnival utterings: He had to learn more.

"Why are you not repelled by me? Do you not find my face offensive?"

"I have seen worse," said Williams.

"Your answer surprises me. I was once told that everybody I met was certain to be disgusted by me."

"And who told you that?"

Ishmael found himself recalling memories that he didn't know he owned: of Ghertrude and Mutter; of the house and its high walls. As his explanations tailed off, he insisted on his question until Williams gave in and answered.

"Yes, back in the city you would be an oddity. Nobody has seen a real, living cyclops for thousands of years. Life would be difficult for you; you would have to hide. But here it is very different; you are but one of a multitude of strange things in this forest."

Ishmael limped along behind Williams, leaning heavily on the stick that the tall man had cut for him. He felt compelled to press the issue further.

"But you could have passed by when I was attacked back there. And you still help me now. Why is that?"

"I suppose I could easily have left you. But everything here has meaning: All my purpose seems to be locked into the secrets of the Vorrh. I don't know how, but it's possible that you are a part of that. And anyway, I would leave no creature to the mercy of those man-eating monstrosities."

"But what if it was they who were a part of your destiny here?" asked Ishmael intently.

"Then it was their destiny to die and my destiny to help them do so. You were simply the trigger to the event."

The cyclops fell quiet; being a trigger to somebody else's event was far beyond his experience, and he was not sure how comfortable he was with the notion.

They walked for three hours on a high ridge that petered out into a solid plane of trees.

"There is the centre," said Williams, "the core." He pointed across into the middle of the dense mass. He unslung his bow and looked around. "Stay here. I shall return in a short while."

Before Ishmael could protest, he walked out of sight, using the shoulder of the ridge as a screen between them. The cyclops sat down and examined his bandaged leg. He heard the arrow loose and felt the strange emptiness in its wake. Ten minutes later, the Bowman came back to stand over him. The same look of loss and confusion had stolen his confidence again. His hands were stained black from the bow and he was searching Ishmael's face for an answer to which neither of them could find the question.

➤→

Tsungali always completed a task once he had undertaken it, but something in him had deserted him this time; his purpose had dwindled. His prey had power and identity, and he was not alone. They were ahead of him, and all he trusted was behind. Last night's dream had coaxed him to another place, a place that no longer existed. He stopped suddenly and looked at his hands, holding Uculipsa. The old rifle with its inscriptions and dents, with its recently splintered stock, suddenly looked as tired as he. The talismans that lined his body felt heavy and sullen. His age and the strangeness of this country passed through all his protections. For the first time, he understood momentum and it stopped him in his tracks. Why was he doing this? For whom? He sat down and forgot his function.

A soft footfall was approaching behind him, and for the first time in his adult life he did not hear it as fear. He stayed still and waited.

"Little one!" the old voice said. "Little one, why are you lost here?"

He could not turn but did not need to. He looked at his hands and the wrinkled blue sheen of the skin. Behind him, his grandfather said, "Come home. This place is full of demons and forsaken ones; there is nothing for you here."

Before him, he heard voices. Williams and his companion were within easy range.

➤

Their silence had become dark and uneasy. Ishmael glanced at his sullen friend apprehensively. "Is something wrong?" he asked. Williams looked into the distance.

"The shot was flawed," he said quietly. "The arrow curved and fell short."

Ishmael did not know how to respond; something in him instinctively preferred to keep the subject of the bow at a distance. In an attempt to change the subject he asked, "Are we walking into the core?"

"In that direction. The arrow leads in that direction."

Ishmael looked back and forth from the slippery path to Williams's face, trying to understand the mood and colour of the other man's introspection.

"She is struggling," said Williams to himself, ignoring the limping cyclops at his side. The sun was becoming strong again, and the breath of the trees was coagulating with it to make the air soupy and moist. "This has never happened before," continued the Englishman. He looked at the bow in his outstretched hand, disregarding the path beneath his feet.

Ishmael did not understand, and the man's mood swings

were worrying him. Doubt had crawled into their relationship; the offered protection and care were threatened by Williams's disengagement.

"I think the bow wants you," announced Williams, and the squirm of fear in Ishmael's gut increased to a shudder. "She bleeds and strains towards your hand."

Williams stopped dead in the track, his arm outstretched, the black bow quivering.

Ishmael blinked at the now-terrifying object held towards him. Williams had shut his eyes against the touch, and the bow swayed slightly, as if its horizontal curve was trying to match the cyclops's straining eyelids. Ishmael had no intention of touching the eldritch thing. "I don't want this. It's your bow; I don't want it."

"It's not about what you want," said Williams, his eyes still pressed shut. "Come; take her from my hands."

➤→

Tsungali knew that the voices of men, like their breath, did not always live in this world alone. He knew they could pass into others and sometimes bring back different sayings. That was what the child, Irrinipeste, was so wondrous at doing: Her voice had passed into many worlds and brought great wisdom back. So it could be the voice of his grandfather behind him; but it could also be the voice of a ghost or demon that had stolen it. If he believed and turned to confront it, he would be lost.

"Come, take my hand," his grandfather said.

In that moment, he heard the echo of those words spoken above him, in the mouth of his prey. Without looking back, he looped up towards the track ahead of them, no longer caring about the noise he made in his approach.

He crept with speed to the edge of the track and saw them

in his path, unprepared and engaged in a type of bizarre white-man's game. They had become silent, and the Bowman, the one he knew, held his weapon away from his body, thrusting it in the face of a smaller man.

All this Tsungali saw in a fraction of a second. Whatever this ritual was, it had left them exposed and unprepared: The field was his. He attached the long-bladed bayonet and bolted a round into the breech, then climbed up onto the track and began to charge, head down like a bull, the blade cleaving through space towards them.

➤→

So intent was Williams in his self-imposed blindness that he did not hear the fast rustle of leaves or the velocity of the twigs breaking behind the cyclops. But Ishmael did, and he swung around, glaring down to where he imagined he would see the squat yellow bodies of the attacking anthropophagi. To his shock, he was confronted by the charging blur of an enormous black warrior carrying a rifle, a vicious knife gleaming at its snout. It was coming fast.

Ishmael did the only thing that he knew would awaken Williams into that lethal moment: He snatched the bow from his hands with such force that it jarred the Bowman's eyes open and alert.

The cyclops turned again to the assailant, and his glare was like a slap across the hunter's eyes. This was not a white man—it was not a man at all. Ishmael's glaring eye hit his sight and he faltered, slipping on the sticky path. He slid almost to all fours but never lost his momentum or his grip on Uculipsa. He caught himself without falling and stumbled forward, pulling his lope upright and back into a charge.

Williams saw the charging man, watched him lose focus and

slither in his approach. Lifting his hand to his shoulder bag, he pulled out the hefty, eager weight of the Mars pistol before the hunter had righted himself and gathered speed.

As he ran, Tsungali saw the creature raise the bow over his head; he saw the quick, unfolding movement of the other man and he knew the voice he had heard below really had been that of his grandfather, not a demon or a ghost. The monsters did not whisper below: They were up here, with him, and he was running straight at them.

Williams cocked and aimed the pistol as he saw the black man's eyes.

The point of the bayonet was within two metres of Ishmael's chest when the great roar put a stop to all motion; all, that is, except for that of the birds, who threw themselves from every branch and beat their wings upwards and out of the forest, into the bright, dazzling air and away from the terrible sound.

Ishmael had dropped the bow, letting it spring away from his fast hands as he grabbed at his ears, a hot, white flame passing over his shoulder. He sank to his knees, howling.

Williams stepped past him, the pistol never wavering from its attention. He stared down the track to where Tsungali lay, lifted off his feet and thrown back to the exact spot where he had regained his momentum only seconds before. He writhed in an excruciating tangle while Williams slowly walked the narrow distance to stand over him, the smoking barrel at his side.

CHAPTER TWENTY-FIVE

Charlotte watched him as he stared out to sea from the quarterdeck of the great white-and-silver ship. He was motionless and uncommunicative; every day spent on the endless water made him drift further and further away. She tried to be close, but a barrier was forming as he fell inward. She had never felt so lonely or so helpless as she did while watching the sea turn from blue to green, pondering its unfeeling and enormous depth.

At night, under fierce stars, they ate in silence, with all her attempts at gentle conversation ignored or rebuffed. She knew he could not help it, that it was not vindictively aimed at her, but it still wounded her. She told herself that her hurt was nothing compared to his; his most overwhelming feelings were attached to an irredeemable absence. Every hour of his waking and sleeping life was given to searching the recesses of his blank memory for a face or a moment to hold and flood with his tidal wave of emotion. But all he ever found was a distant, grey, empty shore, and by the time they had reached Marseille, he barely noticed she was there at all.

He no longer shared his hurt with her. Instead, she became the recipient of the brunt of his disappointment and his growing, aimless anger. Their return to Paris was peevish and numb. He refused to be enlightened by her happiness of homecoming. Every effort she made was wasted and disregarded. He was punishing her inability to solve or reduce his misery, demanding rather than asking her for things, especially his fastidious meals and his increasing supplies of barbiturates. She had to keep a record of his experiments with these, so that he might calculate different alchemies of unbeing and find the limits of his nonexistence to balance against the volume of his pain.

He was listless; he could not settle or write. He roamed the rooms, peering through the curtains into the diminished City of Light; he talked about travelling again, used movement as a surrogate for thought. For the first time, she seriously considered breaking their contract, giving up his mother's money, and fleeing his baleful presence. But she stayed for him, knowing that without her, his life with the indifferent servants would be even worse. His death was the enigma that stalked her life, and she came to recognise that it was not the tangled weight of responsibility that made her care and kept her close; it was something stronger, something strangely unnecessary and totally essential; a kind of love; a constant need to contain and guard with unflinching proximity. It was not maternal and was certainly not fed by perversity from the injuries of his brutality. It was her presence, which had become entangled with his, beyond circumstance and sometimes even personality. She would stay until the end and remove all judgment to do so.

She remembered a conversation she had once heard in her childhood. She was nestled under the thick legs of dark furniture, while a Jewish relation explained stories of his faith. He talked about many peculiar and difficult things, but one stuck in her young mind: the division of day and night, and how dusk and dawn had two characteristics, the twilight of the dove and the twilight of the raven. She now understood that the rest of their time together would be like this, a constant dusk. She would maintain it and work on its luminance. It would be the twilight of the dove, and the raven would never be allowed in.

→ *Part Three*

In some country everyone is blind from birth. Some are eager for knowledge and aspire after truth. Sooner or later one of them will say, "You see, sirs, how we cannot walk straight along our way, but rather we frequently fall into holes. But I do not believe that the whole human race is under such a handicap, for the natural desire that we have to walk straight is not frustrated in the whole race. So I believe that there are some men who are endowed with a faculty for setting themselves straight."

NICHOLAS OF AUTRECOURT, *Exigit ordo*

The grandiosity of "paper buildings" like Brueghel's tower of Babel, Boullée's funerary temples, Piranesi's prisons, or Sant'Elia's Futurist power stations have been realized, and by an amateur, a fanatically motivated little lady from New Haven whose dream palace was crafted with Yankee ingenuity.

JOHN ASHBERY

... and as the disputational .44
occurred in his hand and spun there
in that warp of relativity one sees
in the backward turning spokes
of a buckboard,
                    then came suddenly
to rest, the barrel utterly justified
with a line pointing
to the neighborhood of infinity.

ED DORN, *Gunslinger*

CHAPTER TWENTY-SIX

Muybridge stood before the oval mirror, combing his beard. Now back in America, he had lost weight again, and the furrows under the white strands looked dark grey, deep rills and valleys in a late, gaunt sliver of moon. He wore his finest shirt, one he had bought in Jermyn Street, at London's most renowned tailor, the consort's own shirtmaker. There was a flicker in the peeling glass, tarnished silver curling away from the polished transparency, the shadow of a woman passing. He ignored the unimportant flicker of the past and looked closely at himself, catching the roaming eyes for a moment and holding them out of focus, not wanting to see into their meaning. The glass had warped since the time of his wife, become thin since her fatness had moved away. Perfumed colour and greasy powder no longer wallowed in its gilt frame; now it was only the empty grey of his eyes reflected in its shallows, sphinctered tight against search or understanding.

The doorbell rang: His carriage had arrived. He donned his surtout coat, picked up his cane and his new formal day hat, and hurried for the door, his old bones creaking against the speed. He was on his way to meet the grand dame, and he must not be late.

The carriage rattled as he held tightly to his stick, jittering with excitement and nerves; he had always wanted to meet her.

She had sent the request through the Stanfords, inviting him to take tea with her on this bright March day. He was fascinated by her diminutive beauty and gigantic wealth, having seen the former many years before, across a ballroom as he passed through the garden. She was not a classic beauty, like one of the willowy Long Island sirens who fluttered and coiled in the gleaming white of society's grandest parties. Her attractiveness came from within and radiated her every movement with grace and charisma; not a polished diamond, but an energetic nugget of strength and robust dignity. Since then, she had been over-whelmed with money and grief. The wasting death of her only daughter and untimely demise of her husband left only her lone-liness to break her, and her vast inheritance to haunt every hope of an afterlife.

Sarah was the only benefactor of the fortune earned by the enormous success of the Winchester repeating rifle, the gun that "won the West." It was a greatly evolved version of the clum-sier Henri rifle, and a revolutionary design: A tubular magazine sat under the barrel and fed twelve rounds into the breech by means of an underlever, which also acted as a trigger guard. The lever-action carbine could be rapidly fired from horseback. The firepower and speed of delivery made it a weapon superior to all that had gone before it.

It tidied away the few remaining tribes who refused to yield to the white invasion. The gun, and its heavier-calibre brothers, cleared the plains of the buffalo and every other creature with a price on its tail or horn. At the outbreak of the Civil War, the Northern army bought the gun in vast quantities, and money gushed and splashed into the Winchester coffers. It shot one bullet per second and possessed a trajectory that wiped out half a generation of neighbours and friends.

Sarah's tears never really ended. After the first five years, they simply turned inwards, so that her eyes would well and weep inside her lids, hollowing the flesh beneath the fine skin of her cheeks and finding her throat, so that she might swallow down the wet pictures of little Annie wasting at her breast. The child had nothing except ferocious hunger and pain; between its skeleton and its skin, no flesh or fat grew.

Almost fifteen years later, she would swallow her pain with the rotted lungs of her young husband as disease ate him away. He, like his screaming daughter, shrivelled in her arms. It was said that she balanced precariously on the edge of madness at the beginning of the 1880s, but some kind of resilience kept her from stepping over its line. She wasn't sure where it came from: It certainly wasn't rooted in the mountain of money that grew behind her grief, for she had no interest in that; there was nothing it could buy, and so it stockpiled, a burgeoning model of her ballooning anguish. There had to be a reason why so much horror had quenched so much joy; when she eventually found it, it was appallingly obvious.

He had come to explain. With his pale smile and his gentle hands, she had no doubt that it was her husband being described, standing at her side, beyond the reach of her untrained eye. He was here to explain their evolution and lay her personal guilt to rest: None of this was her fault.

The medium held a handkerchief to her face as she spoke his words for him, consoling him and encouraging him to speak more clearly. He said, through her, that those who had been slain by the terrible weapon were vengeful and returning, that they followed the dollar line back to those responsible, and that she, by default, was the only one left. They had taken William and Annie (who were happily together on the spirit side), but their anger was not extinguished.

Salvation was possible, and it had a physical form. Her

husband told her to build a house, a mansion, for herself and the dead to cohabit; one large enough to accommodate every lost soul, before they came homelessly scratching at her existence. She must never stop work on this ambition, he warned. The house must continuously grow; if its expansion ceased, she would die, and they might never meet again on the other side.

Sarah left the séance that day with hope and a purpose; after years of pain, she finally had something worthwhile to channel her money and energies into. She had been given a first deposit on a new life, a pilgrimage that would divert Leland Stanford's train lines to the building site of her new home in the West, and she thanked the medium for guiding her in the right direction. She employed an army of workmen day and night to construct a monstrous labyrinth of wood to hide herself in. Llanda Villa multiplied around her, its blind corridors and infatuation with the number thirteen snaking in all directions, plumbing the furious demons and mortally wounded ghosts into blocked passages, insane turrets, and flights of stairs that ascended, essentially, to absolutely nowhere—but always away from the nucleus of her grief.

Muybridge had heard it all, but his memory was selective and grievously affected by his need. Sarah Winchester was a woman of influence and beauty; he admired her purity. She had never remarried and was fiercely loyal to the memory of her deceased family. She would understand him—he was sure of it. She must have heard about the incident with Larkyns. He was certain that she would appreciate his justification and see him as a chivalrous gentleman as well as, he hoped, a significant artist.

The carriage stopped before the garden entrance of the growing house. He stepped down and walked up the path, passing by the fountain and up to the porch. The pillared entrance was cool and elegant, a mechanical glade of craftsmanship. The door opened and a hushed man took him inside.

The house was immaculate and squeakingly new. It smelt of polish and sawdust, both scents sharpened by subtle undertones of varnish. The hand-fitted parquet flooring was perfect and infinite; he seemed to follow the man forever, unable to resist occasionally dropping back for a closer examination of each detail and angle. They entered a hall whose possessions outnumbered those of all the other rooms put together. In the centre stood a piano that dominated the furniture and pictures. These were obviously the occupied parts of the house. The other rooms were token, superfluous, but these rooms had life. He could feel her presence in the next room.

The hushed man left him standing and went ahead, closing the door behind him. His anxiety twitched his hat and cane and he longed to lay them down but dared not risk causing offence. He fretted and looked around the room, said belongings tapping against his leg. Murmured voices could be heard, and then the door opened and his host stepped forward, holding her hand out in greeting.

"Mr. Muybridge, thank you for coming."

He was shocked by her appearance. The lady of his historical glimpses was utterly changed. She had thickened, become solid, not with fat or ease, but as if the gravitation of the world around her had changed. She had become compressed by her circumstances, by the weight of the house. Her face was lined and hollowed, yet each line was somehow attached to the plumpness of her skin; she was a contradiction of form, almost as if the contours of her expression had been painted over the wrong surface. The layers of makeup, stencilled over her once flawless complexion, gave her face a strange hint of varnish. Only her teeth remained perfect, though her eyes had retained a glimmer of something constant and disconcerting. In the distance, hammering could be heard, but he tried to ignore it. He bowed slightly and gave her his hand.

"Thank you, Mrs. Winchester," he said, a boyish blush blooming under his pale skin. "I was delighted to receive your invitation." She smiled graciously and led him through to the smaller sitting room, where tea was already laid out on a small dining table. They sat and spoke politely of weather and acquaintances. After twenty minutes of stiflingly obligatory formalities, the conversation at last began to move towards the purpose of her invitation.

"The Stanfords have been introducing me to your work, Mr. Muybridge. I must say, I am quite impressed."

"Thank you, ma'am. May I ask which photographs you have seen so far?" he asked.

"Oh, pictures of mountains, a volcanic place, and the primitives dancing in a circle."

"Ah, the Ghost Dance," he said with glee. "I am the only person ever to have photographed it."

"The Ghost Dance?" she said, her attention caught in exactly the way he had hoped. "What is that?"

"It was a belief held by many native tribes that they could summon their dead to help them stand against the settlers who were moving west. They imagined an uprising and a joining of clans, dead and alive, to hold what they regarded as their sacred lands."

Sarah shifted forward slightly in her hard-backed chair. "When exactly did these dances occur?" she asked.

He gave her the dates of his prints and she fell silent, her mind quickly calculating their significance. A staccato quietness filled the room and she looked at the floor, the corner of her mouth twitching softly, as if something was working in her throat. It seemed wise to change the landscape and the subject.

"My other experimental work is progressing excellently," he interjected. "I have captured the movement of many animals in my cameras, even humans!" His attempt to raise the energies of his host met with a heavy silence.

She raised her forlorn eyes to look into his, and he had to look away.

"I am inventing new cameras," he continued awkwardly, "with faster shutters. Triggers that work repeatedly to grab an image. A bit like your wonderful rifle, ma'am, which I once used in Arizona; a superb mechanism. I aim to develop something similar in my cameras, that same speed and accuracy, dividing time . . ." Her expression silenced him.

She held one hand to the nape of her neck and blinked, clearing her throat as her voice prepared to be used.

"Can you . . ." She paused again, seeming unsure of how to phrase her query. "Have you ever . . . photographed the dead?" she asked.

"I'm not sure I understand, ma'am," he said carefully.

"I am told that certain European photographers are able to capture images of those who have passed over to the spirit world," she stated sternly, burying a wave of emotion beneath her severe exterior. "I am looking for such an artist. According to the Stanfords, you are the best there is. If anyone might be capable of catching such likenesses, I am told it would be you."

Muybridge was appalled, but he stiffened himself towards an answer.

"I have never made such pictures," he replied, trying not to betray his inner wave of disgust.

"Would you be willing to try?" she asked, hope piercing her eyes and his internal complexes. He paused before answering, enthusiasm eluding his disenchanted artistic streak.

"For you, Mrs. Winchester, I will try."

It was with a heavy heart that he carried his cameras, tripods, and other equipment through the polished tunnels of the expanding house two days later. The séances were held in a room designed for the purpose, a circular table at its centre and small, high windows at its edges, which opened onto the interior of the house. There was no direct light; the room was located at the core of the twisted architecture, a long way in every direction from an external wall or the scent of the outside. Not that it mattered: His photographs would all be taken in the dark.

He had seen the "spirit" images she had spoken of. All were conspicuous fakes: double exposures and ridiculous montages, executed without any subtlety or skill. His opinion of Sarah Winchester had collapsed in that moment. How could anybody be taken in by such manipulated lies? It reeked of the worst excesses of affluent, puerile fiction, dressed up as truth. But the fact remained that he needed her patronage, her circle of friends, her wealth. And, with that in mind, one could forgive the beliefs and sad fantasies of a grief-ridden old woman who never left her home. Perhaps when she understood the qualities of his work and the accuracy of his scientific objectiveness, her fanciful commission might lead to more serious work offers.

He positioned his cameras in the far corner of the room and set his face in the great seriousness of an Old Testament patriarch: It was his best posture.

Sarah brought three other people into the room—all devout spiritualists, he guessed. Today's medium was to be Madam Grezach, a striking woman of Polish origin. She had a smouldering attractiveness that hid beneath a face that melted uncontrollably between the ages of eight and sixty-five. She sat at the table, flanked by her sitters. Elder Thomas sat close to Sarah, to the left of the medium. On her right sat a large, horse-faced woman, whose name Muybridge instantly forgot.

A prayer was said. Soon after its finish, Madam Grezach started to sway and softly moan, her eyes rolling beneath their closed lids. It could all be clearly seen by the light of the dim lamp that hung above. Unlike many larger circles, they did not hold hands, but placed their palms down on the table, fingers evenly splayed. Muybridge was vividly reminded of a photograph he had never stopped to take: Mexico; a row of freshly caught deep-sea spider crabs, laid out to dry in the bleaching sun, their salmon-pink shells vacuous and surrendered on the sand. He shook the thought and its attendant smile out of his head without moving a muscle. Madam Grezach groaned again, in a deeper, more masculine tone. She said her spirit guide was called Wang Chi, that he was here now, to help them and guide those who had passed over to the table.

Muybridge took his first picture on a wide-open lens and silently wondered why any butler would help in this way. Outside, on the streets, the Chinese were little more than slave labour, treated like dogs, their ancient culture spat on. Sixty miles from here, he had witnessed a "chink hunt"; four of the best local pistoleros had placed wagers to see how many Chinese they could shoot from horseback. Their targets were the immigrant labourers, recently dismissed after building a stretch of the new railway line. The distressed men had fled in panic, dropping their few possessions to gain more speed. Sixteen fell that day, under a laughing hail of bullets. Nine died. One of the sportsmen was using a Winchester '73. It was unclear who had won the wager, but Wang Chi had gained either great benevolence or vast ignorance on the other side, for he was apparently bringing Sarah's lost child to the table.

The medium's voice tightened into falsetto and Muybridge took his second picture, this time in a blaze of flash powder. All—including the spirits—had been warned about the potential intrusion, so that most closed their eyes when he said *"Now!"* and fired the light.

Afterblurs danced in their heads and added to the sense of aura, the smell of nitrate and magnesium stinging the closed air of the wooden chamber. Amid choked sobs and watery sighs, a child expressed her innocent love for her mother.

Muybridge was preparing to take his third picture when the medium announced that another presence had joined them. As he squeezed the bulb to slice out another long exposure, something moved in the corner of his vision. He jolted to see it, but there was nothing there. The sitters seemed oblivious to his change of attention.

"Who are you?" asked Madam Grezach, in long, drawn-out, saggy words.

She brought her hand to her face and made a few passes over her eyes.

"Someone is here for you!" she said in operatic surprise. "For you, Mr. Muggeridge, for you!"

He flinched to hear his real name being spoken, especially in front of the Winchester heiress. He moved to correct Madam Grezach when she spoke again.

"A poor woman is here. She asks why you made the gins which hurt her so terribly?"

The medium's voice was changing again, and now a slippery Cockney accent emanated from the same mouth, where the child and the butler had so recently been.

"Why did the sun's shadow cut me so?" it wailed. "The face that finished me was white, all white and looking in at the sides of me; inside me."

The other sitters were agitated by the change of direction; their lashes twitched with desire, longing to examine his expression. Muybridge fumbled with the plates and pretended not to hear the tone of these questions and comments. Even though he knew it was all nonsense, he still felt the dread of this charade raking up his troubled past. He half expected the ghost of his idiot wife to waltz into the room and tell stories of his cruelty and lack of manhood, to gabble his secrets aloud from the yapping mouth of this charlatan Pole.

"The lights crawled inside; I had to find the shadows and get 'em out!"

He fired another magnesium flash to banish the vulgar words from their company. White smoke flared from his camera and the voice disappeared. The medium sank into heavy groans and placed one hand drunkenly on her head, dislodging one of the tortoiseshell combs that kept a curly torrent of unruly auburn hair in place. It spilled onto the table unreasonably, covering her face and the groans beneath, giving the now slumped figure a grotesque, simian quality. Just for a moment, he heard a distant flock of birds sing from her dripping and distorted mouth.

Sarah said something to Elder Thomas, who stood up and shuffled to the door. Moments later, the lamp glowed brightly and the room's shadows receded to other parts of the house. The sitters stood up and fussed around Madam Grezach to regain her posture and her hair. Muybridge met the eyes of Elder Thomas, communicating with the slightest of expressions his disdain of this frantic, hysterical woman and the whole façade of music hall nonsense. He expected to see his subtle glance of cynicism mirrored in the elder, to gain a nod of support and agreement. Instead, he saw the opposite: total belief in the procedures and disapproval of his own expression. Worse still, he saw blame and distrust glinted against him. The elder helped the old woman and the medium leave the room, turning his stiff back on the upstart who had contaminated their tabernacle with his past lives and his present bewilderment of irritant equipment.

When all had left, Muybridge stood adrift in the empty room, unable to make sense out of all that had occurred. There was no meaning in any of it, and he felt foolish and mistaken. God knew what he would find on his glass negative. He suspected there would be nothing but blurs and shadows and he would be proved right.

In the red cave of his private darkroom, blood-warm fluids made his hands puffy and succulent. He peered into the night trays and saw patches of light rise against the settling blacks. He moved them to a fixing tray and rocked them to and fro, simmering them into permanence.

He turned on the light to view the first picture. The image showed the whole group leaning towards the medium, whose out-of-focus head and body had been moving during the exposures. Her edges were undefined in relation to the sharp, delineated forms of the others in the weird room, but it was, in all other respects, a perfectly ordinary image.

The second picture was quite different. All the sitters had been caught in the flash powder like victims in a blast. All showed agitation; the old woman and the horse-faced one stared directly at the camera, responding to his call of *"Now!"* Their eyes were blurred on the inside, and their whites gave off a disturbed incandescence as their faces gawped. Elder Thomas was caught staring stiffly away, looking straight at the medium. Madam Grezach herself was stock-still and in focus. She had been speaking at the time and her expression was held in the vise of a twisted smile. He shivered as he recalled her hocus-pocus about the dead child, suddenly noticing a difference in her face, a change of shape, as if a smaller face was being born through it, not violently, but with a rippled plumping. He was horrified by the notion but could not deny the effect the flash had caught.

He dragged his eyes to the third print, another open shutter that held a room of blurs. He couldn't recall any accidental movement, but he must have juddered the tripod or rattled the lens. The sitters and the table were smooth and softened, as if diluted and coming apart at their edges. He laid the print to one side, relief creeping in to cover his initial misgivings.

Then he looked at the last image. The light had not startled the party this time, but they had been upset by something else; he recalled the pitiful voice of the London street woman. They stared at the medium in distaste, the flash catching the repugnance in their postures and on their exposed faces. Madam Grezach looked straight through him, and her expression made his blood run cold: It was no longer life and theatre that illuminated the medium's face; her features and nuances of gesture had been stolen and replaced with facsimiles from another time. The magnesium burn had dredged out a decoy of rank terror, which in turn aimed its shivering wet sinews and pitiless hunger towards him.

He stepped back from the table of rectangular dishes in dismay. Had he really made a genuine psychic photograph? Had he achieved what others had only faked? With shaking hands, he lifted the wet papers out of the fluids and pinned them up to dry. They had already changed. The significant, unique transformations in the medium's face had diminished; now it was only conjecture, a matter of interpretation and not fact. The images of Madam Grezach had become normal, blurred pictures of a normal, blurred woman. What had he seen before? Was he imagining things?

He collected the negatives and set them on a glass table with a light beneath them. Their reversed faces seemed skeletal and goatlike, but without any obvious signs of distortion. He became more perplexed: He had obviously been wrongly influenced by a desire to achieve the images that Sarah Winchester had wanted; her perception must have clouded his defined eye for a brief moment. Indeed, that influence was probably the very heart of the whole meaningless business. The next day loomed in his confused mind; the presentation of the prints worried him. There was nothing to show, and his anxiety at that knowledge forced him to see the inconsistencies in the chemical waters, as if the solutions he sought lay at the bottom of a glass or in the centre of a spinning mirror. He switched off the lights and turned his back on the darkened room, making his way to bed with a desperate sense of having been undervalued again and, in some inexplicable way, tricked.

He slept badly, in a dream of being continuously awake. The pillows aggravated his rest; the sheets clung or slipped; his bladder was the only fact that ruled and divided the short night.

He rose far too early and snatched the dried prints from their stringy line, bustling them into an envelope and a leather satchel. He had not even fully dressed yet, and he roamed about with his lower half naked and ultimately flaccid. By nine o'clock, he was exhausted but did not dare sleep. The outside world was working, and it was time he joined it.

He washed and dressed for his meeting with the Winchester woman, preening disconsolately before his looking glass: If he must present his failure, at least he would do so with some dignity. It had been her idea, he mused in the endless carriage ride, to make these pictures in the first place; he had tried to explain to her from the beginning that it was not his usual subject. By the time he arrived, he had an entire speech prepared, about the true nature of photography and its urgent importance as a scientific instrument. He did not want to insult the old woman or her puerile beliefs; it might still be possible to get her to fund a real project, one worthy of his talents and skills.

He was ushered through the gloomy polished rooms, which

seeped resin from all the fresh wood but refused to shine, and into another reception room, where she waited for him. To his horror, she was not alone: Elder Thomas stood by her side, his lank, dark seriousness absorbing the little brightness the room possessed. He looked at Muybridge with a polite indifference, which the photographer suspected covered his seething contempt. Sarah's eyes drifted from his nervous face to the satchel in his nervous hands.

"Thank you for being so prompt, Mr. Muybridge," she said, generously ignoring the fact that he was forty minutes early. "I do hope your journey over here was not too tiresome."

"It is always a pleasure to call on you, ma'am; the distance is of no importance," he said.

"As you can see, Elder Thomas is joining us today; he is as excited as I to see what you have achieved."

This time, everybody present looked at the satchel. It was time for the speech.

"Photography is seen by some to be an art and by others to be a science," he began. "I believe its future lies somewhere in between. With new cameras and developing processes, it will become possible to catch many of the wonders of nature and hold them for examination forever."

"Excellent," she interrupted. "I am so pleased to see that we are of such similar minds on the subject, that we can envisage the wonders of both worlds being brought together so." She flushed with an infant joy and he wilted in the blindness of it. "Please, may we now see the pictures you made?"

She extended her hand towards him. He had no choice and no more words, so he opened his satchel and brought out the envelope. Elder Thomas retrieved it from him and brought it swiftly to her side. She opened it and fetched the prints out, laying the images in her lap.

"It's not always possible . . . ," he began to mutter, but he was halted by the look on her face.

She turned the print over to see the next, and her expression deepened.

The elder peered over her shoulder, his countenance beginning to reflect the same intensity.

"The third print was more difficult to expose," said Muybridge to deaf ears.

As she looked from image to image, he was lost. He had no idea what she thought. It looked as though her face was shifting through amazement and shock, but certainly not into the disappointment he had expected. Her eyes were moist, and small sighs fluttered under her moving lips. Could this be rage? he wondered. She set the prints down in her lap and lifted her head.

"Mr. Muybridge, I had no idea," she gently said. "I had hoped something might be possible, but this! I thought at first you seemed a little reticent, a little surprised by my request. Yet these!" she said, touching the prints and leaving both hands folded over them. "These are beyond my wildest hopes. You are obviously a man of significant talents."

Emotion swept over her again, and the elder touched her sleeve. She rose and turned to leave the room, the prints pressed hard against her bosom. Muybridge rose with her, watching as she tottered slightly, robustly supported by the anxious elder. At the door, she turned to look at Muybridge once more, to thank him silently before leaving him alone in the cavernous space of her departure.

He stood awkwardly in the odd room at the centre of the winding, empty mansion, in a state of total bewilderment, awash with flows of contradiction. He glowed at her words but turned to ash at their meaning. There was nothing there, just a few blurred, underexposed fools sitting at a table. Could she have seen what he did before? Had she shared in the same dim delusion, or had she seen more?

He closed his empty satchel and made his way out to the hall-way; he was met by the butler, who conducted him to the street. The door shut firmly behind him. A breeze had picked up and rattled the new buds on the trees. Spring was early, and the old energy of the land flowed back into the newly made streets. The green scent of optimism roamed abroad, and he stood on the porch, seeing it with a magnificent clarity. In his heart, another autumn was stirring.

CHAPTER TWENTY-SEVEN

*M*arie assumed Maclish's extended absence was merely a continuation of his increasingly erratic behaviour. She considered for a moment that it was the regret and shame of what had happened on the night of the dinner that kept him away. But that theory did not swill around her experienced mind for long.

She savoured the unexpected solitude, enjoying the quiet space, free for the first time of masculine posture and strut, of those endless noises that men make to convince themselves and others of the necessity and toil of their presence.

She sat and thought about the future of their child. She would be a good mother; she would keep the child safe from any excesses of clumsy love or dictating attitude that her husband might bring to its infancy. She still hoped that he would make a good father, even through all her nagging misgivings. Wasn't he showing eagerness towards the birth? He had tried to be supportive before, when the last child was stillborn. Hadn't he even let Dr. Hoffman examine the poor wee thing to understand what had gone wrong? She convinced herself that William would change when their family began to grow. After all, they were stronger now: Money was being saved; the house and the job were secure; he was becoming a man of consequence.

She lit a lamp in the kitchen against the growing night and started to prepare food. It was a notably dark night, with only a curved rind of moon to light the way of any late visitor to their home. Her eyes were continually drawn to the window, expecting to see him walking down the hill at any moment, his form silhouetted against the glow of the slave house and its reflection on the chain-link fence. Then it dawned on her why the gloom was so unusually impenetrable: The slave house emanated darkness. Its humped shadow was entirely black. An iced apprehension infiltrated the warmth of her blood. She opened the back door and stepped nervously through it, into the night. The yard was unnaturally still; the quiet held the loneliness of cooling embers. She returned to the safety of her home and locked the door, a shiver escorting her around the room until the air was stirred by her bustling and the house had stopped holding its breath.

The next morning, the Chinese cook found the slave house empty; the night guard was gone, and a chair had been turned over. Apart from that, the prison felt unused, as if no one had ever lived in it. They found the cold train later that day, but an extensive investigation revealed no trace of Maclish or the Limboia: they had vanished into the whispering trees.

The Timber Guild immediately started a search; one of their representatives was sent to inform Mrs. Maclish. The man would later report that Marie Maclish had seemed taken aback at first, but as he had delicately reassured her that she would not be left alone to struggle, should something untoward have happened to her husband, she had seemed to become less worried, a little euphoric even. He would put it down to shock and explain that the poor woman was undoubtedly grievously disturbed by the news of her husband's disappearance.

———

They searched for a week but found nothing; they contemplated extending the search area but were unwilling to delve any deeper into the forest. In addition to the loss of their best foreman, there was the more pressing problem of finding another workforce as quickly as possible. Many business empires and livelihoods were utterly dependent on the company's constant supply of forest timber; the panic of commerce far outweighed the concerns of a lost employee and his tribe of soulless heathens.

But when Hoffman went missing, the rumours began to squawk and fly. His working relationship with Maclish was well-known but unclear. Also, for years there had been complaints and rumours attached to the eminent physician's conduct. These had been brushed under the carpet or paid off, while the larger chunks of accusation had been crushed by threat. All began to surface in his absence.

When officers of the Civic Guard started to look into the doctor's affairs and lift some of the more conspicuous stones and lumpier carpets, a scree of innuendo came loose and tumbled onto his reputation. They searched his house and laboratory, discovering more facts than rumours, stopping midway to seal the rooms and leave with grey complexions. Pathologists from foreign cities were brought in to continue the search; the findings were never publicly announced. The Timber Guild absorbed the wrongs of its own, even when they revealed malpractice, illegal experimentation, and crime. All was stifled and kennelled, patted quiet by wads of money or choke-chained by itinerant accident; perfect erasure by perfect symmetry.

➡

The bells of the cathedral were wallowing the city in their depth and counterpoint when Cyrena read of the disappearance of Maclish and Hoffman.

Pacing the room in time with the bells, she tried to hold back a smile, knowing it was all connected in some way to their search for Ishmael. She felt responsible and elated in the same moment. She cared nothing for those men, but the consequences of these portent happenings had a weight that unbalanced her equilibrium, causing a flutter in her ribs and setting her imagination racing. The game was under way. A huge obstacle had been eradicated; her embarrassment had been erased with their departure. She rang for Myra and asked her servant to tell the chauffeur to bring the car as quickly as possible. They were going to see Mistress Tulp.

Fifteen minutes later, they were purring through the streets, the cathedral bells still ringing as she passed beneath the twin spires. She craned her neck to see the silver bridge and laughed aloud. The chauffeur gave her a glance in the mirror and she brought her smile under control. It would not do to be so obviously happy at the rogues' misfortune. But in truth, it was not their disappearance but her reunion with a part of herself that left her so elated, a part that had been imprisoned by their actions and attitude; she had almost forgotten that it was locked away until it had flown out of the rustling pages of the discarded newspaper.

By the time they reached 4 Kühler Brunnen she had composed herself. She rapped sharply on the gate and heard shuffling on the other side. She rapped again. Not even the miserable servant would dampen her current enthusiasm.

Mutter opened the gate a few inches and peered at her.

"Well, open up, man, for goodness' sake; let me in!"

Mutter reluctantly pulled the heavy gate back and stood aside.

"That's more like it," she said, beaming down at the wide man as he seemed to chew on a sticky and knotted word. "Now, go and tell your mistress that I am here," she commanded.

He made a strange gesture, his eyes seeming to roll around in his head, as if he were trying to observe the entire courtyard via his peripheral vision. "Please wait inside, madam," he said in a flush of unsurpassed politeness. She was taken aback at such a remarkable change of attitude and let herself be swiftly escorted across the cobbled yard, away from the stables, and into the house. He left her in the reception room and went to find Ghertrude. She was delighted that Mutter had responded to her firm but polite commands so well: There was hope for the man yet.

Several minutes later, the door opened soundlessly and Ghertrude curved into the pale room. She had changed. Cyrena's first thoughts were that she looked older since their last meeting, larger somehow, but that was impossible. Yet her complexion, it seemed, was also different from what she remembered. Cyrena's new eyes were still hungry for detail, even if the rest of her mind found them rather too unrelenting.

"My dear, how are you?" she said, pushing aside her doubts to greet her friend with the great warmth and pleasure she nonetheless felt.

"Very well, thank you, Cyrena. How are you?" Ghertrude replied, her few words exposing so much—it was obvious that she was anything but well. The speed with which she had politely changed the direction of attention was overly polite, and Cyrena began to suspect that her presence was less than welcome. She quickly crossed the room and made a soft extension to grasp her friend's hand. She saw the flinch. It was involuntary and momentary, but it was there. She held it anyway, shuddering at its coldness.

"My dear, you are freezing!"

She instantly brought the warmth of her other hand to cup

the cold paw. Ghertrude looked away. Cyrena's concern grew; the built-in determination that so marked Ghertrude's character was nowhere to be found: Whatever had happened, it was serious.

"What's wrong, Ghertrude?" she asked in a caring, solid tone.

She felt the movement again, trapped beneath the warmth of her grip. This time, it was not a flinch but a tiny tug of escape.

"Ghertrude? Tell me. You know you can trust me."

Ghertrude wrenched her hand free and looked at Cyrena with an expression that neither of them recognised.

"Don't treat me like a child!"

Cyrena felt the words slap against her face and looked on, speechless.

"We are in serious trouble and you pretend nothing has happened?! You breeze in here as if all those horrors never occurred? You are laughing and I cannot even smile!" Ghertrude was fighting back the tears, her shaking fists beginning to bunch. "I cannot sleep; I keep seeing those men and that horrible monster. Ishmael is lost and we will be dragged into the very depths of this dreadful crime!"

The younger woman was instantly overcome by a great gushing of contained emotion. She erupted in sobs and shudders, collapsing her stance and her speech into uncontrollable, wet convulsions. Cyrena guided Ghertrude to the sofa as she gave in to the tumult and wept until there was nothing left inside. Little sniffs punctuated the growing weight of her body as she fell into an exhausted sleep in her friend's arms.

Cyrena was very still, cautious not to move and wake Ghertrude from the depth of such vital rest; she had been turned inside out by the strenuous action, but sleep would re-form her in its flat, calm wake. They were both soaked from her tears; Cyrena's blouse clung coldly against her bosom, where Ghertrude rested.

From her fixed position, she looked around the room, letting her mind recall their adventures together. Why had Ghertrude said "crimes"? Nothing they had done could be called a crime; their involvement with those dubious men may have been a secret, but it was not illegal: She had paid for their services, which had proved to be less than useless. She moved slightly, to shift her weight; the sleeper gave a quiet moan. Cyrena stroked her friend's head and settled her weight again. She continued her casual inspection of the room, trying to alleviate the growing discomfort and take her mind off the pins and needles developing in her feet.

Sometimes, she thought her inquisitive eyes had a life of their own; they constantly flitted and settled on things to embrace their shape and meaning. They looked into the tangled garden of the Persian carpet, imagining all kinds of arabesque creatures hiding within. They stroked the curved legs of a dark mahogany chair and rolled smoothly over its satin cushion. They took in the squat shadow that crouched behind the chair, swept over to the bright brass of the fireguard, then flicked quickly back to the shadow to look more deeply.

There must have been a shock of recognition, because something awoke Ghertrude. She flinched and pulled herself up, realising her embarrassing position. Still confused and wiping drool from her face, she noticed thin traces of it on Cyrena's blouse. "Oh, oh, I am so sorry!" she spluttered. "Please forgive me—this is dreadful."

She arose quickly and staggered back, still unbalanced from her folded sleep and the sticky webs of its unformed images. Cyrena was on her feet and ready for her fall, her hands outspread. Ghertrude righted herself and looked at her friend, clasping both Cyrena's hands in her own. She had returned, secure in her old self.

"You must think me such a fool. How can I ever apologise? I

am so sorry; I have not slept for three nights and my nerves are worn ragged." She again noticed Cyrena's crumpled, wet blouse and her own dampness. "Please forgive me. You have been such a dear friend and I have treated you terribly. I will get something warm for you to wear and light a fire; it is cold in here; we hardly ever use this room." She fussed, dithered, and twirled, making her way to the door. "I will be back in one moment," she said. "Please, do make yourself comfortable. We will light a fire."

And then she was gone. Cyrena waited for silence, then swiftly crossed the room, searching out the Gladstone bag that skulked behind the chair.

Several minutes later, Ghertrude returned carrying a dressing gown and a tray with a flask of warm milk laced with rum. Mutter followed, holding kindling and logs. Cyrena had returned to her seat, but her colour had changed; she was pallid, and her smile was drawn over clenched teeth. Neither of them noticed; they were too busy lighting the fire and laying out the drinks. Ghertrude offered the dressing gown for her damp friend to step into, holding it out with a smile and a flourish, like a suddenly joyful matador. Cyrena donned the gown and they sat together with their warming drinks in front of the blazing fire. Mutter left the room without a word but with a significant glance at Ghertrude, which they both assumed Cyrena was oblivious to.

"Cyrena, please forgive my appalling behaviour. I am very tired and under the weather."

"I should have told you I was going to visit. I think I took you by surprise," said Cyrena, sipping her drink.

"No, no, you are always welcome. Now, tell me about what you have been doing."

Cyrena was not prepared to change the subject, but she patronised her friend for a moment.

"Oh, this and that, attempting to find another purpose in my life."

Ghertrude raised a quizzical eyebrow and cocked her head.

"Did you hear about Hoffman?" Cyrena quizzed.

"Oh! Yes, he disappeared, didn't he?"

"Off the face of the earth."

Ghertrude changed the subject immediately, though only as far as Hoffman's unfortunate accomplice. "And what about the other one? Maclish!"

"Yes, he, too, apparently."

They put their drinks down simultaneously, as if to mark the end of a difficult conversation.

"I feel I must apologise again," said Ghertrude.

"You mean for not trusting me?" said Cyrena, closing in.

"Well, no, I meant . . ."

"I know what you meant. And I know what's disturbing you," interrupted the older woman.

"I am just unwell," Ghertrude stammered.

"Don't lie to me! I deserve more than this," replied Cyrena, her voice rising and changing pitch. "I truly am your friend; now, tell me the truth!"

Ghertrude was silent.

"Ghertrude, tell me the truth; I already know what you are hiding."

"It is . . . very difficult for me to say," said Ghertrude gently.

Cyrena looked at her silently, her eyes dark and demanding. She would not be deterred.

"Very well," Ghertrude sighed. "I am pregnant."

CHAPTER TWENTY-EIGHT

The ancient black hand shone in the flickering light of the small campfire, its tattoos of spirals and sun wheels spinning as it passed through the circular clearing of the forest. It moved past the two men sitting close to the flames and whispered in the dancing shadows, stroking the cheek of its grandson before vanishing out of the circle and into the night.

Tsungali opened his eyes. The flames made the trees shudder and jump; the world looked unstable and weightless. This must be the other place, he thought, bracing himself for his retribution. Then he saw Uculipsa, lying on the shuddering ground next to his spell pouch; his bandolier, kris, and other possessions were nearby. He extended his hand out towards them, but nothing happened; there was only a wrenching pain. He looked to where his hand should have been, but there was nothing there; his arm was reduced to a stump, from his shoulder to his elbow. He felt sick and groaned loudly. One of the men at the campfire stood up and moved towards him. He stooped down to pick up Uculipsa, lifting her by her carrying strap; the rifle slid apart and swung in two halves. From where Tsungali lay, she looked like a broken bird, hanging mutely from the man's hand. He walked over and dropped her at the invalid's side.

"You should have died," said Williams. "You deserved to."

Tsungali stared into the face, made of shadows and flashes of orange: It was him.

"My bullet hit your arm as you charged. It took your hand and lower arm and snapped the Enfield in two. It was meant for your chest. You are a very lucky man."

It was the same voice. How could this be? Tsungali veered in and out of belief, his broken body unable to keep up with such revelation.

"Oneofthewilliams," he whispered woozily and passed out into a pit of raging black thunder.

When he woke, he was in a different place; they had moved him into the shade and changed his dressing. Williams was sitting next to him, drinking from a tin cup. The creature was sleeping. Without turning, Williams spoke. "You know me?"

The wounded man tried to speak, but his throat was closed with dust. At the pause, Williams turned. Seeing the man's struggle, he poured water into the cup and offered it up to his broken lips. Tsungali drank and dissolved the webs on his voice. "Why did you let me live?" he rasped.

"I would have blown your head off, but he stopped me," Williams said, gesturing towards the cyclops.

"What is he?" Tsungali asked weakly.

"Ishmael? He is something from the old world, something that never really existed. He is unique."

He took the cup and refilled it, drank some, and then handed it back, turning again to stare into Tsungali's face.

"Now, about your words earlier." His tone tightened to a blade. "What did you call me?"

"I called you Oneofthewilliams. You knew me when I was a young man; the rifle was yours." He pointed to the pathetic carcass of the snapped Uculipsa. "You were chosen to survive by the holy Irrinipeste, daughter of the Erstwhile, and I believe you have been changed by her forever."

He finished speaking and slumped a little, fear and fatigue mining his strength.

Williams was very still; he looked perplexed.

"If this is true, why would you try so hard to kill me?"

"I did not know it was you until it was too late. I was working for your old masters; they thought you long dead. Then it was said that you were returning through the coastal lands. They wanted you gone, not coming back. Walking freely through desertion after all this time and relighting old fires."

Williams could not make images for the words, but the depth of his understanding knew them to be true.

"Do you intend to continue your quest?"

Tsungali shook his head wearily.

Williams got up and slowly walked over to Ishmael, who had been woken by their conversation. His hearing, which had been hiding in a constantly ringing place ever since the pistol fired next to his head, had almost returned.

"I don't know which of the three of us is the biggest freak," Williams said, retrieving his bow and quiver. "I will be back in an hour. Don't worry about him. He is going nowhere."

He walked out of the camp, a trio of eyes fixed on his disappearing form.

Long, indecisive minutes passed. Eventually, Ishmael called a greeting to the wounded man.

"I am coming to speak with you. Do not be alarmed!"

The black man waved feebly at him to signal understanding and agreement.

The cyclops sat at his side, so that his face would not shock and he would be able to watch the other man's moves. He had no fear of the wounded man—he had been the cause of his downfall and the preserver of his life. He had purchased him, between life and death, and now the power was all his, unfamiliar and thriving, from a source unknown to him but nonetheless evident: he owned this man. He had stared down the track with Este in his hands, and this man had slipped and faltered. There had been a reaction between the bow and his eye that saved their lives. Now something told him to spare, or rather save, this man's life; there was a purpose in it.

"Why do you pursue me?" he asked quietly.

"I was not hunting you; I sought only the Bowman."

"But you would have killed me if I hadn't stopped you?"

Tsungali glanced tentatively at his interrogator's profile and gave a small nod.

"So you do know that I stopped you?"

Tsungali nodded again and began to tremble.

"Do you also know that I saved your worthless life?"

Again he nodded, tears forming and a great weight growing over his heart.

The cyclops lowered his face and looked into his subordinate's eyes; a great passion rose in him and swelled up, out of his chest.

"You are mine!" he boomed. His voice was commanding and alien to him, bred out of certainty and spite; the hunter shrivelled under its command, triggering some other instinct in Ishmael; he softened his tone a fraction. "What will you do for me?" he asked.

Tsungali directed a nod across the camp, indicating the pile of confiscated possessions; he seemed to have lost his power of speech. Ishmael stood and crossed the space to the small heap. He lifted each item, one at a time, until Tsungali signalled that he had reached the right one. In his hands was a bulky, brown leather belt, strung with pouches and bulging pockets. He inspected it suspiciously before returning to the prone man. Holding it up for a moment, he looked down into the man's soul, then dropped it callously across his body. The buckle caught the stump end of his wound, and Tsungali jounced into spasm. Ishmael watched silently, waiting for the writhing to subside as some developing part of him sipped at the agony.

Eventually, once the throb in his shoulder had returned to an almost bearable rhythm, Tsungali fumbled into the pouches with his only hand. He pulled out a small, unseen item and held it in his loosely bunched fist. Ishmael watched for signs of betrayal but knew there would be none. The hand, which shook a little less than it had, slowly opened, palm up, cupping the small grass ball. Inside its woven cage, the eye stared out, focusing intently on its new owner.

Williams shot the arrow vertically, up through the green shadows and into the bright sky; he did it to consult her in a way that sought no direction, at least not in the physical realm. She had changed; his memory of her had shifted; they were no longer one body. There was no pain in the separation; it was as if they had simply worn out an invisible circulation in which they had once shared everything. The pounding veins and singing capillaries that had held every reflection and nuance of their world had disappeared; the flow between them that had made one soul of their minds and bodies had ceased, somewhere in the Vorrh. Now not even the recollection of their transfusion together existed. They were two things: a man and a bow.

He could never return to all that he had forgotten; the road ahead must be walked alone. He walked back into camp, undone and clear, smelling the new breeze in his tight, half-sobbing lungs.

"He is called Tsungali; he will be my servant from now on," said Ishmael to the frowning Williams, who, though amazed at the turn of events in his absence, was equally intent on his own change of course.

"I know who he is. You are welcome to him." If Ishmael noticed the distance in his friend's tone, he didn't show it.

"He knows a medicine man who can change my face; he has agreed to take us to him."

Williams grunted impassively and started to gather his pack.

"What are you doing?" said Ishmael.

"I have other things to do. Your leg is better and you have a slave to look after you now." At the word "slave," everybody flinched, including its speaker.

"Where will you go?"

Williams paused for a moment, his emotions playing wearily over his face.

"Out of this godforsaken forest."

They fell silent and still, each considering his position in the new pattern of things.

"Maybe straight through and out the other side," said Williams finally, breaking the spell.

"If you travel on, it will take your memory," said Tsungali, in his first unsolicited utterance.

"What memory?" Williams shrugged. "You know more about me than I do myself." He turned away from the questions and stooped to retrieve a blanket, dropping it near his growing bundle of belongings. The rest of the day passed without much conversation. As the evening drew in, Williams gathered his possessions and moved them to another place in the forest. Ishmael assumed he would leave at dawn, and he put together a simple meal, as he had seen others do. He lit the campfire, boiled water, and waited. He and Tsungali were hungry and picked at the food. The bow rested against a nearby tree, its quiver hanging in the low branches: His friend could not be far away. But by nightfall, their comfort was replaced with anxiety, their appetites slipping away as the truth wormed its way into their stomachs: He had gone. The bow was left in the flickering tree, and he had departed, wordlessly, into the enveloping night.

The two wounded men made their way out of the Vorrh, to the island where Nebsuel dwelt. Tsungali's hidden boat could not be used: The cyclops was too skittish and weak to be trusted on the fast water, and because Tsungali had only one arm, the boat was useless. So they went by foot, back through the monsters' hunting ground.

Ishmael carried the bow; it had not left his hands since they realised that Williams had gone. It wormed itself into him day and night, burrowing into his future, drawing a blood line around all his maps of possible tomorrows. He dared not use it yet, fearing the momentum of its power when fully taut and waiting for release. Like a child, that virgin part of him shrank from the full volume and implication of such an act. He held it before him as they moved forward through the Vorrh, and the forest understood its new application of meaning. Not a creature dared approach them, and they were met by muffled silence all the way. The birds knitted their beaks, the animals bit their tongues, the insects froze, and the anthropophagi ignored their passing. The silence infected their journey, making it strange and infuriating for Ishmael: He had many questions for his new servant, but nothing he said could provoke an answer.

The pain amplified Tsungali's introspection: The cyclops seemed to know nothing about the world. How could he begin to explain his history with Oneofthewilliams; his childhood; how he and his grandfather were shut behind glass in another world; the tragedy of the Possession Wars? There was too much to say and too little experience shared; better to be quiet and concentrated, stay on the track and get to the healing man as quickly as their wounds allowed.

Ishmael missed Williams, missed his humour and protection. He had a warmth about him that the tattooed killer who now travelled by his side could never possess. The old man refused to answer even the simplest questions as they pushed through the undergrowth. Ishmael began to think that he had made the wrong decision. He should have stayed close to his friend and not let him leave so sadly. There was, he began to realise, little reason to trust his new companion; his promise of a new face might be a lie or a lure—Ishmael could be following him to death or worse. Why had he so hastily accepted this man's servitude? He could see that Tsungali feared him, but he did not understand his total abasement to him when he held the bow. He guessed it was some kind of primitive superstition and pondered how he might be able to put it to his advantage. He wondered if it could be used to receive the answers he so desired. He changed the bow from one hand to the other and then touched Tsungali's back with its tip.

"Tell me about this medicine man," he said.

The effect was instant and undisguised. The old killer fell to his knees, placing his working arm in the air in a gesture of surrender; Ishmael circled him, looking closely at the trembling man's face.

"Yes, yes, I will say all, yes!" rattled the mercenary, in a fast, breathless assent.

"Then tell me about him. What can he do?"

"He can fix your face, fix like other men; he can put my live eye in, fix it there so two eyes like other men. He can do many things, make a new hand, last time fixed jaw, fix bullet wound. Some say he plays with death so face fixing is easy." He was panting the words out like a running dog.

"Why will he do this for me?" asked Ishmael suspiciously.

"Do because of the bow, do anything for the bow, what bow says," the hunter gibbered in reply.

Ishmael sat down on the earth and gripped the bow, turning

it in his hands. He questioned his slave for an hour on all matter
of things. The trembling man spat out a barrage of answers. Not
all of it made sense, but Ishmael built a picture of his servant,
of what he knew and how he could be used. When he had heard
enough, he stood and pointed forward and the jabbering man
led the way.

The Erstwhile watched the performance peak and fade. They
crept close, keeping themselves concealed; gradually, with the
slow speed of great wisdom, they saw the bow. The self of it
accumulated in them, like a residue of sand forming a mountain, grain upon grain, until it filled the entire landscape. They
had not known of its presence in the forest while it had been
in the grip of the white man. Now, in the hands of the cyclops,
it broadcast its existence loud and far. They turned away and
moved at painstakingly slow velocity, as far away as they could.
Conventional hiding was not enough; they separated and found
their own places to dig, clawing the stubborn earth and roots
aside. All now knew that the bow was here, and they made
grave-like hiding places, crawling in and pulling piles of earth
and leaves over themselves. They lay still in their concealment,
waiting for sleep, hoping to escape the ambiguity of dreams, the
scent of which was most attractive to higher animals and other,
more difficult entities.

➤→

Nebsuel hid his shock at seeing Tsungali on his doorstep. So
amazed was he that he scarcely noticed the hunter's shaded
companion, half-concealed by his hood and scarf. He brought
them into his crowded workroom, a library of objects, bottled
and stacked, shelved and hanging, boiled over, chaotic and alive,
a vast collection of fragmented animal, vegetable, and mineral

from around the globe. He gestured to them to sit and asked them to tell their tale.

Tsungali told of his quest and how it had changed. He said something of Oneofthewilliams, but not all. He told of demons and introduced Ishmael, who began to discreetly unwrap his face from within the scarf. "We have come to you for help. I am wounded again and my master needs rectification," explained Tsungali.

"Master?"

"Yes, master."

"Rectification?" said Nebsuel, like a stranger trying out a word in a foreign tongue.

"He needs a new face."

Nebsuel swung around to view the other man. He looked straight into the cyclops's face, and a strange gleam engulfed his gaze. Ishmael looked at him warily, uncertain of this unusual response; his doubt did not last for long.

"Wonderful!" crowed the healer, unable to control himself. "I never thought I would meet one. *Do you speak?*" he hawked, apparently expecting the response of some cretinous species or another.

"I do, but not in the crippled tongue of your native land."

"By the living gods, he is intelligent!" declared Nebsuel, clapping his hands, a lascivious grin on his beaming face. "Forgive my rudeness, young master; I mean no offence; I am simply staggered by your uniqueness. Please, let me get you both something to eat and drink. Your journey must have been arduous." He turned quickly, leaving a trace of something moist and hungry in the atmosphere around their bare skin. Ishmael's hackles rose. He could not understand why, but he did not like this man; he had the bearing and manners of a jackal, one that was wiser and more complex than anyone he had yet met. But he was a gracious jackal, and Ishmael's stomach urged his trust to be stretched a little further.

They ate and drank, taking freshwater into their parched throats. Their host opened a bottle of wine all the way from Damascus, where, Nebsuel explained, his forebears had come from. The wise man's ancestors had travelled to fish the rich shoals of slaves hundreds of years earlier, building networks of communications that ran in all directions and to all lands.

The exotic things in this room, and the wine itself, still passed through the gradually fading routes.

"Tell me of your home and background," he asked of Ishmael.

"They are unknown to me at this time," the cyclops replied regretfully. "Completely unknown."

"Ah, but you mean to find out?"

Ishmael eyed him warily. "I do," he replied, uncertain of how much he could safely reveal.

"Take care, rare one; origins are mysterious. There are tangles and causes, curves and strangers, which are sometimes best unmet. Stones that should never be turned. Especially in one like you."

It sounded like a genuine and sincere warning, and Ishmael began to warm to the shaman: Perhaps he was only a wolf and not a jackal at all? Even so, Ishmael avoided speaking of the Kin or Ghertrude: His instinct kept them well away from the uncertainty of strange men.

The conversation progressed and they talked about Nebsuel's work. The old warrior promised Nebsuel he had a prize beyond riches and that the medicine man would find time in its company a magnificent exchange for his skills. There was some laughter about the existence of such a treasure; the wine helped silken the conversation's flow.

Tsungali took the eye out with great care, picking bits of grass and dust from its slippery surface and clearing a space on the table to allow closer observation. Nebsuel brought his magnifying glass near and directed a pointed lamp at the treasure.

"You bring me another wonder," he marvelled. "Such bounty; such bounty!"

He became hushed, bending closer to view the impossible again. Here was a new version of the thing he valued most, another demonstration that the world was unfathomable and its resources unlimited, infinitely mysterious and ever changeable. His expertise in anatomy and charm surgery was in a constant state of amazement, but this brought a new pinnacle of surprise: a human eye, active and vital, long after separation from its lifeblood and the protective surroundings of the rest of its body. What nourished it? What let it work so frantically when the optic nerve that operated it had been so definitely severed from the brain? It was like a continually working bucket that had unknowingly lost its well. He turned to Tsungali, enraptured.

"You know my only two prices are objects of use and objects of fascination." Tsungali grinned through his gapped teeth. "You have brought me two bounties of knowledge and fascination: My service is yours. What can I do for you?"

They discussed the hunter's arm, the wise man prodding thoughtfully at the healing stump, mental calculations whirring through the room. But at the mention of Ishmael's face, his expression darkened.

"No," said Nebsuel definitely. "Such uniqueness is untouchable. Why would you want to look like everybody else?"

"Because I want to become myself and live my life as a man, not as a monster. I want to be forgotten for who I am, not judged for how I have been made."

Nebsuel paused to digest this, then said, "Do you choose to be with those who see you the wrong way?"

"Who else is there?"

"I know some."

Ishmael tensed at the suggestion. "No, I want to go back changed." Nebsuel made a clucking, swallowing sound and returned to his beaker of wine, shaking his head. Ishmael and Tsungali sat with him in silence, not looking at each other, eyes focused on their drinks. Too many moments had passed when Tsungali eventually blurted out, "Well? Will you do it? Will you operate on us?"

No answer came. The healer was hardening. Tsungali looked at Ishmael and nodded. "Show him," he said, and Ishmael dipped his head in understanding.

Ishmael pulled the long, thick bundle from under his feet and started to unwrap it. At first Nebsuel paid no attention; he had assumed the bundle to be the stranger's bedroll. But as more and more of the blanket was unravelled, he felt something straining in his solar plexus. He knew from old what that meant, but there was no time to register it or protect himself: The cyclops's possession was disclosed. As the last layer fell away, he began to sweat, his heart drying and fluttering, mites and dust shaken off in the straining, sticky cage of his ribs. He could not believe what he was seeing. The dark maroon of the bow's surface seemed to ripple and bend under his enforced gaze. Ishmael's hand was black with effort and excrescence. The eye rolled from its safe perch on the table, gravitating towards the bow and the floor. Everything in the room seemed to be turning and twisting, yearning towards Este in a curiosity that became mangled midway into abeyance. Ishmael dragged the bow down and covered it with the blanket, crudely smothering its influence under the covering. The eye stopped short of the table's lip; in its passage, it nicked itself on the sharp wire from around the discarded cork of the wine. The room crept back to inertia. Nebsuel sank into his seat as Tsungali grinned at the excellent demonstration. There was an eerie scent in the room: something of the sea and an exotic garden, smouldered together; a flinch of ammonia, at first exhilarating, and then turning to a whiff of dread, like a leeching memory trapped and waiting in a dream.

"I will do anything," said Nebsuel, in a voice from a distant, colourless place, "anything you want."

➤

The bird activated its bell of arrival and the fine sound sleeted down into the lower room like pointed snow.

Sidrus was not expecting a communication; there was very little to be told from the river mouth. He continued rubbing the sticky balm into his porous face. The bell rang again, and he wiped the fat from his fingers, so that they would not slip as he retrieved the scroll from the bird's dry, struggling ankle.

It was a message that should never have been sent, one laced with mistakenness from the moment Nebsuel had penned it, in a stolen pause that had masqueraded as the friendly replenishment of wine. It told of his visitors before he knew who they were and before he understood what it was that they really wanted. It said, simply:

Tsungali here with a cyclops. I think they killed Bowman and took his soul.

Sidrus dropped the note, feeling the consequence hollow him and make room inside for the wrath, which began to boil and brim. The lardish balm melted and dripped from his distorting face without the slightest trace of a flush. As the heat of it settled, he selected his canes and drugs, picking weapons with the detachment of a deadly perfectionist. It would take him three days to reach Nebsuel's pox-ridden island, maybe another four to extract the right amount of pain from the wicked scum for performing such an act of blasphemy.

➤→

"I cannot make you a perfect, natural face," Nebsuel explained. "It would seem that your skull has only one socket, so I will have to make a place for the other one. The living eye will be stitched into folds of constructed muscle and skin, but it will have no real nest to work in. It will not rotate; it will remain blind but, I hope, living. Yet, I cannot promise this. Whatever keeps it vital is beyond my understanding, and nothing to do with the rules of regular anatomy.

"I am anxious about its stability. If it were to die, it would infect the newly grafted tissue around it. But for now it is still animated, and as bright as your other. I pray it will always look like that, alert and active, not like false eyes made of glass or ivory, which always have a dead and lonely appearance. The good news for you is that because your working eye and socket are not quite central, the space between the eyes will seem more natural, if a little close together." The shaman paused for breath, adding, "Which some find most attractive—many of the European royal families have interbred to create this very effect. They might even recognise you as one of their own!"

Sensing that he had pirouetted out onto very thin ice, he decided that it was best to retreat to the more solid ground of surgical details.

"I will build you a nose of normal proportion, to place between the eyes, using the little bulb you have now as a starting point. This will be the easiest part of the procedure. Did you know that surgeons are now treating injured warriors from the great European war with the same methods I have used for years? I am told that they use scrapings taken from diseases and tinctures from rotting moulds to help the healing. My charms and plants are much cleaner, but they take longer. You might look a bit like one of those scarred warriors, a man who has been in a battle and bears the wounds of his heroism with pride. Your face will look like a damaged version of all other humans. Are you sure that you want this, and that I cannot help you find another alternative?"

Ishmael looked from the bundle, which now stayed very close to him, to the doctor, who followed his gaze and his meaning. The conversation ended there.

Nebsuel attended to Tsungali first. Building a new, living hand was out of the question, but a wooden one, with a hinged elbow that strapped onto the remains of his upper arm, was feasible.

The old mercenary seemed disappointed; he had allowed himself to imagine a fully working hand, made of flesh and bone and imbued with magic. Nebsuel explained that if he had kept the fragments and brought them with him, then maybe he could have improvised a kind of weak, articulate hook or claw. But the hardwood version would be better, he assured him. The hunter could have different models, with ivory fingernails and powerful engravings; charms and weapons could be hidden inside. He could have versions of other creatures: Puma paws and boar tusks could sprout from his sleeve, eagle talons and shark teeth might surprise an attacker or a victim.

The old warrior came around to the idea but explained that the days of his mercenary skills were over. His purpose now was to serve Ishmael and use violence only to protect his master. He made this point very clearly, explaining that while they were both healing, any attempts of outrage on their persons would send him and the bow into a frenzy of revenge, especially if he was dead. Nebsuel reassured him that they were both safe, not realising that his message to Sidrus made his promise impossible to keep.

The patient slept in a drugged sea of his mother's milk, his limb wrapped in layers of leaves and ointments, looking more like a papoose than a sling. The new arm was a crude affair but had a certain rustic brutality that Tsungali admired. Considering the short amount of time Nebsuel had taken to hollow and carve it, he considered himself fortunate to have anything more than an old chair leg grafted onto his stump.

Then it was Ishmael's turn, and he was jumpy, even after the numbing drafts he had been given.

"Young master, this is your last chance to change your mind," offered a blurring Nebsuel. "There is no going back once I begin."

Ishmael looked out for the last time through the face of a cyclops, a face that had already begun to disintegrate in the gathering haze. His view of the speaker began to fall away on a long track, shrinking the medicine man, whose own face muffled gibberish at him.

"Do it. Do it!" he said, and he heard his words float up, cooing to sit on his closing eye like a fat, indifferent bird.

CHAPTER TWENTY-NINE

"When is the baby due?" asked Cyrena at last.

"In August," said Ghertrude, sheepishly. "At least, that's when I think it should be, but . . . it seems to be progressing faster than that."

"Carnival?" asked Cyrena.

"Yes, it was conceived then."

"Is it his?"

"I don't know; I cannot be sure."

"You coupled with more than one?"

"Yes," she said, without a quiver of shame. It was too early to be assigned a father. The tiny beast of jelly turned in her soul and tried to speak in drowning verse to anything that might be its parents.

"Can you find out? There are some medical tests available. Maybe Hoffman?"

They met each other's gaze and Cyrena understood that the master of the skulking Gladstone bag would not be returning to collect it. Its doglike presence behind the chair seemed to awaken for a moment at the sound of its master's half-said name. Cyrena felt it. "You'd better get rid of that," she said.

Ghertrude stiffened, thinking she still referred to the unborn child, then saw that her friend was looking elsewhere. "Get rid of what?"

Cyrena pointed languidly and Ghertrude followed her wagging finger to the shadow. She cringed when she saw it, letting out a small shudder. It was as if the good doctor's head had been left under the chair, unnoticed, watching their every action since his removal.

She told Cyrena everything. The threat to her life; his rage; the broken pearls and Mutter's revenge.

"I will protect Sigmund for what he did to save me from that vile animal," she said with gritted determination. "I will protect him against all."

The implication of her words was clear: Cyrena was inside the pact or out of it; there was no middle ground. She would take Mutter's ground against all comers, including her friend.

"Your secret is safe with me," Cyrena replied, and she meant it. The new life and old death in the room were being gifted in a one-way transaction; she was already part of them both and wanted to be active in each of this woman's conclusions. Anyway, the prospect of crossing a raging Mutter was too horrible to contemplate. "I am glad that wretched man is out of our lives," she said decisively. "It sounds like he got everything he deserved."

Ghertrude nodded, nipping anxiously at the edges of her fingernails. Something dawned on Cyrena and she looked at her friend quizzically.

"What did Mutter do with . . . the remains?"

Ghertrude paused, realising that she did not know. They had never spoken fully about that night; she had only thanked him and sworn her silence, a pact she had now broken. "I don't know," she confessed. "Don't tell him you know—don't tell him I told you!"

She was becoming distraught again, and Cyrena wanted her

confidence, not her fear. She reached out and held her hands, looking intently into her anxious face.

"I will do whatever you want. I am with you in everything; you can trust me in this. We will put this whole horrid business behind us and face the future with your child together. I can help in all things."

And so they rebuilt the previous weeks with vigour and companionship. They rolled up their sleeves and scrubbed away all the images and stains of memory that were attached to their dealings with Hoffman and Maclish. They burnt the Gladstone bag and incinerated the days where the monsters, humiliations, and violence had dwelt. In their growing, joyous friendship, Ishmael was almost forgotten.

Mutter watched their daily laughter and the endless tidying and rearranging of furniture; the buying of flowers, the intimate lunches and dinners, their closeness; he knew that she had been told. The haughty outsider was aware of his crime, though she feigned a clever ignorance. He started to observe her more closely, wondering how he would dispose of her when the time came.

Yet Cyrena's gleaming, overactive vision missed nothing; she saw the simple, wicked plans being knotted together behind the old servant's red, veined eyes. If she did not deal with this now, it would soon be permanently out of her control.

Ghertrude was out shopping when Cyrena arrived at the gate. She was let in and made to cross the cobbled yard, coming to a stop on the exact spot where Hoffman had been dispatched.

"Herr Mutter, I think we should talk," she said, peering down at the bunched and ready man. "There is a great secret," she began, ignoring the clenching of his fists and his boots bracing the ground. "A great secret that I think you should know. I am telling you because I know of the loyalty you have for your mistress. In the future we will need your help even more, and that is why I am telling you, because Ghertrude is still too shy."

Mutter frowned and relaxed his attack stance.

"The truth is, your mistress is going to have a baby."

He had known it, had felt it days ago. He had smelt the glow, the warmth hidden in milk. His house and his life had been full of it for years. He had known it and put the idea aside as being impossible.

"Only the three of us know about this. She will tell her family later. I know this places an extra burden on you and I think it only fair that you should be remunerated for all you have done and will do in the future."

The old yeoman had no idea what she was talking about—"remunerated" meant nothing to him.

"So, Herr Mutter, please, accept this for your troubles."

She handed him a small cloth pouch, which he took gingerly, holding it in uncertain hands.

"Do open it—it is for you and your growing family."

He pulled a document out from inside the pouch, awkwardly unfolding it into his blank stare. She suddenly realised that he could not read and was ashamed at her own ignorance. How could she have been so stupid?

"I am afraid it is rather a complicated legal paper. Essentially, it is your house. It is the ownership of your home. It is now yours and your family's, forever."

Mutter stared blankly at the paper, her words beginning to stick to it with an uncomfortable mixture of amazement and distrust. He wondered if it was a payoff, or some sort of lever, to prise him away from his job. But no: His father had always paid rent to the Tulps, and so had he, endlessly. His cynical heart began to understand that it was, in fact, a gift. A gift for saving Ghertrude from that foolish man. A gift of freedom for his children and their children to come. He stared at her, changing gear from silence to awestruck speechlessness. She smiled at him from the bright clouds and said, "You are not to work today, Sigmund. Go, tell your good wife the news."

She fluttered her hand towards the door and he slowly started to move towards it, walking backwards in a crablike fashion. His smile began as he reached the wall and grew with every step that brought him nearer to home. He did not notice Ghertrude pass on the other side of the cathedral square as he hurried along, cap clutched to his chest.

Ghertrude entered through the side gate and found Cyrena still standing in the courtyard. She looked at her friend in bewilderment.

"I have just seen Mutter rushing through the streets, with an insane expression on his face."

Cyrena beamed at her. "Perhaps he is happy?"

"I have never seen him like that before, I do hope he is all right."

"I am sure he is fine," said Cyrena, opening the door of the house and motioning for her friend to enter.

Mutter was out of breath by the time he reached home. He stumbled inside, through his narrow door, catching his rigid boot noisily on the frame, dislodging minute traces of the vanquished Dr. Hoffman. The commotion made his wife stop her duties in the kitchen and rush to see what was going on.

"Whatever's the matter, Sigi?"

He laid his cap aside, still grasping the crumpled paper and cloth bag. "What on earth is the matter? You look like a giddy ox—look at the colour of you. What is it?"

He could say nothing through his breathless gasps, but his scarlet face looked as though it was ready to burst. He placed the paper on the dining table, which was the focus of the small room. He lovingly flattened it out, caressing its folds into careful submission.

"Thaddeus! Is he in?" he asked his wife excitedly.

"Yes, my dear, but what—"

"Thaddeus!"

The young man loped into the room, bending almost double to avoid the low doorways and sloped ceiling.

"Thaddeus, please read this for us."

They crowded around the nervous paper, Thaddeus skimming the document to see what he was dealing with, before moving into oratory mode. He stopped short and looked at his father.

"Father, do you know what this is?"

"Yes, yes, read it!"

Thaddeus read it slowly and carefully, announcing the long legal words carefully.

"Oh, Sigi, what is it? I don't like the sound of it. Are we in trouble about the rent again?" said the frantic wife, who had screwed her thin apron into a ball.

"No, Mother," said her son. "It says that we now own the house. It is ours forever. None of us will ever pay rent again."

The other children now joined the table, having been attracted by the unique sounds and vibrations in the room. The wife looked back and forth between the paper, Thaddeus, and Mutter, waiting for one of them to speak.

"It's been given to us by Mistress Tulp and the Lohr woman. It's a present for my loyalty to them and for being quiet about the baby."

"Whose baby?" said his wife quietly, the hope draining from her face.

"Father, this is overwhelming. Your services must have been remarkable to be given such a generous gift."

"Whose baby?" she said again, suspicion furrowing her brow.

Mutter blushed through his cooling face; praise was an experience previously unknown to him, and he looked shyly at his son.

"Your grandfather and I have cared for that house for years, long before these good people arrived. It has been very different working for them in there."

"*Whose baby?*" squawked the infuriated wife.

Everybody looked at her in surprise and Mutter said, "I don't know whose baby it is. It's a carnival mite, I think."

He saw her confusion crush her accusation and realisation set in. "You thought it was mine? With one of them?!"

He started to titter, which very quickly turned into a roar of snorting laughter. They all joined in, the children not knowing why and the wife no longer caring. Under his mirth, Mutter felt a great pride that his wife thought him capable of siring another child, of tupping those genteel ladies, pleasuring them with the girth of his masculinity. He grinned again and opened a bottle. It was much better to think about being paid to bring new life into the world, especially when his real reward had been for dragging life out of it, screaming.

CHAPTER THIRTY

The silver bell rang, and again its glitter rained into the lower part of Sidrus's dwelling.

But this time the bird was ignored, as was its message from Nebsuel saying that he had been wrong about these strange ones. He told Sidrus to come in peace and talk gently with them to find the answers he wanted. The bird pecked at its food tray, jumping from the perch into the cage. Again the bell chimed, and its sound melted to nothing in the quietness of the empty house.

➤→

Singing: Somewhere in the beige, vague world outside of his sleep, there was singing. His mouth was full of clay and dry holly leaves; he was aware of a dull throbbing and itching between himself and the melody. He tried to speak, and the itching turned to lines of glittering tinsel: shimmering pain. Ivy? No! Scarabs! Running under his skin! Encrusted and fast. Glass decorations. Christmas; a tree in a house?

He touched his face, expecting the soft contours of normality, but found only a huge, misshapen ball of rags where his head should have been. It had all gone wrong, but how? Think, remember. "Him's," she had called them, the endless dirges;

him singing. Pine and wax smoking inside the room, where? The singing stopped.

"It is all well, master. You are well, and you are safe."

The voice was close and without meaning. Something touched his lips; it was wet and cool, and he sucked hard on it. The knife! His throat cleared and his horror dispersed. The knife; he felt its pressure, and then it was gone. The knife to carve a feast, or him, or hymn. Hymns. Or a place in life and a socket of death.

"Tsungali," he said feebly, touching his bandaged head again.

A larger hand closed over his and he felt its radiance and smelt pine again—the pine of disinfectant, not Christmas. As he slid back into a painless sleep, Tsungali continued to sing an ancient chant to keep the ghost bound tight in the body.

"Hold him," ordered Nebsuel.

Ishmael was propped up on the bed, Tsungali's rock-like good arm bound around him.

"The last layers of leaves and bandage might hurt when I take them off." In the fetid darkness, Ishmael braced himself. The drugs had kept the pain at bay, but he knew that it was only sheltering, that it would emerge with vengeance when given half a moment. He was weary and mute; his body strained for experience, and his brain was exhausted through a lack of dreams. Now he could feel it all focusing in his itching face, sense it being rubbed awake under Nebsuel's unwrapping.

Murky, stained light seeped in, and his hackles rose as the dressing tugged at the split nerves and sewn flesh. The final mass came away in one piece, letting the raw light play on his open wound. With the stained mass in his hands, Nebsuel silently studied his handiwork. He touched the new eyelids, and Ishmael yelped. It wasn't pain, but a curdling flinch of nausea that made him jump.

"Hold still now," said Nebsuel, nodding to Tsungali, who gripped the swaying patient more firmly.

After ten minutes of probing and squinting at his face, the medicine man smiled and said, "It is good, young master. Welcome to the mundane world of normal men."

Ishmael wanted a mirror but was denied. "Not yet," ordered the shaman. "You must wait for the swelling to go down. Your first impression is very important. It will stay in your mind forever; you must wait so that you will retain a good image, not a half-healed one."

Ishmael saw the sense in this and decided to allow his good eye a few more days to be alone.

"I am leaving to fetch provisions, news, and wine," announced Nebsuel. "My senses are tired and I need time away from the smell of your raw flesh. Look for me in a day or two, and do not look on or touch that face; let the air and sun mend it."

Ishmael thought about threatening him over his return, but it seemed wrong, so he simply waved and said, "Be careful!" through the lower, working part of his face.

He settled back in the bed and allowed himself to imagine a new life, one without strangeness and hiding, a life full of lessons and couplings, of carnivals and friends. Unexpectedly, the Owl rose in his memory on silent and elegant wings, wings as white and pure as her silk bed linen; as powerful and soft as her hungry body and her lessons of kiss. He would see her again. She would not know him, but he would know her. He refused the pain-killing potion that Tsungali had been instructed to feed him. He had been dull for enough time. He wanted to focus on whom and what he knew, and who he was ready to become.

———

Tsungali was cooking in a small alcove behind a hanging carpet. He was still getting used to his new hand and forearm, and he muttered occasionally at its errors over the stove. The rich smell of simmering grain infused with thyme was settling across the room. Ishmael had found a book containing images of gardens, hand-coloured woodcuts printed on thick, crafted paper that itself still showed plant fibres crushed into its surface. He believed them to be fabled gardens from all over the world. He was looking at one from Tunisia, turning the book sideways to gaze at the interior depth, when he heard the door open.

"Nebsuel!" he called out. "I have taken one of your books to look at."

The wrong kind of silence greeted his statement, the kind that made the house suddenly brittle. Tsungali sensed it, too, and quickly drew back the carpet screen.

"What is it?" said Ishmael. "Is there somebody here?"

Tsungali reached forward towards his weapons, then stopped, yanked upright, standing to attention. Ishmael nearly laughed but could not understand the expression on the grimacing face. They looked into each other's eyes, both seeking some kind of solution, and then Ishmael saw it move: Midway down the old man's body a small, silver fish twitched and shivered. It was growing in length, and Ishmael could not take his eyes from it. Tsungali, seeing his master's stare, looked down at the point where the bright blade protruded from his chest. It turned and lengthened again, and he gave out a terrible cough as his heart was sliced through. He fell to his knees and landed facedown. The fish vanished.

Behind him, in the shadows, stood a man with a floating white melon head. His face looked like it had no bones beneath: a puffed-up bladder, smooth, immaculate, and totally unnatural. Had Nebsuel constructed this face? Is this what he would look like in a few days' time?

Sidrus stepped over Tsungali's body, keeping the long, razor-sharp blade held before him, never wavering from its aim at Ishmael's neck.

"Don't scream. Open your mouth and I will open your throat," he said in a clear, foreign accent. "Answer my questions quietly. Where is Nebsuel? What have you done to him?"

"Done? We have done nothing; he is out buying wine." Ishmael's voice shook, but his new face held its defiant composure. The blade moved closer.

"Don't lie to me, freak. Why would he trust you and this old dog, alone in his home?"

He kicked at Tsungali and the sound of his death throes rattled so loudly that his last words were obscured. Ishmael's heart contracted in mortal fear of the cold-blooded killer, but he managed to scratch out an answer.

"He has been operating on both of us."

This made no sense to Sidrus. Why would the healer bother with them after what they had done to the Bowman? And yet he could see the raw, stitched meat of this one's face. He twisted Tsungali over with his foot and saw the strap that held his new arm. He nicked through it with the point of the blade and the hollow wood tumbled off. He put the flat of the blade against the stump and brought it up to his face. He sniffed at the fresh sutures and knew it to be true.

"Did you injure or kill the Bowman?" he asked.

"Do you mean Oneofthewilliams?"

"Yes," said Sidrus, startled at the creature's knowledge of that name.

"No. We left him in the Vorrh. He left without us."

"And the bow?" Sidrus's blade twitched.

"He . . . he gave it to me."

Sidrus was dumbounded; how could any of this be true? Why would Oneofthewilliams give the sacred thing to this meat-faced youth?

"I will have the truth!" he said, drawing another blade from concealment and advancing towards Ishmael's shrinking bed, his small, cold eyes calculating where to cut first.

There was a sharp, metallic click from across the room, like somebody standing on a twig of iron. Sidrus knew what it was, even before he heard the voice.

"Twelve grams of splinter round at four metres," it said. "Put the blades down where I can see them, old friend."

Sidrus obeyed in slow motion, sneering at Ishmael.

"Nebsuel, I thought this scum had disposed of you."

He started to turn towards the rifle's muzzle, which peered at him from across the room.

"Very slowly, old friend. I know your ways and I am not alone."

"But it was you who summoned me here," said Sidrus.

"Yes, but I was wrong, and so were you to slay a man in my house."

A rope was swiftly lowered from the ceiling, a loop tied at its end. "Put your hands in the noose," said Nebsuel.

"There is no need for this; you can trust me. It will be better for you in the long term if you do."

"Put your hands in the noose."

"You tempt my anger," snarled Sidrus.

"Put your hands in the noose! You are tempting your death, and you know I will do it."

Sidrus thrust his hands into the looped rope; there was a small tug from above to tighten it and then a great wrench, which lifted him from the ground and high into the space above. A dry, rumbling sound filled the room with its mechanical power. It halted, and Nebsuel shouted up.

"You hang between two great wooden drums. If you displease me, you will be mangled through them and crushed to a rag before you can take a breath. Do you understand me?"

"I do!" came a faint voice.

"Now, tell me exactly what weapons and charms you have about your person."

Sidrus began to recite an inventory of his possessions; Ishmael was astonished at the length of the list. When it was over, Nebsuel stepped out of the shadow; he held a black dove in his hand. He winked at Ishmael and threw it into the air.

The bird disappeared towards the sky, and he pulled a wooden lever concealed in the wall. The drums turned, slowly this time, and Sidrus was lowered to the ground. He was white from the strain of hanging by his twisted arms, dangling like a puppet. He glared at Nebsuel, who put a small ball of leaves in the wide muzzle of his short rifle and pushed it into Sidrus's face.

"Eat it."

"Fuck you!"

"Eat the sedative or eat the charge, and the splinters waiting behind it." The hanging man knew Nebsuel would do it, so he sucked the sticky ball into his wide mouth. Nebsuel helped by jarring the rifle, chiselling the barrel onto Sidrus's teeth.

"No man soils my house. No man murders in my healing room. Now swallow."

He thrust the barrel again, hitting Sidrus in his Adam's apple. Sidrus choked and swallowed the mouthful down, his eyes raging. The lever was pulled again and he fell to the ground. Nebsuel was at his side with a sharp, curved knife. He slit the rope from Sidrus's hands with a deftness that demonstrated how easily he could have done the same to his throat.

"Put your weapons and charms on the table and go." Nebsuel stood by the door, splinter gun at the ready.

"I could still take you both."

"Maybe, but you would pay a terrible price for it. Anyway, we have the information you need to find your Bowman. Information that will now cost you dearly. You will never come here again. If you cross this threshold, you will die. In the future, we will communicate only by bird. Do you understand?"

"I want to know all, *now!*" Sidrus barked.

"I doubt you have the time."

"I have all the time it takes," he spat back.

"How long did it take you to get here?"

"*What?*"

"How long?"

"Three days."

"As I thought. I have given you forty hours to get back."

"What are you gibbering about, old fool?" snarled Sidrus.

"I told you, from now on we only communicate by bird. I sent a black dove to your abode, a quarter of an hour ago. It carries my last supply of the vital antidote for Mithrassia Toxia, the spore of which you sucked from my rifle a few minutes ago."

"Mithrassia? You gave me Mithrassia?!"

"Yes. I lied about the sedative. That is why you don't have the time to discuss what we may do for you."

Sidrus was speechless for a moment and then bolted for the door.

"Pray there are no hawks in the skies between us," shouted Nebsuel at the swinging door.

The healer started to clear up and remove the sad, scarred body of the old black warrior. Ishmael attempted to get off the bed to help but was stopped and told to rest.

Nebsuel disappeared outside to dispose of the body, then returned to the hushed interior to start to prepare for the cleansing ritual, which would last for five days. Ishmael watched him for many minutes before eventually asking, "Please, what is Mithrassia?"

The shaman groaned and sat down wearily on the edge of

the bed, gently patting Ishmael's hand. "Young man, you really don't want to know; you have already been surrounded by too much shadow and chill. I will not be responsible for telling you more. You must heal now; you need to set your mind and body in light and warmth." He started to get up, then turned, his face creaking into a reluctant grin. "Let me only say that the symptoms of Mithrassia are tenacious and unspeakable."

➤

Tsungali sat with his grandfather during the five days of purification. He did not know who had killed him, or why, only that it was not the healer; not like that. He hoped that Nebsuel would remember the oath he had taken, his vow to be more vengeful in his death than in his life. He hoped that the cleansing would stop short of his exorcism; part of himself needed to remain viable to be able to feast on the revenge; he needed his ghost in that world for a while longer, to protect Ishmael until he had reached his home. Need was the only thing that still remained, and he did not want the healer to rub it away; it would wear out in time; the spirit would depart—there might be the occasional, fleeting return, but his time was not without limits and he would have to make it count.

His grandfather was pleased to welcome him. He would have preferred him well and walking, back in that world, but this, though early, was always expected, and there was contentment in their reunion.

Nebsuel was as just as he was wise. He remembered Tsungali's words, and in honour of his wishes, he did not make the final scouring. Instead, he shushed away the last, scattered remnant, sweeping his ghost out into the world, to wait with the dry leaves and dust until Ishmael was healed.

The day of the mirror arrived. Nebsuel showed Ishmael how to wash in the warm, pine-scented liquid in the bowl before him; he dried the new face with care and patted down the hair, which had grown long.

"Very well, young master," said Nebsuel, fetching an oval mirror with a red cloth draped over it. "The time is here. Now you will see my handiwork and the way you will look in the world." He set the looking glass before the young man, whose apprehension made his cheeks turn pale. With a small theatrical flourish, the healer removed the cover to reveal a blinking man, framed within.

Ishmael could not move or speak; he touched his nose and the inset eye, dabbing at its reality. As the silence grew, Nebsuel became nervous: If this was not to Ishmael's taste or requirement, there was nothing he could do. It was impossible to read Ishmael's expression; he had not yet become used to flexing it, and the inevitable nerve damage made parts of it permanently impassive. The shaman watched with growing trepidation. The cyclops still had the hideous bow close by; his displeasure might become horrendous with its use.

"What do you think?" ventured Nebsuel. "I have used all of my knowledge; it is the best of my work—of that you can be sure."

The words nudged Ishmael. He stood up and very slowly approached Nebsuel. He took the old man's hand and brought it to his lips. This was another kind of kiss, one that nobody had ever taught him.

The days passed quickly, with each better than the last. He gained strength and learned much from Nebsuel, who found it novel to have such a keen and sagacious student; he could show off his knowledge and tell tales of wonders and impossibilities all day without the young man's attention ever failing.

The face became pliant as Ishmael practised with it. His

moods could be read, and communication became more fluent. The bow lived in a corner of the house, wrapped and silent, recognised but unengaged.

Nothing had been heard of Sidrus. The dove did not return, so they could not know whether he was healthy and fuming with rage or if he had painfully rotted apart. As the weeks passed, they became less watchful; Nebsuel removed some of the more virulent charms that he had placed about the house for protection.

An unexpected friendship grew between the unlikely pair; for a time, they played at father and son. Tsungali occasionally came knocking at night, not to frighten them, but to announce his presence and register an anxiousness about the length of Ishmael's stay. For a while they disregarded him and continued to work together in the ramshackle house. But growth and satisfaction can hold a young heart for only so long, and one morning, without apparent reason, Ishmael announced that it was time for him to leave and find his place in the world.

"What's wrong with this being your place in the world?" grumbled Nebsuel.

"Nothing," replied Ishmael, "but I have another one that I must confront first."

"I suspect you're right," said the old man grudgingly.

They spent the coming days making preparations for his departure. Like the experience of all about to separate, the strain of an imagined elsewhere bore a hurtful torque on the moments they actually inhabited. The night before Ishmael's departure, when they heard the impatient ghost moving back and forth outside, Nebsuel became bad-tempered and melancholic.

"Begone, you midnight nuisance. He will be yours tomorrow. Allow us a final evening together without your tramping."

The words seemed to resonate with the spirit of Tsungali; they heard him change direction and walk away.

"Do ghosts ever sleep?" Ishmael found himself asking.

"Yes, but not the sleep of men; theirs is an emptier kind of slumber. Our sleep is always full: From catnap to coma, it brims over. Those hollow ones have thin, dangerous dreams." There was a pause, as if the air might be listening. Then Nebsuel continued. "It is contagious to some; thin sleep can last for centuries. It can allow its owner to become modified or change themselves entirely. Some say that the creatures that infest the Vorrh use it knowingly for that purpose, that they bury themselves deeper and grow young, in their desire to return to nothing. It's the only way they can ever escape the Vorrh and their charge at its centre."

"If they lie buried and forgotten, how is this known?"

"Because some get dislodged, dug up by animals or men, dragged to the surface. These are the dangerous ones, because they no longer know what they are, and if they enter the world of men, they grow back deformed into its shape."

"You mean that some of them walk with us out here?" Ishmael sounded at once fearful and defensive of his new world.

"It is said to be." There was a pause while both men seemed to ponder the impossibility of such a thing.

"Do they breed with women?" said Ishmael.

Nebsuel laughed. "It is better and worse than that. Some mix the contagion of their sleeping with a knowing human, and fuse with humans inside its influence."

"To what advantage?"

"If an Erstwhile and a willing human enter that condition and seal themselves away from the world, they become something else, something quite different, without form, like a memory, a tangible genie of the place where they hide. It can insist itself into the imagination of all those who pass by, stirring up great feelings and powerful emotions in the unsuspecting traveller. Some say that such a thing has been used in the defence of holy places. Jerusalem is said to be guarded that way, guarded by longing. It is even said that the spirit of the forest himself is composed of such an unmitigating force, that the Black Man of Many Faces is held together by it."

These were big thoughts for Ishmael, whose head was already full of the melancholy of departure. He asked no more questions, and Nebsuel offered no further wisdom. They stared into the fire as it flickered in its raised iron grate in the middle of the room. They stared and sipped wine and said nothing.

The next morning they embraced in the doorway. Nebsuel had prepared a travelling bag full of potions and charms; it sat awkwardly in the doorframe between them. The bow was already outside, and the old man felt a lightness and relief at its departure. As they said their goodbyes, Nebsuel gave his warnings and advice, and Ishmael offered his deepest thanks. They vowed to meet again, and parted.

CHAPTER THIRTY-ONE

*M*uybridge was beginning to feel his age. Not in a depleting sense—he was strong, lean, and agile, with the physique of a man half his age—but the shortage of time before him had begun to vex. He was becoming aware of how much work there was to do and how little time he had left to do it in.

Almost every day, he was talking in public, producing interviews and articles, a man on display. The zoopraxiscopes were as popular as ever, and he had managed to shelve his disillusionment with them; they were making a small fortune and had become a clarion for his reputation, much more so than his more serious work, which seemed to continually be overlooked and underestimated.

It had been after his meeting with Edison, where they had discussed the possibility of adding sound to moving images, that he had started thinking again about his lost machine in London. Edison was impatient and somewhat shallow for Muybridge's taste; he found the inventor to be little more than a mechanic, with an ego dedicated and driven towards fame and fortune. The American seemed more like the new breed of entrepreneur showmen, rather than a son of science; he had more in common with Barnum and Bailey than Newton and Galileo.

However, their meeting had been a clear pointer towards the deeper significance of his own knowledge and its meaning, which lived a long way from the production of toys for petty entertainment. So he went back to the hidden charge he had observed in photographic images. He would return to his machine, when the chance arose, to catch the phenomenon and explain its workings to a more select and dignified audience.

In the meantime, some of the flock of patients he had treated had come home to roost; his investments were paying fine premiums and the Stanfords still patronised his work. He was justified and rich, and he could do whatever he chose.

To his amazement, nothing had ever come from the Winchester coffers; the mad old woman hadn't given him a bean. After the embarrassment and time that he had wasted on her, she had commissioned nothing. He thought about her sometimes, still shut up in that wooden mausoleum, letting nobody in and building brick upon brick of empty rooms for the dead. He thought about the millions of dollars still flowing in from that old gun, a cent for every time it was cocked, a cent to buy another nail for her timber fortress, just another mad hag shut up in a box. What was the name of that old woman in the Dickens story?

Many years earlier, he had bought his wife a magazine subscription for her birthday; it was for an English publication. He could still see the expression on her glum, sour face as he had given it to her. He had thought it a good present: It, and its postage, had been expensive but worthwhile. It could have educated the stupid bitch if she had ever read it; enlightened her and brought culture into her prairie mind. But no, he may as well have burnt his hard-earned money for all the appreciation she had shown. In the end, he had read it himself; he hated fiction, but not quite as much as he hated the sight of the unopened packages from the publisher.

He had read Mr. Dickens's story and recognised many coincidental features of his own life in it. Perhaps Mr. Dickens, he had pondered, had met the crazed Winchester dowager on one of his trips to the USA? Met and stolen her, so as to lock her insanity up in his words forever. But he did not need Sarah Winchester's money now; he was independent. If he could only find the time, he would remake that mysterious and powerful machine and carve himself a proper place in history with it.

It had been this chain of thoughts that led him to dig out the logbook from those distasteful times. It carried the scent of Gull's rooms, and when he undid the clasp, he heard the sound of the crank spinning the light, humming. What he read still made sense, was still the work of a balanced and creative mind. He closed the book backwards, vowing not to let such valuable work go to waste, and that's when he saw it, like a black shadow at the back of the book: a drawing of the solar eclipse. She had drawn it from memory, from his photograph, directly into his book; the nerve of the filthy woman! Then he saw the other: It was instantly recognisable as a map of Africa, but distorted and scribbled in, upside down. Near its edge was the same signature, the crippled "A" for Abungu, scrawled in a hand that he knew to be hers. He had once asked Gull if her name had any meaning, and the doctor had told him that "Abungu" meant "Of the Forest." He turned pale looking at it, knowing it had been secretly drawn and inscribed for him.

For the first time, Muybridge was getting tired of his long transatlantic shuffles, but he was returning to London out of public demand, and in spite of criticism he had received from a new generation of scientific sceptics, he was being honoured, and Great Britain owed him that. He also came to confront the endless nightmare of Whitechapel.

Each trip seemed to take a little longer. The jewels of the night sky and the luminous waves seemed less and less bright and appealing, and he spent more time in his claustrophobic cabin, planning and brooding about what might await him.

He would anticipate the criticisms of those who constantly whined about the "validity" of his work and would rehearse for their unprovoked attacks. He had hounded his critics ruthlessly with his letters to the press. The ship rocked against his adversaries and all who would disclaim him: the cowards who hid in the shadows and waited for the moment to belittle him; those who objected to his retouchings, his improvements on the original, slightly blurred pictures; the artless, who envied his talent with the brush and the lens. He would have them all, open them up from crotch to craw for such impertinence. Again the ship rocked, and he thought about those who had betrayed him or let him down. There were many, and in some ways they were worse than the obvious foes.

He had wondered why Gull had stopped writing to him. The last four letters had gone unacknowledged; then the news of his death was rumoured. But no proof was found.

On arrival, Muybridge moved into the Great Eastern Hotel, the only establishment for miles that offered the grandeur that he had become accustomed to. It was also within walking distance of the filthy slums where his machine had so perfectly worked. An hour after unpacking he packed his pistol and was back in the hive of Whitechapel again.

Nothing had really changed, and he found his way to the building that still haunted him. He looked up towards where he knew the door would be. Snow swirled in from the freezing streets.

For once, the city and its buildings were not swarmed with people; the cold had driven them inside to huddle in silence and sleep.

He climbed the familiar stairs of the exposed landing, where the ice had made the cold stone treacherous. Frost glistened on the banisters. The steps creaked, along with his long, cold bones. He had aged seven years since they had last met, enough time for every cell in his body to change. A different man climbed these shadows and stairs, so why did he feel the same?

The dull brass key in his hand felt unchanged, yet he knew she was not there. She had sold the cameras and bought a passage back into her origins. She was in Africa with the sun and heat. So why were his insides hollowed with dread as he climbed towards the rooms?

The door opened easily and he paused to listen, straining for those sounds that humans make, even when holding their breath: the uncontrollable vibrations that are emitted as they sleep. There were none. The rooms were empty, their silence clad and reinforced by the snow outside.

He shut the door and peered into the studio; his machine was still there, in exactly the same place. But his nerves were spliced and unsettling his abilities: He could not leave the other rooms unchecked. He quickly paced through them and found them to be clinically empty; every scrap of their previous tenancy had been cleaned away. Her metal bed was stripped to its frame; the sink was bare; only the crockery of their golden-memoried breakfast remained, in a stacked, unbroken pile.

He returned to the machine, removing his gloves to touch his fingertips to its smooth, cold mechanisms. The crank turned, free and easy; age had not atrophied his engineering. The lenses and shutters fluttered in obedience, albeit far too quickly. He bent closer to see that all the polished surfaces were clean and free from dust.

As he touched the gears again, he felt oil on his fingertips. He looked closer: There was wear on the head strap. Somebody had used it, not once, but a number of times. Who would have done such a thing? And what for? His mind raced. Apart from Gull and his men, the only other with keys had been the black woman. He shivered. Did she still come here, addicted to the effects of the machine? He looked edgily around the rooms again, fondling his pocket where the revolver nestled. Nothing moved.

He came back to the table and walked to its other side. Something lumped under the thin, stained carpet beneath his feet, something akin to a long, slender pipe. He knelt and pulled the shabby rug away. A tarred, black electric cable ran along the floorboards and across the room, its end snaking up the inside of the table leg and under its top. He peered under the table, crouching to see what was hidden below: Here was the greatest find. Two incandescent lamps, held beneath the table by sturdy clips. He pulled one out and examined it. It was Edison's work: one of his handmade, electrically powered lamps—new, unique, and incredibly expensive. But where had it come from? And what would this extravagance give his machine?

He stood up and stared at the machine, the wire and bulb still in his hands. He imagined her in it, serene and seemingly unaffected, and tried to push the images of her transformation out of his mind. He looked at the wire, which split to join each of the two bulbs, a metal ring on each brass stem holding the lamp in place. He searched below the counter with his fingers and quickly found the two holes drilled into the tabletop. The surface of the table near the holes was burnt, its varnish scarred from the continual heat of the lamps. He traced the cable back to an empty cupboard. By his calculations, the batteries would have been stored here: Somebody had been using his device in the dead of night. That would be the only reason for such expense—to operate it and transform another while all else slept. He shuddered at the idea. His machine of daylight, which had proved sinister enough in the sun's presence, had taken on an ominous, unnatural function in his absence. He wished he could have talked to the almighty surgeon about this, but the moment had passed.

On his way home through the slow snow, he reflected that perhaps the locked room was best left that way, with nobody except the dead doctor knowing of his involvement here. If the machine had been used for some untoward purpose, then it was nothing to do with him. He was innocent of any of the effects that it might have produced. Yes, better left that way.

His trusty instinct was sharp in the cold, and it told him that yet again he had only a few days left in this city of crime and intrigue. He would lay low and let the snow keep all muffled until he was on the ship again. There, between his worlds, he could decide whether to take the matter further or drop the brass key like a bullet into the starless, churning water.

The gaslights around the Great Eastern glowed and fluttered in the falling snow. He had little time to rest, bathe, and dress for his lecture that evening. He was a world-famous celebrity; now others were taking photographs of him. His vast portfolio of human movement had been a colossal success, and he knew at last that it had all been worthwhile: His place in history was assured. The century was turning, and his work was on the crest of it.

The institute was bustling, and he could hear by the muffled roar that every plush seat had been taken. His new evening suit creaked as he combed his titan beard, which dazzled white against the lustrous blackness of the fine cloth. He checked the mirror again: "justified." The stern dignity of science rested on his strong shoulders.

He strode upon the stage to waves of applause. He had the newest batch of movement photographs ready to project, as well as some old favourites, which he had turned into glass slides and was looking forward to seeing projected large for the first time: everything from elephants to studies of dancing girls, modelled in classical poses. He had made lantern slides of all of his studies to share with a wider audience and to advertise the desirability of purchasing the published works. He felt the vast audience sway closer and closer; sensed their appreciation and wonder as tangibly as one feels heat or smells the sea.

Looking out across the hundreds of faces staring at the screen behind him, he could watch their concentration without being seen. So fixed were they on his magnetic images that he became invisible. He saw his fame in their wide-eyed wonder, heard his applause in their startled sighs. They were all his devotees, his prisoners of illumination.

And then he saw the impossible, sitting in the audience and staring directly at him, ignoring the screen and its changes of animals and humans: Gull. He was supposed to be dead. The doctor's demise was supposed to have coincided with Muybridge's last departure from England; wasn't that what everyone had told him? Had everyone he trusted lied to him? Even the fellow he paid to read the British newspapers?! He did not have time to read every bit of tittle-tattle the papers printed; the man had been instructed to scour newspapers for articles about himself or for letters of his that had been printed. He had been provided with a list of men of interest to spot; he had reported Gull's passing almost two years ago! Even the hospital had said so, yet here he was, as large as life, his dense, rectangular face flickering in the projection light.

In more private circumstances, Muybridge would have had a few things to say to the good doctor: Questions about the use of his machine instantly sprang to mind. But the animal slides had finished; he was on. He had a short time to fill with explanation as the next set of pictures was loaded. The spotlight moved to him and he could no longer see the audience or the doctor. For a moment he was lost and forgot what he had to say. There was an uncomfortable shuffling; murmurs could be heard. He coughed and hummed, spluttering the flywheel into action. It turned over and his speech began, capturing the attention of his audience again.

Five minutes later he got the nod from the projectionist and brought his dialogue to an end; the spotlight went out. The slides flickered into life; *Athletes from the Palo Alto* series; *Men and Women in Motion.* He looked back at Gull. He was gone, but two blurs remained in the darkness where he had been sitting. Muybridge strained his sight into the auditorium. The blots looked like eyes, made from smears of light. It rattled him and confused his next speech. He waved the projectionist on, not trusting himself to speak, wanting only to peer into the audience and make some sense of his sight. *Women and Children; Running and Jumping with a Skipping Rope; Miss Larrigan Fancy Dancing.* He stepped forward to observe the empty seat with greater certainty. They were still there, glaring back at him; amorphous balls of glowing intensity. Why did nobody seated see them there, floating so close? Was Gull playing tricks on him with his mind mechanics, or was he imagining it? Had he become sick again? He searched every face nearby, but they were locked onto the figures on the screen that rattled past their measuring lines, their muscles and curves bracing against the stillness, the same old charge of strangeness echoing between the bodies and the time they were clad in.

He felt the eyes even after they had gone, as afterimages, scorched into his retinas. He rubbed at his lids, turning the blurs into dark stain, so that when he opened them and looked at the illuminated screen, he saw two dark, unfocused holes; pits, like Marey's dugout cameras of slowness. He rubbed them again, growing angrier at the irrelevance.

He thought he saw something move at the back of the hall, a shadow that ducked to avoid detection. Could it be? Was it Gull? There must be an intelligent solution; he would hold no truck with ghosts. The latecomer scratched a painful scramble to his feet, his bruised knee exacerbating the embarrassment of his mid-aisle tumble, none of which Muybridge's blinded logic registered.

Miss Larrigan danced on the screen, her costume made to resemble the garments of ancient Greek friezes and lofty temples. Its diaphanous nature displayed the elegance of her rhythmic dance and the sensual contours of her body. Projected to this size, it also clearly displayed her erect nipples and the shadow of her pubic mound; her nudity danced gigantically, out of the accepted space of the naked and into the highly charged arena of the erotic. Muybridge had not anticipated such an effect; his audience was noticeably taken aback.

The fallen man at the back of the auditorium stood with his back to the screen, wholly unaware of the delightful vision playing out to his companions. His friend reached out to help him, and the fallen one let out a short chuckle, to show that he was perfectly all right; by some acoustic whim, the laugh carried and was heard everywhere. Muybridge spun towards the noise, peering down like a wrathful Jehovah.

"Who dares to snigger? These are images of art and science, not brought here to titillate prurient minds! I have not slaved over their perfection so that they might be debased; I have crossed the Atlantic to demonstrate my technique to an educated audience, not to entertain an insolent rabble with the morals of a Turk!"

There was a stunned silence. He looked at the empty seat again.

"Next slide!" he bellowed at the cowering projectionist.

At the end of his lecture he stalked off the stage, the audience overclapping as a means of apology. Muybridge left the theatre to the sound of their applause. When he never reappeared, the claps gradually petered out and the crowd left in silence like hunched, mute sheep.

That night, he dug out every obituary to be sure that Gull was indeed dead. What he had seen was obviously somebody playing an elaborate hoax in an attempt to undermine him and turn him into a laughingstock.

CHAPTER THIRTY-TWO

*E*ssenwald had changed: Ishmael sensed it the moment he entered its outskirts. It had grown impatience out of its security, become frantic and hectic inside the dynamo of its industry. All this was worn in the air: the scent of qualm.

Walking through the streets, he shaded his face from the crowd: he was not yet used to showing himself openly. His was still a face that caught glances, made strangers gawp, but no longer in abject horror. Their reaction now was rooted in something else, a compulsion he did not fully understand, though he recognised at least three of its components as surprise, curiosity, and pity. Of the few who had seen him so far, none had run or cried out in shock; either they had searched for a deeper understanding or simply turned away. It was a transformation of wonderful importance, and it fuelled an excitement that bubbled and pumped inside him.

In the five days it had taken him to reach the outskirts, he had used almost all of the money and food provided by Nebsuel on his departure. He thought about his ability to survive in a world that was so expensive.

Previously, he had been sheltered from such realities; now, the mechanics of existence were dawning, and he found them baffling and rather crude. His instinct was to head for 4 Kühler Brunnen; at least there he would find a friendly face. He would be invited in and fed, even if it was by the sour old man, Mutter. A plan finally in mind, he began to stride through the tangle of streets with purpose and exhilaration.

➤——➤

A mild panic had begun to grip life in Essenwald. The established pulse of the city's great heart of timber had fluttered and slowed, the supply of wood withering, while the demand blocked the arteries with its swollen need. Since the Limboia had vanished, only a dribble of trees left the forest. The scant workforce that brought the wood out was expensive, and their labour was hasty and sporadic. No one wanted to work in the Vorrh day in and day out, and no amount of wages could pay for the devastating effect that such exposure produced. At first, the new work teams consisted of volunteers, collected from the industries that fed from the forest. This system quickly broke down, only to be replaced by foreign labour, lured there by rumours of rich payment. But it took no time for the outsiders to discover the city's secret, and they added their own layers of myth to the brooding trees.

Now the workforce consisted of a mixture of the desperate, the criminal, and the insane, most of whom had been dragged into enforced labour. Nobody knew what effect might be produced by adding such a volatile mixture into the mind of the forest. It was a desperate measure, and the elders of the Timber Guild met daily to try to devise the next alternative. The old slave house became a hostel for the unstable, itinerant crew who now cut and ferried the trees: It was undeniably a place to be avoided, and Marie Maclish had acquiesced to that understanding, taking the guild's compensation and fleeing to raise her child in more stable lands.

➤——➤

Ishmael was lost. He had walked past the same garden four times in two hours, each time approaching it from a different direction. Eventually he stopped and looked for the spires of the cathedral to guide him home, but they could not be seen from the elegant streets he was walking through: He needed to get higher. He searched out a street that seemed to head vaguely uphill and followed its lead.

He had been walking for ten minutes when he sensed it, not with sight, but with familiarity: He had been here before. He looked confusedly at the dozen or so vast houses that lined the street, at their imposing walls, grandiose towers, and long, sliding roofs of immaculate tiles. Why would he have ever been here? At the very moment the question was formed, it was answered: It was the street of the Owl! He had found it—or it had found him. His visual memory of the outside of the mansion was scant, so he walked up and down the street, lingering a little longer each time at the house with the ornate metal gates in its wall. He had nothing to lose. He smoothed down his long, black hair, now grown to shoulder length, dusted down the blue riding coat that Nebsuel had given him, and approached the gates, pausing momentarily before pulling the metal ring of the bell. He adjusted his collar, turning it up about his face, and waited.

A dim, absent little man came to the gate and peered through. "Yes?"

"May I speak to the mistress of the house?"

"What is your business with Mistress Lohr, sir?"

"It is private. Quite private. But she will know me."

The little man peered more eagerly at the suspicious figure hiding in his ill-fitting clothing and his upturned collar.

"Your name, sir?"

Ishmael looked at the man in dismay, seeing the problem a second too late: He had only one name, and the Owl did not know it. Furthermore, he knew that saying just one name would be considered strange: Most other people he met had two names, if not three.

The man behind the gate was getting agitated, believing less and less that this individual could ever have any legitimate business with his mistress.

"Please, tell her it is Ishmael, from the night of the carnival."

Now the gatekeeper was sure that this shabby figure, with his crude, long bundle and scruffy rucksack, had no real business here. "Mistress Lohr will not be able to help you, sir. Be off with you! Be off!"

Ishmael tried again to explain, but his words served only to raise the man's guard higher.

"*Be off!* No beggars here; we've had enough trouble with your kind!" Ishmael gave up trying, picked up his bundle, and wearily walked off.

"What's wrong, Guixpax?" called Cyrena from the balcony.

"Nothing, ma'am, just another beggar."

"Ringing the bell?" she asked, surprised yet again at the rising levels of boldness that poverty seemed able to induce.

"An insolent rascal who claimed to know you, ma'am."

"Really? Whatever next?!" She turned and started to walk away from the balcony, but something outside of sight stopped her. She closed her eyes and stepped back to the rail, almost afraid to voice the question on her lips.

"Guixpax—did the beggar give a name?"

"Why, yes, ma'am. Ishmael, I think it was."

He was almost at the corner when he heard the sound of shouting and someone fast approaching behind him. He stopped, sensing that running would be seen as a sign of guilt, and hunched his shoulders, waiting for trouble to descend. He had only rung a bell and asked a question, but he realised this was probably enough to cause outrage in this neighbourhood. He heard the footsteps stop behind him and braced himself.

"Ishmael?" said the gentlest of voices. "Ishmael, is it really you?"

His heart leapt. It was the voice of the Owl, and she knew him! He turned slowly into his hope, hesitant in her sudden company, his face half-hidden by hair and uncertainty. She stared at his presence, her vivid eyes reading and absorbing every detail of his sheltering features.

"You have two eyes!" she said in amazement. "Ghertrude said you only had one."

"You know Ghertrude?"

"She has become my dearest friend; I found her when I was searching for you."

"For me?"

"Yes. I looked for you at once; there's so much ..." She became abruptly aware of their surroundings and shivered at their exposure to unseen ears. "There's so much to say. Shall we return to the house? It may be better to discuss things there."

She took the arm he offered and they walked slowly back up the road, past the gate, where the bemused Guixpax was waiting and watching.

Inside the mansion, they sat like strangers, in chairs that faced each other. His hand returned repeatedly to his face. Neither quite knew what to do next, though their hearts strained palpably towards each other; their passions and unfamiliarity clenched together, forming a barrier of embarrassment between them.

"May I ask to wash?" Ishmael requested politely. "My journeys have been long and arduous."

"Of course! I should have suggested it immediately!" Cyrena rang the bell and Myra came into the room, subtly observing the injured young man from the corner of her eye. Her mistress ignored the question in her eyes and instructed her to prepare a bath and bring towels, perfumed salts, and a dressing gown. Guixpax was summoned and sent to town to buy suitable clothing.

When alone again, Cyrena listened at the bathroom door and heard him splashing with what she hoped was pleasure.

Dim, bewildered old Guixpax returned with the weirdest selection of clothing she had ever seen. She pawed through the tangled mass on the polished table while the gatekeeper stood behind her, proud of his unique purchases.

"Thank you, Raymond. A fine choice. You can leave it to me now."

Guixpax left, glowing with achievement but confused by the situation that his mistress appeared to be so enjoying. Cyrena waited for him to depart, then selected a choice of garments and placed them outside the bathroom door.

"Ishmael, there are clean clothes outside the door."

"Thank you, er . . . ?"

She realised, with some embarrassment, that she had not yet told him her name. "Cyrena," she replied. "My name is Cyrena."

"Cyrena," he repeated, the room of steam and perfume echoing the name.

Tsungali's ghost had followed its master as far as the garden; he had neither the will nor the desire to enter the elaborate and confusing dwelling.

He watched from the dense colour of the unusual foliage. It was a pleasant place, and he passed through the plants and trees with idleness. His master was safe and at peace inside the house, with a woman and servant to look after him; the villain who had threatened Ishmael's life was nowhere near, so Tsungali let himself be diluted by time, so that no one saw him crouching among the energetic growth and high, containing walls.

Ishmael padded softly down the hallway and found her in her favourite room, drinking golden wine from a long-stemmed glass. She did not hear him arrive, so light was his footfall. He was wearing Chinese silk slippers that she had left for him. Very quietly, he said, "Thank you, Cyrena."

She stood up and looked at him, allowing herself to linger on the details of his presence, basking in his proximity. He was wearing silk pyjamas and the blue dressing gown that she had left him. His hair was still wet. She looked at his face, at how the scars around his eye seemed to gather his features together at that point, giving it a bunched squint. His nose was a little worse for wear; the straight line of it veered a little between loose folds and taut stretchings. Apart from this, it was the normal face of a slender young man who looked as though he had lived a troubled and weather-beaten life. He began to raise his hand again, insecurity blooming under her gaze, but she crossed the room to stop him, reaching out to his hand and holding it in her own. She led him to the window seat and they sat looking at each other for an endless, unruffled time, the evening darkening around them.

"I don't know where to start," she said eventually. Handing him her glass, she moved away to fill another, then turned back to him. "It's been a long time since the carnival, and many things have changed for us both, I am sure, but . . . perhaps we should begin where we left off before?"

He stared at her for a moment and then smiled, his new eye

gleaming almost as brightly as the other. He reached for her hand and together they walked up to her bedroom.

Outside, the swallows were changing to bats, to count the space of the sky with sound instead of sight. Inside, contentment had come to the house of Cyrena Lohr—for all except for the bow, which seethed in its wrappings.

Cyrena and Ishmael had not stepped outside the house for almost a week. The world beyond the mansion's walls had dissolved in its own continuum of noise and bustle. They never left each other, talking and touching and succumbing to their courtship through all the hours of the day and night. Even the division of light and dark held no meaning for them: The richness of their realm was more than all else.

The servants ferried food and drink and kept out of their way. So powerful was their love in the house that it evaporated all gossip and belowstairs speculation. The staff just grinned knowingly and shrugged their shoulders and grinned again.

The bow lay neglected in the hall; Ishmael no longer moved it with him from room to room. Occasionally it would fall in the night, clattering noisily against obscure items and leaving unpleasant odours and resistant stains. Eventually, he placed it as far from the heart of the house as the walls allowed, resting it in the small porch that joined the garden to the cellar. The servants were warned not to disturb it under any circumstances. It was a somewhat unnecessary order: The long black bundle was loathsome to all.

Under a nearby bush, Tsungali's ghost dozed peacefully. His grandfather had caught up with him a few days after he arrived. He had decided to wait with him for their business to be concluded, so they might travel together into the awaiting worlds. Tsungali slept to conserve the strength of what was left

of him. His grandfather kept a wary eye on the bow while he
dozed.

The arrival of the letter dislodged the peace of the house.
Its sharp white envelope was like a porcelain blade. It was from
Ghertrude.

MY DEAR FRIEND,

*Have you forsaken me? Please tell me what I have done to
cause your silence? I felt such relief at your support in this
strange, incomprehensible time; I cannot begin to express
my despair at your absence.*

*I am so alone. Nobody comes. I only ever see Mutter,
and I cannot speak to him—his smile unnerves me; it is
more than I can tolerate at this moment.*

*The house has never been so empty. I am racked by
nightmares, which I think might be omens; the evil spirit
of the doctor comes to steal the life from within me and I
wake in terror every night. Please, if I have not offended
you in some unknown way, come to me soon. I need your
strength and friendship to see me through these desperate
times.*

YOURS ALWAYS,
GHERTRUDE

Cyrena was mortified. She had not considered Ghertrude's
needs for days, even though she and Ishmael had talked about
her frequently with warmth and care; she had to go to her friend
at once. She called Ishmael and showed him the letter.

"What is the significance of this doctor?" he asked.

She shut her eyes to the answer that tangled in her throat.
There was so much to explain, and so much more to forget.

"He was one of the men we paid to find you. He was a vile man, corrupt and dangerous."

"Where is he now?"

"He disappeared," she lied, "ran off somewhere with the other vermin who tricked us."

Ishmael was content and asked no more questions, letting her rush about as she dressed for the first time in days.

"I don't know how long I will be," she said at the door.

"I am coming with you." He had his shoes on and was buttoning his shirt. "I am coming to see Ghertrude."

The car sped through the city and she gripped his hand tightly, moving back and forth in her seat as if it might help the lilac Phaeton gain speed. Ishmael tried to talk, but it was impossible to engage her, so he sat back, enjoying the speed and the vista of the city without the disguise of a mask or a scarf. He was beginning to feel grand, in his new face and the plush elegance of the car's interior.

They arrived at 4 Kühler Brunnen minutes later, and she rattled at the gate and the bell. Ishmael stepped into the street and was suddenly overwhelmed; he was transported to a very different place, with a tide of memories flooding back.

When a dishevelled Ghertrude eventually came to the gate, the sight of her friend unhooked her and she immediately began to weep. She yanked the barrier open, throwing herself, sobbing, into Cyrena's arms. Cyrena held her tightly, patting her back in soft, soothing strokes, heavily aware of their unseen companion but overcome with a maternal sense of responsibility. "I am so, so sorry for deserting you. Please forgive me; it will never happen again."

Ghertrude pulled back slightly from her friend's damp shoulder. "I am sorry for crumbling so again; I have just been so lonely and scared."

"No, my dear, it is I who must apologise; we have been so locked up in conversation that all else faded."

"We?" Ghertrude sniffed, only then realising that they were not, in fact, alone. Her eyes transcended Cyrena's shoulder and found the face of the stranger; it took far too long for her to be certain. She frowned calculations at the mangled face, which returned her gaze apprehensively. Pushing herself back from Cyrena, she examined her friend's expression before looking again at the man with long black hair and two independent eyes.

"Ishmael?"

He relaxed his doubt and smiled. "Yes, Ghertrude. I have come back much changed."

She moved past Cyrena, who allowed their reunion a respectful space. With one hand still grasped by her friend, her other reached out and rested on his chest; he gently covered it with his own. The three of them stood, wordless, welded into a silent tableau that slowly softened and flowed, through the yard and into the house.

Mutter was just arriving as they got to the front door. They turned to acknowledge him and the young man waved. Mutter frowned back and nodded, attempting to smile while groaning inside. More strangers in the house. More odd doings and unpredictable relationships. A stunted root of defensive jealousy started sucking at the earth of his foundations. Who was this new boy, and what did he want with his ladies? Why had they picked up another one, after all they had been through? Could they not be contented with what they had and let him take care of them, make sure that they were safe from intruders and parasites? He had never quite seen them in the same way since his wife had confessed her anxiety about his desirability to them. In the months since, he had come to see her point of view, that she could have been right all along; it was only a matter of circumstance that the growing carnival mite was a stranger's and not his.

Their conversation was long. Though they sat close to one another, the spaces between them were growing and flexing in all directions. Cyrena and Ishmael did their utmost to conceal their intimacy; Ghertrude and Cyrena did not speak of the baby, and Ishmael did not seem to notice its obvious presence. He had mated with both women, and, in each other's company, both felt possessive and maternal about him in very different ways and to varying degrees. Surface tensions crackled and buzzed, building a static charge between their words and shaping the conversation into irregular troughs and peaks; doldrums of reflection mingled clumsily with elated memories; lows of tongue biting were interspersed with peaks of overly jovial camaraderie.

Cyrena ached to be closer to him, to touch and be touched again. She wanted to be at home with him, but her duty was here: She had pledged her presence.

Meanwhile, Ghertrude tried desperately not to stare at his new face and to fight back her overreaction at seeing their blatant love. She did not want him—indeed, she never had—but his distance was proving to be too much, too soon.

Ishmael sensed the women's hunger and felt suffocated by it. He felt deeply for Cyrena, but he longed to breathe freely, and he made a bid to escape.

"Ladies, would you excuse me for a short while? It's been a long time since I have been in this house and there are so many memories. Ghertrude, would you mind if I roamed around for a while and reconnected with my past?"

Ghertrude and Cyrena exchanged glances. Ghertrude nodded her assent, and he took his leave, closing the tall, elegant doors behind him on a conversation that he had no desire to hear.

He immediately bounded up the wide stairs to where his

room had been. The proportions had changed again, another reflection of recollection, rather than scale. So much had happened so early, shunts of life that suddenly revealed themselves to be ill matched and opposite.

His room was unlocked and unchanged. He touched the bed and opened the wardrobe to see his history hanging there: so many textures and smells, so many memories of isolation. He went to the window and thoughtfully traced his finger along the spot where he had picked the paint off the shutter.

"What will you tell him?" said Cyrena.

"I don't know. Nothing will be known until the birth. I don't want to raise a false alarm for him; he has already been through so much."

Cyrena nodded her agreement. "You are right, I'm sure. Until we are certain, it's probably best to say nothing."

"We are becoming very good at saying nothing."

Cyrena agreed again in silence.

In the attic, he opened the shutter into the breeze and the courtyard below, leaning out to get a better view. He saw Mutter moving back and forth, changing the straw in the stables. He looked towards the cathedral and watched the jackdaws circle over the spires.

He needed to see more. He climbed into the tower and opened the swivelling eye of the camera obscura, observing the activity below, changing lenses to see inside it. The curved white table flooded with his memory of Ghertrude, the exposed parts of her body made whiter by the table and the squeezed light. He remembered watching her confusion turn into annoyance, then transform into abandonment and, eventually, satisfaction. He recalled the same transformation in himself, only in reverse.

"You mean you intend to live together as man and wife?" Ghertrude sounded disapproving and a little horrified.

Cyrena said nothing.

"Do you really feel so much for him? You hardly know each other. What about his past? I have told you something of his dubious origin. Doesn't that concern you?"

Cyrena's eyes were changing colour and shape, bracing themselves to protect what sheltered behind them.

"There are many things that I have not yet told you," Ghertrude continued, "things you would not believe."

"I don't want the details about how he made love to you," Cyrena blurted.

"Not that; things before any of that happened, when he was kept downstairs."

"Ah yes! The mysterious teachers who lived in the basement, those that you saved him from." Cyrena was turning on her friend, disbelief becoming her advancing weapon. "And then they disappeared, vanished into thin air. Am I right? Is that not what you said?"

"I boarded and locked all the cellar rooms after I got him out—"

"You mean they might still be living down there?" said Cyrena with a dismissive, unpleasant laugh. "Or did they vanish like Hoffman?"

Ghertrude glared at the question, feeling the restraints of their friendship being pulled taut.

"Well? Did they? Did Mutter spirit them away?" pushed

Cyrena, the bit between her teeth, her tastes changing from defence into attack. "How many others have you removed to have him for yourself? Am I next?!"

The truth instantly quenched the rage flaring between them.

"It wasn't as simple as that," said Ghertrude. "They weren't human; they were machines, puppet-like machines."

He was tightening the strings, softly strumming them to adjust their pitch. The task gave him a place to think and recollect. The matter-of-factness of balance and modification separated his mind and let him wander back into the Vorrh. Nothing had happened to his memory. He had suffered no adverse effect. Was he immune to its legendary influence? Certainly, Tsungali had been confused, and Oneofthewilliams had seemed positively deranged by it.

Cyrena's jaw was hanging in astonishment. Ghertrude had told her everything, in great detail, with a delivery that was sparse and without emotion. There had never been the opportunity before, and she was finally released from the burden of her own disbelief. The naked facts of the impossible sounded firm and clear in the air, rather than forever tumbling around in the depths of her uncertainty, where they nagged and clotted, shifting focus into possible delusion.

When she had finished, both women sat in silence, a quietness that was unexpectedly gilded by sounds that seeped in from above. Wafts of celestial chords rolled and hovered down through the house, their beautiful eeriness making Ghertrude's tale all the more strange. The tang of disquiet was smoothed out by the poignant resonance, and they sat in bemused silence, while Ishmael set more and more of the Goedhart device into action. The vibration passed through them, through the turning ball of life, through the furniture and the floors, and all the way down to the well, where its harmony increased and spun, igniting tiny engines that ignited tiny engines that ignited tiny engines.

On the way home, Ishmael tried to gently quiz Cyrena about their friend; he wanted the core of Ghertrude's reaction, to know which way her thick waters flowed. The car slipped smoothly through the dark city; Cyrena's thoughts were burrowing too deeply to answer. An odd tiredness was guiding her towards hibernation, to a place other than the previous glow she and Ishmael had generated, somewhere far from the cooling distance of Ghertrude and her latest stories of hidden monsters. In this brittle, shifting world, ruled by sight, Cyrena did not know what to believe or whom to trust; she wanted sleep and darkness and the hope she had always had before. She begged exhaustion, promising to speak about it later. She huddled deeper in her travel blanket and looked out at the bleary city, its house lights and fireflies wavering sympathetically to long-stringed music that still sang in her heart.

The ivy and some of the smaller, more tenacious plants had begun to entwine themselves through his nothingness. It brought them pleasure, an irresistible tingle that ran through them, almost to the tips of their roots.

The ancient ghost tapped his dozing grandson.

"You will sleep yourself to nothing."

There was no reaction, so he tapped again.

"It is time to wake and thicken. She is troubled and moving, shrugging the rags off. You must gather yourself."

Tsungali opened one eye, catching the old man's meaning in his other. He had felt the friction from her unrest; he knew the bow longed to be naked, her every fibre straining towards meaning. He stretched unnecessarily, his muscles untaxed and absent. If he could, he would take her back, carry her into the Vorrh; she needed to be given there before rage and insanity consumed her. His fingers flexed involuntarily and he looked at his arm, something stirring in his psyche as the one that should not be there, the ghost arm of a ghost, lay expectantly at his side. It was normal now, as normal as dead arms could be, but surely that was not possible—it had died before him. Did he dare to try to grip the bow?

He knew his grandfather would disapprove; the old man was of the generation where the dead knew their place and trod the haunting track with unerring vigour. Tsungali quietly arose and slipped away towards the house. The breeze of his intentions swung the porch door on its whispering hinges, and he knelt before the bow, speaking to her in gentle, respectful tones.

"Great sister, I am of your own people, a common warrior who wants only to obey. I have heard your needs and ask for your blessing in bringing you aid. It is my wish to lift you and carry you in your journey."

There was no response; the bow remained still. As he stretched out his twice-spectred arm, the wrapping fell away, letting his fingers close around the supple maroon sheath; it did not struggle or shrink from his touch. He felt his hand enter into its apparent substance, the bow gripping him even as he gripped it. They fused together without hesitation and he was flooded with warmth.

A single arrow was left in the vacant quiver, white and old and imbued with history; the wood of the shaft was stiff and twisted; the fletchings had lost their perk and gained a dingy yellowness about their edges. He retrieved it from its lonely perch and walked back to his vaporous ancestor.

His slow grandfather turned towards him and immediately sprang back. For a second or two, Tsungali thought the old man had been petrified, but then his mouth opened and a thunderous, ethereal roar emanated soundlessly from him, rattling the leaves like seeds in a husk. The ancient ghost sprang from one foot to another, clapping his hands and bouncing in place. It was not the reaction his grandson had expected, yet in some indefinable way, his arm was not taken aback. As he stood in the awareness of the new sensation, it spread along his shoulder girdle, flowing into his other arm and curving in to embrace his neck and spine.

"It is you," the old man yelped. "It is you! You are the final one!" His nostrils flared and he whistled his short breaths, completely overcome with joy.

Tsungali's arms were one with the bow. He walked to the far corner of Cyrena's garden, where the wall blocked the view of anything, and placed the warped arrow against the bowstring, bracing it against all his strength. Gravity was dissipated in the straining, swallowing the rest of his body in the act. The arrow pointed up, over the wall, in the direction of the Vorrh.

In that second, everything stood still. The plants turned to face him, the lazy sunflowers most obviously, their heavy yellow crowns lolling around. The roses, drooping with scent, lifted their drowsy heads as tiny anemones strained up on delicate necks. The blind heads of worms, muscled out from their clinging arteries of mud metres below his feet, kept a breathless stillness, and the stalk eyes of snails swivelled into the scene. The kaleidoscopic lenses of a thousand bees and flies focused on him, their wings floating to a stop as the moment drew itself out to full length; the birds above came to a standstill, midflight, their attention locked on the unfolding below. Everything twisted towards the bracing, from the servants in the house to the citizens of the city.

Then the arrow was loosened and breath was restored, before most could register its absence.

With his grandfather matching his every step, the final Bowman left the house, relinquishing his care of the young man. Together, they walked the path of the arrow, following the rippling turbulence that it left, a humming song that vibrated in the air.

A solid line of twisting swallows swam above them, forming a frantic, parallel shadow to guide the way and lead them through Essenwald's glowing streets; past the towering cathedral and the balconied hotel; past the church of the Desert Fathers and the slave house; past memory and meaning and beyond the city's walls, out onto the train track and into the heart of the Vorrh.

CHAPTER THIRTY-THREE

*T*he first stabs of illness and return of the horses in his waking dreams made Muybridge relinquish his demands of his homeland. He would retire. He demanded to live with his cousin back in Kingston upon Thames. He would spend his last years there in quiet and splendid old age. England would have his bones and his triumph to immortalise.

The last thing he expected was a commission from Her Majesty's government—a commission to kill a horse.

He stood proud and erect at the centre of a great barn. He looked like God. A mane of unkempt white hair, a long, fearsome white beard, and wild smoke eyebrows cocked ragged over piercing, unforgiving eyes. A stern, knowing face that saw the world in a hard light with gauged contrasts. He wanted to look like this—biblical, austere, and imposing. He was seventy-three years old and justified. He had remained justified all his life, and now, as a celebrated patriarch, he was not a man to be disobeyed or questioned. He had the certainty of Abraham.

Five men and a horse waited on his commands as the cold air and light streamed in from the tall open doors at one end of the hollow building. He spoke to them quietly and they nodded to his instructions. One man led the horse outside; the others took up their positions in the delineated interior. The walls and the floor had been painted black, immaculately clean and precise.

White lines were drawn into the controlled darkness in chalky paint, grid patterns that framed the space into a stiffened concept and held the smells of the farm at bay. When the generated light came, it scrubbed the rural out, a fizzing brightness that tightened the interior into a fiction.

Her Majesty's men had made him a replica of his previous studio, where he could photograph what he wanted without anybody knowing. They had dragged him out of his docile years for these images, built his equipment into the old barn, followed every instruction and requirement he had given. He even insisted on the colour of the horse.

"It must be white, pure white," he had told them. "Preferably with a flowing mane."

Some of the government men had speculated, behind their hands, that this was a narcissistic whim, that he wanted an animal that looked like him. But they had been wrong: The photographer had another horse in mind, one from a stable of madness and violent dreams. But that was his business, not theirs; he was ready to make a picture that the world had never seen.

Muybridge picked up a handful of cables and nodded to the two men at the far end of the barn. One put his fingers in his mouth, while the other lifted a gleaming Gabbett-Fairfax Mars pistol from a wooden box. It looked like a forging hammer.

Muybridge called to the other, lesser man, who shuffled nervously at the far end, by the doors. The signal was given. The man outside whipped the horse hard into a stampede. The man with the fingers in his mouth whistled, a series of tearing notes. The horse bolted between them into the glaring, disembodied light of the fathomless hall. The other man lifted the gun. The thunder of the hooves rattled the painted grid as the horse steamed into the light. The camera shutters twitched in insect frenzy and divided the time. A vast and unexpected fist of fire leapt from the Gabbett-Fairfax, and the sound that followed swallowed everything else. The horse collapsed onto its running legs, sending up a cloud of black, swirling dust, its thrashing body digging into the white grid and splattering the walls from the exit wound in its spine. It snapped its neck in the violence of its death throes, which, like everything else, seemed to be instantaneous. With its last snort of breath, the cameras ceased and a tidal wave of silence wallowed into the barn.

All stood still in the settling air. After a moment, the nervous new electricity was turned off. The scene became operatic in the sliding light of the opening doors. The whistler and the horseman put on overalls and began to clean up around the corpse; the shooter put the monstrous gun back in its icon-like box and unpacked a maroon rubber apron and gloves and a box of equine surgical instruments. Some of the black dust still eddied, high in the shafts of daylight that flooded the barn, giving celestial animation to the actions of the industrious men. Muybridge seemed totally uninterested in the current activities and busied himself with the cameras, collecting their precious thoughts and taking them away, to be unlocked next door in his night-black chapel of chemicals.

Muybridge entered the lightless room, out of focus and red. The darkroom's proportions were shunted into afterimage by a scarlet lamp that did not illuminate, but swallowed any traces of normal white light or perspective.

Water flowed ceaselessly, and the occupant moved with determination in the thick, urine-scented air. He soaked his hands and the glass plates in blind tanks of warm fluids. Sealing them, he counted aloud as he rocked them into waking under the hollow red of the mournful light. When they were complete, he released them and set them aside, the glass dripping dry while he prepared the next batch of chemicals. Once they were cured, he gently inserted them into the projector and opened them out as light and shadow on the flat screen below. Peering sideways into the focused surface, his eyes almost touched the image, seeking errors and imperfections: None were there. It was another immaculate work. Every grain of dust and spit of flying blood could be seen—sharp white sparks against the inverted black of the horse's skin. He quickly blocked the flow of light and, with something close to glee, slid the sensitive paper beneath it, unsheathing the glow from the lamp once more. He set a loud clock ticking and adjusted the preciously kept temperature of the bloods. When the alarm bell sounded, he gathered up the paper and drowned it in the floating tray of liquid chemicals, lulling it back and forth until gradually, under his moving hands, a shadow appeared, a shadow darker than anything else in this bolted chapel, a shadow grown to become a space around the screaming void of a horse.

Muybridge lifted the image of the spilling animal from one tank to another, where it floated with more of its kind in a circulation of fixatives. He dried his hands and pulled his long white beard out from his shirt collar—it had been tucked in so as not to stir the chemicals and spoil the process. He stepped back, straightening into a position of satisfaction and unbolting the door to the intensity of the world.

An hour later, he laid out the sequence of photographic prints on a long, narrow table in his temporary study, which adjoined the barn. Four men moved together towards the images as Muybridge stepped aside to give them space around his pride.

The running horse had been delineated, flattened to silhouette on a scaled grid. The cameras had erased the noise and the sickening third dimension. Now it could be studied, uncluttered by the stink of actuality. Great beauty strode across the dense chemical papers. The horse had become classical and otherworldly as it charged, buckled, and collapsed in a dignity of aestheticism.

The men were delighted as they pored over the prints. Theirs was a world of mechanical precision, and this gridded slaughter had proved the value of its latest device. They packed away the evidence that would lead to manufacture and thanked Muybridge on the doorstep of his domain, shaking his hand enthusiastically.

He closed the door on their departure. For a moment, in the narrow corridor between rooms, he mused on the effect that monstrous gun would have had on the anatomy of the despicable Major Larkyns, and how his last expression of stunned surprise and pain would have been so much greater. Even after all these years, he would have liked that. He would have liked his treacherous young wife to witness her lover being cut in two.

It was a moment of delightful speculation before he returned to the serious business of the negatives. His military clients had their prints, but he had the negatives, and he had his own plans for the images. He had been at the pinnacle of a life's achievement when he decided to chase another quality in his work: an elusive ghost that permeated everything he photographed. It had led him into deep speculation and personal violation, but still he could not put it aside. He was an artist, photographer, and inventor of prodigious importance—that was all secured, acquired against all the odds. The last few experiments were his, and they would answer the questions. He pictured a horse that never touched the ground, or one that charged under it, or another that stalked his sleep like a bedsheet phantom. This was to be his ghost dance. Process thrown over anxiety to flap in the corridors of then and his few remaining tomorrows and what beckoned beyond.

Horses had guided his life and crippled his journey. The glass negative was the removal of that splinter in his soul. The last machine he would create would look through the world. The glass negatives of the dying horse in a box of earth, using water to shutter its time and process a glimmer of far-off light that he thought might just be in Africa.

Muybridge died a year later, but only after digging up half of his cousin's garden. When somebody finally summoned the courage to ask him the purpose of the huge holes he had made, he replied, "I am making a scale model of the Great Lakes of North America."

No further questions were proffered or answered. His last two names were misspellings. Eudweard Muybridge written in the crematorium register. Eadweard Maybridge carved on the stone that marked his ashes.

CHAPTER THIRTY-FOUR

On the night of their return from Ishmael's reunion with Ghertrude, they made a strange mating. Ishmael made love to assert himself, while Cyrena's endeavours sought a reassuring balm: Neither was achieved. The hybrid resonance that followed them into their sleep disturbed the house for days. They were only fortunate that the bow was already gone; she would not have fed well on the atmosphere they had created.

Ishmael did not notice that Tsungali and the bow had gone. So absorbed was he in finding his place in his new life that he temporarily forgot his old one; he could hold no reflection on anything other than Cyrena. He longed for her to see his truth, not because he was deformed and rare, but, conversely, because of his growing normality and commonness. He hungered for her to mirror him in the depth of the love she so strongly professed. He watched her continually, when he thought she was unaware, to see if there were cracks or blemishes in the perfection of her surface. He wanted her to prove his existence in hers; all else had been empty, and the attempts of those who marked his passage had always failed: Even Nebsuel's ministrations now seemed lost. His place in the world had been slippery, unfounded, and without a single trace of purpose, as hollow as a bottomless well.

Cyrena visited Ghertrude once a week. She took care to do it alone; it was easier that way, and she could concentrate on her friend without distractions. She found relief in being clear of the house, to have a break from Ishmael's constant attention. It was not his fault, she realised; he simply wanted to be close, but she had lived alone for years, and most of that time had been spent in a space that no other human could truly enter. The difference between the now and then was like the difference between the sound and the sight of the swallows. In her crossings of the city to visit Ghertrude, she would try to revert to those times, and her imagination and sensitivity would glide gleefully in advance. Sometimes they would warn of obstacles, but mostly they would tug her impatiently and joyfully forward.

At the house, Ishmael always sat close to her; her feelers never seemed able to extend beyond him. He smothered her perception with his love and need, and she sought ways of stretching around it, for both of their sakes. She was aware that he sometimes watched her, as if listening to her heart for irregular beats and uncertainties. She assumed it was care, but at times it felt like custody.

Ghertrude was regaining her strength, that confident energy that had so defined her from her first day in the world. But now it was turning inwards, no longer seeking to pry and investigate into the lives of others. Hoffman no longer stalked her dreams—he had been banished by the first visit of Cyrena and Ishmael. Her instincts told her that it was Ishmael who had done it, that it had something to do with the sounds from the attic. The eerie music, without structure or form, slid into the subconscious and opened pathways and doors previously closed. It had filled the entire house and had been the only thing to enter the basement in the years since her foray down there.

Since she had told Cyrena about the incident with the Kin, she realised her memory of it had changed, as if sharing her story had given her space to reflect and see it from different angles. The facts remained the same, and the events occurred in the same sequence, but their meaning had somehow shifted. The puppet guardians no longer seemed uncanny and full of dread; instead, their actions appeared to have a calmness, care, and purpose, rather than the cruel, mechanical coldness she had so automatically and fearfully interpreted.

How could this be? What had changed to allow her to give them such a great benefit of the doubt? In their absence, she realised that the only variable factor was herself. She considered the child growing inside her and wondered at the effects it might be having on her attitude, but surely that should be making her more protective, more hostile to anything that could be unnatural or threatening? Perhaps it was the harshness of recent events—the reality of violence, and the blind selfishness that so often instigated it. She had, after all, witnessed it firsthand. Hoffman, Maclish, even Mutter, had behaved in ways abhorrent to all that she treasured and believed; blood and anger had washed the innocence from her eyes. Ugly conceptions and spiteful deceits had hacked at her heart until it had shrunk and burrowed deeper into its meaty cage. In such a fearful setting, those brown things were turned into the dreams of another place, as opposed to the nightmares of this one.

Her thoughts carried further than she could have known; as she sat and pondered her past with a warmth and tenderness unfamiliar to her upbringing, locks withered and fell away, and the nailed-up doors grew soft, warping ajar.

Three days earlier, Ghertrude had enlisted Cyrena's support and made the difficult journey to her parents' home to tell them about her pregnancy. She had long been dreading it, and the drive there in her friend's purring car was fuelled by trepidation. Cyrena held her hand, letting her feel the firmness of her purpose and her total support.

Ghertrude's mother greeted the pair and showed them into the dining room; a strange choice, Ghertrude had thought, among the myriad of other, more suitable rooms in the house.

"Your father will be here presently," she said in a hard, agitated voice.

Did she already know? Was she already upset and angry with her? Had Mutter let the cat out of the bag? Ghertrude sensed a strain, an unease showing in fractured white marks through her mother's agitation. She looked older and worn. Her buoyant ease had disappeared, replaced with a distance and distress.

"Mother, is something wrong?"

The answer to her question chose that moment to walk in the door: Her father was shrunken and hunched, his eyelids red rimmed and his clothing dishevelled. Where had Deacon Tulp gone, and who was this poor imitation that had replaced him? She looked on apprehensively as he waved them to the chairs.

"Sit, sit down, please," he said, in a voice that had none of the stride or wit that he was so famous for. "My dear child, you are shocked to find me changed so; you are not alone in that. Sometimes I shock myself." A weak smile flickered across his face, and he looked at his wife, whose lips were pursed tightly together, squeezing the blood elsewhere.

"The truth is, I am near the end of my tether. The business is dying and our savings have gone."

"Gone, Father? Gone where?"

"Gone with August Daren," Mrs. Tulp interjected. "He has closed his bank, taken all the money, and disappeared."

"He must have predicted the collapse of the industry; he saw the imminent destruction of the Timber Guild and the downfall of the city and he got out while he could, taking everyone's savings with him."

"But, Father, why is this all happening?"

"Because there are no trees, my dear. Without a workforce, there's no one to bring the logs out of the forest, so they sit in desolate heaps, cut and rotting. No one will work there. We have tried everything!"

Ghertrude had never seen him so despondent.

"The only thing we can do is take what we have and leave," sighed her father.

"Where?"

"South."

"But where?!"

"I don't know!"

They sat in silence for a long time, until Cyrena, uncomfortably intrusive in the unexpectedness of the family's revelation, could hold her tongue no longer. "Is there anything I can do to help?"

There was a glint of annoyance in the old man's eyes, which smoothed out as he shook his head.

"No, thank you, dear. You are very kind." And then, as if it had only just occurred to him to remember, he said, "You can do one thing for us: Keep an eye on this little one. Always be her friend."

Cyrena nodded gravely and he brightened for a moment.

"Anyway, my daughter, let's talk about you. What is the important news that you have brought us today?"

The three days since her visit should have given Ghertrude time to get used to the idea of her family's upheaval, but she could not erase the image of her father's anger at her news. He could not speak and had left the room distraught and furious. Since her disclosure, she had slept soundly for only one night, and her dreams had been full of displacements and endings; this was not the nutrient she had intended to feed her child.

She sat alone in the house, searching for a positive stance, when she heard a sound, something moving outside the kitchen door.

"Sigmund!" she called out, knowing that it was not he.

She stood up and walked to the door, cracking it open to listen at its gap. Hearing nothing more, she stepped into the hall and looked around. Though she saw it on her first scan, she did not allow herself to acknowledge it. The second look, however, was more deliberate, and it could not be ignored: The white envelope had not been there before. She knew what it was and was terrified of what it had to say.

G. E. TULP

The period that has passed since I last addressed you has been much longer than I suggested; it was not necessary to contact you before now. You have performed beyond my hopes. Your conduct and intelligence in all matters has been excellent, and you shall be rewarded.

Firstly, do not fear for your family. They shall be provided for, as will those who have assisted you in our quest, even Herr Mutter. No one will discover the fate of H; you may rest assured on this matter.

You will stay in this house and bring your child up in its safe confines. Help will be offered to you, but you should consider all factors very carefully before making any decisions. Your child will be healthy and well and somewhat different from others. This will be a blessing for all. Over the next few years, much will change around you. The city may fall and rise, but this house will remain the same; it always has and always will.

------

*Ishmael now has his own life and will be left alone to
use it.*

I will contact you again after the birth.

➤━

Cyrena sat on the balcony looking out at the city, beyond the city
walls, to the distant Vorrh. Ishmael brought her a glass of wine
and gently laid his hand on her shoulder.

It was difficult to believe that so much change was occur-
ring. Everything looked the same. Ishmael thought of the camera obscura; Cyrena watched the swallows. Their skin was warm
in its contact and reassuring. Between them, they would endure.

➤━

Ghertrude's hands were damp and she was flushed with the
child as she walked through the echoing, empty hall. Mutter was
elsewhere. He spent most of his time in the stables or cleaning
the yard; only invitation lured him into the house these days.
Now that she was larger, he seemed more bashful, yet incapable
of averting his eyes from the protuberance.

She walked over to the basement door and unlocked it with
the key she had carried in her wet hand for the last two hours.
The nails were loose and fell to the floor with the soft, disinte-
grating sounds of liberation. She unchained the padlocks and
pushed into the waiting kitchen; the warmth of disinterest still
pumped at its enigmatic heart. She ignored its invitation to stay
and think, to let time drift, and went to the dented panel.

She was a very different shape now and had to adjust her new
balance in the tightness, easing herself down the stairwell and
squeezing through the narrow entry, stepping at last into the
room where the puppet had broken beneath her feet so long ago.
The memory of her most forgotten dream enveloped her. She

edged, catlike, across the space. No trace of that haunting action was evident: no stains; no cobwebs; no history. She entered the next room and was somehow unsurprised to see Luluwa, sitting on the crate that had laid open since Ghertrude's last visit; she was still and soft, her stiff brown hands resting on her thighs, head bowed. Ghertrude observed her calmly, waiting for direction.

"You are the one that broke Abel," Luluwa said in her high, singsong voice.

"Yes," said Ghertrude.

Luluwa raised her polished head; her eyes swivelled between their brown surface scars, looking for the question that Ghertrude's observation had not yet formulated.

"I hear the child," Luluwa said. "I hear the squalling of the movement; the child sucks at your interior and thrashes with its limbs."

Ghertrude suddenly understood why she had not recoiled from Luluwa instantly, why she had not been immediately shocked to see her. Two eyes of cunning observation adorned her face, surrounded by scars, as if the sockets and lids had been smeared with a hot knife. Her features had been altered with an amateur technology that had misunderstood the perfection of both the new and the original material: it was a botched and graceless job at rendering her more human.

"We will be your servants now," said Luluwa. "I and the remaining Kin will be teachers to the child."

Ghertrude was running out of emotions, or at least the connective tissue that made sense of them.

"I did not mean to kill him," she said.

Luluwa bobbed her head in understanding. "Life is not durable. There is no blame." She got to her feet, then looked again at Ghertrude. "You did not know that the camera tower is aligned over the well?"

To emphasise the point, she walked over to Ghertrude, placing one hand on her abdomen and the other above her head, where a halo might float. She made a small rotating movement; Ghertrude could smell the hum of Luluwa's Bakelite. She realised that they were the same height.

Luluwa had grown and stood looking at her, shoulder to shoulder and eye to eye.

CHAPTER THIRTY-FIVE

*T*he figure at the crossroads tensed his muscles and drew himself up to full height: There would be no passing this day.

No one had ever passed through the forest untouched; the figure before him had lived in it and traversed it a second time with apparent effortlessness. He had worked hard and suffered much to keep the man before him alive—soon, he alone would possess all elements of the knowledge and their connotative power.

In his altered condition, Sidrus had taken weeks to circumnavigate the outskirts and reach this point of interception. His anxiety to be enlightened peaked and crested within his broken body, sending torturous spasms of adrenaline into his healing wounds. He tolerated the sensation unflinchingly: It would not last long. When he finally entered the sacred ground, in command of the Erstwhile and able to touch the most sacred centre, all things would be put right.

Sidrus had not reached the vial in time. The Mithrassia had begun to thrive before he had even reached the outskirts of the city: The evil old cunt must have lied about the hours he had to spare. When Sidrus had the knowledge of the Vorrh and was properly healed, he would return and slowly split the medicine man apart, at a far, far slower pace than he had ripped open the dove with the antidote.

The contents of the bottle had stopped the horror from finishing him, but his body was a shattered wreck: His genitals were gone; three of his toes had fallen off and only two of his fingers were left intact; most of his teeth had been eaten away and his face was a putrefied mess; a quarter of his adrenal system was blighted to smithereens. It would all be rectified when he entered the sacred core.

The Bowman had stopped, as if jarred by the sight of him. Sidrus had seen this before and made some quick mental adjustments.

"Come closer, friend. I mean you no harm," he slurred, his twisted mouth diffracting the intensity of his words. "I am Sidrus, a Boundary Holder of the great forest. I hold warrant for these lands."

Williams stepped closer to the insatiable hunger.

"I will not shake your hand. It is no longer a custom in these parts, and anyway, you would find the sensation displeasing. As you can see, I have been the victim of a terrible illness. It is not infectious and I am not ashamed of my injuries. Please, do not be worried about my appearance."

"I am not," answered Williams, almost truthfully.

"You do not know me, but I have been aware of you for many years. I have protected you from much danger at the hands of hired mercenaries." Williams seemed blank and disinterested in these facts and did not show the slightest degree of gratitude.

"You no longer carry your bow?"

"Bow?"

"The living bow that guided you for years."

Williams shrugged and said, "I have no knowledge of these things. I think you are speaking to the wrong person."

Sidrus was astonished at the effrontery of these lies; Williams saw the eaten face shift into the expression of the spectral vision from the slip of vanishing paper. He understood it as a warning and held his bag closer to him.

"You can trust me; I have done much to protect you."

"So you keep saying, but why? And from who?"

Sidrus enjoyed games of cat and mouse only when he was undeniably the feline; this display of churlish arrogance was beginning to annoy him, but he played along, the act of ignorance not distracting his sights from the end goal.

"You have enemies and adversaries who did not want you passing through the Vorrh again. Your previous colleagues branded you a deserter, a murderer, and worse. They wanted you dead or banished, not wandering through the lands of uprising. A bounty was put on your head; all manner of scum have tried to slay you and collect the reward."

Williams realised that this man's disease had gone deeper than his face; it must have chewed at his brain. "I don't know what you are talking about."

"About the Possession Wars?"

Williams shook his head, writing disbelief and disinterest in deep marks around his eyes.

"About the Vorrh?"

"The what?"

"The Vorrh. The great forest."

"What forest?"

Sidrus's face could no longer be described. In fury, he pointed behind Williams, who turned, looked, and irritably slumped back. "I see no forest."

"I have given flesh, money, and years to save you. I suffer like this and you mock me?!"

Sidrus was in a rage of tears.

He drew two black canes out from beneath his coat.

"I mean you no offence," said Williams, "but what you speak of holds no meaning for me. There is nothing like a forest out there; I know because I have been walking for days. There is only a vast, dismal mire."

Sidrus, so eternally contained and controlled, was finally undone. The truth that he had sought for so long, and come so very close to, slipped further from him with every word. Had the Bowman really forgotten all and been blinded into an illusion? Was this the ultimate effect of exposure to the forest, its greatest defensive irony? Or was this all a foul, vindictive game, a vicious lie to keep him from a life of riches and wealth beyond all imagining?

"Have you ever travelled through or lived in a forest?" asked Sidrus, searching out any avenue that might separate truth from lie.

"I have the dimmest recollection of a forest destroyed; broken stumps and hacked roots; a place of mud and death, illuminated by thunder and lightning that tore men into pieces. But that was a long time ago and far from where we now stand."

More lies.

"Were you alone? Apart from men, what other creatures dwelt there?"

Williams paused, as if in thought, his hand moving slowly into the corner of his canvas bag. "I can think of only two: mules and angels." The pistol clicked into gear and he swung it up, letting the bag drop to the floor. But he was no match for the speed of indignation. Before he could commit to a shot, Sidrus bounded across the space between them, arcing one of the sticks up and over, its practised blade exposed. It severed the bag and its strap, slicing through the tendons of Williams's arm. Sidrus spiralled around him in a blur; he was standing behind the Bowman before his cry had reached Sidrus's ears.

"I have had enough of your mocking lies!"

Williams grabbed at his bleeding arm; the rest of the world fell away from under him.

➤→

When he came to, it was darker; the shadow, which seemed to construct the room he was in, smelt rank. He gagged against his consciousness and tried to move. Nothing shifted; he was held in some sort of constraint. He could hear the wind nearby; it sounded as though he were outside, on some desolate landscape. Then he made out the snapped lead and its fringed remnants of light: a stained glass window, long, meagre, and broken, its coloured frames all stolen years before. He recalled the tiny chapel behind the figure at the crossroads; its description fit his rudimentary assessment of the space he strained against: He had been tied to the simple altar.

Sidrus's voice had changed: There was no sign of his earlier emotion. The anger had been distilled.

"I mean to have my answer from you today. I will not tolerate any more of your foolishness. I have been a servant to the Vorrh all of my life; I have tended to its needs and commands; I have engaged with its watchers and culled its predators. I know that the child they call the Sacred Irrinipeste opened your soul to it, and I know you carry its essence locked in your heart and head. My knowledge of it is extensive; yours will make it complete."

Williams choked against his restraints of rope, throttled by his own ignorance.

"If you will not give it to me," continued Sidrus, "then I will take it."

"I have nothing to give!" spluttered Williams with all of his strength.

"Then I shall cut you down and peel you away, until you are only your voice. You will have no choice but to tell."

The wind cascaded through the broken window, flickering the last of the afternoon light. It bent the puckered fragments of clear glass and the fatigued lead arteries that held them in their tenuous position.

"It is said by some that parts of memory reside outside of the brain, saturating themselves into the muscles and running the length of the spine. I believe that to be true, and so I am going to dig them out, one by one; wake them and release them, so that what you know of the core will be free to reach my ears."

The purposeful torturer attached a tourniquet to Williams's upper thigh. A small brazier smouldered nearby, a quenching iron glowing in its heat. Sidrus saw the Englishman's terrified eyes staring at it.

"Not a drop of your precious blood will be wasted. By the time I finish, it will exceed the organs it has so faithfully served. It will rush and buffer your brain with overrich oxygen; only your pain will equal its need to empty its power. Together they will shriek the truth that you refuse to give."

The first cut felt like only pressure, until he skinned the nerve and everything in Williams's mind turned white.

He did not know how many times he had passed out or how many times he had come to. New agonies awaited him with every breath. The night arrived and the wind dropped; he was about to scream again when he felt it change, its velocity fluttering and calming into a whisper.

"Now," he heard himself say. But now what?

He felt something, far outside the chapel, searching him out, rushing to his side. Was this what Sidrus searched for? A secret approaching, to be given to him and then passed on? A secret whose journey was triggered by blood? Sidrus moved closer.

"Speak up, Oneofthewilliams: Your time has come, as I told you it would."

The whistle outside was shrill and fast, only moments away. Sidrus was oblivious; he pushed his disgusting face closer to his prey's mouth, but the sounds he heard had no meaning.

Williams saw the voice from the corner of his eye. It flashed white in the window for a fraction of a second, and he recognised it as the first arrow, the one that Este had made for him; he almost smiled before it sliced through his throat, pinning his words to the altar.

Sidrus sprang back in a shower of blood, his white face drenched pink.

"No!" he bellowed at the dying man, tugging desperately at the white arrow impaled in his neck. But it was no use: Williams was gone, and the arrow would not move. Sidrus slumped backwards, defeated and dejected. He wiped a shaking grey hand over his bloodied face. He sat there until the dawn's grey sheen made the chapel hover. The thin light moved across the room, momentarily highlighting a tiny painting of a heavily bearded prophet, standing in a flat black landscape of featureless insistence. The colourless prism illuminated the dead man's face to reveal an expression of pleased contentment. No man who died in such pain should look like that. Sidrus scrabbled to his feet and grabbed at the ropes around the corpse. There was a smile somewhere in that face, under the bone, working like a battery and powering an expression of total peace. Sidrus shook the dead body in rage. The arrow fell loose, as though it had merely been resting there.

He could bear no more. Grabbing his things together, he speedily shovelled the blunted probes and knives into a sack. The brazier had not fully cooled and he left it behind, pushing impatiently out into the damp, brightening air.

He ran towards the forest. It took him an hour to reach its sanctified enclosure; it already felt different, less troubling: He felt at ease there. Had he got it? Were those words, those few, strange words, the secret? Could he at last go deeper and contact the Erstwhile directly, communicate with them in some tangible way? The forest warmed and flamed with beauty as the full power of the sun rose over it: He was welcome here. He had it. It had begun.

He dropped the sack of tools and made straight for the core. His patience had run out: He needed to find the older being and be cleansed of the wounds he had already carried for too much of his life. It was midday; huge shafts of light flooded down from the canopy, shuddering with life and birdsong. He could see the swallows darting in the sky between the spaces of trees; something rustled in the undergrowth, followed by a trill in the air; the swallows spun into a line and parted the leaves above. A great arc formed and glided down from the clouds to the forest floor. It approached at speed, almost upon him before he understood what shrilled inside the arc. It was another arrow, old, white, and twisted. It spun to the ground with huge purpose. It struck its target: a grey-skinned creature that had been hiding in the undergrowth. It fell to the ground in front of Sidrus with a force that echoed through his bones. It cried out, thrashing momentarily before falling silent.

Birds spiralled upwards, fluttering through the chattering leaves and out to quietness. He bent to examine the creature's grey skin, unable to decide if it was man or animal; it seemed much too shrivelled, as if it had been dead for years rather than seconds. His interest faded with the recollection of his purpose; he walked away from it, not noticing the two black ghosts who approached in his departure.

➤

Tsungali disregarded the mangled presence in the chapel: There was nothing to be gained from such a lost and empty being; he was like a white sack, limp and vacant, standing only because he did not have the wisdom to fall. Tsungali and his grandfather approached the other dead thing. The old man pulled the arrow they had shot from Cyrena's garden out of its parched grey skin. He gave the arrow to Tsungali without his eyes ever leaving the carcass. His other hand circled above his trembling head. He knew what they had killed but could not believe that it had strayed so far from perfection. He lifted the creature's hand and parted the fingers, removing moss and lichen that clung there. The fingernails had turned into horny claws. He pulled away tendrils of ivy that grew under the skin and what might have once been veins and arteries. The distorted covering fell away like parchment and revealed what had once been a human hand. The first human hand. The grandfather turned away and told Tsungali to shoot the same arrow out of the forest, pointing his attention into the shafts of swirling light.

➡

From the moment the arrow left the bow, followed on its journey by the duo of earnest spirits, Sidrus's vision started to fail. The sound of the bow echoed behind his eyes; they quivered in his head and lost focus. His skin crawled with a shiver that had previously been the avatar of Mithrassia, but this was something else, something altogether different. It must be the blood, he thought, or else the thrill at the beginning of his repair. It was as though his entire body was alive with thousands of ants, running over and inside his changing skin, rewriting his structure and purpose. He came to a murky pool and plunged his white head into its brackish waters to wash off any last traces of

Williams's death. The water felt cool and cleansing against the heat of his purpose, his exposed body embraced by the closeness of the trees. He emerged and dried his wrecked face carefully on his shirt, breathing heavily into its comfort. When he opened his tight, button eyes, all that lay before him was mile upon mile of desolate black peat.

EPILOGUE

The book was a present
Best to throw it away, to the bottom
Of the sea where ingenious fish may read it
Or not.

JOHN ASHBERY, *A Snowball in Hell*

BELGIUM, 1961

*T*he streets are livid with bright cars; they seem to run at the same speed as their horns. The sunburnt boulevard is engorged with primary colours. The American poet looks at his map once again. Brussels seems to be based on an irrational grid. Eventually, he locates the cul-de-sac, snatches up his briefcase, and strides on, past clipped gardens that are manicured to retentive perfection. As he walks on, the buildings become older and more dishevelled. He arrives at the entrance of the public nursing home, enters, and is met by the universal smell of old age, an indelicate ambience of urine and sour cooking; here in central Europe, it is tinged with perfume and garlic. He talks to the staff in a remote French from his high school. Most of them are peasants, or foreigners with accents weirder than his. He claims good, proper French, taught to him and his classmates by a tutor from Montréal.

A Moroccan woman in a stained, threadbare uniform of

blue and white takes him through the old house, which has been embalmed in magnolia and disinfectant. They climb two tasteless flights of stairs. The American is nervous and keeps pushing his spectacles back onto the bridge of his nose. She takes him into a large room full of seated women.

"Madame Dufrene, your visitor is here."

All the old women look around. He panics: He has no idea what she looks like. Then a hand waves from a seat by the window.

The once grand room has crumbled into institutional decay. He carefully crosses it, avoiding the damp patches and dropped objects that redesign an exhausted carpet. She is frailer than he expected, double wrapped in a heavy shawl as the sun floods the streets outside.

"Madame Dufrene, good morning! Please allow me to introduce myself," he begins.

Charlotte listens and smiles kindly at the incorrect precision of his French. He pretends to make an effort to engage in polite conversation but soon tires of the charade and pounces on his only interest. For the next hour, he asks endless questions about the Frenchman. Most of what he says is incomprehensible to her. She grows weary of the strain it takes to understand him, becoming more and more uncertain about what it is that he actually wants.

"May we talk a little about the last days in Palermo?"

She is aware that he does not see her, does not look in her eyes. He is so appalled by her fall from grace that he cannot bear to acknowledge her tired gaze. He buries himself in the questions and pushes on relentlessly.

"Is it true that he could not sleep in his bed, that he had a fear of falling from it? Is that why he was on the floor next to your door when they found him?"

She thinks of the genius of the man and knows it is not what this large, lumpy American wants. For her, his brilliance was not in his books or his words, but in the moments when he became a unique, infused, individual human being, doing what he loved most. She thought of him sitting at the piano, playing, improvising voices. He could mimic everything from the trams squealing outside to exotic animals, from opera divas to common street singers. It made them both laugh, in that time when he still could.

"Do you have any pictures of your time together?"

She expected this and pulls a large, crumpled manila envelope out from under her shawl. She digs into it and, after a few moments, produces a dog-eared photograph. They are posed like a married couple: she seated, him standing behind her chair; her kindness radiates, even lending beauty to her startling hat, which resembles the neck of a dead, inverted swan. The American is mesmerised: this is the best image of his literary hero he has ever seen. It shows a taut, immaculate man of precise, if diminutive, proportions.

"This is wonderful, truly wonderful!"

She warms towards him and relaxes. He listens as she begins to unwrap an explanation of what their relationship truly was. It has become quiet in the room; even the incessant coughing has stopped. The ladies subtly strain to catch the details.

As he is about to leave, he remembers the gift he has brought her and rummages about in his briefcase. He presents her with the chocolates and asks if they can meet again. She is delighted and says nothing would please her more.

They meet four times more; on the last occasion, he visits her in her own room in the elegant, private nursing home that houses her final days in peaceful dignity.

He had worked hard ever since he had first left her in the crumbling decay. He had instigated the move, and surrealism had paid for it. Now she shone in her reflective surroundings. She beamed at him when he arrived and showed him around the room, pointing out her prized possessions, which had been locked away in storage for the last nine years. She wanted to tell him everything, but there was so little detail that he really wanted to know, and she had already forgotten so much. Only the joy and spite remained, embedded over the years; the rest had fallen away. Nevertheless, they talked for hours. She enjoyed the company of the soft, shapeless man and did not welcome his final departure; he started to rummage in the briefcase and she knew he had already left.

Like a disappointing conjuring trick, the chocolates had transformed into a book. She stared at it as he adjusted his spectacles.

"I thought you would like this: It's just been published, the latest edition."

She took it from him; it seemed unfinished, without a spine or hard covers.

"It's the first publication in paperback," he said gleefully.

She thanked him and held it close. They said their goodbyes and he slipped away, waving back to her along the diminishing corridor: She knew she would never see him again. She crossed the plush carpet and lay down on the bed, bolstered slightly by the crisp white pillows, her thoughts soft edged and reminiscent.

The dove had won over the raven, at least up to the very last days. She had fought hard and dogmatically for its victory. His cruelty had been painful to her, but nothing like the carrion bird that had stabbed at his own heart continually. Now she would banish that and see him only as she wanted to: mimicking music hall stars, or playing Max Kinder's hopeless decadent fop, seated at the piano again, his fingers skipping across the keys, his warbling voice dimming into a plaintive hum.

The book was in English; its title sounded more emphatic that way. *Impressions of Africa*—he would have liked that. She imagined him reading it out in the mock British accent he so enjoyed. She smiled, closed her eyes, and put the book aside. She would never read it, not in English. She had never read it in French.